THE CAULDRON OF GOD

JOSEPH FINLEY

TARASTONE PRESS

The Cauldron of God
Copyright © 2024 by Joseph Finley

Published by TaraStone Press

Edited by Brett Berlin
Cover Design by Jessica Bell
Map of Constantinople by Jeff Mathison
Map of the Otherworld by Joseph Finley

ISBN: 978-0-9884108-6-2 (paperback)
ISBN: 978-0-9884108-7-9 (hardcover)

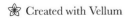 Created with Vellum

A NOTE ON PRONUNCIATION

Because the novel is set throughout tenth-century Europe, it contains a few Old Norse, Old French, and Gaelic names that can be a bit difficult to pronounce. The following is a rough pronunciation guide for some of the trickier words.

Aurillac—OHR-ee-YAK
Alais—AH-lay
Ciarán—KEER-in
Columcille—KULL-im-kill
Évrard—eh-VRAAR
Gerbert—ZH-eh-RBeh-R
Jarl—YArl
Jörmungandr—YOOR-muhn-guhn-dahr
Jorundr—YOR-uhn-dahr
Maugis—MO-zhee
Nimue—NEE-moo-ay
Poitiers—PWA-tee-ay
Tuatha dé Danann—Thoo-a-haw-day-dah-nawn

And war broke out in heaven; Michael and his angels fought against the dragon. The dragon and his angels fought back ...

— Revelation 12:7

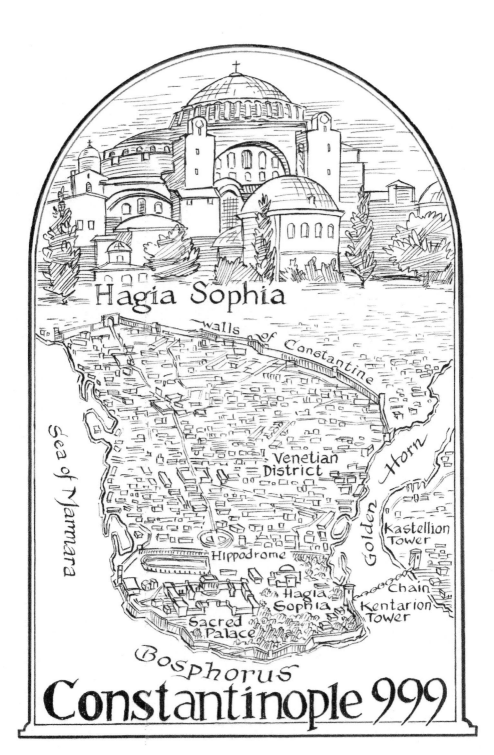

Hagia Sophia

walls of Constantine

Sea of Marmara

Venetian District

Golden Horn

Kastellion Tower

Hippodrome

Chain

Hagia Sophia

Kentarion Tower

Sacred Palace

Bosphorus

Constantinople 999

PROLOGUE

Theodora questioned whether she was still trapped in a nightmare as the boat glided beneath the towering stone archway. Gigantic gargoyles flanked the entrance, their stone-gray eyes gazing down from above hooked beaks, resembling fiendish birds of prey.

She sat in the damp hull with her wrists shackled in iron manacles linked by a short chain. Sweat coated her long platinum hair and soaked through the delicate fabric of her pale dress. Her captor, Naberus da Roma, towered over her. Dressed in the black woolen robes of a Benedictine monk, he propelled the boat with a long oar up a river as dark as cuttlefish ink. Each stroke of the oar released the dank scent of a cavern untouched by sunlight. Naberus's complexion had grown ashen, a ghostly pall emphasizing his sunken cheeks and the edges of a beard that tapered to a pointed chin, its once-dark strands now shot with silver.

"Master," he cried, "we are coming!"

His words echoed off walls of dark gray basalt on each side of the river.

"*Master … aster … aster … We are coming … coming … coming …*"

As the river snaked through a ravine beneath a gloom-filled sky, Naberus screamed louder. "Master, show me where you are!"

"Are ... are ... are ..."

His ravings caused Theodora's head to pound as if she had consumed too much wine. But she did not recall any drinking or revelry, just a vague memory of Naberus forcing a bitter elixir down her throat. It had happened in the ruins of the old Roman Forum. The ruins were flooded, as was half of Rome. They had traveled there by boat. Her, Naberus, and Rumeus. Yet Pope Gregory was there, too.

We had abducted the young Saxon pope ...

She remembered wanting to kill the pope herself, but knew that vengeance had been denied her. After swallowing the elixir, her memory of what happened afterward was gone, like a flame snuffed from a candle. The next thing she knew, she had awakened in the boat.

When I heard the pope scream.

The events that followed seemed elusive, like piecing together the fragments of a dream. She recalled a cavern with giant faces carved into the rock. And fire. So much fire. She saw Pope Gregory chained to two pillars, his body hanging lifelessly like some crucified messiah. Then Naberus summoned the being from the black waters. She remembered its luminescent skin and its transformation into a giant winged creature forged from the flames blazing around the cavern. *A dragon.* There was a battle and more fire, but most of the details were shrouded by the fog still clouding her mind. Except one, a lance piercing the being's side before it shed its serpentine form and stole away on the remnants of its dragon-like wings.

Holding her aching head in her hands, she questioned whether any of this had been real. But why else was Naberus searching so desperately for the being now?

"Master," he cried again, "we will not abandon you!"

Trying to clear the haze from her mind, Theodora surveyed her surroundings. The sheer cliffs were unlike anything she had ever seen, not even the rugged Apennine or Alpine Mountains. The fear that should have draped over her like a suffocating shroud did not come. Instead, she was filled with a strange numbness, as if Naberus's mysterious elixir still dulled her senses.

Something bumped up against the hull, and she saw a glistening snakelike shape crest briefly out of the inky water. The sight sent a flicker of terror through her veins.

"Naberus," she stammered, "there's something in the river."

He turned, answering her question with a furious glare. "I was wrong about you." His bloodshot eyes were filled with anger—and something more. *Madness.*

Naberus returned his gaze upriver. "Master, give us a sign. Show us how to find you!"

"You ... you ... you ..."

The echoes of his cries faded away, and soon, the only sound was the splash of the oar. Naberus rowed deeper into the ashen gloom. Then, in the distance, a golden light flared.

Theodora gasped.

"Master!" Naberus cried. He paddled frantically toward the light.

As its radiance pierced the twilight, Theodora saw the river parted around a small island. The being sat on its ash-like sand, reclining against an enormous boulder. His muscular physique reminded her of a Roman statue of Apollo. Any remnants of the dragon-like wings had disappeared, and his naked skin shone with golden light. He clutched his side above his hip, where a lance pierced his flesh.

Naberus began shaking. "You're hurt."

The being looked almost amused. His hair spilled over his broad shoulders like thick spun copper, framing a flawless face that was both beautiful and terrifying.

"My apostle," the being said with a voice as pleasant as a song. "Fear not the wound. It cannot kill me. But the lance is cursed to my touch. I will need you to remove it."

"Whatever you ask," Naberus replied breathlessly. He leaped from the hull. In one long stride, he reached the being. Still shaking, he grabbed the lance and drew it from the being's side. The being grimaced as the massive spear tip withdrew from his flesh, then his

3

hand flew to the gaping wound. Luminescent blood flowed from the laceration, seeping through his fingers and running down his leg. Light flared from his palm, and within its glow, the flesh around the gash sealed shut. When he removed his hand, only a six-inch scar remained, marring his flawless skin.

The being stood. While Naberus was one of the tallest men Theodora had ever known, the being towered a foot and a half above the top of his head. Her mouth fell open as she gazed upon him, more perfect than any man she had ever seen, like Apollo made flesh. Like an angel from heaven.

He noticed her now. His irises shone with a golden hue that matched the light emanating from his skin. "She was not the one?"

"No, master," Naberus confessed. "I beg your forgiveness."

"You will have time to earn your redemption," he said almost breezily. His gaze fell to the manacles around Theodora's wrists. "There's no need for those."

Her eyes widened as he stepped toward her and reached into the boat. His hand was large enough to envelop both her wrists, and the heat from his touch warmed her skin. He closed his grip, and with a crack, the manacles crumbled around her wrists as if the iron was nothing more than brittle clay. She drew in a startled breath, watching the remnants of her bonds cascade into the hull like metallic grains of sand.

The being turned to Naberus. "Toss the lance into the river where no man will ever find it again."

"As you wish." Naberus hurled the lance into the river. The weapon bobbed like a cork for a breath, as if resisting its fate before surrendering to the black waters.

Naberus looked to the being. "Now what, master?"

"We move with divine purpose." The gold within the being's irises shined brighter as he spoke. "The cycle nears its end, drawing us and our enemy toward Dudael, where we shall bathe the ground in our enemies' blood. We will kill the woman, take the Key, and free my people. And with their liberation, the vengeance for which I have waited four thousand years shall finally be mine."

The being spoke with an edge in his voice, and a hint of rage flashed across his flawless face. Theodora had seen that rage before. In the cavern, in the fiery eyes of the dragon. She had witnessed what he could become. Her lower lip began to tremble, and she wrapped her arms tight around her chest. For she knew who it was that stood before her.

And that realization sliced like a cold knife deep into her soul.

PART ONE

Then I saw in the right hand of the one seated on the throne a scroll written on the inside and on the back sealed with seven seals; and I saw a mighty angel proclaiming with a loud voice, "Who is worthy to open the scroll and break its seals?"

— Revelation 5:1-2

CHAPTER I
THE DRAGONSLAYERS

With a torso as large as two oxen and wings as broad as a barn, the practice dragon swooped and soared above the sprawling compound that long ago served as the Baths of Diocletian.

The dragon's wings, covered in huge leaves of parchment, caught the wind like twin sails, lofting its body and tail, built of a light wooden frame wrapped in sheepskin. As it banked and dove through the slate-gray sky, the dragon's slanted red eyes painted on its triangular face gave it a fearsome appearance, as did the fiery orange ribbon dangling from its mouth and whipping in the wind.

From the walled structure's spacious courtyard, Ciarán gazed at the dragon, then glanced at the teams of Danes manning the three ballistas arrayed across the north end. Gerbert had designed the ballistas based on the crossbow-shaped siege weapons the Imperial Romans used centuries ago, but with a few modifications. Unlike the old Roman ballista, which was built on a heavy frame and could only aim in a single direction, Gerbert mounted each weapon on a massive wheel lying flat atop a cart-like structure. This allowed the operators to turn the weapon in a semi-circle, increasing its range. He called the ballistas his "Dragonslayers," naming each one after a

9

legendary saint who vanquished a dragon: Saint George, Saint Theodore, and Saint Radegonde. This morning was the first time they would test the weapons against a moving target, and as Ciarán looked on, butterflies roiled his stomach. If they had any hope of winning this war, they needed these weapons.

The wind coursing through the courtyard caught the hem of his scarlet cloak, sending it snapping against his leather boots and tousling his thick hair. Just a year prior, that hair had been cropped at the crown in a monk's tonsure, and instead of the gleaming mail coat and leather baldric he wore now, he'd been cloaked in a black habit and cowl. His longsword, Caladbolg, now hung by his side, a far cry from his past. It felt as though a lifetime separated him from his days as an Irish monk beneath the shade of Derry's fair oaks.

Beside him, Gerbert put his hands around his mouth and hollered across the courtyard. "Loft it higher!" The ginger-haired cleric made for an unorthodox field general in the white cassock and skull cap he often wore since his coronation five weeks ago as Pope Sylvester the Second. "The real Dragon won't be such an easy target."

At the courtyard's south end, Alais nodded back, her long raven hair dancing in the breeze. With a wave of her hand, the practice dragon soared skyward, a full sixty feet above the courtyard. Ciarán watched in awe, for Alais effortlessly wielded the Fae arts, and through the words flowing from her lips, the wind obeyed her every command.

"Aim for the heart!" Holger hollered. Clad in his bear-fur cloak, the tall golden-haired jarl paced behind the ballistas manned by his fellow Danes.

Holger's hirdman, a handsome Dane named Magnus, and the pair of crewmen assisting him, spun Saint George toward the dragon. Magnus cranked the winch, tilting it skyward before yanking the lever that triggered the weapon. With a loud *ka-chunk*, a bolt as long as a spear launched from the ballista. Ciarán tensed as the bolt sped toward the dragon, but the shot was too late. The dragon banked left, and the bolt sailed harmlessly past.

Magnus swore under his breath. He and his crewman cranked

the winches to ratchet back the bowstring while a third Dane grabbed another bolt to reload the weapon. While they struggled to rearm the ballista, Jorundr, a hulking Dane with white-blonde hair, fired a bolt from Saint Theodore. *Ka-chunk!* The spear sailed toward the dragon, but the artificial serpent dove beneath the bolt's path. "Bah," Jorundr cursed.

With one missile left, the youngest of the Danes, a seven-foot giant nicknamed Strong Bjorn, took careful aim with Saint Radegonde. He tilted the massive crossbow ninety degrees and pulled the trigger. *Ka-chunk!* His bolt flew straight. The practice dragon banked right, but not in time. The bolt nicked the corner of the dragon's left wing, shearing off a strip of parchment, though not enough to affect the dragon's flight.

Strong Bjorn pumped his fist and gave a triumphant yell, but the dragon wheeled in a swift arc and dove straight for the line of ballistas. The Danes, scrambling to reload their weapons, ducked as the dragon streaked past, mere feet above their heads. Ciarán grimaced. He imagined a torrent of fiery breath erupting from the dragon's mouth, engulfing the Dragonslayers and their crews. In that instant, the battle would be lost. And with it, the war.

"The heart," Holger bellowed. "I said *aim for the heart!* Clipping its wing will only fuel its fury."

"And God help us then," Ciarán muttered to Gerbert. "They'd never survive the flames."

"I'm working on a remedy for the fire," Gerbert sighed. "But I fear the immediate challenge is the aim of our marksmen."

"Then let's pray to the Holy Father they can sharpen their skills."

Ciarán looked back at the practice dragon as it descended in a circular arc before landing gently on the courtyard's flagstones. Around them, the wind died until only a wisp of a breeze remained.

That's nothing like what we'll be facing, Ciarán thought. He had seen the real Dragon in that otherworldly cavern beneath the Palatine Hill, and ever since, it had haunted his sleep. The real Dragon was a gigantic creature of fire and fury with scales like glowing embers, eyes like molten slits, and a mouth filled with teeth as long as daggers. Fire gathered in the beast's throat as its gaze seared into Ciarán night after night. Through that pair of molten eyes, Ciarán could feel the Dragon's presence boring into his flesh. An evil as old as time itself, the ancient Enemy of God. When Ciarán had first witnessed the Dragon, the sight of it shook his limbs and stole his breath. And ever since then, as it tormented his dreams, Ciarán felt helpless under the weight of that gaze.

How in God's name will we stand a chance against that?

His thoughts returned to the present when he noticed Alais crossing the courtyard, heading toward them. The dark blue dress she wore accentuated her graceful stride. Because of her captivating appearance and noble blood, some of the Romans had taken to calling her the Lady of the Lateran Palace. Meanwhile, Magnus and a few other Danes referred to her as Lifthrasir, the goddess Freya reborn. And while there were slivers of truth in that belief, the reality of it all was a bit more complicated. To Ciarán, Alais stood apart as the most extraordinary woman he'd ever met, and his feelings for her were more profound than he'd ever fathomed. Yet, he'd kept those feelings locked away, often reminding himself of the cautionary words of his late mentor, Brother Dónall: *"Lad, remember your vows."*

Alais met their collective gaze with her storm-gray eyes. "I fear they'll only have one shot each. The Dragon won't give them a second."

"We'll only need one of the three to hit its mark," Gerbert said, scratching the chin of his silver-flecked beard. "One shot to bring him to the ground, where Brother Ciarán can use Enoch's device to end it."

"I doubt it will be that easy," Ciarán said, feeling a chill as he tried to keep the Dragon's image from his mind. He eyed the ballistas. Only Magnus's team had managed to reload their weapon. "Just three shots against the Dragon—against the Devil himself. Could we have worse odds?" He shook his head. "Perhaps trying to confront him is the wrong strategy."

Gerbert raised an eyebrow. "The prophecy appears to compel

that confrontation, does it not? The Dragon and the champion meeting in the final conflict?"

"But why does it have to be that way?" Ciarán pressed. "If we believe the Dragon remains confined to the Otherworld, and if he needs the key Alais holds to fulfill his plans, then why not simply protect her? Go somewhere far away where he can't touch her."

Alais sighed. "Ciarán, wherever we might go, the Dragon would find us. There's nowhere we'd be safe. Our only path is to take the fight to him and make our stand in Dudael. Which means these three need to work on their aim."

In his heart, Ciarán knew she was right. Their late colleague, Brother Remi, once warned of the Dragon's servants and their reach. *It has servants—men in dark robes who hide in the shadows. And not just men.* Ciarán had encountered plenty of those servants since Remi's passing. The furies, the demons, the Nephilim—all drawn from the darkest regions of the Otherworld.

He glanced back at the Dragonslayers. Jorundr and Strong Bjorn's crews had finally rearmed their ballistas. If these weapons were all they had, they might as well make the most of the situation. "They say practice makes perfect, right?"

"Indeed, they do." Gerbert clasped his hands together. "My lady, are you up for another go-around?"

"Of course," Alais replied.

She started her way back to the southern end of the courtyard when the sharp clack of sandals on marble resounded from the dilapidated archway of the bathhouse. Emerging from the shadows, a monk rushed toward them, moving as swiftly as his corpulent frame permitted. Many in the Holy See had mockingly dubbed him Pietro Bucca Porci—*Peter Pig's Snout*—for his pronounced nose and full cheeks. Ciarán, however, refrained from using such a moniker for the twenty-eight-year-old Roman, whom Gerbert had entrusted as his Papal Librarian. Above the beard that framed his face, Pietro's cheeks radiated a warm flush, sweat glistening on his brow. Yet his eyes sparkled with an unmistakable fervor.

"Pietro," Gerbert asked, "what is it?"

"Most unexpected news, Your Holiness," Pietro replied between breaths. "You demanded to be informed immediately if a priest named Father Michele returned to Rome? Well, earlier this morning, we received such word."

Alais looked at Ciarán, her eyes wide. Ciarán sucked in a sharp breath. The old man Alais knew as kindly Father Michele—likely the same being Ciarán encountered a half-world away as the terrifying gothi, Blind Mikkel—was back in Rome.

Gerbert blinked twice. "Are you certain of this?"

"Archdeacon Niccolo bore the tidings," Pietro said, "and his spies are second to none. He reported that Father Michele was seen visiting the Convent of Minerva." Pietro's face filled with awe. "If Father Michele is who you believe he might be …"

"Then perhaps the prophecy's final act has begun," Gerbert mused. "For Scripture holds that *he* will return at the End of Days."

Ciarán could hardly wrap his mind around the implications. Michele and Mikkel were both derived from the ancient name Michael. *Father Michele … Blind Mikkel … Saint Michael.*

The pope gave them a thoughtful look. "You three should get going. If an archangel *is* afoot in Rome, then you'd best not keep him waiting."

CHAPTER 2

MINERVA

lais and Ciarán followed Pietro through the veil of mist surrounding the Baths of Diocletian.

Even though the Viminal Hill, on which the baths sat, had been largely abandoned for centuries as the city's population clustered around the Tiber, they could not risk panic among the citizenry if someone saw a dragon circling above one of the Seven Hills of Rome. So before their exercise began, Alais had summoned the mist from the morning dew to conceal their activities. Misty mornings were common this time of year, and few people would pay much attention to the thick cloud of mist covering the hilltop and flowing into the valleys flanking the hill. It also helped that the sky this morning was gray and thick with clouds, blending seamlessly with the mist.

The cool vapor kissed her skin as Alais emerged from the misty veil. Pietro led the way down the road of broken flagstones that descended to the shallow valley between the Viminal and Quirinal Hills.

Ciarán walked beside her. "When I woke this morn," he said, "I didn't expect to be doing this today."

"Neither did I," Alais admitted, running her fingers through her damp hair. "Though I knew we'd see him again."

Ciarán raised an eyebrow. "Is that a hunch? Or is it, uh ..." He chewed his lip as if trying to find the right words. "You know, something you remember from the last time all this happened?"

Alais feigned a wounded look, her hand fluttering to her chest. "Ciarán mac Tomás, the last time all this happened was a thousand years ago. Are you suggesting I'm that old? You know, it's impolite to comment on a woman's age."

"You nary look a day over twenty-three, milady," he replied with a charming grin. "But what about the prior versions of you?"

"Ah, all those pesky past lives," she said with a smile. "I've no memory of most of them, and what I recall of the others are like bits and pieces of shattered ceramic scattered across the ground. I can't tell how to piece them back together. But what I remember about Michael—if that's who Father Michele truly is—comes from what I was shown back in Avalon. When I saw how he and Sirra put all of this in motion."

That vision, revealed to her in the scrying pool of Avalon, was one Alais would never forget. Michael stood in the hull of a boat with a prow carved like a heron's head, the glowing waters of the Lethe lapping at its hull. His robes, as white as ivory, shone with light, reflecting off hair the color of beaten bronze and a face both ageless and perfect. Sirra waited to board the vessel, her silver hair spilling over her shoulders. Together, they forged a plan. Sirra would sacrifice her immortal form, allowing her to be reincarnated through an endless series of lives, all to protect the Key, a sacred power imbued within her spirit.

"If Michael started this plan with Sirra to protect the Key from the Dragon and his servants," Alais continued, "he'd need to make sure whichever incarnation of Sirra existed in this lifetime knew who she really was so she could use the Key when it was needed. Which brings me back to Father Michele. When I first met him at the ruins of the Temple of Venus and Roma, I swear he knew who I was. He told me that if he weren't a Christian man, he might think that Venus had returned to her temple. He knew that's where I'd discover that Sirra was the first of my former lives. It was as if he was guiding me to that place because the situation depended on my being there on the night of the Awakening."

Ciarán stroked his chin. "If Father Michele's the same man as Blind Mikkel, I suppose he guided me, too. He knew who I was by name, and he told me a story about the Key. It allowed me to realize it was not the physical object we'd been searching for, but a power residing within Sirra. But even more, his words led me to Stonehenge, where you found me."

"Because he knew you and I had to do this together," Alais said with a thoughtful nod. "He's been guiding us all along, and I won't be surprised if he wants to give us one more piece of guidance before we embark on the final leg of this journey."

Ahead, Pietro turned around and ran a thick-fingered hand over his tonsured scalp. His expression suggested he'd been quietly eavesdropping on their conversation all along. "Here's what I don't understand. If he's who we suspect he might be, and he's truly looking out for you two, why didn't he just drop by the Lateran Palace? It's not like we couldn't use some help to figure out what we're supposed to do next or how to get to Dudael, wherever that might be. I have a list of questions for him longer than my arm."

"If Father Michele is the same person as Blind Mikkel," Ciarán said, "I can assure you he's not a very direct fellow. He's fond of riddles and mysteries."

Alais thought about that. "Father Michele was never mysterious, but he was subtle. He offered clues, but I think he wanted me to discover the answer on my own."

Ciarán tipped his head toward the clouds. "That reminds me of something Dónall told me when he showed me Maugis d'Aygremont's riddle about the sphinx and the key to the prophecy." He imitated his mentor's gruff Irish tone. "'*Knowledge of any value has to be earned, lad. So if there's any value to those theories, you're going to have to sort it out yourself.*' Then he told me to solve the damn riddle."

A gentle smile formed on Alais' lips. "I suppose if we're in for more riddles, we're fortunate you've become so good at solving them. And you, Pietro, seem to have a knack for that, too."

17

Pietro blushed. "But none like yours, My Lady. Of the three of us, you might have the keenest knack of all."

Alais gave Pietro a fond look as they continued up the road before the mammoth remains of the Baths of Constantine came into view. Half of the structure had collapsed, exposing the crumbling remnants of its dome-like apse. One portion still had a roof with terracotta tiles, though others were roofless shells with pockmarked walls where the marble facade had long been pilfered to adorn some of the many basilicas the popes constructed throughout Rome. Beneath one of the towering archways, five cloaked figures huddled around a cookfire. One of the figures craned its neck to look their way.

Alais' muscles tensed; Pietro gave a worried glance.

"They're likely just outcasts," Ciarán said, "but no need to worry." He made a deliberate turn toward the huddled figures and drew Caladbolg from its scabbard. The sharp sound of steel scraping against the scabbard's mouth rang through the ruins. The blade was imposing, broader than a typical longsword, with a cross-shaped guard and round pommel set with an opaque gemstone. Alais knew that if Ciarán invoked the blade's true power—the power of the weapon Gerbert had called Enoch's device—these people would flee like field mice from a burning barn. But even in its current state, the double-edged sword was fearsome enough to cause the cloaked figures to look away and huddle more closely around their fire.

"They won't give us any trouble," Ciarán assured them.

"I hope you're right," Pietro replied, hastily touching his forehead and chest in the sign of the cross.

Alais put a comforting hand on the monk's shoulder. "He's right."

Ciarán sheathed his sword, and they walked briskly past the ruins where the colossal statues of the Horse Tamers stood in a plaza paved with flagstones. Only the massive pedestals, where the naked Tamers posed alongside their gigantic stallions, stood unmarred by the vandalism that plagued the surrounding ruins. The two statues were protected by the Crescentii, the powerful Roman family whose patriarchs had served as the prelates and princes of Rome for most of the century. They were the makers and unmakers of popes, ruling the city with a king's ruthlessness before the Holy Roman Emperor Otto the Third returned to Rome and defeated Crescentius of the Marble Horse. Crescentius's banner even depicted one of the Tamers' mighty stallions. Alais remembered that banner flying above Castel Sant'Angelo where Crescentius made his last stand before it was torn down and replaced by Otto's standard of Saint Michael. *Once again,* she thought, *everything points to Michael.*

East of the Horse Tamers, the road cut through a weed-choked field more than a quarter-mile wide before ending at a cluster of buildings that looked like a small town. Tendrils of smoke wafted from hearths of two and three-story buildings made of wood and brick, and behind them loomed the massive domed structure the Church had christened as the Basilica of Santa Maria Rotunda. The Romans of antiquity, however, had known it as the Pantheon.

As they neared the buildings, where a flock of chickens scratched and pecked the edge of the field, Alais caught her first whiff of the odors of urban life: the stench of refuse and animal dung mixed with the aromas of cookfires drifting from the chimneys. The road led to a narrow street flanked by frame houses, shops, and storehouses. Shopkeepers, hawking their wares, crowded the lane before the street ended in a familiar plaza. At the plaza's eastern end, where pigeons foraged between the flagstones, stood the columned portico of the Basilica of Santa Maria Rotunda. Atop the columns, the basilica's triangular pediment bore the inscription "M. Agrippa L.R. Cost Tertium Fecit"—*Marcus Agrippa, son of Lucius, three-time consul, made this*—and above it rose the structure's magnificent dome.

"Around the corner, there used to be a temple to Minerva," Pietro said. "It was in ruins, of course, when Pope Zachary allowed a group of Basilian nuns to build a convent atop the site."

He took them down a narrow street between the basilica's curved wall and a row of sheds and close-packed houses. "Here it is."

The narrow street opened into a modest plaza where a white-faced church with three circular windows stood on the east side. A litter with exquisite woodwork and prominent crosses between the screens on its side sat in front of the church while its bearers, dressed in plain gray tunics, sat against the convent's facade. Next to the litter, two hard-looking guardsmen leaned on their spears, eying the trio as they approached. Alais felt their gaze crawl over her body until their eyes focused on Caladbolg strapped to Ciarán's side.

Pietro approached the guardsmen. "Peace be with you, friends. May I ask who that belongs to?" He gestured toward the litter.

One of the guardsmen, a towering, broad-shouldered Lombard with a jagged scar down his left cheek, answered brusquely. "It belongs to His Excellency, Cardinal Bishop Beno, whose business with the abbess is none of yours."

Ciarán leaned close to Alais. "He's a charming fellow."

"I see that," she replied under her breath.

Pietro wrinkled his nose, turned away from the guardsman, and began ushering Ciarán and Alais toward the church's main entrance.

"Who is Cardinal Bishop Beno?" Ciarán asked as they stepped into the church.

"Cardinal Bishop of the Suburbicarian Dioceses of Tusculum and a kinsman of the late Crescentius," Pietro explained, keeping his voice low. "Pope John the Fourteenth appointed him to his current office, and he's had his eye on Saint Peter's throne ever since."

"Can I help you?" asked a woman's voice from the nave.

Alais turned away from Pietro to find a nun, not much older than herself, glaring at them.

"Ah yes, blessed sister," Pietro answered. "We come from the Lateran on word that a Father Michele may be visiting this convent. We would very much like to speak with him."

"I'll have to see if he's still here," the nun replied tersely. "He comes here to visit one of the orphans. But you'll have to wait in the cloister. And you cannot bring a weapon into a house of God." She made a frustrated gesture toward Caladbolg.

Ciarán gave her a sheepish grin. "My apologies, sister. I would have left my sword outside had those guardsmen looked more trustworthy."

The nun's expression softened. "You can call me Sister Priscilla. Just follow me."

Sister Priscilla led them to a door halfway down the nave that opened into the cloister. It looked like every other cloister Alais had ever seen, with four covered walkways arranged in a square shape with rows of archways along the interior walls opening to an herb garden in the center. The cloister's outer walls were stone with doorways to the various buildings that comprised the convent: the church, the chapter house, the dormitory, and the refectory.

"You can wait here," Sister Priscilla said. "I'll try to find the old priest." She turned on her heels and strode down the walkway before rounding a corner. When she reached the opposite side of the cloister, she disappeared into one of the doorways.

"Let's pray she finds him," Ciarán said.

Alais clasped her hands. "Let's hope."

Sister Priscilla did not return quickly. As they waited, the three of them wandered down the walkways surrounding the garden. Halfway down, they heard voices from behind a slightly open wooden door. Pietro bent an ear toward the sound, then mouthed a word. *B-e-n-o.*

Alais crept beside Pietro to listen.

"I've uncovered some damning information about our Frankish pope," an older man's voice said.

"Do tell," a woman replied eagerly.

"It's about his time at the Cathedral School of Reims before he tried to usurp the office of archbishop."

Pietro's eyes widened. Alais clutched the sleeve of his habit.

"The pope was a member of a cabal of heretical monks who obtained a forbidden book, undoubtedly discovered by the pope in his youth when he studied among the infidel Moors. I'm told there were twelve of these monks at Reims, a mockery of the blessed apostles. Do you know what happened to seven of them?"

"What?"

"They burned at the stake."

Alais sucked in a sharp breath. Beside her, Ciarán grimaced. One of those seven monks, Alais knew, had been Ciarán's father. Ciarán's mother died alongside him.

"For what crime?" the woman asked.

"Sorcery."

The woman gasped.

"If seven of them practiced the Devil's ways, I have little doubt our pope did too."

"Will you take this to the emperor?"

"When I have a bit more," Beno said slyly. *"The young emperor is still fond of his former tutor, but I believe more digging will yield finer gems. The pope's wickedness has infected the Lateran. Just look at this woman he has taken in. The one they call the Lady of the Lateran Palace?"*

"Scandalous!"

A chill pricked Alais' skin when she realized they were talking about her.

"I have spies inside the palace," Beno continued, *"and once we've secured enough evidence, we'll convince the emperor to move against the pope. After all, the thousand years are ending …"*

"And when the Savior returns," the woman hissed, *"no foreigner shall sit on Saint Peter's throne."*

"Blessed Sergius," Pietro muttered under his breath. Ciarán shook his head in disbelief while Alais' stomach tightened into a knot.

As footsteps echoed in the cloister, they withdrew from the door. Alais' gaze shifted to find Sister Priscilla approaching, accompanied by a young girl who seemed no more than twelve or thirteen. Dressed in a simple gray frock, the girl had an air of vulnerability, her olive skin setting off a heart-shaped face and bright brown eyes. Her dark hair, reminiscent of Alais', was neatly pulled back, save for an arresting streak of white that cascaded down the center. Such a premature hint of gray was unusual in someone so young, but it detracted nothing from her youthful beauty. Alais had little doubt the girl would mature into a stunning young woman. Yet, in the absence of Father Michele accompanying the girl and the nun, Alais felt a twinge of unease.

Before Sister Priscilla could utter a word, a door creaked open behind them. A priest in somber black robes adorned with a golden cross stepped into the light, followed closely by a nun whose face was heavily creased by age. The priest had to be Cardinal Bishop Beno, his face gaunt, with jaundiced eyes smoldering in deep-set sockets. His skin looked as if it were parchment, stretched taut across a skeletal frame, and errant wisps of silver hair escaped the confines of his black skullcap. Initially, he regarded Alais with a flicker of surprise, but as it evaporated, his eyes took on a disquieting gleam, eventually resting on the young girl. The corners of his mouth lifted in a ghost of a smile—subtle, but enough to make Alais' skin crawl.

"Peter Pig's Snout," Beno sneered, "to what pleasure does this convent owe your presence?"

Pietro stuck out his chin. "His Holiness has interests here we must attend to."

"His Holiness has many interests, it seems." Beno made a subtle nod toward Alais, earning a grin from the abbess. "I must be going. I have the Lord's business to do elsewhere." As he turned to leave, he cast a parting glance at the girl. Alais stepped between the two, and Beno scowled at her before retreating with the abbess toward the church.

Sister Priscilla looked at them, puzzled by what had just transpired.

"Did you find Father Michele?" Alais asked.

The nun turned to the girl. "Tara, tell them."

"He arrived yesterday before breakfast, milady," the girl said. "But he left before nightfall."

"Did he say where he was going?" Ciarán asked.

The girl shook her head.

"The old priest brought Tara to us seven years ago after her mother died," Sister Priscilla explained. "As I said, he comes to check on her now and then, but he never stays long. If he returns, I'll tell him you wish to speak with him. But for now, you must go. It's almost the holy hour of Sext, and the sisterhood will be gathering to worship. You can leave the way you came."

Alais' heart sank. Had Father Michele just come for the girl?

As they turned to leave, the girl reached for Alais' hand as if to shake it. But, instead, she pressed something into Alais' palm. Alais looked at the girl, but her face was unreadable.

Alais waited until they had left the convent. Cardinal Bishop Beno's litter was gone, and the plaza stood empty. She opened her hand to find a piece of stained parchment folded into a small triangle.

"What's that?" Ciarán asked.

"The girl gave it to me."

Alais unfolded the parchment and sucked in a breath. It was a curious message addressed to her.

My dear Alais, I'm sorry I missed you.
Remember to protect the Witness.

CHAPTER 3
THE MAP ROOM

C iarán hurried through the marble hallways of the Lateran Palace.

He had overslept after another night tormented by a nightmare of the Dragon. The vividness of that dream still shook him. A memory of the creature rearing back his head before unleashing a torrent of fire, stopped only by the wall of black water Alais had summoned to save them. But when the wall of water collapsed into steam, the Dragon remained, gazing through those molten eyes, boring into Ciarán's soul. He had awoken in a cold sweat sometime after midnight. Eventually, he fell back asleep, slumbering straight through Prime, and finally crawling out of bed when the bells tolled for Terce. He had lost most of the morning, but the last thing he wanted to do was be late for his meeting with Archdeacon Niccolo. It was never a good idea to keep the pope's chief spymaster waiting.

The hallway ended in a foyer, its final doorway granting access to the palace's expansive map room. Ciarán stepped onto a floor of alternating porphyry and white marble tiles. Narrow windows summoned midmorning sunlight into the chamber, where it danced upon mosaics depicting biblical scenes: Jonah in the belly of the whale and the Apostles wrestling with tempestuous seas. At the chamber's heart stood an imposing table, and behind it waited Archdeacon Niccolo. Dressed in a severe black cassock adorned with a silver cross, his angular face wore its customary pinched expression, as if he were perpetually caught between a sneer and a frown.

"Brother Ciarán, good of you to finally make it."

"My apologies, Your Eminence," Ciarán answered with a slight bow. "I trust Pietro already briefed you about what we overheard Cardinal Bishop Beno saying yesterday at the convent."

Between his weak chin and long nose, Niccolo's lips curved into a frown. "He did. Sadly, Beno is a pit viper. He's heavily supported by Crescentius's widow and son in Spoleto, who would like nothing more than to return the Crescentii to their former glory. I also fear that Beno has fallen in with the remnants of the Brotherhood of the Messiah. It's unfortunate you and your Danes didn't kill them all earlier this year. That would have been good of you. They remain hellbent on ensuring that by the end of the millennium, no foreign pope will sit on Saint Peter's Throne."

"Our goal that night was to find the Key, not end the brotherhood."

"I know it was." Niccolo's frown gave way to the hint of a smile. "Oh, and I'm sorry you missed this Father Michele. I'll let you know if I catch word of his return. I have eyes and ears everywhere in Rome."

"And, thankfully, outside of Rome, too." Ciarán glanced down at the map spread across the table. The map was as large as a tapestry, depicting all of Europe and portions of Africa. Illuminations decorated much of the map, transforming it into a work of art created by a master craftsman. Throughout the seas, great whales spewed water, sailing ships caught wind from billowy clouds, serpentine sea monsters rose from the ocean, and mermaids and giant crabs nestled on islands. On land, banners waved above cities, eagles soared over vast mountains, long-horned aurochs roamed the valleys, and satyrs danced near dense forests. As one who grew up illuminating manuscripts as a young monk at Derry, Ciarán could marvel at the map for hours. But today, the information he hoped to receive from Niccolo was more pressing than his artistic admiration. For somewhere in that wide world was a ship called the *Reaver*, and Ciarán was determined to find it.

The *Reaver* was captained by an ally of Naberus da Roma named the Varangian. After Naberus led the Viking attack on Ciarán's ship, *La Margerie*, nearly a year ago, the Varangian purchased *La Margerie's* surviving crew as slaves. This included Ciarán's crewmate Mordechai and his dear friend Josua, whom Ciarán had convinced to join their campaign, even though it meant leaving his wife and three children. Josua had already lost his eldest son, Eli, on their earlier voyage to Córdoba, yet another young life sacrificed for this terrible cause. So, ever since their capture, Ciarán had vowed that he'd free Josua, Mordechai, and *La Margerie's* crew before they gave their lives, too.

When Ciarán noticed the smooth stones marking various cities along the coastlines, his hope swelled. "Does this mean you've received tidings about the *Reaver*?"

Niccolo grinned. "I believe so. South of Rome, the Tyrrhenian Sea is awash with Saracen pirates. Fortunately, however, this Varangian is of the Rus, and a giant of a man no less, so he's not hard to spot among a crowd. I have word that three months ago, the *Reaver* was moored in Constantinople. The Greeks refer to the Rus as *Varangians*, and I suspect he may have hailed from there before relocating to Rome and working for the Crescentii. After being spotted in Constantinople, his ship was sighted in Amalfi." He pointed to a greenish stone next to a town on the Italian peninsula south of Rome. "And then in Tropea," he continued, noting a marker on a city farther south, near the toe of the boot-shaped landmass.

His finger drifted to a stone marking an island farther south in the Mediterranean Sea. "More recently, the *Reaver* was seen in Malta, and I have a report, though unverified, that the ship had moored in Carthage at one point." He gestured toward a fourth marker on the tip of Africa.

Niccolo retraced the points on the map, moving from Amalfi to Carthage, then from Malta and Tropea, forming a roughly rectangular shape. "As you can see, in the center of it all is Sicily, which is where I suspect the Varangian has made his new home. Now, Sicily is ruled by Ja'far bin Yusuf, whom the Egyptian caliph has dubbed the 'Sword of the Faith.' But lately, that sword has not been very sharp, for Sicily stands on the brink of a civil war. Rumor has it Ja'far's brother has aligned himself with the Berbers and is trying to convince them he would be a more fitting ruler. I doubt the Sword of the Faith would house a foreign and infidel pirate as notorious as the Varangian at Palermo. But I would not put it past him to keep the man as an ally close by. My hunch is that the Varangian is based here, somewhere near Trapani." He pointed to a town on the coast of north-western Sicily. "Or perhaps here, in the Egadi Islands." He placed a finger on a cluster of five small islands west of Trapani.

Ciarán rubbed his forehead as he worked through the possibilities. Jarl Holger's longship, the *Lindworm*, could make the voyage in a few days with fair weather. But when would they have time to undertake such a journey? The Dragon's threat remained, and they were nowhere close to deciphering the location of Dudael, the place where the prophecy says they'll face the Dragon in the final battle. Still, now that he knew where the Varangian might be, his goal never seemed nearer.

He had one more question, however. "Have you any word of Naberus da Roma?"

Niccolo pressed his lips into a thin line. "None. Although wherever he's surfaced, there's a chance this Varangian may know where to find him."

"Yet another reason to track down the Varangian."

"True," Niccolo said. "But I must caution you, Brother Ciarán. There are slave markets throughout North Africa and Sicily, so there's no guarantee your friends are still with him."

"Aye," Ciarán replied, "but I must keep the faith."

"As we all should."

Ciarán clasped his hands. "Thank you, Your Eminence, for all of your aid. If you learn more, please let me know."

"You have my word." Niccolo's pinched expression returned to his face. "Good day, Brother Ciarán."

By the time Ciarán left the map room, he figured he had an hour before his training session with Jarl Holger. Since their return to Rome, the Danish lord had been teaching him swordcraft, and Ciarán welcomed the lessons. Having spent most of his adult life as a cloistered monk copying manuscripts and illuminating their margins, he had none of the skills to be a swordsman. But serving as an oarsman on Holger's ship had developed his muscles and given him the strength to swing a sword like a warrior should. All he needed now was training. Though with his lesson still an hour away, he had time to check on Pietro, who had thrown his energy into deciphering Father Michele's cryptic note.

Ciarán navigated a labyrinth of columned corridors, their grandeur accentuated by the sculptures that stood like silent sentinels along the way. Eventually, he arrived at a deep alcove, home to a shrine dedicated to Saint Sophia of Rome. Guarding the shrine was Gaido, the captain of the Papal Guard—a clear indicator that the Pope was sequestered in the papal archives below. A towering man hewn from Lombard lineage, Gaido wore chainmail beneath a crimson tunic that bore the image of two crossed keys over his broad chest. Beneath his crested helmet, a pair of blue eyes surveyed Ciarán. Those eyes were set in a stern, clean-shaven face marked by furrows of age, suggesting a man who had lived at least two decades longer and seen worlds more than Ciarán.

"Brother Ciarán," Gaido said in a husky voice, "I can guess why you're here."

Ciarán clasped his hands together. "And by the fact you're here, Captain Gaido, I can guess His Holiness is downstairs."

"A fair guess," Gaido replied with a hint of a smile. "He's with Brother Pietro, as you might expect."

"Then I ought not to keep them waiting."

Gaido nodded before welcoming Ciarán into the shrine.

As Ciarán entered the shrine, he inhaled the sweet scent of beeswax candles. Atop an altar that appeared to be built into the wall, the candles surrounded a small statue of a veiled Saint Sophia holding three young girls, representing hope, faith, and charity. However, there was more to the altar and statue than met the eye, for the construct was actually a doorway that led to the papal archives. Constructed in 452 by Pope Leo the Great, the underground archives originally existed to protect the Holy See's most precious books and artifacts from Atilla and his Huns. And it always amused Ciarán that Pope Leo was clever enough to hide the entrance to the archives behind a shrine to a saint whose name meant "wisdom."

Passing through the clandestine doorway, Ciarán descended a stone stairwell that unfurled into a corridor, its brick walls dimly illuminated by flickering rushlights. As he ventured deeper, the walls gave way to a series of alcoves, each a shrine unto itself, marking his entry into the sanctuary known as the Hall of Relics. These hallowed niches cradled the most sacred treasures and artifacts in Christendom. One alcove enshrined a colossal golden menorah—plunder from Rome's sacking of Jerusalem. Next to it, a magnificent reliquary shaped like a towering crucifix safeguarded fragments of the True Cross, discovered by Saint Helena at the Holy Sepulchre. Yet another featured a statue of Saint Veronica, her likeness standing guard over a jewel-encrusted chest containing the holy veil bearing the image of the Savior's face. Further alcoves housed elaborate reliquaries, each enclosing the bones of saints or other invaluable ecclesiastical artifacts amassed through the centuries. Each step Ciarán took through this sanctified chamber filled him with profound reverence and awe.

The Hall of Relics gave way to an elongated chamber bathed in the warm glow of candles, a space Ciarán had come to know as the Reading Room. Volumes and scrolls, each a repository of ancient knowledge, filled the wooden shelves that adorned the walls. Suspended from the vaulted ceiling, a grand wheel-shaped candelabra cast its luminous aura over a table strewn with manuscripts and arcane objects positioned at the chamber's heart. There, the pope and Pietro stood engrossed, bent intently over the table's cluttered surface.

"Ah, Brother Ciarán," Gerbert said, looking up. "We were just going to find you. For it seems Brother Pietro may have solved the riddle surrounding our mysterious witness."

CHAPTER 4
THE WITNESS

Ciarán could hardly believe his Irish luck. Already this morning, Archdeacon Niccolo may have located the Varangian, and now Pietro might have deciphered Father Michele's puzzling note.

The message had vexed Ciarán ever since he read it. It spoke of a witness, but a witness to what? And whoever this witness was, why did he need protecting? Ciarán glanced at the table and the mess of unfurled scrolls and leather-bound books, breathing in the scent of dusty parchment and ancient vellum. Had the answer been so simple that Pietro discovered it in a day pouring through these old writings? Ciarán knew the papal librarian was as bright as they came. Despite that, he found it hard to fathom.

"Go on, tell him," Gerbert said.

A satisfied grin spread between Pietro's plump cheeks. "I believe the witness might be part of the prophecy."

That struck Ciarán as odd. He recalled the night with Dónall in the crypts of Saint-Germain-des-Prés more than a year ago. The day he learned the secrets of the prophecy etched in the heavens. "When Brother Remi told me about the prophecy, he said nothing about a witness."

"As I'm sure you'll agree," Gerbert remarked, "Remi's interpretation was less than clear in places."

"It's just a theory," Pietro said, walking over to a large square of parchment displayed on an easel. The parchment had been Ciarán's attempt to recreate an image that Brother Remi had scrawled on the walls of the crypts of the old Merovingian kings. It was a picture similar to a hieroglyph in the book of Maugis d'Aygremont: a circle surrounding a seven-pointed star, and along the circle's outer ring were the twelve symbols of the zodiac. Illuminations of nearby constellations hovered near the symbols to replicate Remi's original drawing. In his book, Maugis had called it "The Prophecy of Arcanus," referring to the Atlantean king who first discovered the secret three thousand years ago.

"You've always said the prophecy is etched in the heavens," Pietro began.

"Aye," Ciarán replied. "That's what Maugis wrote in his book. The interpretation lies in the symbols of the zodiac, so long as you read them in the right order."

"The riddle of the sphinx," Gerbert added. "Maugis d'Aygremont's clever key to the prophecy."

Ciarán nodded. "A creature with the head of a woman and the body of a lion. So, the prophecy begins with the woman, Virgo, and ends with the lion, Leo. But I'm unaware of any symbol of the zodiac that's supposed to represent a witness, whatever that's supposed to be."

"Bear with me," Pietro said. He pointed to the first four symbols: Virgo, Libra, Sagittarius, and Scorpio. "We know the meaning of the first act of the prophecy, for you've already experienced it. The champion of men, symbolized by Virgo's seed, is measured—or tested, as suggested by Libra's scales—in an early battle against the enemy, represented by Scorpio. The key is Sagittarius, the weapon we refer to as Enoch's device. That's how you survived the prime conflict."

"I'm well aware," Ciarán added.

"Of course." Pietro clasped his hands together. "The meaning of the second act, the one you call the journey, is also clear. The journey, symbolized by the running waters of Aquarius, begins and ends with a sacrifice, represented by Capricorn, the goat, and Ares, the ram. Sadly, these were Orionde and our dear Pope Gregory, though it's the third symbol in the quartet, Pisces, that reveals the journey's purpose."

Above the symbol, Ciarán had illustrated two fish bound by a chain connected to two other images. The first was the constellation Cetus, which Ciarán had tried to recreate from Remi's drawing, a beast like a great whale with the scales of a fish and the jaws of a shark. The second was the constellation Andromeda. Remi had depicted her as a shamelessly naked woman, but Ciarán's version was clothed and bore a vague resemblance to Alais.

"Pisces," Ciarán acknowledged, "represents the Key to the Abyss. It binds the fallen angels, represented by Cetus, to the woman—Andromeda or, rather, Sirra—whose spirit lives in Alais. Only the Key can free the fallen from their eternal prison."

Gerbert gave a sly grin. "Our old friend Remi hadn't put that one together."

"No," Ciarán admitted. "None of us did until Alais learned its meaning in Avalon."

"Which brings us to the last act," Pietro said eagerly. "It begins with Taurus, the raging bull, a symbol of conflict. It also ends with Leo, another symbol of the champion, and his final confrontation with the Dragon."

Next to the symbol for Leo, Ciarán had illustrated the constellation known as the Hydra. The seven-headed serpent embodied the book of Revelation's seven-headed Dragon, an incarnation of the Devil himself. It was a grim reminder of what awaited Ciarán at the end of all this.

"Before Leo, there's Cancer," Pietro continued, "whose meaning means to bind or encircle. We all agree it symbolizes the place where the final conflict occurs."

"Dudael," Ciarán said. The Hebrew word translated into the Cauldron of God. "Alais believes that as much as she believes anything. But that leaves us only with Gemini. Brother Remi believed it meant 'united'—the forces of mankind coming together in the battle of Armageddon. So, where's your witness?"

Gerbert looked down his aquiline nose. "Sometimes a symbol can have more than one meaning."

Ciarán scraped his fingers through his hair. Gerbert was right, of course. Ciarán had confronted symbols with dual meanings on the cover of the Book of Giants, and understanding both meanings allowed him to solve the puzzle. Yet here, a second meaning eluded him. "I'm afraid I'm no expert in astrology."

"Neither am I," Pietro admitted, "though my research reveals that Gemini also symbolizes Castor and Pollux, the twins from Greek mythology."

"Were either of them witnesses?" Ciarán asked.

"Not that I'm aware," Pietro said. "The important part, however, is that there are two of them."

Ciarán sighed. "As is always the case with twins. I don't see how this relates to Father Michele's note."

Gerbert pressed his palms together. "Don't focus on the astrology or the mythology. There are other sources about the subject of this prophecy."

Pietro lifted a leather-bound book from the table, which Ciarán recognized as a copy of the book of Revelation. "Scripture," Ciarán admitted.

Pietro leafed through the pages, stopping halfway through the tome. "Among all the malevolent things John of Patmos warns us about—the Dragon, the Whore of Babylon, the Beasts of the Earth and the Sea—he also writes of two benevolent beings. The two witnesses."

"In Revelation," Gerbert said, "the two witnesses are prophets. Some in the Church believe they are Enoch and Elijah reborn to warn about the End of Days."

Pietro touched the symbol for Gemini. "What if Gemini marks the arrival of the two witnesses? We still do not know how one finds their way into Dudael, but suppose the two witnesses are the key to getting to this place?" His plump finger shifted from Gemini to

Cancer. "And if Scripture is any guide, these two will need plenty of protection."

Ciarán scratched his head, unable to recall this precise portion of Revelation. "Remind me."

"It's written right here." Pietro began reading from the passage he had turned to. *"'When they have finished their testimony, the beast that comes up from the bottomless pit will make war on them and conquer them and kill them.'"* He closed the book.

"You must admit," Gerbert said, steepling his fingers, "Pietro's theory is worth considering."

Ciarán rubbed his forehead. So far, each act of the prophecy had focused on something from Scripture critical to surviving this conflict: the device from the Book of Enoch and the Key to the Abyss from Revelation. So, why couldn't these two witnesses from Revelation be essential to the final act? But there was one detail that did not fit Pietro's hypothesis. "Father Michele spoke of one witness, not two."

"Yes," Pietro conceded, "but Scripture also doesn't say the two witnesses must be found in the same place."

Gerbert held up a finger. "Which means it's plausible that Father Michele was warning you that one of the two is in Rome—and in grave danger."

"That would certainly explain Father Michelle's note," Ciarán conceded.

"It also supports another theory I've been pondering about the prophecy and the number seven," Gerbert said.

"Seven?" Ciarán asked. "What do you mean?"

The pope's eyes shone with a clever gleam. "The Book of Revelation is replete with references to the number seven. An angel opens a scroll with seven seals, the seven angels sound seven trumpets and pour seven bowls of wrath, and John of Patmos wrote the Book of Revelation for the seven churches. Also, Christ stands among seven candlesticks, and there are seven spirits around God's throne. All *metaphora* to some degree, but I believe it's no coincidence that the hieroglyph of the prophecy from Maugis d'Aygremont's book has a seven-pointed star as its primary symbol."

Gerbert reached into his pocket. "Then there's this." He held out a disk-shaped amulet, one Ciarán had seen before. Made of gold, it showed the familiar Seven-pointed star, but within its center was a dragon's head shaped like an inverted pentagram. "As you know, we found this on one of the Nephilim warriors that Jarl Holger and his men killed on the Palatine Hill. At each of the seven points on this heptagram, there's a crown. It's another symbol from Revelation: the seven-headed Dragon who wears seven crowns. We believe Naberus da Roma summoned the Nephilim through the gateway in the shrine to the Etruscan god Orcus, so it seems even our adversaries in the Otherworld find significance in the number seven."

Ciarán eyed the amulet. Maybe Gerbert had a point. Ciarán had seen a similar symbol with a seven-pointed star on the cover of the Book of Giants they discovered in Castel Sant'Angelo. "So everyone's fond of seven-pointed stars, but what does it symbolize?"

"Let me show you." Gerbert slipped the amulet back into his pocket, then gestured to a sheet of parchment laid out among the scrolls on the table. A series of squares had been drawn up and down the parchment, upon which sat six small polished stones. Three were obsidian black, and three were bone white. A handful of like-colored stones lay off to the side.

"The Moors call this game Tables," the pope explained. "The idea is to conquer your opponent until only one piece remains, either black or white. Now, imagine the Table board as Dudael in the final conflict. Revelation tells us of several beings associated with this conflict." He pointed to the three obsidian stones. "First, there are the three servants of the Dragon: The Beast from the Sea, the Beast from the Earth, and the Whore of Babylon."

Ciarán knew this portion of Revelation well. He had illuminated each of those terrible beings in the manuscripts at Derry, and he was aware of similar beings in the mythology of the Danes. At the battle of Ragnarok, they are the three children of Loki: the great wolf Fenrir, a beast from the land; the Midgard Serpent, a beast from the sea; and Hel, the goddess of the dead.

"You've already faced one of the beasts," Gerbert continued.

"Adémar of Blois, who we know now, was a Nephilim prince of the Dragon's bloodline. Although you slew him during the Prime Conflict, I have no doubt another of the Dragon's bloodline will take his place in the final battle."

"Adémar of Blois came to Derry on a ship," Ciarán realized, "from across the sea."

Gerbert nodded thoughtfully. "Indeed. I also believe you have faced the Beast from the Earth—Naberus da Roma, who murdered Pope Gregory and freed the Dragon from his prison. From the documents we retrieved from Castle Sant'Angelo, Naberus may have been operating in Rome for more than a century, so we must consider that he, too, is not entirely human."

A chill pricked the back of Ciarán's neck. He'd always believed the race of Nephilim dwelt in the Otherworld, where they had been imprisoned since biblical times. But the thought of one of the Nephilim living secretly among humankind was unnerving. Naberus da Roma, however, had never seemed anything but mortal.

"What of the Whore of Babylon?" Pietro asked, causing Ciarán to wonder if this was the first time Pietro was hearing this theory, too.

"She has not been revealed to us yet," Gerbert replied. "But I suspect that's only a matter of time." He reached down and lined up the three obsidian pieces in a straight row. "Until recently, I never connected the Dragon's servants to the number seven because there were only three. But now, with the addition of the two witnesses, my theory began to take shape." He arranged two of the white pieces until they touched one another. The two witnesses."

"And the sixth piece?" Ciarán asked.

"Revelation reveals her identity." Gerbert moved the last white piece in front of the other two until they formed a small triangle. "The angel who holds the Key to the Abyss. The angel is mentioned twice in Revelation, and we know now that angel is Sirra, whose power flows through Alais."

Ciarán furrowed his brow. "That's six pieces. Who's the seventh?"

Gerbert plucked two more pieces from beside the game board,

one white and one black. "I believe the seventh is the victor." He set the black piece on the board's center. "If it's the Dragon, all will be lost. The End of Days will be upon us."

He scooped up the black piece and replaced it with the white one. "The alternative is the champion. Revelation tells us when the original war broke out in Heaven, that being was Saint Michael who battled the Dragon. On the Day of Judgment, it will be Christ. And in the context of the prophecy, for the conflict that lies ahead, it will be you."

Ciarán stared at the white piece in the center of the board, feeling the weight of Gerbert's words—until he heard his name being called from the Hall of Relics.

"Ciarán!"

Jarl Holger burst into the chamber. The urgent look on the Dane's face sent a flutter through Ciarán's stomach.

"It's Alais," Holger said between breaths.

"What happened?" Ciarán gasped.

"She was with Breda when a crier announced some bishop plans to burn a young witch at the stake. Alais flew into a rage. Breda said she's never seen her so filled with fury."

"Where's she now?" Ciarán pressed.

"Breda's gone after her, but Alais rode off to stop them."

A jolt of dread surged through Ciarán. In France, Bishop Adémar had tried to burn Alais at the stake. Back then, she was helpless. But now, after discovering her powers, Ciarán could only imagine what she was capable of.

From the dire look on Gerbert's face, he shared the concern. "You have to stop her."

"Aye," Ciarán said, his heart beginning to race.

Then he followed Holger, rushing down the hall like the palace was on fire.

CHAPTER 5

THE SORCERESS
OF ROME

A flock of pigeons burst into the air as Alais rode furiously through the narrow, cobblestoned streets leading to the Piazza della Rotunda. It felt as though she was charging down a darkened tunnel, her ears filled with the deafening clatter of her mare's hooves against stone.

The anger that sparked when she learned a witch was to be burned now blazed into blinding rage. She would never forget the day Adémar of Blois accused her of witchcraft, to hide the fact he had raped her. That's what depraved priests did to conceal their crimes—accuse their victims of witchcraft. And by God, she would not stand by while an innocent woman burned at the stake.

Since she raced out of the Lateran Palace, tearing past the ruins of the Old Roman Forum, the terrible memories of that December day seventeen months ago had assailed her mind. She recalled the bishop's men tying her to the stake. The rope being pulled around her neck, and then her waist and ankles. The harsh smell of pitch being slung onto kindling and brushed onto her dress while the craven monks of Selles-sur-Cher looked on. Not one of them protested when the bishop's men dropped torches onto the pyre,

40

sending the first tendrils of smoke rising from the pitch-soaked straw. Or when the baking heat reached her toes, and her body shook with sobs as the flames crackled and flared.

Back then, Ciarán had saved her, along with Brother Remi and Brother Dónall, wielding the power of the Fae. But now, she knew, that same power flowed through her veins, and she would use every ounce to stop this from happening again.

She veered down a crooked street that ended in the small plaza in front of the Convent of Minerva. From beyond the convent and the curved dome of the Basilica of Santa Maria Rotunda rose a narrow plume of smoke that caused her stomach to harden like a rock. Alais kicked her mare forward, but it slowed around the corner, its hooves clacking on the flagstones. A crowd of people had gathered in the plaza outside the basilica. From her saddle, Alais could see that many in the crowd were nuns dressed in their Basilian habits, but others were priests and monks mixed with shopkeepers, merchants, housewives, and even children. They gathered around a pyre in the plaza's center. A tall wooden stake jutted from the smoking kindling, and Alais gulped down a breath when she looked upon the girl tied to the post.

The witch was no older than thirteen with a bolt of white in her otherwise dark hair—Tara, the girl from the convent. Bound by her neck, waist, and ankles, Tara stared in terror at the flames crawling up the kindling. Tears streaked down her smoke-stained face as she gasped for air amid the fumes from the burning pitch.

And Cardinal Bishop Beno presided over the atrocity. He raised a bony hand in the air, his voice rising above the murmur of the crowd. "Her eyes rolled back into her head, and she spoke words of blasphemy!"

Gasps erupted from the mob.

"It was a verse of scripture twisted into lies that threatened my holy personage." Beno put a hand on his chest to act as if he had been wounded. "Does not the gospel prove the Devil knows scripture and that he can pervert it to his evil ends? Such artifice is beyond the comprehension of a simple girl. So what must she be?

One who communes with the Devil. She even has the Devil's mark —the witch's streak—in her hair. And she spoke the Devil's words like only a witch could do!"

"Let her burn!" a man yelled from the center of the crowd. Others joined him.

"Kill the witch!"

Heat surged up Alais' neck as she shouted, "Stop this!'

Her voice rippled through the nearest bystanders, their heads turning to regard her. Some wore expressions of confusion, taken aback by the sight of a woman on horseback disrupting the moment; others glared at her with open hostility. Yet it was painfully clear that her plea had been swallowed by the cacophony of the mob.

Sensing her mare's growing unease amidst the throng, Alais dismounted. She began shouldering her way through the sea of onlookers, each step a struggle against the human tide.

"But what of a trial?" demanded an indignant priest from the steps of the basilica. "The girl cannot be properly condemned without a trial!"

"I witnessed this witchery with my own eyes!" Beno hollered. "There's no need for further proceedings unless you mean to accuse me, *a cardinal bishop*, of being the blasphemer. This pyre shall be her trial. If she is not of the Devil, but of God, let Him save her!"

A cheer rose from the mob as Alais pressed her way toward the front. She inhaled the acrid stench of burning pitch. "Stop!" she cried again, but the clamor from the assembled masses smothered her voice.

Alais spotted Sister Priscilla in the crowd. She grabbed the nun's habit, spinning her around. The nun gasped. She held her hands over her mouth, her face swollen from tears. "She was only alone with him for a moment," Priscilla sobbed.

Alais dug her fingers into the nun's robes. "Did he touch her?"

Priscilla began shaking. *"I don't know,"* she mouthed as her voice caught in her throat.

Clenching her jaw, Alais relinquished her grip on the nun's arm and muscled her way through two more layers of gawking spectators. She finally broke free, emerging into the plaza like a tempest. Her gaze locked onto Beno as she shouted, "She's an innocent girl!"

Standing beside his hulking Lombard guardsman, Beno's jaw fell for a heartbeat; then his lips twisted into a feral grin. He pointed a bony finger at Alais. "Look who sides with the witch—the palace whore!"

Another gasp erupted from the mob. The Lombard warrior gave Alais an amused look before reaching for the hilt of his sword while a half-dozen other guardsmen near the front of the crowd trained their eyes on her. Then, from the pyre, Tara screamed. A flickering tongue of fire had flared up from the burning kindling to lick the girl's toes.

"Seize the whore," Beno cried, "and we'll build a second pyre!"

As the guardsmen stepped towards Alais, a newfound rage pulsed through her veins. A fury summoned from her ancient spirit. *From Sirra.* She spoke only three words, known to her since the beginning, born of the language of creation. As the first two words flowed from her tongue, the air sizzled, and the flagstones beneath her feet began to crack. The guardsmen stopped in their tracks. When Alais uttered the final word, she felt the power surge from her palms and focused on the blazing pyre.

With an earsplitting roar, the pyre erupted in a torrent of fire, radiating out from the stake like a hellish wave. Cardinal Bishop Beno was hurled through the air, landing with a thud amidst the petrified throng. Guardsmen were knocked off their feet, as if slapped by an invisible hand, while embers and flaming straw rained down on the gaping mob. The wave of heat and flames parted around Alais as if the fire did not want to harm its master, but all around her, people screamed.

And burned.

With most of the kindling blasted away, the area surrounding the stake was little more than a pile of ash and charred wood. From its center, Tara stared wide-eyed at Alais as if witnessing a miracle.

The mob's terrified screams filled the plaza.

Alais ignored their cries, stepping over ash and debris to rescue the girl.

~

A THUNDER of horses filled the alleyway. Ciarán clung to his palfrey's reins, racing behind Magnus and Holger on their geldings. Holger craned his neck. "I see Breda!"

Ciarán leaned left in his saddle to peer around his companions. Holger's red-haired wife sat astride her bay mare at the end of the alley, although a wall of people barred her path to the plaza. But more alarming than the packed mob and rising smoke were the ghostly blue flames flickering over the rooftops like Saint Elmo's fire. *Alais' using the power!*

When they reached Breda, he jerked back on the reins to slow his mount. A look of concern seized her face. "She's——"

The roar of an explosion cut off Breda's words.

Ciarán's horse bucked in fear, and he had to grab its mane to stay in his saddle as a chorus of terrified screams burst from the crowd.

Beside Ciarán, Magnus looked on in awe, a word falling from his tongue. *"Lifthrasir."*

His heart hammering in his chest, Ciarán spurred his horse through the smoky haze until he could finally glimpse the chaotic scene in the plaza. What was once a neatly stacked pyre had transformed into a hellish scene, its explosion sending the crowd into frenzied disarray. Men, women, and children scattered like startled birds, tripping over one another in their panic. Nearby, the shockwave had flattened a disoriented cluster of priests in dark robes and guards in chainmail, who were now struggling to regain their footing. Amid the smoldering wreckage, jutted a stake. Tied to it was a small woman, and, through the chaos, Alais dashed toward her.

"Get to Alais!" Ciarán urged, as fear-stricken men and women scrambled into the alleyway, pushing past the horses.

"Ha!" Breda yelled, spurring her mare into the oncoming crowd. People leaped away at the powerful mare's advance, and Holger, Ciarán, and Magnus pressed on behind her.

Ciarán forced his way through the panicked crowd, his gaze

darting between people beating flames from their clothes and others writhing from burns, ash blackening faces and tunics. From the gaggle of priests, a man's voice rose over the cries of the crowd. "Stop her!"

Turning his head, Ciarán saw the speaker was Cardinal Bishop Beno. Smoke steamed from his robes, and soot marred what skin of his face was not red with rage. "She is a sorceress! The Whore of Babylon—the sorceress of Rome!"

Four of the guardsman clambered to their feet, and one drew his sword.

"Help Alais!" Holger called to Ciarán. "We'll handle these dogs."

Ciarán gave a curt nod, and Holger and Magnus kicked their horses into motion, positioning themselves like living barriers between Alais and the advancing guardsmen. For a split second, hesitation flashed across the faces of the guards. It was as if they were taking stock of the towering Danes—men whose sinewy muscles bore the marks of relentless oar-pulling and whose rugged faces were hardened from countless battles. The moment Holger unsheathed Curtana, his gleaming longsword, and Magnus drew Corpse-maker, his own formidable blade, the guards wavered, then took a step back.

"Begone, you heathens!" Beno screamed, waving his arms at the Danes. "You are opposing the will of Almighty God!"

Ciarán glanced at Breda, who had reached the stake. Alais had unbound the small woman, whom Ciarán realized was no more than a girl—and one he recognized, too. *The orphan girl Tara.* Alais helped her onto Breda's saddle.

Guiding his horse over the remnants of the pyre, Ciarán held out a hand for Alais. She grasped it, and he pulled her onto the saddle.

She wrapped her arms around his chest. "To hell with all of them," she whispered in his ear.

"Aye," he replied, sharing her anger. They tried to burn a girl at the stake; the act was unforgivable. But his contempt for the cardinal bishop and his priests mixed with growing dread. For the priests and the mob had witnessed her wielding the power, and the consequences of that were inescapable.

As he cantered his horse behind Breda's, heading toward the alleyway, he heard Cardinal Bishop Beno shouting above the wails of the terrified mob.

"She flees, she flees, the sorceress of Rome!"

CHAPTER 6

WHAT DREAMS MAY TELL

Tara was shaking, her eyes wide with fear, as Breda led her away from the palace stables toward the relative sanctuary of a guest chamber. Alais followed at a respectful distance. The surge of anger that fueled her actions in the plaza was beginning to fade into an anxious concern for the girl. Alais had asked Ciarán to ensure that no men would be present during her conversation with Tara. For whatever Beno had done to Tara, the last thing she needed was to face more scrutiny under a masculine gaze.

The guest room was small but comfortable. Breda placed Tara on the bed before handing her a woolen blanket. The girl wrapped the blanket around her body and sat at the edge of the bed. A lock of white hair curled over her forehead.

Breda spoke in broken Latin, which she had picked up since she arrived in Rome three months ago. "You're safe here."

Tara gave a faint nod. Her tears had left a trail through the soot that settled on her cheeks as she stared in awe at Alais. "The bishop called you a sorceress ..."

Alais inhaled sharply before releasing a warm smile. "I'm no sorceress, I promise."

47

"But I saw what you did!" Tara clutched the blanket to her chest. "You spoke to the fire, and it went away!"

"I did what I needed to do to protect you," Alais said firmly. "The power is a gift, but it's not sorcery, just like whatever you said to the bishop was not witchcraft."

Tara lowered her eyes and spoke softly. "Maybe I am a witch, like the bishop said."

"I don't believe that," Alais replied. "Men like Cardinal Bishop Beno often try to conceal their own sins by lying through their teeth." She placed a hand on Tara's arm. "What did he do to you?"

Tara shuddered.

"You can tell us," Breda said. "We've both experienced terrible things at the hands of men."

Tara let out a quiet sob. "I was sweeping the refectory when he came in and asked me to give him a hug. I did so because Sister Priscilla always says we're supposed to obey priests. He made me sit on the edge of a table and touched my leg." She took a deep breath. "Then he slid his hand under my dress."

As she listened, Alais felt renewed anger simmering inside her. She looked at Breda and could tell from the fierce expression on the shieldmaiden's face that she would have gutted the bishop like a salmon had he been in the room.

"He tried to kiss me," Tara went on, "but then I passed out. Like going to sleep and waking up in a dream—a frightening dream."

Alais had not expected this, though she remembered what Beno had said in the plaza. *Her eyes rolled back into her head, and she spoke words of blasphemy!* Alais wondered if this "vision" was Tara's way of coping with Beno's assault. "What happened next?"

"If I tell you," Tara began, brushing a white curl out of her eyes, "you'll know I'm a witch."

"Why would you say that?" Alais asked.

The girl stayed silent, her eyes shifting between Alais and Breda. Finally, she spoke. "My mother could do things like you did. Make fire disappear. If she was a witch, couldn't her daughter be one too?"

Alais' eyes widened. She had known no one who could use the

power except men like Gerbert and Dónall, who had studied the book of Maugis d'Aygremont. There was more to this girl than met the eye. "Did you ever mention this to Father Michele?"

She nodded. "He told me my mother had been touched by God. He called her a magus. I asked the abbess what a magus was, and she told me it's a witch from Persia."

Alais frowned. "What did Father Michele say about you?"

"I asked him if I'm also a magus. He said only time will tell. But he told me I'd been touched too and would become an oracle. When I asked the abbess what an oracle was, she said it's a witch from Greece. So I think the bishop might have been right after all."

Alais shook her head slowly. What must this girl have thought about herself growing up? The bishop and the abbess were as ignorant as they were cruel. But Father Michele was not, and he'd obviously taken a particular interest in the girl.

"The bishop's a fork-tongued liar," Alais told Tara. "And I doubt the abbess even knows what she's talking about. But if Father Michele believes you're an oracle, I want to hear what you saw in your dream after you fainted. I've had dreams too, and they were often trying to tell me something."

Tara took a deep breath. "I was standing before an oak tree with leaves that burned like fire. In the branches were four creatures, like the monsters I've seen painted in the margins of some of the books in the convent. Their bodies were like a huge cat's with wings like a falcon's, but each had a different head. One looked like a lion. Another had the head of an ox. A third had the face of a man, and the last one had the head of a bird—an eagle, I think."

That's no ordinary dream, Alais thought.

"They gave me a warning," Tara said. "I must have spoken it aloud when I woke up."

Alais recalled Beno's words. *It was a verse of scripture twisted into lies that posed a threat to my holy personage!* "Do you remember what you said to the bishop?"

"They told me to speak it."

"The creatures?"

Tara made a slight move of her head to indicate yes. "They said,

'Four seals broken, three survive. On judgment day, the horsemen ride. Their leader's horse is pale of hue. His name is Death, and he comes for you.'" Tara chewed her lip. "Don't you think that's an awful, witchy thing to say?"

"I wouldn't call it witchy," Alais said. "Though it sounds like a prophecy." *Something an oracle would say.*

The girl's brown eyes brimmed with apprehension.

"What is it?" Alais asked.

"When they told me to say it, I imagined the bishop's face. But I also saw your face, from your visit to the convent."

Alais tilted her head in confusion.

"The warning was not only meant for the bishop," Tara said, her voice full of worry. "I think it was meant for you, too."

CHAPTER 7

THE BROKEN SEALS

Gerbert rubbed his forehead as he listened to Ciarán's account of what happened with Alais outside the Basilica of Santa Maria Rotunda.

The pope sat in a high-backed chair beneath a domed ceiling decorated with a mosaic of Christ and the twelve apostles. Sunlight streamed through an arcade of windows, illuminating the chamber and dancing off the mosaic tiles.

From across a round table, Ciarán described their escape from the plaza.

"Oh dear," Pietro muttered to Gerbert's left when Ciarán explained what Alais had done to the pyre.

When Ciarán finished, Gerbert sighed before taking a long drink of wine from a narrow chalice.

As the pope set down the chalice, Archdeacon Niccolo entered the chamber. "How bad is it?" Gerbert asked.

Niccolo closed the door behind him. His normally pinched expression looked bleak. "My sources have spoken with several priests and nuns who were in attendance. According to one, the pyre exploded like a ball of fire into the crowd. Another said it was as if the Devil himself appeared as a woman to cast fire and brimstone over the assembled faithful. To a man, all claimed to have seen Lady Alais utter foreign words, whether a magic spell or the names of demons, before the explosion. The injured among the crowd promptly overwhelmed the hospital at the Convent of Minerva, but according to the nun in charge of the infirmary, none of the wounds were mortal. Fortunately, most were minor burns or people who fainted during the ensuing panic."

As Ciarán listened, the knot in his stomach tightened. Things were worse than he imagined.

Meanwhile, Gerbert groaned. "What of Cardinal Bishop Beno?"

"I understand his eyebrows and hair were badly singed, and he's quite livid." Niccolo frowned. "I fear he'll make trouble."

"I don't doubt it in the least," Gerbert said.

Pietro wrinkled his nose. "Why does Beno get to play the role of victim? He tried to murder a thirteen-year-old girl, for God's sake."

Pietro's question gave Ciarán a glimmer of hope. "Doesn't the law demand a trial?"

"There is precedence for dispensing with the trial," Niccolo explained, "particularly when a priest himself has witnessed the crime."

Ciarán's hope extinguished like a candle in a stiff breeze. *That same case could be made against Alais.*

"There should have been a trial," Gerbert insisted. "None of this was handled properly. But that doesn't change the fact that scores of citizens witnessed Alais' actions. And while we know there's a benevolent explanation for how she did it, we won't convince the Church or the citizenry of that. Many in the Church are quick to conclude that anything they don't understand must be witchcraft or deviltry. Could you imagine a pope trying to explain the Fae and their origins and the source of their power? Half of Rome resents a foreigner sitting on Saint Peter's throne. Just imagine what they'd do if they saw me trying to rationalize what they believe to be sorcery. The mob would drag my body through the streets like they did to Pope Boniface the Seventeenth."

"We won't let that happen, Your Holiness," Pietro said.

"Though Beno undoubtedly will try to use this to undermine your papacy. We know he was scheming to do so before this happened."

Holger rapped his knuckles on the table. "If only the bishop's guards had raised arms against us." He spoke in stilted Latin. "Magnus and I could have dispatched them and maybe killed this Beno, too."

"The murder of a cardinal bishop would not have helped the situation," Gerbert said disapprovingly.

"It would have eliminated an enemy." Holger crossed his arms. "A dead enemy cannot plot against you."

Gerbert shook his head. "You're a Christian now, Jarl Holger. That's not how we settle things."

Holger grumbled under his breath and took a sip of wine from his cup. On a leather cord around his neck, the silver crucifix he had worn since his baptism gleamed in the sunlight.

"Can't we use the fact that Beno was going to kill a child against him?" Ciarán asked.

"At thirteen years old, she's hardly a child," Niccolo pointed out. "Under the law, she's old enough to marry. But more importantly, the sympathies of the mob will not turn against Beno if they believe the girl is a witch."

Ciarán rubbed a hand over his face, trying to fathom how they could avoid the trouble Beno would cause, when someone knocked on the door. Niccolo opened it, and Alais stepped into the chamber.

She was met with Gerbert's disapproving gaze while Niccolo's expression turned from pinched to scowling. Ciarán wondered how much she had overheard through the door.

Alais' storm-gray eyes simmered with anger. "Beno tried to rape her."

"Blessed Sergius," Pietro muttered.

Niccolo looked away; Gerbert's mouth fell open. Suddenly, Ciarán appreciated the depth of Alais' fury. *They both suffered similarly at the hands of bishops.*

"Tried?" Gerbert asked in a bewildered tone. "How did she stop him?"

"She blacked out," Alais explained, "but then experienced a

vision, like a dream—the kind meant to deliver a message. And there's more. Father Michele told the girl she's an oracle and that her mother was a magus."

Ciarán blinked. During the last cycle of the prophecy, a thousand years ago, the magi—each a magus—were its champions. Even more, their friend Khalil had long believed the Persian magi would have prepared for the prophecy this time around. But this was the first Ciarán had heard to suggest the magi still existed.

"The Oracle of Delphi was a prophet," Pietro said, the surprise still lingering in his eyes.

Gerbert's gaze narrowed. "Tell us about this dream."

Alais reiterated everything Tara had told her about the tree with the burning leaves and the four creatures, but when she mentioned the different heads of the beasts, Ciarán drew a sudden breath. By the astonished look on their faces, he could tell Pietro and Gerbert shared the same realization.

"The four living creatures," Pietro said, "with the heads of a lion, an ox, a man, and an eagle. In the book of Revelation, they are the Cherubim, the agents of God."

"Some scholars equate them with the archangels," Gerbert added.

"Would this child have known enough Scripture to imagine such a thing?" Niccolo questioned.

Ciarán felt certain of the answer. Since the prophecy had begun, both Alais and Holger had received messages through their dreams. Father Michele and Blind Mikkel played a role in both instances. *And if they're indeed the same person …*

"The girl was raised at the convent," Ciarán said, "but I doubt they've turned her into a scholar on the book of Revelation. Though if she's an oracle, as Father Michele claimed, then as Pietro said, she's a prophet. Just like the two witnesses from Revelation."

Gerbert wrinkled his forehead. "You think we've found one of the witnesses in a thirteen-year-old girl?"

Ciarán glanced at Alais, who looked like she was struggling to follow their rapid remarks. She had been gone when Pietro developed his theory about the witness, so Ciarán began from the beginning. "At the Convent of Minerva, we were told that Father Michele brought the girl there seven years ago—*seven years*. He also had the girl give Alais a message to 'protect the witness.' So now, we have this girl—this oracle or prophet—claiming to receive messages from the very agents of God referenced in that same book of scripture. On top of that, she's in mortal danger. *She's* the one Father Michele warned us to protect. She has to be the witness."

Pietro's eyes widened. "If she *is* the witness, then Alais had to save her, or everything might have been lost."

Gerbert rubbed the chin of his ginger beard. "On the chance that Father Michele is who we suspect he might be, we must consider your theory, Brother Ciarán. Though I suppose before we settle on any conclusions, we should hear from Lady Alais about what the creatures supposedly said to the girl in her dream."

Alais surveyed the men seated at the table. "The creatures," she finally said, "gave her a warning, and it sounds very much like a prophecy. They said, *'Four seals broken, three survive. On judgment day, the horsemen ride. Their leader's horse is pale of hue. His name is Death, and he comes for you.'"*

"Oh, my," Pietro said. "I imagine *that* got Beno's attention."

"She warned him he was going to die," Ciarán added bitterly, "so he accused her of witchcraft."

Gerbert gave a thoughtful nod. "That seems plausible for a man like Beno. But I'm struck by the fact this girl has given us another reference to Revelation—and to the number seven."

"Aye," Ciarán said, having caught the reference too. "The Seven Seals of God. In Revelation, they herald the End of Days. The first four seals unleash the four horsemen of the apocalypse. Their leader rides the pale horse." He quoted the verse from scripture. *"'And there was a pale green horse. Its rider's name was Death, and Hades followed with him.'"*

"Still," Gerbert said, thinking aloud as he often did, "the girl's words—or the creatures' words—if she's to be believed, warn that the end is near. We already knew that. Yet why would she give this warning to Beno? What do the four horsemen have to do with him?"

"I can answer that," Alais said, her expression darkening. "Tara said the message was not just intended for Beno, but for me, too. Whoever is coming wants the Key."

As the chamber grew quiet, Ciarán's stomach hardened, and Brother Remi's warning echoed in his mind. *The Dragon has servants —men in dark robes who hide in the shadows. And not just men.* This was everything he had feared. They were coming for Alais, and he would have to fight them.

Even if it cost him his final breath.

THE IDEA of something coming after Alais dominated Ciarán's thoughts for the rest of that day and kept him up for most of the night. But, worst of all, he had no notion of what might be coming. Were they human servants, like Prior Lucien and his devil-worshiping monks? Or something more fearsome, like the Furies who had pursued them to Córdoba or the Nephilim who they had fought on the Palatine Hill? The only thing worse than not knowing *what* was coming was knowing they wanted Alais.

These thoughts tormented Ciarán as he tossed and turned in his bed until exhaustion finally overcame him, and he drifted off to sleep, left only to his dreams. Though since the night of Pope Gregory's murder, Ciarán's dreams had become nightmares.

As it had done so many times before in his sleep, the Dragon glared at him with molten eyes. Fire gathered in the depths of its throat behind a forest of razor-sharp teeth until it exploded into a searing blast of flame.

As before, Alais raised the wall of water as black as cuttlefish ink, transforming the fire into hissing steam. As the wall collapsed, Ciarán expected to feel the beast's molten eyes boring into his soul. But when the billowing steam dispersed into a swirling gray mist, the fiery Dragon was gone. In its place was a man floating in the mist, dressed in dark robes and a broad hood. The hood's shadow obscured the man's face, save for a pair of eyes with gleaming golden irises.

Even though those eyes had taken on a more human form, Ciarán sensed he was staring into the eyes of the Dragon.

"Ciarán mac Tomás," came a menacing voice from the shadow of the hood.

At the mention of his name, Ciarán's blood ran cold. *This is just a dream,* he tried telling himself. But it felt *real.* As he stared at the hooded figure, coils of chilling mist wrapped around Ciarán's limbs, and he found himself lifting off the ground as if his body had become weightless. He glanced at his hands, noticing a faint luminescence clinging to his skin.

This can't be real, Ciarán insisted, fighting back the terror welling inside him.

"Ozam!" the voice said as if speaking a command.

Around the fingers of Ciarán's left hand, the mist sizzled. A strange heat settled in his palm, warm but not scalding. From the surrounding mist came a faint whisper, as if the vapor was humming a haunting verse. *Ozam, odamma, cialpor, mir, agrit ...*

What is happening? his mind screamed.

"I've been watching you," the voice replied as if answering his question.

How? Whether Ciarán thought the question or spoke it out loud, he could not tell.

"Nothing escapes my gaze."

Ciarán felt the power of that gaze searing into him. "You're the Dragon." His words were barely a whisper.

"But one of many names. They call me the Morning Star, the Shining One, the Son of the Dawn, the Night-Bringer. You know who I am."

Panic surged through Ciarán's veins. He wanted to turn and flee, but his body floated helplessly in the seething, whispering mists.

Ozam, odamma, cialpor, mir, agrit ...

"What is this place?" Ciarán gasped.

"The Greeks called it the astral plane. When you dream, your astral form touches this realm—a realm I, too, can reach from the place you call the Otherworld. Finding you took time, but as long as you dream, you cannot escape me."

The terror within Ciarán swelled. He could hear his heartbeat thrashing in his ears, barely noticing the heat pressing into his left palm or the whispers in the mist.

"Why are you here?" Ciarán stammered.

"To show you the truth." The golden eyes narrowed. "You remember my servant, whom you knew as Adémar of Blois? Do you recall what he told you the first time you met?"

Ciarán's memory flashed to that day in the candlelit oratory at Derry, more than a year and a half ago. Adémar of Blois had grabbed his arm with a grip like a blacksmith's. The bishop glared at him with feral eyes. His dark mustache and beard, flecked with gray, added to his wolfish appearance. *"All you need to know,"* Adémar had said, *"is that everything you have come to believe is a lie."*

Beneath the hood, the golden irises flared brighter. "You do remember."

Ciarán clenched his jaw. "I killed Adémar of Blois."

"So you did, but your victory was pyrrhic. One has already taken his place—his brother, who is eager to avenge him. And what did that fleeting victory cost you? How many lives have been sacrificed for your cause?"

"No," Ciarán murmured. Their names haunted him. *Khalil, Dónall, Isaac ... his brothers at Derry ...*

The image of the hooded man faded. In its place, Ciarán found himself staring at his dearest friend. The closest thing he ever had to a real brother. *Niall.*

Clad in his fleece-gray habit, Niall stood on the grassy Irish hillside with a blood-stained sword. Two Frankish warriors lay wounded at his feet near the bodies of their friends, Murchad and Fintan. Adémar of Blois grabbed one of the swords and parried Niall's strikes.

The bishop's face burned with rage as his blade arced out with a cleaving strike.

A scream caught in Ciarán's throat.

Niall's body staggered backward, a yawning red wound opening from his shoulder to his waist.

Ciarán shut his eyes. He could not bear to watch any longer.

58

"You drove me to this," he heard Niall say.

Ciarán opened his eyes to see Niall slowly crawling toward him on the blood-slick grass. "You let me die," he insisted through gritted teeth.

"Not true," Ciarán stammered.

"You're going to let them all die!"

"No!" Ciarán screamed.

He awoke panting, his chest slick with sweat.

"What's wrong?" Pietro asked in a startled tone, sitting in the bed beside Ciarán.

As his breathing calmed, Ciarán realized he was back in his chamber, safe inside the Lateran Palace.

"It's nothing," he said. "Just a bad dream."

CHAPTER 8

THE TORMENTOR OF SOULS

An hour before midnight, Ugo Grassus trudged up the path that climbed the Palatine Hill. The ruins of the imperial palaces loomed over Rome. Swathed in a voluminous black cowl and cloak, sweat permeated the fabric and trailed down his ample, bearded jowls, each droplet a testament to the discomfort weighing on his ox-like frame.

"How much farther, quaestor?" growled one of the sellswords following behind him. Ugo had brought three of them on this trek, all huge, muscular men who had served Crescentius before the boy Emperor Otto the Third took his head. The three wore swords at their sides, but on this night, they carried sacks and shovels.

"The shrine is across the hill," Ugo replied between deep breaths, "near the House of Augustus."

"Why would Naberus da Roma hide his money there?" the sellsword asked. "Anyone could find it?"

"The entrance to the shrine is hidden," Ugo explained. "It was made nearly two thousand years ago by the Etruscans to honor their god Orcus. And it is one of many places throughout Rome where I believe Naberus hid his wealth."

"And what if he finds out we took some?" another of the mercenaries asked. "I wouldn't want to get on his bad side."

Ugo craned his neck to look the hard-faced mercenary in the eye. "Naberus is *never* coming back to Rome. That, I can assure you." It was the first thing he had told the sellswords that had not been a lie. Naberus would never return to Rome. His master had assured him of that.

The last time Ugo had seen Naberus da Roma was at the Basilica of Santa Maria Nova. The Tiber had overflowed its banks and flooded the ruins of the ancient Roman Forum, and that night, Naberus had used Greek Fire to set the water ablaze. He and three others had arrived by boat only so Naberus could drop off Countess Theodora. He had some need for her in the ruined Temple of Venus and Roma that abutted the basilica, and before he departed, he made her drink some intoxicating liquid that affected her like milk from the poppy. Then he had rowed away in his boat with Pope Gregory, bound and gagged in the stern. On the oar bench beside him sat Rumeus, the traitorous archdeacon who had helped arrange the pope's abduction. They told Ugo they were taking the pope to the Palatine Hill. That was the last Ugo ever saw of the three of them.

Back then, Ugo did not know what had become of Naberus. Crescentius's notorious consigliere had not been seen anywhere in Rome, nor had Rumeus. The pope, however, was found dead, and some claimed he had been murdered. A few even whispered that Ugo Grassus had a hand in his death. By then, Ugo had been declared a traitor and forced to flee his position in the Holy See. He had been a quaestor, a pardoner of sins for the Church. But at heart, Ugo Grassus was always a thief.

Not long after the floodwaters subsided, Ugo decided to search for the place Naberus had taken the pope. Ugo had long suspected that Naberus kept sanctuaries hidden throughout the city where he stored his vast wealth, and there were rumors he would frequent a place within the ruins on the Palatine Hill. Greed had lured Ugo to that place, which he discovered after several tedious days of searching. It was an old Etruscan shrine beneath the ruins of a temple to

Apollo. Feverish with anticipation and the prospect of untold wealth, he descended the long, crumbling stairway leading down to the shrine. Yet there, in its depths, he had not found wealth but something else—a presence.

That was many weeks ago. Since then, Ugo had waited patiently to return to the shrine, spending his time surveilling the Lateran Palace, stealing glimpses of the raven-haired woman who held the Key within her veins. She would be his ultimate prize. But he had been ordered to wait until the others could arrive, for his master wanted to handpick his horsemen. And now, finally, it was time to greet them.

Ugo and the three men reached the crest of the hill, where moonlight cast shadows off a grove of cypress trees. They skulked through the ruins of imperial gardens near the hulking remains of the old palace of Emperor Domitian. "Over there are the ruins of the temple of Apollo." Ugo pointed across the gardens, where the broken remains of columns jutted like gravestones from the overgrown weeds. "That is where we'll find the entrance to the shrine."

When they reached the ruined temple, Ugo gestured to an enormous flagstone that sat near the ruins of Apollo's temple. All that remained was a foundation of mortared gray stone covered in moss and vines amid a scattering of broken columns. "The stairway down to the shrine is under that flagstone," he said. "It will take a few of you boys to lift it."

One of the sellswords shrugged before wedging his shovel under the flagstone's side. He grunted while veins bulged from his muscular arms, which shook as he pushed on the shovel. After all that effort, he managed to raise it but an inch off the ground before the flagstone thudded back in place.

"See what I mean," Ugo said.

The next time, two men used their shovels to raise the stone enough for the third man to move it aside. The muscles in his back bulged from the strain. With the flagstone pushed aside, the men stared down as a stairwell of ancient stone that plunged into darkness. "You'll need to light torches," Ugo instructed.

After they did, Ugo followed them as they carefully descended the stairwell, whose steps were crumbling in places. After climbing down more than a hundred steps, one of the men gasped. "What is that?"

In the sputtering torchlight, they faced an archway carved to look like the face of a roaring giant. Beneath wide-open eyes and broad flaring nostrils, two fangs jutted from the top of its mouth, which created an opening large enough for a man to pass through.

"That is Orcus," Ugo said reverently, "and this is his shrine. He was a great, great god. A god of death. A lord of the Underworld. The punisher of broken oaths, the tormentor of souls!"

Two of the men looked at him wide-eyed, while the other glared at Ugo as if he had gone mad.

"I don't like this bloody place," the man protested.

"Do not worry," Ugo assured them, "that is just what the Etruscans believed. And it was long ago, before the founding of Rome. Enter, and I'll show you where the treasure is buried."

"This better damn well be worth it, Grassus," another of the sellswords griped.

"If Naberus da Roma was as wealthy as some suspect, your reward will be handsome."

"It better be."

Warily, the three men stepped through the carving's gaping mouth. Ugo followed them into what was little more than a cave. A shallow alcove stood at the far end, where dark stains marred the small flagstones that covered the ground. "There," Ugo said, "in the alcove. Dig beneath those stones."

The burliest of the men was the first to enter. Jamming his shovel between two of the flagstones, he pried the first one loose. Worms slithered from the dark soil where the stone had been. The other two men joined in, digging with their shovels.

One of the men tapped his shovel on a dark, reddish stain on one of the stones. "What is this?"

Ugo's broad lips stretched into a grin. "The blood of the innocent."

The burliest man shot him a cross look. "Stop trying to scare us, you sick bastard."

Ugo chuckled. "You should be very scared."

The burly man stared back daggers; his mouth formed into a snarl. "What did you say?"

Then, without warning, Ugo charged. He threw his full three hundred pounds of girth into the sellswords, slamming them into the alcove's wall. Before they could shove the quaestor off them, ghostly hands emerged through the stone like glowing wisps of smoke. The spectral arms grasped at the men, who let out terrified screams as phantom fingers clawed into their skulls.

Ugo stepped back and watched the attack play out until the three men stopped struggling and the spectral forms disappeared. When it was done, the men just stood there, staring at Ugo, their collective gaze filled with a fiendish gleam.

The being that once was Ugo Grassus stared back. For when he came to the shrine many weeks ago to steal Naberus's treasure, Ugo had discovered a presence—an ancient and malevolent force that enveloped him, just like the demons who had possessed the sellswords. The spirit spoke inside his head and dominated his will until it came to control all of his thoughts.

"Welcome, brothers," he told his companions. "I am Orcus."

CHAPTER 9
MERIDIANA

C iarán's concern for Alais had not eased by the following day. Nor could he dispel the memory of last night's terrifying dream. The golden irises of the Dragon in human form and Niall's terrible last words: *You're going to let them all die …*

That didn't happen, Ciarán reminded himself. Niall had died at the hand of Adémar of Blois, but he never spoke those words. Ciarán had convinced himself it was just a bad dream, but these thoughts still weighed on his mind during his lesson with Jarl Holger.

Since Gerbert's coronation as Pope Sylvester the Second, Holger had held daily lessons with Ciarán in the art of swordcraft. They practiced in a small, inner courtyard framed with columns and archways, away from the priests and monks who frequented the Lateran Palace's many halls and passageways. Holger insisted they train in chainmail so Ciarán could get used to the armor's weight while fighting with wooden swords designed to weigh more than their steel counterparts. After five weeks of this conditioning, Ciarán felt comfortable with the weapon's weight and had improved his parries and thrusts. But Holger's lifelong experience in fighting allowed him to school Ciarán before the lesson's end, landing a sweeping blow to Ciarán's gut when he had raised his sword higher than he should.

Had the weapon been a real sword, it would have sheared through his mail into his flesh and stomach; instead, Holger's strike only knocked the wind out of him.

As he doubled over, struggling to regain his breath, Ciarán wondered why in Heaven God had chosen him to wield Enoch's device. He had spent nearly his entire life as a cloistered monk in a remote monastery in northern Ireland, while men like Holger had spent their lives honing their swordcraft instead of copying manuscripts with goose-quill pens. Holger also stood almost a foot taller than Ciarán, with broad shoulders and muscular arms as thick as an average man's thighs. Surely, Ciarán thought, a warrior like the Danish jarl would have been a far better choice than he was.

Holger handed Ciarán a cup of watered ale. "Drink this, and next time, keep your sword down."

There was a time when Ciarán would have answered, "Yes, lord," for almost a year ago, he had been one of the jarl's thralls—his slave—after being captured along with his friend Khalil during the Viking attack that claimed Évrard's life. Ciarán had hated Holger and his other captors back then and even devised a plan to escape during one of Holger's trips to Dublin. But Khalil became convinced that fate—*kismet*, as he called it—had determined their destiny lay with Jarl Holger. Holger's sword belonged to one of Charlemagne's paladins who, along with Maugis d'Aygremont, protected the secret of the prophecy two hundred years ago with the aid of Orionde the Fae. Khalil saw this as a sign. Even more, Holger dreamed of fighting alongside Ciarán at Ragnarok, the great battle in the Northmen's mythology like the Christian Armageddon. Both men now believed that was the conflict toward which they were heading, and, joined by this destiny, the two men had become friends of sorts. Three months ago, Holger had made Ciarán a free man.

Ciarán gulped down the ale and then sat down on a bench. Holger joined him.

"I have been thinking about the girl Tara's dream," the Dane said. "The tree she saw with leaves like fire reminded me of the stories about Yggdrasil."

"Yggdrasil?" Ciarán thought for a moment. "I remember Blind Mikkel using that word."

"Yggdrasil is the great tree whose branches spread out over the nine worlds and reach up to the heavens. At one of its roots, three old hags called the Norns spin the fate of men. The fate they have spun for us lies at Ragnarok, as Blind Mikkel told us. And now, I fear, the destiny of that girl Alais saved has been woven into our own."

"If Blind Mikkel and Father Michele are one and the same," Ciarán said, "that may be true."

"When I think of Yggdrasil," Holger continued, "I think of our fate. We're supposed to fight this battle in Dudael, yet we have no idea how to get there or where it even is. You, Pietro, and Gerbert have been rummaging through those dusty books in the archives for weeks. And what have you found? Nothing. And now, we have this bloody priest causing trouble that threatens to set us back even further. Half the priests in Rome think the world's going to end before your year one thousand, and yet this Beno is out trying to burn witches and scheming for ways to usurp Gerbert's throne." Holger's face reddened. "It reminds me of a story I heard about an old emperor of this place who played a fiddle while the city burned."

"Emperor Nero."

Holger nodded. "Like Emperor Nero, this priest is fiddling away while the drumbeat towards Ragnarok grows louder, and now we must deal with his machinations when we could be finding our way to Dudael. Had I known yesterday who this troublemaker was, I would have separated his head from his shoulders, and I don't give a damn what the priests might have thought about it."

Ciarán let out a weary sigh. *If only it were that easy,* he thought.

"You look tired," Holger said. "Have I worked you too hard?"

Ciarán shook his head. "It's not that. I've been worried about Alais, but ..." He considered not mentioning the dream, but he had to tell someone. "I've been dreaming of the Dragon ever since we fought him. But last night, in my dreams, the Dragon spoke to me. I know it sounds foolish."

Holger raised a brow. "In the legends of my people, dreams are not to be taken lightly. Sometimes, they show us the future, like my dreams about Ragnarok, as Blind Mikkel has said. But other times, dreams are how men are contacted by the spirits or the elves. Even the gods."

Ciarán suppressed a shudder. "You think he could have reached out to me in the dream?"

"If he has, and if the Dragon is like the Loki of our legends, you need to be on guard. Loki is known as the Lie-Smith, the Shape-Changer, and the Sly One. Lies are his weapon. He will use them to poison you."

"He said he wanted to show me the truth."

"I hope you didn't believe him."

Ciarán thought about that, holding his head in his hands. *It must have been a lie; Niall didn't speak those words.*

Hearing footsteps, Ciarán glanced up and caught sight of Magnus striding through an archway. Adorned in a knee-length mail hauberk—once the property of Maugis d'Aygremont—Magnus radiated a roguish air. Ciarán had originally lost the armor to him during his time in slavery. Yet, in a twist of fate, he'd allowed Magnus to keep it, negotiating the return of his leather baldric instead. The intricately designed strap secured Caladbolg's scabbard to his side. Magnus's shock of blonde hair framed his forehead, giving way to bright blue eyes that almost always held a gleam of mischief.

"Irish," Magnus called, using his nickname for Ciarán, "you'll want to see this. The shaven men are making trouble. A small army of them is gathering outside the palace."

Ciarán and Holger glanced at one another. The pagan Danes called priests and monks "shaven men" because of their tonsures. While many of Lindworm's crew had become Christians like Jarl Holger, Magnus had remained steadfastly pagan. His contempt for Christian priests was well known, and Ciarán found it ironic that Magnus was now living in the Lateran Palace, the home of the most important priest in all of Christendom. Magnus's tidings, however, alarmed Ciarán, who had little doubt Cardinal Bishop Beno had something to do with it.

After slinging his baldric over his shoulder and securing his scarlet cloak, Ciarán fell into step with Magnus and Holger, navigating a labyrinth of marble corridors. They ascended a stairwell, eventually reaching the columned hall that opened onto the papal balcony. Out on the terrace, Pietro and Archdeacon Niccolo stood side by side, their eyes trained intently on the unfolding scene below in the plaza. As Pietro heard the footsteps of Ciarán and the Danes, he craned his neck and met Ciarán's gaze, mouthing three words: *"This is bad."*

A wave of unease roiled Ciarán's stomach when he saw the size of the crowd. Amassed in the plaza below, the mob numbered five or six hundred, mostly gathered around the massive statue of Emperor Constantine on his stallion. There were scores of black-robed priests, monks, and nuns, and among them, Ciarán noticed the long pointed hoods of the Brotherhood of the Messiah. He counted at least thirty members of that poisonous cult among the mob, which was still growing. Merchants and laborers, men and woman, and even their children joined the rabble, which included Romans from all walks of life: beggars dressed in little more than filthy rags, citizens in plain tunics and dresses, and gentry in their fine-spun clothes accompanied by hosts of mailed guardsmen. Ciarán suspected the nobles were likely members of the old Roman families, the same people who supported the powerful Crescentii. A hostile murmur rose from the mob.

"Have you seen Beno?" Ciarán asked Pietro.

"He's here." Pietro pointed to a line of men pushing their way through the crowd toward the palace. In the front of the line, four servants carried a wooden dais, while behind them trailed an entourage of guardsmen and priests surrounding the cardinal bishop. He waved to members of the crowd, who cheered him on as his servants set down the dais, and he climbed its wooden steps.

"Yesterday," Magnus said under his breath, "I should have stuck that shaven man like a hog."

Holger nodded. "We should have."

Beno's priests and guardsmen circled the dais and raised their arms to quiet the crowd. Among the guardsmen stood Beno's hulking Lombard warrior. He looked up at the balcony and caught Ciarán's eye. A leering smile spread across his lips to the jagged scar on his left cheek.

Ciarán glanced at Niccolo, who stood, arms crossed, glaring at Beno.

Beno lifted a finger and leveled it at Niccolo. "We are here for the Lady of the Lateran Palace. She stands accused of sorcery and witchcraft!"

An angry grumble rose from the crowd.

"Yesterday, in the Piazza della Rotunda," Beno went on, "she was witnessed speaking a language most diabolical to the burning pyre, where another of her coven would have received the fire of God's holy justice. Through her unholy magic, the fire did her evil bidding and caused grave injury to me and twenty-six Roman citizens, including six priests and seven monks. She is accused of the crimes of sorcery and witchcraft, and, as the book of Exodus commands, no one of God shall permit a sorceress to live!"

"Burn the witch!" A man cried from the crowd, encouraging others to follow.

"Kill the witch!" they hollered.

"Roast her alive!"

As their anger rose, Ciarán felt a stab of concern that the mob might try to break into the palace.

Then Niccolo spoke. "This is a holy place. The lady is entitled to seek sanctuary here. She will not be turned over to a bloodthirsty mob."

"See," Beno cried accusingly, "the pope's own archdeacon seeks to defend her!"

Shouts of protest filled the plaza, but Beno raised his voice. "This proves the extent to which her demonic influence has infected the Holy See. For hear me now and listen as if the fate of your immortal souls depended on what I am here to tell you. The woman they call the Lady of the Lateran Palace is, in truth, *Diablos Meridi-*

ana, the sorceress of Rome and the Devil's concubine! She has seduced the pope and taught him all her wicked spells in exchange for sins of the flesh." His face bore a perverse look of ecstasy. "The witch, Tara, is her apprentice, and together they seek to corrupt the Holy See!"

Bile rose in Ciarán's throat as the crowd's chants rang anew.

"They cannot live!"

"Both should burn!"

"Quiet!" Niccolo demanded. A red hue flushed up his neck. "We will not tolerate mob justice on mere accusations. The law requires a trial."

Beno scoffed. "I, a cardinal bishop, witnessed her crimes, as did sixty-six other priests, monks, and nuns. There is no cause for a trial. Open the doors and let us take the witch and her apprentice and bring them to God's justice!"

As the mob's front line lunged forward, Ciarán's hand instinctively shot to the hilt of Caladbolg. But just as suddenly, the crowd halted, as if hitting an invisible wall. A sea of scarlet emerged on the nearby palace balconies—papal guardsmen, their bowstrings taut, aiming arrows downward at the restless crowd. The air grew thick with tension; if they released their arrows, it would be a massacre.

"Cardinal bishop," Niccolo shouted, "any bloodshed today will be on your hands. There shall be no sentence without a trial. That is the law!"

"This is outrageous!" Beno's eyes bulged with fury. "I shall appeal to the emperor. Even his foreign pope cannot defy the word of God, for no sorceress shall be permitted to live. *That* is God's law!"

A roar erupted from the crowd—cheers of approval intermingled with hisses of derision aimed at Niccolo and his guardsmen. Beno, basking momentarily in the discord he'd sown, lifted a defiant fist into the air. With that final gesture, he pivoted on the dais and melted back into the seething mass of humanity below.

As the mob began their slow retreat, Niccolo gestured for the archers to lower their bows.

Ciarán, meanwhile, felt ill. "What do we do now?"

Niccolo's face was grim. "We must get to the emperor before Beno does."

CHAPTER 10

TRIALS AND TRIBULATIONS

C iarán sat on the pedestal of the magnificent statue of Constantine astride his mighty stallion, waiting for Gerbert's return.

He had been gone for hours since leaving for the emperor's fortress on the Aventine Hill, and the wait left Ciarán on edge. The plaza was strangely serene. There was no sign of the angry mob who had packed the area earlier that morning, though a half-dozen armed guardsmen protected the entrance to the palace. The sky above was blue with wisps of white clouds, and across the plaza where the flagstone ended in a patchy field of grass, Breda and Tara were playing fetch with Breda's dog Rosta.

Tara hurled the stick as far as she could, sending the massive boarhound bounding after it while Breda clapped and cheered. After Rosta fetched the stick, he dropped it at Tara's feet and gave the girl an eager look, his tongue wagging from his jowls. It never ceased to amaze Ciarán how a dog bred for hunting boar and who had killed men in battle could be so kind and playful with the people he loved. Breda, meanwhile, looked as happy as Ciarán had ever seen her. Holger once mentioned the two of them had been unable to have children, and Ciarán wondered if Breda had found in Tara the daughter she never had.

Ciarán's head turned at the creaking sound of the palace doors swinging open. Alais emerged, swathed in a dress of muted slate-gray that matched her headscarf. Despite knowing her for well over a year, her beauty never ceased to make his breath catch in his throat. She crossed the plaza with purposeful strides and settled beside him on the pedestal. "I've made a mess of things, haven't I?" she exhaled with a wistful sigh.

"You did what you had to do. Besides, maybe Gerbert can put an end to all the trouble Beno has caused."

Alais looked skeptical. "You really think he can convince the emperor to make this all go away?"

"If anyone can, it's Gerbert. He's known the emperor his whole life. He tutored him and served as his private secretary before the emperor appointed him archbishop of Ravenna. After Pope Gregory's murder, the emperor could have appeased the Romans by naming one of their own to the papal throne, but he chose Gerbert instead."

"Still," she said with a frown, "men like Beno—evil men with power—aren't easily stopped. Especially with the threat of a mob. Would the emperor risk the peace he's tried so hard to keep for someone like me? I doubt it."

Ciarán harbored that same doubt, and it was fueling his growing sense of dread. He let go of the thought when Alais reached out and gently touched the hair above his left ear.

"You have flecks of silver in your hair," she said.

"Silver?" Ciarán liked the feel of her touch, but did not know what she was talking about.

"I've never noticed it before. Don't worry; it's just a little. Not nearly as much as Gerbert."

"I'd hope not. Gerbert's thirty years my senior!"

"You don't look *that* old," she said with a smile.

Ciarán combed his fingers through his hair as though he could actually feel the strands of silver woven into it. His attention shifted when the rhythmic clatter of hooves echoed down the road. Led by

Captain Gaido, a dozen papal horsemen escorted a litter bearing Gerbert into the plaza. As the litter bearers settled near the palace entrance, Niccolo was the first to disembark, followed by a stern-faced Gerbert. The pope's sour demeanor did little to quell Ciarán's growing apprehension. Soon after, Pietro emerged from the litter. Spotting Ciarán and Alais, his unsmiling expression left a bitter taste in Ciarán's mouth.

"What happened?" Alais asked as soon as Pietro was in earshot.

"Beno reached the emperor first," Pietro said, wringing his hands. "He must have gone straight to the Aventine palace after he left the plaza. By the time we arrived, he was gone." He looked at Alais. "He nearly convinced the emperor you should be executed without trial because so many nuns and priests had witnessed what happened."

Ciarán grimaced. "You said nearly. Did the pope change the emperor's mind?"

"Only to a degree," Pietro replied. "His Holiness argued a trial would best serve God's will. After all, Beno might have misperceived what he thought he had witnessed, which could mean the accused was innocent." He gave Alais a sympathetic look. "The emperor wants to hear your plea and judge your sincerity before committing to a trial. So, he's summoned all of us to his court at noon tomorrow. Right now, however, the pope wants to speak with the two of you in his study."

Alais shot Ciarán a look of concern. He took her hand and gently squeezed it. "I'm sure Gerbert will think of something."

They found the pope in his study with Archdeacon Niccolo.

The two men huddled over an open book on the pope's dark oak desk. Behind them, neatly filed books and scrolls filled bookshelves that dominated the far wall, casting off a musty scent of vellum. When Ciarán and Alais followed Pietro into the room, Gerbert looked up at them with a humorless expression. "I presume Pietro's told you there will be a trial. Assuming, of course, that the emperor accepts your plea of innocence as genuine."

"I can swear to my innocence," Alais insisted.

Niccolo raised an eyebrow. "Convincingly?"

She crossed her arms. "The charges are witchcraft and sorcery. The power I wield is born of the language of creation, and the spirit within me that enables it is light, not dark. So, yes, when asked if I am innocent of witchcraft and sorcery, I can swear on God's name that it's true."

Ciarán could hear the conviction in her voice. He hoped the young emperor would recognize it, too.

"That may convince Otto," Gerbert said. "The trial, however, will present a very different challenge."

"What will it entail?" she asked.

The pope let Niccolo answer the question. "Beno will demand a trial by ordeal, and if history is any indication, the ordeal will be boiling water. A small iron cross is placed at the bottom of a boiling cauldron. If the accused can reach into the cauldron and remove the cross without being scalded, then God is on her side, and she shall be proclaimed innocent. However, if the flesh of the arm or hand blisters or swells, she must have been in league with the Devil and will be condemned."

"If you take God and the Devil out of it," Gerbert added, "it is pure *scientia*. Flesh burns when exposed to scalding water, so you can imagine how often the accused is convicted."

Ciarán felt his stomach tighten, but Alais appeared undaunted. "I could manipulate the water," she said, thinking out loud. "Lower its temperature during the ordeal."

Gerbert shook his head. "I'm afraid that won't work. There are telltale signs when anyone uses the power. The shimmering blue light that dances along the rooftops like Saint Elmo's Fire. The faint sizzle in the air and the steam that will inevitably rise if you release the heat from the liquid. And not to mention the Fae words you'll need to utter, even if under your breath. If people were to witness you performing what they perceive to be sorcery to escape your trial, you'd convict yourself. Even I could not stop Beno from condemning you on the spot."

"Then what do we do?" Ciarán asked with an edge of panic in his voice. "There's no way she'll survive the ordeal unscathed. You know that." He turned to Alais. Her expression had paled. "We should leave tonight. We could flee to France. To one of your relatives, perhaps."

"Where would you be safe?" Gerbert pressed. "Any bishop in Christendom who learned of the charges would have you arrested and tried."

Ciarán's mind raced for answers. "I grew up in Ireland, at the edge of the world. True, there are bishops, but far fewer of them. And news from the continent takes a long time to reach there."

"Fleeing is out of the question!" Niccolo snapped. "The damage it would do to the papacy is impossible to overstate. The situation is fragile enough with a second foreign pope on Saint Peter's throne. If Beno were to convince the masses that His Holiness aided and abetted the flight of an accused sorceress, the whole of the Church would turn against him. The emperor too. As Archdeacon of the Holy See, I could *never* let that happen."

Anger flushed up Ciarán's neck. "So you'd let her die to protect His Holiness?"

"Enough, Brother Ciarán," Gerbert said sharply. "We mustn't lose sight of the larger picture. A far more dangerous enemy awaits than Cardinal Bishop Beno. We're preparing to face that enemy, and we've built the weapons to do so. We can't have you halfway across the world when we discover the way to Dudael. And what about the witness you're supposed to protect?"

"We could take Tara with us," Ciarán said.

Alais drew in a long breath. "The larger picture matters most."

Ciarán mouthed a word. "*No.*"

"We must protect Lady Alais at all costs," Gerbert spoke in his most authoritative voice. "But we must protect the papacy, too. Men like Cardinal Bishop Beno would drag the Holy See back into the swamp of corruption that consumed it for much of this century. Which means only one thing—we must find a way to win this trial."

Pietro, who had stayed quiet until now, raised his hand. "As a novice, I studied law at the monastery. There's a way we can win, but it comes with considerable risk."

Gerbert's eyes narrowed. "What do you have in mind?"

Pietro told them. As Ciarán listened, he felt a mix of hope and apprehension. The plan would be risky—very risky. But he would do it for Alais.

CHAPTER II

THE EMPEROR'S COURT

O tto the Third, King of Germany, Lombardy, and Italy, and *Imperator Romanorum*, sat on his throne like a young Caesar.

Ciarán hadn't laid eyes on the nineteen-year-old emperor since Gerbert's coronation. The young monarch still looked much the same: clean-shaven, with keen blue eyes set into a delicate, almost effeminate face. A golden circlet of grape leaves crowned his thick auburn hair, and he wore a long burgundy tunic trimmed with gold. A dark green cloak lay draped over his chest like a Roman toga. Despite the gravity of the occasion, the emperor seemed more intrigued than tense. Yet Ciarán was a knot of anxiety. This was only the first of two trials they faced. If the emperor rejected Alais' claim of innocence, he might sanction her summary execution at the hands of Cardinal Bishop Beno. And if it came to that, Ciarán couldn't even begin to think how they'd prevent it.

The emperor's hall, though modest in size, was packed with armed, mail-clad Germans. Four of the hard-faced men guarded the exit, while eight more flanked the dais containing the emperor's wooden throne, half on each side. On the emperor's right stood a rugged Saxon lord whom Ciarán recognized as Margrave Eckard of

Meissen. Archbishop Heribert of Cologne, a handsome cleric who served as Chancellor of the Holy Roman Empire, positioned himself on the emperor's left. He was the only man near the dais not wearing a sword.

Though dressed in his mail tunic and scarlet cloak, Ciarán was unarmed. Guests were not permitted weapons in the emperor's presence, so he had left Caladbolg with Breda back at the palace. Jarl Holger had also left Curtana with Breda, so he, too, stood unarmed alongside Ciarán and Pietro on the hall's west wall. Gerbert headed their group, clad in his white cassock and skull cap, flanked by Archdeacon Niccolo and Alais. She wore a plain dress and a headscarf, both made of white linen to proclaim her innocence.

Across from her stood her accuser, Cardinal Bishop Beno. His pale skin, stretched over his bony skull, creased into crow's feet at the edge of his jaundiced eyes. A gaudy golden crucifix hung to the chest of his scarlet robes. Behind him gathered a gaggle of black-clad priests and nuns, including the bone-thin abbess of the Convent of Minerva. To her left loomed Beno's brawny Lombard warrior with the jagged scar down his cheek. From the look in his eyes, the man seemed to be enjoying this.

"Let the accused step forward," Archbishop Heribert commanded.

Ciarán tried to steel his nerves as Alais took two steps into the hall's center and faced the emperor.

The young monarch regarded her with a thoughtful expression. "You are Lady Alais of the House of Poitiers, are you not?"

"Yes, Your Imperial Majesty," she said.

"Cardinal Bishop Beno calls you the sorceress of Rome. He accuses you of witchcraft." He cocked his head. "Is this accusation true?"

Ciarán drew a quick breath. He felt as if the sincerity of her next words carried the weight of the world.

"No," she declared. "I'm innocent of the charges." Her voice held the same conviction it had in Gerbert's study.

The emperor gave a subtle nod, though his expression did not change.

Then Beno interjected. "Your Imperial Majesty," he began, raising a bony finger, "her plea is meaningless. The consort of the Devil is the princess of lies. Listen instead to the witnesses behind me, who, along with myself, saw this woman commanding the fire to do her sinful bidding. She conjured her black magic to save a rightfully convicted witch whose blasphemous words burned my humble ears. Scripture states, *'no sorceress shall be permitted to live,'* so there's no cause for a trial. You have but one choice in God's eyes."

The emperor looked taken aback. He glanced warily between Alais and Beno, and Ciarán felt his worst fear was coming true. *The emperor is afraid of defying God.* Ciarán looked to Gerbert, who calmly cleared his throat.

"My ever august Caesar and glorious lord Otto, exalted Imperator of the Romans." The words rolled off Gerbert's tongue. "Cardinal Bishop Beno assumes that what he claims to have witnessed was an act of sorcery. He also assumes the orphan he tried to burn at the stake was guilty of witchcraft. But what if those assumptions were wrong?"

"Wrong?" Beno scoffed. "Fire does not have a mind of its own. It was sorcery. I witnessed it with my own eyes!"

Gerbert clasped his hands together. "When Emperor Diocletian ordered that Saint Philomena be shot with arrows, did not the arrows turn back in mid-air to kill the archers who fired them? And when Diocletian sought to burn Saint Florian at the stake, did not the saint command the fire not to burn? And what about Saint Polycarp of Smyrna? When they tried to burn him at the stake, the fire jumped from the pyre and formed the shape of a great shield that did not singe the saint's flesh. Were these acts of sorcery? Or holy miracles?"

The emperor gave a subtle nod. It eased Ciarán's immediate fear, but his anxiousness remained.

Gerbert pointed a finger at Cardinal Bishop Beno as if he was the man on trial. "What if the thirteen-year-old girl he tried to burn was as innocent as Saint Philomena? Could not the phenomenon they witnessed involving the pyre have been a holy miracle to save an innocent life?"

"Outrageous," Beno growled. "These women are sinners, not saints."

"If there are two possible causes to what they have witnessed, there must be a trial. Leave the answer for God Himself to decide."

Beno's lips twisted into a snarl. "I *know* what God's will is. The sorceress must burn!"

"Cardinal Bishop!" Gerbert retorted angrily. "The last time I checked, I am Christ's vicar on Earth. Do not presume to tell me what is God's will."

Ciarán wanted to cheer. Beno's lips were trembling with rage.

Then the emperor spoke. "There will be a trial."

"Thank the Lord," Ciarán muttered under his breath.

He saw Alais breathe a sigh of relief; Gerbert could not hide his grin.

The emperor turned to Beno. "What manner of trial would you propose?"

Beno tried to compose himself. "Ordeal by boiling water." He raised his hands theatrically. "If she is innocent, God will protect her flesh as she pulls His holy cross from the cauldron. Yet if her flesh is harmed, her secret as the Devil's concubine will be laid bare for all to see."

Ciarán braced himself for Gerbert's next move. The pope stepped to Alais' side. "The accused objects," he said.

"On what grounds?" Beno asked incredulously.

"On grounds the law gives the accused a choice to reject trial by ordeal." Gerbert paused for effect. "In favor of trial by combat."

Beno's eyes bulged in their sockets. "Outrageous!" He thrust his finger toward Jarl Holger. "This is *rigged*. The pope employs the services of pagan barbarians who have a bloodlust for battle. He seeks to use this pagan warrior as her champion to spare his mistress. This cannot be allowed!"

The emperor's mouth fell open. "Is this true?"

"No, Your Imperial Majesty," Gerbert said calmly. "For one, Jarl Holger is not a pagan. He has been baptized a Christian. I

82

performed the ceremony myself. And second, he is *not* her champion."

The emperor's head flinched back slightly. "Then who is?"

"I choose Ciarán mac Tomás," Alais announced.

Ciarán had been waiting for this moment, and now that it had happened, his chest swelled with resolve. He would fight to save her life.

Beno, however, choked back a laugh. "Him?" He gestured to Ciarán. "The bastard Irish monk who obviously has abandoned his vows?"

"You wish to be her champion?" the emperor asked skeptically.

Ciarán stepped forward. "As God is my witness, Your Imperial Majesty."

A cunning smile spread across Beno's lips. "We accept this challenge. Let us see if God favors this unfaithful monk over my devout captain, Gundoald of Pavia." Standing head and shoulders above Beno, the brawny Lombard—likely Gundoald—let out a disdainful chuckle. His eyes, cold and calculating, seemed to belong to a man well-versed in the art of killing. When those eyes locked onto Ciarán, a shiver of apprehension coursed through his veins.

The emperor clapped his hands. "Very well then, let the trial happen tomorrow. The old Theatre of Pompey should be a fitting venue."

Ciarán whispered to Alais. "It worked."

She nodded and wiped back a tear.

Ciarán glanced at Beno. The cardinal bishop was not finished.

"Your Imperial Majesty," Beno said. "There is still the matter of the sorceress's apprentice. If the accused is found guilty, her apprentice, too, should suffer the same punishment. For if scripture says no sorceress shall be permitted to live, should not her apprentice die with her on the pyre?"

Alais shook her head. "No, she's innocent."

"*That* is for God to decide," Beno insisted.

Gerbert opened his mouth to speak, but the emperor had already made up his mind. "That appears just," he declared. "But by the same logic, if Lady Alais is exonerated, the girl should be too."

Gerbert nodded. "Wiser words could not be spoken."

Beno grimaced. After a curt bow, he led his followers out of the hall. When Gundoald reached the doorway, he glanced back at Ciarán and smirked.

Ciarán drew a long breath.

Once Beno's party was gone, Gerbert left to speak privately with the emperor. Alais touched Ciarán's hand and mouthed two words. "*Thank you.*" Pietro joined them, his plump face beaming with pride. Though standing beside him, Holger wore a solemn look.

"What's wrong?" Ciarán asked. "You don't think I can beat Gundoald?"

"It's not that," Holger replied. "It's the girl's warning that troubles me. For now, we know what tomorrow is—it's judgment day."

PART TWO

When he opened the fourth seal, I heard the voice of the fourth living creature call out. "Come!" I looked and there was a pale green horse! Its rider's name was Death, and Hades followed with him ...

— Revelation 6:7-8

CHAPTER 12
THE HORSEMEN

Beneath the faint light of a half moon, the ancient being that inhabited the body of Ugo Grassus rode with his three companions through the deserted Roman streets. The being knew that later today, he would savor the taste of victory. For once he seized the Key to the Abyss, this war would be over before it had even begun.

The horsemen reached the ruins of the Stadium of Domitian two hours before sunrise. A lone cat stalked quietly across the field in the center of the crumbling stadium, whose entire south end had collapsed, ravaged by time. Heading towards the shadowy warrens at the north end of the stadium, the riders entered the arena. The warrens beneath the old stadium were haunted by prostitutes and beggars, but they also served as the hideout for the Brotherhood of the Messiah. The cult had moved here three months ago after the pope's soldiers raided their former hideaway in the ruins of Trajan's Market. While many in the brotherhood were religious fanatics desperate to place an Italian pope on Saint Peter's throne, more than a few were unscrupulous men like Ugo Grassus—conmen, thieves, and scoundrels—all under the influence of Naberus da Roma. Yet today, those men would serve the Dragon.

Ugo Grassus slid his three-hundred-pound body off the saddle of his pale gray charger. A chink of mail accompanied the sound of his boots landing on the muddy ground. He had ornamented himself for battle with an oversized chainmail coat and a pot-shaped helmet beneath the hood of his cloak. A broad sword hung from his belt next to a sheathed dagger, and his right hand gripped a spear with a vicious barbed head. His three companions, each possessing the muscular body of one of the sellswords he had recruited two days ago, were similarly clad and armed. They dismounted their horses and followed their leader into the warrens.

The air reeked of piss and dung, and the warrens were quiet, save for the chatter of rats. Three black rodents scattered as the four men approached the wooden door to the brotherhood's lair. Ugo Grassus set his spear against the ancient stone wall and drew the dagger from its sheath. He brought his meaty left hand to the door and gave three hard knocks. Moments later, the door creaked open to reveal a gatekeeper who couldn't have been older than twenty. Pockmarks marred his face, and he wore the black habit of a monk. However, his pointed cowl lay draped behind his neck rather than covering his head. With bleary eyes, he regarded the man who had knocked. "Ugo?"

That was the last word he spoke before the dagger ripped through his throat. Ugo smothered the gatekeeper's mouth with his free hand to stifle his dying scream. When he was confident the gatekeeper was dead, he let his body slump to the floor. Then he turned to his companions. "The rest should be sleeping. Kill them all."

The slaughter did not take long. When the four men were finished, they dragged the bodies into the spacious chamber that had served as the brotherhood's chapter house. They arranged twenty-one of the dead men into a circle, with eight more forming a star in its center. As the being within Ugo Grassus looked down upon the corpses laid out to create a necromantic symbol, he felt pleased. Living men were troublesome, filled with anxieties, and prone to treachery. But the dead were obedient—and fearless.

Standing outside the circle, the being and his companions joined hands and began to chant. The words were not Latin or any other language spoken by men, but their collective sound was haunting, like a requiem. The chanting stirred the air until it swirled around the circle, whipping the hems of their cloaks. Electric energy pulsed through the chamber, like the instant before a lightning strike. In the surrounding darkness, motes of light winked into existence. Ten motes became twenty, then thirty, then sixty. They danced in the swirling air like a swarm of fireflies, slowly descending toward the corpses, where they disappeared into the lifeless bodies.

The chanting rose to a crescendo; the words formed from the ancient Nephilim tongue:

> *Spirits of Rome, lost and forsaken,*
> *With unholy purpose we summon thee,*
> *To serve the Dragon, our lord and god,*
> *And make the dead awaken!*

The being glanced down at the body of the gatekeeper near his feet. The man's palms lay open, as still as death.

Then, one by one, his fingers began to twitch.

CHAPTER 13

JUDGMENT DAY

In light of Tara's warning, Jarl Holger determined that *Lindworm's* crew should accompany them to the trial. So that morning, twenty-two sword Danes and spear Danes rode alongside Captain Gaido and a score of the pope's crimson-cloaked guards in the cavalcade that accompanied his litter to the Theatre of Pompey.

They traveled beneath an ash-gray sky past the ruins of the Old Roman Forum. Ciarán wore his chainmail tunic and an iron helm, slightly pointed at the top, with a triangular nasal. Caladbolg hung in its scabbard at his side, buckled to his leather baldric, and he had slung a round wooden shield behind his back. The shield's leather casing bore the image of a white cross over a crimson field. The cross had been Pietro's idea to convince the people that Ciarán fought on the side of God.

Sitting in his palfrey's saddle, Ciarán felt weary. The law governing trial by combat demanded that the combatants fast the night before, and his stomach growled. On top of that, he had barely slept. The only benefit of not sleeping was that he had not dreamed of the Dragon. But throughout the restless night, troubling questions harrowed his mind. He wondered if he had what it would take to defeat Gundoald and save Alais. Gundoald must have been near thirty, with more than a decade's worth of training with a sword, and Ciarán knew he would be no match for such a warrior without Caladbolg. The blade was a thing of legend, having bourn many names throughout time: *Flamberge, Caledfwlch, Excalibur.* Yet would the weapon be enough to even the scales? If he could whisper into the gemstone within Caladbolg's pommel and summon the light, he had no doubt he would prevail, for the sight of the blade blazing with white fire struck fear into the hearts of men. But he could never invoke the power of Enoch's device in a trial for witch-craft. He, too, would be accused of sorcery, and then three people would burn at the stake. No, he concluded, he would have to defeat Gundoald in ordinary combat, as difficult as that would be.

Just as concerning, however, was Tara's prophecy about death coming for Alais. Could this death be the threat of this trial? If so, Ciarán could prevent that by defeating Gundoald. He would not even need to kill the man; just get him to yield. But what if this death was something else entirely? Something coming for the Key to the Abyss, the power that flowed within Alais' veins? These ques-tions gnawed at his mind during their journey to the theatre.

Ciarán rode behind Jarl Holger and Breda, with Rosta padding alongside Breda's mare. Breda was a shieldmaiden, and she came dressed for battle in her mail vest with her sword at her side and a shield strapped behind her back. Tara rode with her, sitting at the front of the saddle. The two were becoming inseparable.

Magnus rode beside Ciarán. As they passed the triumphal arch of Septimius Severus, the handsome Dane leaned toward Ciarán. "Don't look so glum, Irish."

"Forgive me," Ciarán replied. "There's a lot at stake."

"You've been in fights before. Besides, you've been training with Jarl Holger. The only thing better would have been if I'd trained you myself." He flashed a grin.

"I've never fought in a duel, only in battles. And never alone."

"One-on-one is easier than a melee. You only have one foe to worry about. I've heard this man is bigger than you and undoubtedly stronger. So you don't want this to go long. You'll start to wear down, and *that's* how you lose. So, use that magic sword of yours. Parry his strikes and shatter his blade and then make quick work of him."

Magnus's confidence helped ease some of Ciarán's fears about the trial, but it did nothing to ease his concern for Alais. "Promise me something," he asked. "Whatever happens to me, make sure nothing happens to Alais."

Magnus glanced at the litter where Alais was traveling with Gerbert, Pietro, and Niccolo. "Ah, Lifthrasir," he said breezily, using his nickname for her. *Freya reborn.* "I promise, no harm will come to her. And if for some reason you lose to that Lombard, I've already spoken with Jarl Holger and the crew. We'll spirit her out of there and head straight for *Lindworm*. And if anyone tries to stop us, they'll have to go through a shield wall. I don't care what the shaven men think about it. That's what we'll do."

Ciarán knew Archdeacon Niccolo would be furious with Magnus's plan, but it gave Ciarán comfort. It was one of the things he loved about the Danes. Like the Irish, they protected their own above all else.

As they neared the Theatre of Pompey, Ciarán spied the dome of the Basilica of Santa Maria Rotunda rising over the terra-cotta roofs of the surrounding shops and homes. The theater stood south of that village-like cluster near the more densely populated city on the banks of the Tiber. From the road, Ciarán could see that the entire eastern portion of the massive theatre complex had collapsed. It must have been a monumental building in its day, but now it was no more than a roofless series of toppled walls and broken columns. The rubble spilled into the remnants of what must have been a walled garden, now home to a copse of cypress trees and a field of yellow weeds. A building at the garden's west end also lay in ruins; its marble facade pilfered throughout the centuries, leaving only a knee-high wall and an arcade of broken pillars between the garden and the large outdoor amphitheater at the westernmost side of the complex. Although cracks marred its walls, the theatre remained intact, but it had been stripped of any statues or ornaments. Rows of stone benches climbed more than sixty feet up the crescent-shaped amphitheater, ending at a row of shattered columns. In its center stood a square structure framed by pillars and topped by a triangular pediment that reminded Ciarán of an old Roman temple. People were already filling the stands. As best as Ciarán could estimate, the crowd must have numbered about four hundred or so, as if Beno's entire mob from two days before had come to watch the trial.

One person he did not see in the stands was the emperor. Gerbert had persuaded Otto to stay away, claiming that attending such an odious spectacle would be beneath His Imperial Majesty. But Gerbert's rationale was a lie. He wanted to protect the young emperor from whatever might transpire here this day. And the thought of that unknown added to Ciarán's unease.

"Ignore the crowd, Irish," Magnus told Ciarán. "They're going to go home disappointed."

Ciarán answered with a wary nod. His muscles tensed as he waited for the cavalcade to enter the theatre through a tall archway beneath a square tower whose roof had long ago collapsed.

Ten paces ahead, Archdeacon Niccolo stepped out of the litter. He proceeded through the archway, flanked by Captain Gaido and three more papal guardsmen, to announce the pope's arrival. "All hail Silvester the Second," he bellowed, "Pontifex Maximus, Servus Servorum Dei, Vicar of Christ, and Lord Pope of the Apostolic See of Rome!"

Gerbert disembarked the litter, followed by Pietro and Alais. When the pope strode beneath the archway, along with ten more guardsmen, Ciarán knew it was his cue to dismount. He handed his palfrey's reins to a fair-haired, clean-shaven Dane named Freybjorn and met up with Alais. She was wearing the same white dress and headscarf that she wore at the emperor's court. She looked at him with her storm-gray eyes. "It's brave of you to do this."

He laid his hand on Caladbolg's pommel and brushed his

thumb over the embedded gemstone. "I've been in worse fights," he said, sounding more confident than he felt.

Holger and Breda joined them, along with Rosta and Tara. Like Alais, Tara wore a white dress, and she looked scared.

"We'll be alright," Alais told her. "I saw Brother Ciarán defeat a giant once with his sword."

"A real giant?" Tara asked.

"Indeed," Alais replied.

"We've slain giants, too," Breda told Tara. "So we won't let that bastard of a bishop hurt you. I swear it."

Tara seemed calmer after Breda's words and even more so when Rosta licked her arm as if the boarhound had sensed the girl's need for comfort.

Soon, they were joined by Magnus, Jorundr, and the rest of *Lindworm's* crew, except for Freybjorn and Hári Grayhair, who would guard the horses. Ciarán walked beside Pietro and Alais as the group passed through the archway. When they emerged, hundreds of spectators looked their way. Gasps rose from the crowd as Beno's followers watched Alais and Tara escorted into the theatre by a Viking war band armed with shields, spears, and swords.

They entered onto a wide brick path framed on the right by the broken pillars and the collapsed wall of the ruined structure that once stood between the theatre and the garden. To the left, the path stepped down to a vast semicircle of broken flagstones choked with weeds, which Ciarán suspected once served as the theatre's stage. At the northmost end stood Cardinal Bishop Beno, dressed in his scarlet robes and skullcap. His eyes widened as he saw Alais surrounded by *Lindworm's* fierce-looking crew, though beside him, Gundoald looked on with a steely gaze. The burly Lombard stood head and shoulders above Beno, peering from a pointed helm with curved cheekpieces and topped with a horsehair plume. Gundoald's chainmail tunic was polished to a silvery shine, and his round shield, painted sky blue with a thick iron boss, bore a stylized image of a white horse. The image reminded Ciarán of the colossal statues of the Horse Tamers and something Pietro had told him: Beno was a kinsman of Crescentius of the Marble Horse.

94

Ciarán pulled his gaze away from Gundoald and stared into the amphitheater filled with rows of benches. A twenty-foot-wide stairway climbed up the theatre to the temple-like structure behind the stands, splitting the seating area into two sections. Beno's faction crowded in the northern section, while the benches in the southern-most section closest to the floor had been reserved for the pope and his entourage. Gerbert was already seated beside Niccolo and flanked by two ranks of guardsmen. When his eyes met Ciarán's, the pope gave an approving nod.

"What do we do next?" Ciarán asked Pietro.

"You and I will wait here until the trial begins," Pietro said before turning to Alais. "My lady, you should take a seat in the section to the right of His Holiness."

Alais nodded, but before she left, she took Ciarán's hand and squeezed it. As he gazed into her eyes, he wanted to pull her toward him and hold her, possibly for the last time. But he knew he could not do that here. It pained him to watch her walk toward the stairs.

Behind Alais, Magnus winked at Ciarán. "She'll be safe."

Meanwhile, Holger clapped Ciarán on the shoulder. "You and I shall stand together at Ragnarok, just as Blind Mikkel said. The gothi has never been wrong."

Ciarán forced a smile. He looked on as the Danes made their way to the stands. Magnus and Jorundr sat beside Alais, with Holger, Breda, and Tara taking the bench behind her while Rosta sat in the aisle. The other members of *Lindworm's* crew occupied the nearby benches, casting dark looks at Beno's mob.

"It's time," Pietro said.

Ciarán turned to see Beno and Gundoald striding toward the center of the stage. The cardinal bishop held a leather-bound book.

"Peter Pig's Snout," Beno said mockingly. "Is the sorceress's champion still up for the challenge?"

Pietro's cheeks flushed red. "The accused remains *innocent* until proven guilty, and her champion stands ready to defend her."

"Ah, yes," Beno sneered. "The monk who abandoned his vows." With his free hand, he touched Gundoald's thick right arm. "I assure you, *my* champion is ready, and he fights on the side of God."

Gundoald stepped toward Ciarán. Between the curved cheek pieces of his helmet, the Lombard's lips twisted into a snarl. From the gambeson beneath his mail came the rancid stench of sweat-stained leather, a reminder of how often he must have worn this armor in battle. Ciarán tipped his head to look into Gundoald's eyes. They were blue but hard. The eyes of a killer.

Ciarán drew a sharp breath, and his right hand drifted to Calad-bolg's pommel. As he gripped the pommel, the embedded gemstone emitted a faint warmth, helping to steel his nerves.

From the stands, Gerbert's voice shouted above the murmur of the crowd. "Cardinal Bishop, let this trial begin!"

Beno huffed before giving the pope a feigned bow. "As you wish, Your Holiness." He raised the book, holding it high for the crowd to see. "The Gospel of our Lord," he announced vigorously. "May each combatant swear an oath upon it!"

When Beno presented Gundoald the book, the Lombard placed his large hand upon the cover.

"Gundoald of Pavia," Beno began, "do you swear in the name of Almighty God that you shall do all in your power to best your adversary, Ciarán of Hibernia, defender of the accused sorceress, Alais of Poitiers, and make him yield himself up to your hand in vanquishment? Or else make him die by your hand, so help you God and all the saints?"

"I do," Gundoald grunted.

Beno turned his jaundiced gaze on Ciarán, who laid his hand on the book. "Do you, Ciarán of Hibernia, swear in the name of Almighty God that you shall do all in your power to best your adversary, Gundoald of Pavia, defender of the innocent accusers and the citizens of Rome!" He roared the word to stir the crowd while speaking the next verse in a low voice. "And make him yield himself up to your hand in vanquishment? Or else make him die by your hand, so help you God and all the saints?"

"Aye," Ciarán replied.

Before he departed, Pietro leaned toward Ciarán and made the sign of the cross. "May Christ and his saints be with you."

Ciarán answered with a grateful nod, thinking of one saint in particular: Columcille, the patron saint of Derry. His name had been the battle cry Niall and his brothers had used when they charged Adémar of Blois, and one Ciarán had hollered ever since. As he backed away from Gundoald to ready himself for the trial, Ciarán whispered a prayer to that brave Irish saint.

Across from Ciarán, Gundoald drew his blade. The longsword hissed from its scabbard. It was a fearsome-looking weapon in the brawny Lombard's right hand with a cross-guard and square-shaped pommel. He raised his shield with its white horse and looked ready to pounce.

For an instant, Ciarán's thoughts flashed to a memory of Khalil stepping between the hazel rods in King Svein's hall. That night, Khalil had given his life to save Ciarán's, and now Ciarán would risk his own to save Alais. He thought of her as he reached behind his back to unsling his shield bearing the white cross. He slid his left arm through the shield's brace and gripped its handle. Then he unsheathed Caladbolg. The blade rang like a chime as it slid from the scabbard's neck.

Beno backed away from the combatants, raising the Gospel over his head. "God sides with the victor," he cried. "Let His judgment be rendered!"

Ciarán's heart drummed in his chest when, like an angered bull, Gundoald charged. He hammered down his sword. Ciarán caught the blow on his shield, but the force of it sent a jolt of pain up his left arm. Gundoald followed the strike with another massive blow. Once again, Ciarán blocked it with his shield, but the fierce attack drove him backward. In the stands, Beno's followers roared their approval.

Gundoald continued hacking, and Ciarán heard a shield-board crack. He grimaced from the effort of warding off so many powerful blows; a bead of sweat streamed down his forehead. Another thundering strike caused Ciarán to stagger and almost lose his footing on the uneven flagstones. As more cheers erupted from the crowd, Magnus's warning rang through Ciarán's skull: *You don't want this to go long; you'll start to wear down.*

The next time Gundoald struck, Ciarán punched his shield into the blow. He paid for it with a stabbing pain in his left arm, but the move opened up his stance and allowed him to swing Caladbolg. Gundoald ducked under his own shield as the flat of Caladbolg's blade clanged against the shield's iron boss. Spinning to his left, Gundoald hewed his sword. This time, Ciarán could not parry the cut with his shield, but he leaned back. The glancing blow sliced through rings of mail on Ciarán's chest but did not penetrate the leather gambeson beneath it. Gundoald followed with a backhanded strike designed to drive his blade through Ciarán's shoulder, but this time Ciarán parried the attack with Caladbolg. Steel clanged against steel. Gundoald's strike was more powerful than Ciarán's parry, but his sword was not. The razor-sharp edge of Caladbolg's blade sheared through the longsword, severing it in two.

The crowd gasped. Gundoald stared at the broken sword in his hand.

Huffing for breath, Ciarán spat out a word. "Yield."

That only enraged Gundoald. With a defiant growl, he threw away the remains of his sword and drew a foot-long dagger from his belt. He crouched, both shield and dagger at the ready. But Caladbolg's blade was more than three feet long, and Ciarán knew the Lombard was outmatched. So this time, Ciarán charged, bellowing his battle cry: "*Columcille!*"

He swung Caladbolg hard. Gundoald raised his shield, but Caladbolg splintered the wood. Now it was Ciarán who was driving his opponent backward. A second strike sheared off the top quarter of the Lombard's shield, and Ciarán could feel the rush of battle fueling his attack. Gundoald's eyes flew wide as a third blow split the shield's iron boss. The blade kept going until it cut through the willow boards into the mail and muscle of Gundoald's left arm. The huge Lombard roared in pain. Ciarán wrenched his sword free and then aimed a backhanded strike at Gundoald's right hand gripping the dagger. Gundoald leaped back to avoid the blow but caught his heel on a protruding flagstone. His arms windmilled as he crashed onto his back before Ciarán rushed forward and stomped his boot on Gundoald's right arm, pinning the dagger. Then Ciarán touched Caladbolg's tip to Gundoald's throat.

"Yield," Ciarán demanded.

Amid roaring cheers from *Lindworm's* crew, Beno's voice cried out: "No!"

Ciarán turned toward the sound. Beno stood on the brick path a step above the stage, waving his book in the air. "Mistrial! I demand a *mis-trial!*" His eyes bulged in his skull. "The Sorceress of Rome enchanted that blade. For how else could it shear through steel and cut through an iron boss? There's only one explanation—it's a witch's blade ensorcelled with the magic of her concubine, Satan himself!"

"Build the pyre!" a man cried from the stands. Beno's supporters erupted in cheers.

"Burn the witch!" others yelled to applause.

Ciarán felt a sudden stab of fear that the trial was about to be overwhelmed by a violent mob. But then he heard another sound—a rumbling noise accompanied by a chorus of shrieks and wails. The sound came from behind Beno, past the ruined walls and broken columns from the garden beyond.

Oblivious to the sound, Beno continued to shout. "Through witchery, the sorceress and her apprentice have *forfeited* their right to trial!"

Gerbert called for order, but the crowd's protests drowned out his demands. "Burn them!" they roared. "Burn them both!"

Ciarán glanced between the frothing mob and the raving bishop as the rumbling grew into a thunder of hooves. The breath caught in Ciarán's throat when he spotted the four black-clad horsemen stampeding through the garden toward the theatre. And behind them loped a throng of crazed men wearing monkish robes.

Beno's voice rose to a crescendo. "As the holy book says, no man can allow a sorceress to live!"

He must have finally heard the horses, for he turned just as the lead rider leaped his pale gray stallion over the crumbling wall. The rider was an enormous man in a black cloak and cowl, and his charger was equally massive. Its hooves landed on the brick path before the horse plowed into Beno. His gospel book went flying, and he let out a desperate scream cut short by the stallion. The horse barreled through the priest, trampling his body beneath its pounding hooves as it charged onto the floor.

Ciarán cried out. The hulking rider gripped a spear, cocked back, and ready to throw.

With a roar, he launched the weapon toward the stands—aimed straight for Alais' heart.

CHAPTER 14

DEATH'S RIDE

Alais felt frozen in place. She was standing as she had been since Gundoald toppled backward, and Ciarán held Caladbolg to his throat while around her, the Danes cheered victoriously. But then the horsemen leaped over the broken wall, and the rider on the pale horse trampled Beno to death. Tara's prophecy rushed to her mind. *Their leader's horse is pale of hue. His name is Death, and he comes for you!*

The lead rider heaved a spear. The weapon sped through the air. *Move!* her mind screamed.

She felt an arm push her back onto the stone bench as Magnus threw himself in front of her. She heard the thud. The spear's tip burst through the chainmail covering his back, misting the air with blood.

"Magnus!" Holger cried. He reached for his friend while Breda grabbed Alais beneath her shoulders and hefted her up to the benches behind her. Next to Breda, Tara was screaming.

The enormous rider cursed when his spear missed its mark. He tore off his cowl, revealing a bloated face with huge bearded jowls. Alais had seen the man before, but with her mind racing, she could not place where.

Galloping toward the stands, the rider had a deranged gleam in his eyes. He raised a broadsword and yelled at the top of his lungs: "I AM ORCUS!"

As the stallion leaped into the stands, only Holger and Jorundr stood between Alais and the horseman.

"Get her out of here!" Holger hollered to Breda. Then he ripped Curtana from its scabbard.

CIARÁN WATCHED in horror as the spear sped toward Alais, then gasped when Magnus dove in front of her.

The sound of hooves striking brick caused him to spin to his right, just in time to see another black-cloaked rider clear the broken wall. The rider, who held a spear like a lance, bore down on Ciarán. In half a breath, the spear would have punched through his mail tunic, but he swung Caladbolg in an arc to bat the weapon away. Caladbolg's blade struck the spear shaft and sheared through the hardwood. The severed spear tip glanced off his mailed shoulder.

The rider who had tried to impale Ciarán flew past him, but tried to curb his horse for a second attack. Meanwhile, two more horsemen had galloped across the stage and had their horses climbing up the stands where hundreds of Beno's supporters had flown into a panic. Ciarán's mind reeled at the implication of what was happening. *On Judgment Day, four horsemen ride—and they had come for Alais!*

Ciarán's attacker pulled a broadsword from his side and wheeled to face him. Beneath his black cowl, the horseman had a hard face and merciless eyes. Ciarán desperately wanted to invoke the power of Enoch's device, but the rider's imminent attack would not give him the time he needed to do so. He lifted his shield, preparing for the horseman's charge, when Pietro rushed into the stallion's path. The monk had been watching the trial from the outskirts of the stage, but now he was a heartbeat from being trampled.

"In the name of Christ Jesus!" Pietro yelled, waving his arms. "Cease now or risk your immortal soul!"

The horseman bristled at the words and then spurred his stallion. Ciarán was five paces behind Pietro, too far to pull him from the horse's path. "Pietro!" he cried hopelessly, knowing the monk would die like Beno. Then steel flashed through the air. The stallion whinnied as a dagger's hilt protruded from its neck. The stallion bucked, altering its charge enough for Pietro to dart safely to his right as the horseman fought to rein in his panicked mount.

From where the dagger had flown stood Gundoald. The Lombard grabbed Pietro by the arm and pulled him away from the horseman.

The unexpected diversion was all Ciarán needed. He sloughed off his shield and grabbed Caladbolg's hilt with both hands. Placing the sword's pommel to his lips, he focused on the embedded gemstone and whispered the word of power to imbue it with his soul light—"*Eoh.*" The stone blazed with light and heat, and he felt that heat pulse through the hilt, into his fingers, and up the steel blade. As he pointed the weapon at the horseman wrestling to control his mount, bright white fire erupted from the sword like a thousand torches.

And in its light, Ciarán saw the truth.

A monstrous luminescent spirit enveloped the rider, its essence bleeding into every pore of its host. The demon's face, covering the rider's skull like a mask, was a bestial visage with jagged teeth, broad nostrils, and long auroch-like horns jutting from its temples. Similar phantoms clung to the other three riders, who were driving their stallions into the stands where people clambered over one another to get out of the horsemen's way.

The horseman facing Ciarán regained control of his mount. The demon's smoldering eyes fixed on Enoch's device.

Come and taste it! Ciarán thought. He raised Caladbolg in a battle stance and met the horseman's blade. It was a savage strike, but when the mortal blade struck Caladbolg's fire, the steel shattered. Caladbolg, however, continued on, cleaving into the horseman's thigh. The blow severed the leg while Caladbolg's fire rushed over the demon's wraith-like form. The demon let out a hellish wail as the flames became crimson in color, devouring every facet of its being.

Hissing with smoke, the horseman tumbled from the saddle.

Then, behind Ciarán, a voice cried out. He spun to find Pietro wrestling with a man in a monk's habit. The pointed cowl trailing behind the man's neck marked him as a member of the Brotherhood of the Messiah. Pietro's hands clutched the man's arms as he forced a long knife toward's Pietro's throat. The monk's neck bore a gaping wound that should have killed him, and his eyes bulged from their sockets like a man possessed. In Caladbolg's light, a wispy spectral form clung like spidery webs to the monk's flesh.

Ciarán did not hesitate. He lunged and thrust Caladbolg through the monk's ribs. Again, the fiery blade flared, and the ghostly essence clinging to the monk hissed into vapor. When Ciarán pulled the sword free, the man crumpled into a lifeless corpse.

Three paces away, two more of the raving monks were assaulting Gundoald, who bellowed with a mix of rage and pain. One of the men slashed at his chainmail with a reaping hook, while the second one had plunged a pitchfork into the side of the Lombard's left leg. Behind them, more black-robed men leaped into the stands, attacking every man, woman, and child in their way.

They're fighting to get to Alais, Ciarán thought urgently. With an angry backhanded strike, he decapitated the pitchfork-wielding monk and swung back the opposite way. The blow caught the man with the reaping hook below the armpit, hewing deep into his torso. The wound did not bleed, for the man was already dead, judging by the yawning gash on his neck. But as Caladbolg's fire flared, the specter animating the cadaver steamed into smoke.

Gundoald, huffing for breath, gave Ciarán a grateful nod.

He tipped his head to Gundoald, then looked for Alais. He spotted her, Breda, and Tara scrambling up the stands while the horsemen and the horde of black-robed monks fought through the terrified crowd.

Ciarán felt a surge of fear for the woman he loved. Then he raised Caladbolg and charged.

ALAIS FELT DAZED by the suddenness of the attack.

The amphitheater had devolved into chaos, and everywhere, people were screaming. Spectators scrambled from the stands onto the stage while two more horsemen pressed their way through the panicked crowd. Others fell to the horsemen's swords or the attacks of shrieking men in black robes, swinging knives with careless abandon. The air smelled of blood, and somewhere nearby, a young girl was wailing.

Breda was pulling Alais up another step-like bench as the horsemen closed in, followed by the mob of black-robed killers. They were coming for her.

Fight! a voice screamed in her head. *You are Sirra!*

Like the light of a bright morning sun, the words cleared the fog from Alais' mind. As she assessed the urgency of their situation, she saw Holger and Jorundr four rows below battling the horseman on the pale steed. A host of Danes had joined them, though some had fallen. Meanwhile, spectators scattered as the second horseman drove his mount up the stair-like aisle in the center of the bowl. A third advanced toward the aisle from the other side, slashing his sword through the crowd of fleeing spectators. Eight members of *Lindworm's* crew had retreated up the theater's step-like benches, forming a crude shield wall between their attackers and herself, Breda, and Tara. But the Danes would soon be outnumbered by the horde of madmen in monkish robes tearing their way through the crowd.

Casting a glance at Tara, whose face had paled to the color of chalk, Alais felt a torrent of fury rise within her. The arcane wisdom etched into her soul flared to life, coursing through her mind. With newfound resolve, she advanced toward the aisle.

Breda grabbed Alais' arm. "Where are you going?"

"To end this," Alais replied. She pulled away from Breda and called out to the Danes forming the rough shield wall. "Fall back, and protect Breda and Tara!"

The Dane closest to her, a thick-bearded warrior named Ormr, glanced at her wide-eyed as if she were touched. But the warrior next to him, Stóri Red Beard, nodded in agreement. *"Lifthrasir,"* he said to Ormr before the Danes backed away from the aisle, forming a semi-circle around Breda and Tara.

Meanwhile, the horseman climbing up the stair-like aisle was only three rows down, having cleared a path through the fleeing spectators with his spear. Alais knew she had but seconds to act. Dropping to a knee at the aisle's edge, she placed her palm on the stairway's cold surface. She recalled the words to crack stone, and the verse began flowing from her lips. She felt power pulse down her arm to her hands, then into the stone. Cracks spread from her fingertips across the aisle. The cracks widened into fissures, crawling up and down the aisle and advancing into the northmost section of stands. A rolling vibration seized half the bowl, growing more violent as crevices gnawed through the arena like the roots of a giant oak.

Scores of panicked spectators trying to escape the quaking stands gasped and wailed. *Those are Beno's people,* Alais reminded herself. *And a moment ago, they wanted me to burn.*

The nearest horseman's charger hesitated as the tremors rolled like an earthquake down the aisle and across the bowl. Alais repeated the verse as the fissures crept into the archways and walls supporting the stands. With a loud crack, the aisle in front of Alais collapsed, and the crash of crumbling stone drowned out the crowd's screams. The steps beneath the horseman gave way next. The horse whinnied in fear as it fell along with huge chunks of the stairs into the vast space beneath the stands. But as his mount tumbled down, the rider leaped from the saddle. With his left hand, he grabbed the edge of the collapsed aisle just a row beneath Alais. And to her horror, he was uttering the same words of power she had used to crack the stone.

As the horseman hung from the ledge, fissures spread from his fingers up the rows. Now, Alais' section of the theater was shaking as the crevices spread like a spider's web through her side of the bowl. The broken ledge on which the man clung cracked and crumbled, sending him plummeting into the yawning breach where dust billowed from the collapsing stone. Then, with a loud crackle, the stone gave way beneath Alais' knee. As debris tumbled into the growing rift, she threw herself backward, landing near Ormr as the theatre shuddered violently.

She heard Tara let out a cry. The Danes protecting Breda and Tara retreated up the next row, trying to outrun the cracks permeating the amphitheater. Alais scrambled to her feet. She tried to follow them, but the floor caved in beneath her.

Shards of stone cascaded around her as her stomach dropped, and she plunged into the chasm.

CHAPTER 15

DEMONS' FURY

The moment before the theater collapsed, a flickering blue light wreathed the broken columns of the ruined temple atop the theatre.

Ciarán cried out when the center of the aisle collapsed. As the tremors spread, the northern half of the bowl succumbed next, caving in sections, beginning with those closest to the aisle. The horsemen in the stands disappeared into the wreckage, as did black-robed men and spectators who had not made it to the stage. The crash of collapsing stone filled the air, along with plumes of dust, as the ground quaked beneath Ciarán's feet.

A chill flashed down his neck when the southern half of the bowl collapsed. An avalanche of stone benches and flooring spilled into the widening chasm. Halfway up the stands, a band of Danes vanished in a thunderhead of dust, and Alais was nowhere to be seen. Ciarán's free hand flew to his forehead, and he staggered back, suddenly dizzy as the Theatre of Pompey imploded around him.

Something bumped up against his shin. He looked down to find the head of Fótr, one of *Lindworm's* crew. His blue eyes stared life-lessly, and blood ringed his neck where it had been severed from his body.

"Ciarán!" someone yelled.

He glanced up; it was Jorundr. The hulking Dane was climbing to his feet, five paces away from two battles raging at the bottom of the southmost stands. Near what remained of the aisle, six of *Lindworm's* crew fought a dozen of the gibbering monks. Many of the monks sported mortal wounds, and some had even lost limbs, but they continued their onslaught as if the injuries were nothing. Meanwhile, the enormous horseman on the pale gray charger was hammering his blade onto Holger's shield. Strong Bjorn fought at the jarl's side, as did Birghir, a fierce red-headed Dane, though Fótr's body and that of two more of their crewmates lay sprawled on the blood-soaked stage. Rosta clung to the horseman's meaty shoulder, sinking his jaws into the muscle below the horseman's neck. That wound inflicted by a hundred-pound boarhound should have unhorsed the rider. But this man was far from ordinary, for the light of Caladbolg's flames revealed one of the most fearsome demons Ciarán had ever seen clinging to the man's mortal shell. The demon was larger than a bear, with wild, luminescent hair covering its body and massive, curved horns framing its beast-like head. He roared as he fought. "I AM THE TORMENTOR OF SOULS!"

"The bastard's stronger than a Jötunn," Jorundr yelled. He was bleeding from a gash across his ribs. "Holger stabbed him through the gut, yet he fights on like a demon."

"That's because it *is* a demon," Ciarán said through gritted teeth.

The horseman reached a thick-fingered hand behind his back and grabbed Rosta by the scruff of his neck. He tore the dog off his shoulder, ignoring the mangled flesh in the boarhound's teeth, and then hurled him halfway across the stage. Rosta yelped as he tumbled like a barrel over the flagstones just before the horseman landed a massive sword blow on Strong Bjorn's shield that knocked the giant Northman over the bench behind him.

Ciarán set his jaw and gripped Caladbolg with both hands. "Columcille!" he yelled as he charged. When he was a pace away from the horseman, he jumped, raising the fiery blade high above his head. The demon turned toward him. Huge tusks jutted from its lower jaw, but beneath the fiendish visage, Ciarán swore he saw the face of Ugo Grassus. As he brought Caladbolg down with all his strength, he saw fear in the demon's ember-like eyes. The blade's edge landed on the horseman's right shoulder, shearing through mail, muscle, and bone as fire rushed into the wound. "NO!" the demon roared as the flames spread across its incorporeal flesh before the self-proclaimed tormentor of souls exploded, leaving only luminescent wisps of the being that had possessed Ugo Grassus.

With its rider slumped dead in its saddle, the stallion bucked and bolted from the stage. Holger stared at Ciarán before turning to where Magnus lay against a bench with a spear protruding from his chest, his right hand resting on the pommel of his sword. A tear streamed down the jarl's bloodstained face.

"Save Alais!" rang out another voice, unmistakably Gerbert's. The pope stood on one of the surviving lower tiers in the stadium's still-intact southern bowl. Flanking him, Captain Gaido and his guardsmen had formed a human shield around both Gerbert and Niccolo.

Locking eyes with Ciarán, Gerbert spoke with a sense of urgency. "She fell when the stadium collapsed—"

But before the pope could even complete his sentence, Ciarán was already scaling the debris before plunging into the wreckage to find her.

THE FAE WORDS Alais uttered as she fell saved her life. The verse summoned a torrent of wind that rushed skyward from the ground. Wind blasted against her back and limbs, slowing her fall enough to prevent bones from breaking or her skull from striking the remains of the stone bench she landed on.

The gust cleared the dusty haze, leaving only motes of powdered stone drifting through the air. The theatre's underbelly was a warren of broken archways and ruined stone filled with shadows. Seven paces away, the horseman who had invoked the power lay half-buried under huge chunks of rubble, not far from his dead stallion. The man moved his head, but he looked dazed.

Alais could not imagine a horseman had knowledge of the Fae arts. There was more here than met the eye. With a word—*"Eoh"*—the palms of her hands flared with bluish light, which she scattered across the wreckage like an inferno of Saint Elmo's fire. In the light, she saw the demon's true form enveloping the horseman. It was a brutish thing, with a grotesquely prominent forehead, vulgar lips, and teeth filed to points. Overlaying the horseman's eyes, the demon's orbs glowed like hot coals.

She knew the demon could free itself from the horseman's broken mortal shell, but like its host, it was stunned from the fall, giving her precious seconds to act. She picked herself off the rubble and spoke another verse. The air thrummed, and the demon cried out as the words of power bound its spirit to its host. So long as the horseman lived, the demon could not escape. The fiend gnashed its teeth, its eyes smoldering.

"You failed," Alais told it. "The Key still flows through my veins. You'll never be able to break the pillar that seals your ancestor's prison."

The demon's mouth widened into a fiendish grin. "You don't remember, do you? Is that the price of living so many lives?"

Alais clenched her hands into fists. "What do you mean?"

The demon let out a chuckle laced with taunting amusement. "When the thousand years have ended, the Dragon's bonds weaken, allowing him to be freed of his prison, but so too does the power that sustains the pillar atop the Hill of Skulls. Already, cracks have formed on its surface, and they are spreading, just like the fissures you created in this arena. Soon—*very* soon—the power will dissipate into the air around Dudael, and the pillar will collapse beneath its weight. And when it does, smoke shall rise from the bottomless pit, and our forefathers shall be freed."

The demon's grin spread between its vulgar lips, displaying its mouthful of sharpened teeth. "You should be making your way to Dudael, yet instead, you linger in Rome. You are too late to stop it!"

As the demon spoke, an icy chill washed through Alais. "Demons lie," she said with a shudder.

"Look inside yourself, to the life you lived a millennium ago, and you'll know I speak true."

Alais shook her head. *Demons lie,* she assured herself. *But what if it spoke the truth?*

She jerked her head at the sound of something moving through the rubble. From a pile of broken stone crawled one of the men in a monk's habit. Half of the man's skull had caved in, but in her light, she saw the phantom animating the dead man's limbs. Two more monks emerged from the wreckage, their habits covered in dust and their dead eyes fixed on Alais. A rasp hissed from one of their throats. To her left, another shambled around a broken column with a reaping hook clutched in its hand.

Alais' heartbeat quickened. Then, to her right, another man hefted a huge stone block that stood in his path and tossed it onto a heap of ruined stone. The well-built man wore chainmail instead of a monk's habit, and rather than a mere phantom clinging to his skin, this one was possessed by a demon. The demon's face, like an opaque mask, was cruel and cunning, and its thin lips smiled as it pulled a longsword from the scabbard at its side.

Alais found herself surrounded.

"The Key is mine," the demon said, raising his sword.

As he stepped forward, Alais saw a flash of light burst through the shadows of the warren-like ruin. Where darkness had been, Ciarán charged. The demon whirled to parry the blow, but Caladbolg cleaved through its sword and buried its tip deep in the man's chest. When the fire engulfed its spectral form, the demon let out an unearthly wail.

Alais watched the demon die, but an icy hand grabbed her arm, pressing fingernails into her flesh. She tried to wrench her arm free, but the monk's grip was too strong. It was dragging her toward its undead brethren. "Slay the demon," she cried to Ciarán. "Their necromancy gives life to these dead men."

Ciarán spotted the demon pinned beneath the rubble. In two quick strides, he cleaved Caladbolg into its head. As the flaming blade sunk into the horseman's skull, the demon's ghostly form hissed into vapor.

The fingers digging into Alais' arm lost their strength. She pushed the man off her, and he toppled over. The other men in black habits crashed to the ground, as lifeless as a gang of scare-crows, until no one stood in the ruined space except Ciarán and Alais.

"Are you hurt?" he asked.

"No," she said, trying to suppress a swell of emotion. She needed to tell him what the demon said, for if it was true, their situation was far worse than they imagined.

But surveying the wreckage, all she could think about was that Breda, Tara, and a host of brave Danes might lie dead beneath the rubble.

CHAPTER 16

THE UNBELIEVERS

An hour before midnight, the streets of Constantinople were as quiet as the moment of silence before a funeral.

Shadows cast by the moonlight off the Hagia Sophia shrouded the entrance to the tomb-like structure, which stood across from the emperor's ceremonial plaza framed by colonnaded porticos. Dressed in a black cassock of finespun wool, Naberus da Roma blended into the surrounding darkness as he slipped through the entranceway to the Sunken Palace.

The ten men who followed him inside moved as quietly as ghosts. They were but shadows, clad in cloaks and hoods as black as midnight, with dark ribbons wrapped around the sheaths of their foot-long daggers. When they were all inside, Naberus lit a torch while one of his men sealed the door behind them. As he approached an archway that led to a descending stairwell, Naberus drew a deep breath. *The last time I came here,* he thought, *I had come begging for help. Not this time …*

The air became more humid as he descended the stone steps, nearly forty feet below the entrance, until he reached a second archway. There, the steps disappeared beneath the dark water that flooded the cavernous chamber beyond. Over five hundred years ago, it had been a basilica, and a marvelous one at that, built by seven thousand slaves. But over time, the city had grown around it, and then over it, before Emperor Justinian flooded the structure in 532 and turned it into a cistern.

Naberus stepped into the water. By the time his foot touched the basilica's floor, he stood knee high in the cold liquid, gazing upon the haunting beauty of the Sunken Palace. Oil lamps hung from a vaulted ceiling, and their light reflected off the scores of marble columns that rose from the water. Corinthian capitals crowned the columns, connected by a series of archways that ran hundreds of feet down the length of the nave. He tossed his torch into the water, extinguishing its flame with a hiss, then waded deeper into the basilica. Behind him, the footfalls of his men descending the stairwell were no louder than the water dripping into the cistern.

Naberus scanned the forest of columns for the sentinel, but saw no one among the shadows. *He must be hiding in one of the transepts— time to draw him out.*

Naberus's voice boomed down the nave. "Your prodigal son has returned!"

From the darkness of the north transept, the sentinel stepped into the flooded crossing. He stood a full seven feet, clad in a breastplate and helm as ancient-looking as the basilica itself. His hands gripped a long spear, and his eyes glared angrily from the slits in his helm. "How dare you?" he snarled. "In the chamber of the elders, you shall only speak when spoken to!"

Naberus flashed a cunning grin. If he had been a pettier man, he might have taken the sentinel's anger as a challenge and shown him who truly held power here. *But our cause will need warriors.*

"Then take me to the elders," Naberus replied, "and let us hear what they have to say."

"First, announce yourself!"

"Let him pass!" a woman called from deep within the chancel. Naberus's grin widened at the sound of his mother's voice. *Everything is going as planned.*

The sentinel grunted and drew back his spear, allowing Naberus to enter the crossing. From there, he could see the bowels of the chancel, where the nine elders awaited. From their high-backed thrones atop the curved dais rising above the waterline, they gazed down on Naberus. Within their broad cowls shone the golden masks that hid their faces, alight with the glow from the oil lamps hung around the chamber. Each mask had been forged in the image of an ancient Greek deity, six gods, and three goddesses. Zeus sat in the center. A golden amulet shaped like a disk and etched with a seven-pointed star surrounding a dragon's head hung at his chest.

Naberus knew the mask of Zeus, with its angry brow and pleated beard, hid the face of Malthus, a relic of a man who had ruled as chief elder for the last one hundred and sixty years, longer than Naberus had been alive.

"Naberus of Rome," Malthus announced, with a hint of rasp in his voice. "The last time you were here, you left with eight of our finest warriors and the giant, Antaeus of Gog. Where are they?"

Naberus should have bowed before speaking to the chief elder, but he stood defiantly. "Dead, I'm afraid."

A woman in the mask of Hera let out a gasp, followed by another from a man disguised as Dionysus.

"You fool!" cried an elder wearing a mask of Ares. Naberus knew the speaker as Moloch, one of Malthus's staunchest allies.

Malthus's eyes narrowed within his mask's hollow sockets. "Who could kill eight of our warriors and that giant?"

Naberus tried to hide a smile. "There was a ship full of Danes—"

"Danes?" Moloch scoffed. "Barbarians slaying our finest warriors? Impossible!"

Hera and Dionysus nodded their agreement. Meanwhile, the woman masked as Hecate crossed her arms and leaned back in her chair. Through the eyeholes of her golden mask, Naberus felt the warm touch of his mother's gaze.

"They were led by a Celt," Naberus continued, "who had the weapon known as Enoch's device."

"That weapon is but a myth," Malthus hissed.

Naberus feigned a sigh. "It's quite real, I assure you. In fact, everything I warned you about last time has come true. The demons' whispers, and the prophecy about the Morning Star and the Prince of Rome."

"Words of a charlatan," Moloch growled.

Naberus feigned a wounded look, knowing that by now, his men had crept silently down the aisles and should be infiltrating the shadows deep within the chancel. "The prophecy spoke of the path to our salvation."

"Salvation?" Disdain dripped from Malthus's tongue. "A millennium ago, the warlocks spoke of salvation, and their false prophecies deceived our kind into pursuing war. It nearly brought us to ruin. The victory you seek is an illusion. The world is as it is, and it cannot be changed." Malthus leaned forward on his throne. "The ones who accept that truth, who see the world's weaknesses and exploit them, are the ones who thrive. Or have you already forgotten that lesson? You practiced it long enough, and it made you rich and powerful in Rome, as it has made all of us rich and powerful in Byzantium. *That* is how we get by in this world. By ruling from the shadows instead of clinging to religious fantasies of old gods rising from bottomless pits to return the world to the way it was before the Great Flood. That world died thousands of years ago, and there is no savior who can bring it back."

"Oh, our savior exists." Naberus opened his palms. "Now may be your last chance to become a believer."

Moloch made a dismissive wave of his hand. "We shall not entertain your lies, charlatan."

Naberus steeled his gaze. "Do as you wish, but hear my demand. I need more men. All of your men, to be precise."

"Hah!" Malthus scoffed. "So you can get them killed and bring our race to the brink of extinction? You are reckless." He pointed a crooked finger at Naberus. "And you are risking condemnation. You could be tried for losing the lives of the men we loaned to you, and the punishment for such recklessness is death."

"Why wait?" Moloch urged. "Seize him now!"

The towering sentinel gave Moloch a nod. Clutching his spear in one hand, he reached for Naberus with his other. But as Naberus calmly backed away, two black figures rushed from the shadows.

117

One launched at the sentinel, wrapping his arms around the sentinel's shoulders, while the other tore at the sentinel's legs. Gasps exploded from the elders as the sentinel fell forward, splashing face down into the water. The black-robed attackers piled on his back, holding his head beneath the surface.

As if on cue, the rest of Naberus's men struck. Emerging from behind the thrones, their daggers flashed from their black cloaks. Steel blades pressed against the flesh of each elder's neck—all of them except the woman in the Hecate mask.

"What treachery is this?" Malthus rasped with an edge of fear in his voice. A trickle of blood dripped down his neck where the dagger nicked his flesh.

Naberus's mother rose from her throne.

"Astarte," Malthus asked incredulously. "Is this your doing?"

"They say a mother's love for her son knows no bounds," she replied coyly, "but I'm afraid you have made your own bed, Malthus." She pointed to three of the elders, a woman wearing the mask of Nike and two men masked as Poseidon and Hermes. "You may release these three, but bind the others."

Naberus felt a surge of triumph when the young warriors his mother had recruited wrestled the other five elders from their thrones. Moloch and his cohorts shouted protests while Malthus appeared resigned to capture as Naberus's warriors bound their hands behind their backs using the black ribbons that had been wrapped around the dagger sheathes. Meanwhile, two of his men dragged the sentinel half-drowned from the water and bound his wrists, too.

Moloch huffed. "Our people won't stand for this insurrection."

"I'm certain they will," Naberus said dismissively. He never liked Moloch.

Malthus glared at him, his gaze swelling with hate. "What will you do with us?"

"You've been summoned."

"By whom?"

Naberus's lips widened into a wolfish grin. "You'll see soon enough."

CHAPTER 17

THE KING OF WRATH

N aberus led the grim procession down the winding passageway that descended deeper beneath Constantinople.

They had reached the tunnels through a hidden door within the Sunken Palace. The exit had been marked by the gaze of a massive pedestal beneath one of the northwest columns carved in the shape of a giant head, faced upside down and bearing the visage of Medusa. From there, the procession ascended a flight of steps that climbed above the waterline. The stairway led to the tunnels beneath the city, which connected to the passageway that would descend once more forty feet below the cistern.

Naberus carried one of the torches that his mother, Astarte, had procured beforehand, its flame sputtering in the dank tunnel. Behind him strode his mother and ten black-clad warriors escorting the five prisoners and the three elders whom his mother insisted were allies.

"Where are you taking us?" the woman behind the Hera mask demanded. His mother had identified her as Achlys, a devious old woman who was the matriarch of a wealthy family of assassins-for-hire.

"To the Gate of Ahriman," Naberus replied.

"What?" she snapped.

Naberus stopped and cocked his head. "Have our legends become so stale and unimportant under the leadership of our elders that you've actually forgotten them? Perhaps I should remind you. A hundred and fifty years after the Greek prince, Byzas, founded this city, it was captured by the Persian Empire. They held it until the Peloponnesian War, seven centuries before the Roman emperor Constantine would make this place his home. The Persians—"

Achlys huffed behind her mask. "We're not ignorant of history."

"But you appear to be when it comes to the writings of the warlocks." Naberus was enjoying this game of cat and mouse. "My grandfather was the last of them, you know."

"Your grandfather was a doddering old fool," Moloch said contemptuously.

Naberus thrust his torch inches from Moloch's mask. "Doddering and old, perhaps, but not a fool." *Though I had been the fool,* Naberus had come to realize after his revelation a year ago in the shrine to Orcus beneath the Palatine Hill. But now, it was these arrogant elders who needed enlightenment.

"According to my grandfather's dusty old scrolls," Naberus explained, "when the first warlocks arrived here from Rome, they discovered an underground temple built by a sect of Persians who revered Ahriman, the ancient enemy of the Persian god Ahura Mazda. It turns out the Persians chose the temple's location for a reason, as you'll soon discover."

Malthus, who had remained silent during their procession from the Sunken Palace, finally spoke. "Stop acting so mysterious, Naberus. Do you mean to kill us?"

Naberus put a hand on his chest. "I'll do no such thing. You have my word."

He continued his descent, and the procession followed. The air became cooler and dryer the deeper they descended before the passageway emerged into a rectangular chamber paved with ancient flagstones. Light from his torch danced across the far wall where a crumbling relief had been carved into the stone. The massive carving depicted a bearded giant thrusting a sword into the gut of a lion-like monster with eagle-like wings.

Naberus gestured toward the relief. "The warlocks knew that the being called Ahriman had many, many names. He's portrayed here defeating the winged lion, one of Ahura Mazda's divine incarnations. His priests founded this ancient temple because they believed the ground held a sacred connection to their god."

Moloch grunted. "You said this was a gateway, you insufferable fool. You've led us to an empty chamber."

Naberus's lips curved into a smile. Moloch's insults were only adding to his amusement. "A sacrifice is required to open the gate." He held out his right hand, and one of his warriors handed him a foot-long dagger.

Achlys gasped.

"You said you wouldn't kill us!" Malthus cried.

"Not you, Malthus," Naberus said. He spun and tore the Hephaestus mask off one of the elders, sending it clattering across the flagstones. A familiar face stared back from beneath the dark cowl, his eyes wide and his skin ashen. His name was Thais, and they had grown up together as children. Naberus grabbed the back of Thais's cowl and dragged him toward the relief of Ahriman.

Thais's lower lip was trembling. "As boys," he pleaded, "we were friends."

"Yet you aligned yourself with Malthus," Naberus said under his breath as he slid the dagger across Thais's throat. This time, Achlys screamed.

Naberus pressed hard so the dagger cut deep through Thais's jugular and into his esophagus. Thais made a gurgling noise before blood began pumping from the wound. Naberus held the man's head over the flagstones as his blood pooled on the ground. Then Naberus began uttering words in the ancient tongue of his ancestors. Around him, the air sizzled, and a red mist began rising from the pool of blood. With each spoken word, the steam billowed, growing into a ruby-hued cloud that obscured the image of Ahriman.

The elder disguised as Dionysus doubled over and spewed a mouthful of vomit from the hole of his golden mask.

"You'll die for this," Moloch vowed.

Naberus ignored him. "Leave the torches," he told his men, "and bring them through."

The captive elders erupted in protest, struggling to resist as Naberus's warriors forced them into the mist. They should have plowed into a hard stone wall, but instead, they disappeared deep into the cloud as if the wall had vanished. Naberus set down his torch and followed them. A chill washed down his skin as he entered the vapor, while a thrum pulsed in his ears. The mist carried the slightly sweet, metallic taste of blood, and for a moment, it felt like it would fill his nose and lungs, drowning him in its icy embrace. But Naberus did not panic. He had experienced this sensation before when passing between the mortal world and the Otherworld.

He emerged from the gateway into twilight, his feet stepping onto a beach of ash-gray sand. The surrounding air was thick and oppressive. Around him, the elders were huffing to catch their breath. Some of his men stood with their hands on their thighs, breathing heavily.

In the distance loomed a series of tall, dark shapes. Then, without warning, a reddish light flared. It emanated from a gemstone in the palm of a woman who strode toward them. She stood taller than any of the elders, with pale skin that reflected the gemstone's crimson glow. She might have been beautiful had her look not been so severe, with steel-gray eyes, long black hair tied behind her neck, and a jet-black stone set into her pale forehead. Spidery symbols crawled up her lithe arms and legs, and the gossamer robes that covered her torso left little to the imagination. She nodded at Naberus. He had been expecting her.

"Who are you?" Moloch asked bitterly.

The woman stopped ten yards away and answered with a voice as severe as her appearance. "I am Lovetar, the Lady of Pain."

"You're the one who dared summon us?" Malthus scoffed. "What are you?"

Lovetar ignored him and turned her gaze toward Naberus. "Are these the unbelievers?"

"Yes," he responded.

"Bring them to me."

Naberus's men nudged the four elders forward until they stood facing Lovetar.

Beside Naberus, his mother, Astarte, beckoned the other three elders to move away from the captives. "You shall witness from here and assess your loyalties," she told them under her breath. Naberus joined them. All he could do now was watch the spectacle unfold.

"Pull back their cowls and unmask them," Lovetar demanded.

Naberus's men did as they were told. Unmasked, the four elders glared at Lovetar, although worry shone in the lines carved across their haggard faces. Using her glowing red gem, Lovetar drew a circular symbol in the air and traced an inverted star within it, all while uttering an arcane verse. When she finished, the air sizzled, followed by a whiff of ozone. The elders appeared to stiffen until they stood ramrod straight.

"I can't move my legs," Moloch muttered.

"So you can't run and hide," Lovetar said. She removed the disk-shaped amulet from Malthus's neck and hung it on the sash wrapped around her narrow waist. Then she gestured for the warriors to join Naberus and his mother. With a bow, they obeyed, leaving the four captive elders standing before Lovetar with para-lyzed limbs.

She took several steps backward, moving with a sultry grace. Then, like a dancer at a mummers' show, she threw up her arms. "Behold!"

Forty yards behind her, a semi-circle of flames erupted in the chamber, penetrating the shadows. The fire burned from massive braziers atop pillars thirty feet high. They rose from the shore of a vast underground harbor filled with black water where a dark-hulled ship was moored. Larger than two Byzantine galleys, its bowsprit jutted like the tip of a jagged spear, and a tattered sail hung from its yard with rigging like a spider's web. But it was the pyramid-like structure in the center of the sprawling semi-circular harbor that drew everyone's attention. The pyramid was built of stone, with steps that led to its summit shaped like a giant high-backed throne. And atop it sat Naberus's master.

His naked, muscular body filled the colossal throne. His flawless skin shone with a golden light, as it did when Naberus had pulled the lance from his side. Scripture had called him the Morning Star, and his terrifying beauty proved how fitting that name was. The ancient Persians had called him Ahriman, and as he lorded over the elders standing beneath his temple, his eyes burned with sheer power as if this subterranean kingdom and the entire world above were his to command. Naberus could hardly bear to look straight into those eyes, and he could only imagine the white-hot fear coursing through the elders as they were forced to gaze upon his master as if they were staring into the sun. The being's presence filled the air with electricity and drew a murmur from Astarte's lips. *"My god."* For that is what they gazed upon—a god. A being who, throughout the ages, had had many names. And one of those was the name of their savior, the name by which Lovetar called him now.

"Behold," she cried, "the lord, your god, Samyaza!"

Samyaza looked down upon the elders and spoke with a thunderous voice. "Am I a religious fantasy?" He let the question linger. Moloch's lower lip began to tremble.

"I," Samyaza continued, "who waged war in Heaven and brought paradise to Earth? Who led the Watchers to this world to lie with the daughters of men, the act that gave birth to your race? I am your creator, yet you perceive me as some myth to be forgotten?"

"Please," Malthus begged. Unmasked, he looked frail and pitiful, with wispy white hair combed over his feeble skull. "We didn't know."

"You mean you did not *believe.*" Samyaza's voice hardened. "Because you lacked faith. As you will see, *that* has consequences."

As the elders stared helplessly at Samyaza, Lovetar joined Naberus and his mother. The light within Lovetar's gemstone died in her palm.

Meanwhile, Samyaza stood. He was a towering presence, nearly eight feet tall. Then he spread his arms, and his feet left the pedestal. An elder beside Naberus gasped as Samyaza rose into the air. When he floated ten feet above his throne, he said in a booming voice: "I AM THE PRINCE OF LIGHT. THE LORD OF HELL. THE KING OF WRATH!"

With a roar to match Samyaza's own, the braziers atop the pillars flared. Their soaring flames arched toward Samyaza as if he were summoning them. Flames crawled up his arms, legs, and chest until he appeared made of fire. What were his arms spread into fiery wings. His torso expanded, tripling in size, while his neck elongated and his head stretched into a serpent-like shape. As the flames began to die, Samyaza's once-golden flesh was now covered in ember-like scales. Smoke hissed from his wings, and flames still danced along the ridges of long spines that jutted from the top of his head down his serpentine neck. Naberus watched, awestruck, while Samyaza transformed into his other guise. One that gave rise to another of his names—*the Dragon.*

A flap of his mighty wings sent a gale-like rush of air over Naberus and those around him, so fierce it blew the golden masks off Astarte and the other three elders. The woman who had disguised herself as Nike held her hands over her face, unable to look upon the Dragon.

High above the throne, the Dragon's eyes burned like molten fire, fixed on the captive elders. They were crying out, but Naberus could not hear their words above the roaring braziers. The Dragon's chest flushed fiery red as he filled his lungs and opened his jaws ringed with dagger-like teeth. Fire gathered in the back of his throat and then, with a deafening sound, exploded into a torrent of flames.

Fiery breath flooded over the elders. Skin blackened, and the sickening stench of burning flesh filled the air. Naberus and his mother had to step back, for the heat of the Dragon's breath was more intense than he had anticipated. And it continued to wash over the elders. Limbs began to shrivel as fire consumed flesh and bone. With a loud pop, Moloch's skull exploded while Malthus collapsed, his legs turning to ash.

Beside Naberus, the three surviving elders stood speechless. Astarte's eyes held a look of fear and awe.

The Dragon drew in his wings and glided to the ground. He landed at the base of the pyramid next to four smoking piles of ash and bone. His massive claws dug deep into the sand. When he craned his neck toward Naberus, heat emanated from his mouth like a furnace.

"KNEEL!"

The word shook the ground beneath Naberus's feet. His men dropped to a knee, and his mother and the three elders followed. Naberus bent his knee to the ground. "My lord," he said, bowing his head.

Lovetar stepped toward him, holding Malthus's amulet. The golden disk reflected the braziers' reddish light, illuminating the seven-pointed star with seven crowns surrounding the face of the Dragon. She placed it around his neck. "You shall rule your people now."

Naberus felt the amulet's weight on his chest. He had never desired to rule over men, having spent his life as the counselor and manipulator of prelates and popes, growing fabulously rich in the process. Until Samyaza called to him beneath the Palatine Hill in the darkness of Orcus's shrine. And Naberus knew he must answer that call. For like Paul on the road to Damascus, he had found his savior, and his life's purpose had become undeniable.

He drew a long breath and looked into the Dragon's eyes.

"I shall not fail you."

CHAPTER 18

THE SURVIVORS

F ollowing the attack at the Theatre of Pompey, Gerbert turned the chapel of Saint Sylvester on the second floor of the Lateran Palace into a secret infirmary.

Given the urgency of the situation, none of the traditional practices employed by the Holy See's infirmerers would do. Few of the priests and monks who tended to the sick in Rome employed skills beyond leechcraft, and even fewer had studied the medical texts of the ancient Greeks and Arabic physicians, as Gerbert had done over the years. But none of them knew how to use the power of the Fae to heal wounds, and they would have been horrified at Gerbert and Alais' use of such arcane methods to tend to the survivors of *Lindworm's* crew.

Eight patients rested on straw pallets that lined the chapel's walls, where the wavering light from a score of candles glittered off the colored glass and ceramic tiles of mosaics depicting the life of Saint Sylvester. The air was thick with the scent of mint and vinegar to cleanse wounds and chamomile to induce rest. In the narrow aisle between the pallets, Gerbert hunched over twin bookstands containing copies of works on human anatomy by a Greek scholar named Rufus of Ephesus and the Persian physician Ali ibn al-Abbas. Gerbert glanced between the texts and Alais.

"There are two bones in the lower leg," he instructed her. "The tibia and fibula. They come together at the ankle, and you'll need to mend them both."

Alais nodded back. Her patient, a black-bearded Dane named Úlfarr, grimaced as she ran her hands across his red and swollen left leg. While she had never used the power for healing before, she knew that the human body was made of millions of particles, just like iron and stone, and all such particles could be manipulated through the language of creation. Gerbert had shown her the way when he taught her to heal Breda. Her back had been broken, and Holger feared he had lost his wife in addition to Magnus. But Gerbert had used the knowledge gleaned from his books, as well as his keen understanding of the power of the Fae, to guide Alais and her soul light as she healed the damaged vertebrae. The painstaking process took hours, but when it was over, Breda would live and walk again, leaving Alais grateful for Gerbert's keen knowledge of Arabic and Greek medicine.

Clearing her mind, Alais drew a calming breath before speaking the words of power that would let her mend bones. As the words Gerbert had taught her rolled naturally off her tongue, she felt heat pulse down her arm into her palm resting against Úlfarr's leg. She gently pressed the bones back together as the Fae words made the once rigid bone pliable before the fracture mended and the bones became hard and strong once more. When it was over, Úlfarr let out a grateful groan and wiped the sweat from his brow.

"Brother Ciarán," Gerbert said, "get Úlfarr some wine mulled with chamomile. I want him to sleep before he puts weight on that leg."

"Aye, Your Holiness," Ciarán replied. He and Pietro had been assisting in the infirmary, and though neither knew much about mending bones, both were quick to follow Gerbert's orders.

As Ciarán handed Úlfarr the cup of mulled wine, Alais went to check on Jorundr. The tall, muscular Dane sat on his pallet with his back against the wall. The sword blow he had taken from the possessed Ugo Grassus had sheared through flesh, muscle, and two ribs. Had the blade reached his heart or lung, the Dane would not be here. Fortunately, a bandage torn from Holger's cloak was able to stop the bleeding until Alais could mend the ribs and close the wound.

"How does it feel?" she asked him.

Jorundr rotated his arm above the scar where the wound had been. "Stiff, but I'll live." He glanced at Breda, sleeping on one of two pallets beneath a large mosaic of Sylvester baptizing Emperor Constantine. "I'm grateful you saved her," he said. "Had Holger lost her along with Magnus, it might have broken him."

"Thank His Holiness. Were it not for him, I would not have known how to do it."

"I could say the same for you, my lady," Gerbert interjected. "Had I tried to summon the power for as long as you have, I'm quite certain I would have died from exhaustion by now."

Alais smiled fondly at Gerbert. Ever since she had awakened to the realization that Sirra's spirit lived within her, using the power had come naturally and without the taxing fatigue that accompanied such use before her awakening. Yet her moment of contentment melted away when she peered at the patient beside Breda. Tara looked as if she were sleeping peacefully, but Alais knew that was not the case, and it pained her that Tara's condition appeared beyond her power to heal. Tara must have clung to Breda when the bowl collapsed, and Breda's body broke her fall. But debris had struck the girl's head, opening a bloody gash beneath her dark hair. When they had stopped the bleeding, Gerbert concluded her skull had not fractured, which likely would have been fatal. However, the blow had knocked Tara unconscious, and while she still breathed, they could not wake her, no matter how hard they tried.

"She's fortunate to be alive," Gerbert said. "She'll wake, eventually. Give it time."

Gerbert's words did little to ease Alais' pain. According to Father Michelle's note, Tara was the one person she was supposed to protect. And look what happened.

The theatre's collapse had killed two of *Lindworm's* crew and more than fifty spectators, all loyalists of Cardinal Bishop Beno. Niccolo's network of informants was already spreading the Holy See's version of what had occurred: that the remnants of the fanatical Brotherhood of the Messiah had made a brazen attempt on the pope's life. During the ensuing panic, the old Roman structure gave way, resulting in the tragedy that must have been the talk of everyone in Rome. But Alais knew the truth of what she had done, and she wished more than anything that she had found a different way to deal with the rampaging horsemen.

Gerbert put a gentle hand on Alais' arm. "If you're ready, we have more wounded to attend to."

Alais swallowed hard. "Of course."

She followed Gerbert to their next patient when Pietro entered the chapel carrying a stack of clean blankets. "Pardon, My Lady," he said, maneuvering clumsily around her in the narrow aisle between the pallets.

"You're fine," she said to Pietro before kneeling beside Ormr. The thick-bearded Dane lay grimacing from pain despite the several cups of wine he had consumed to numb himself.

"Our friend Ormr must have landed on his left arm," Gerbert said. "He's broken two bones in the arm and three ribs. I suggest we start with the humerus, the bone between his shoulder and elbow."

Ormr proved to be an unruly patient, but after a half hour, Alais was able to mend all five broken bones. She sighed when it was done. This was the first bit of fatigue she had felt from the effort, and her stomach had started to grumble. She could not remember when she had last eaten. She thought about resting herself when Pietro cried out. "Blessed Sergius!"

She turned to find him leaning over Tara. The girl's eyes remained closed, but her head thrashed back and forth, and a faint moan escaped her lips.

"What's happening?" Alais asked with alarm.

Pietro glanced up, his eyes wide. "I think she's having a nightmare."

CHAPTER 19

THE TREE OF FIRE

T ara found herself trapped in a memory. One that clung ferociously to her mind, unwilling to let go.

It began in the boat, as it always did. She was six years old, wrapped in a dark blue cloak to protect her from the biting wind. It was nighttime, and as the boat sped away with its sail full of wind, the city's lights rising above its massive seawalls faded from view. However, the brightest lights blazed from the windows of the city's most prominent building, a vast domed structure, as if a giant eye were watching their escape.

A four-man crew sailed the boat. Tara never learned who they were. Friends of her parents, perhaps. Two men frantically worked the twin rudders while the other two struggled with the rigging on the mainsail and the smaller sail attached to the foremast. Her father, tall, bearded, and handsome, aided the sailor on the prow. They were yelling orders at one another. Their tone was not angry, but desperate.

Her mother, regal and slender, stood between the deckhouse and the mainmast, her dark, hooded cloak whipping in the wind. Her right hand gripped her long, blackened staff. The one her mother said had been carved from a tree struck by lightning during a storm.

Her other hand closed tightly around Tara's. Her mother had always been as strong as steel, but tonight her eyes filled with worry.

"Don't let go of your sister," her mother commanded.

Tara's left hand clung to Sara's. They were twins, so alike it was as if Tara were looking at her reflection in a silver mirror. Sara was shaking.

A brass lantern hanging from a bracket on the deckhouse creaked in the wind, casting its fluttering light about the deck while the sea heaved against the boat's hull, rocking the ship and roiling Tara's stomach.

When they spotted the other ship in the starlight, her mother squeezed Tara's hand so hard that she almost crushed it. The ship was behind them but closing in from the direction of the city. Its sail bowed, and a half-dozen oars beat into the water.

"Yusuf!" her mother cried to her father.

"I see it," he said. His tone was firm, but Tara could sense an edge of fear.

As her father began barking orders to the crew, Tara's heart pounded. Their pursuer was moving faster than they were. Sara pulled her hand free and threw her arms around Tara. "They'll catch us!" Sara cried.

Time became a blur. Tara's heart jumped when the grapplings slammed onto the deck and bit hard into the rail. With its momentum arrested, their boat lurched violently. Sara lost her grip and went sprawling. Their father dove after her and scooped her off the deck and into his arms. Mother pulled Tara close, wrapping her free arm around her chest.

The other ship's prow crashed into the boat's stern. Men leaped from the vessel, flying like phantoms in the night. They were long-limbed, clad in close-fitting garb darker than midnight, with masks covering their faces except for their eyes.

Tara gasped when the assassins plunged long knives into the two crewmen in the boat's stern. She opened her mouth to scream, but the cry stuck in her throat when a third assassin jumped into the boat. He crouched, dagger in hand, ready to pounce on Tara and her mother.

Her mother shoved Tara behind her before whipping her staff and shattering the lantern hanging from the boathouse. Tara's eyes flew wide when the lantern's flames erupted into a plume on the tip of her mother's staff. Uttering words that Tara did not comprehend, with a melody like a song, her mother swung her staff toward the assassin. The fiery plume leaped from the staff, ballooning into a melon-sized ball of fire that struck the assassin in the chest. Her mother uttered more words as the fireball exploded, hurling their attacker overboard. A pair of explosions followed before a billow of smoke hissed from the water. Tara glanced over the gunwale. To her horror, the sea was on fire.

Smoke obscured the boat's stern, but through the dark vapor, another figure emerged. A woman taller than any Tara had ever seen. As she stepped into the glow of the fire burning impossibly on the water, Tara saw her face. Beautiful, but cruel. Her dark hair was pulled tight behind her head, but it was the mark beneath her left eye that Tara would never forget—a violet birthmark shaped like a crescent moon.

The woman spoke to her mother. "Hand over the girls, Shirin."

A chill shivered down Tara's chest. *The woman knew her mother's name.*

Her mother embraced Tara with her free arm. "Never."

The woman drew a dagger and flipped it into the air, catching its hilt with catlike grace.

"Hold on to my arm and don't let go," her mother whispered into Tara's ear. She did as her mother told, feeling lifted into the air when her mother lunged toward the gunwale.

As her mother leaped over the side, holding Tara tight, she heard her whisper: *"Yusuf, forgive me."*

They plunged overboard, dropping into the raging sea of fire.

THE FLAMES DID NOT SEAR Tara's skin, for she was no longer surrounded by the burning sea. She had escaped the memory but now found herself lost in a dream.

Tara stared up at the massive, ancient oak. Its thick, knotted branches reached towards the heavens, its leaves burning like a million tiny stars. She could feel the heat emanating from the fiery tree, and for a moment, she thought she was back in the burning sea. But her bare feet stood on soft, damp ground, cool beneath her toes.

The four creatures rested on broad tree limbs, their golden coats glimmering in the fire's light. Massive paws, much larger than Tara's head, dug claws into the branches, and their long tails lay draped over them. Differing from their lion-like fur, the broad feathers of their raptor-like wings shimmered reddish bronze in the flames. The first beast's thick mane was a flaming golden red, and his eyes, nestled in his massive lion's head, held a warm orange glow. Tara felt its gaze on her skin as if the beast was staring into her soul.

"Greetings, child." The lion spoke in a voice so loud and deep it rumbled through the earth beneath her feet.

From a high bough, the beast with the shaggy head of an ox and long curved horns spoke next. "It is time."

Near the center of the tree, the human-headed beast regarded her with golden eyes set into a flawless face framed by long hair like beaten bronze. "We speak to you again."

The great eagle-headed creature opened its curved beak. "Of the mysteries."

As they delivered their message, one by one, a warmth washed over Tara, and the words burned into her ears and nestled in her mind.

When they finished, the lion's blazing eyes fixed on Tara. "You have heard what you were meant to hear. Now open your eyes, and tell them."

CHAPTER 20

THE FIFTH SEAL

Ciarán gasped with relief when Tara bolted awake.

Alais rushed to her pallet and dropped to a knee. "Are you alright?"

Tara's gaze drifted from Alais to Ciarán, then to Gerbert and Pietro, who huddled beside him, and finally to the pallets of wounded patients lining the walls in the small chapel to Saint Sylvester. Her eyes settled on Breda.

"Is she …" Tara's lower lip trembled.

"She's just resting," Alais said calmly. "She was hurt in the collapse, but she'll wake up as good as new. How is your head?"

Tara rubbed the back of her head and winced. "Sore."

"You looked like you were having a dream," Gerbert said.

Tara's mouth fell open; she looked at Gerbert with a sense of awe. Ciarán imagined this must have been her first time speaking to the pope. A girl raised in a convent likely viewed him as the most important man in the world.

"They told me to speak to you," she said.

Gerbert arched an eyebrow. "The four creatures?"

Her eyes widened. "You know about them?"

Pietro glanced sideways at Ciarán, who waited on Tara's next words, anticipation welling within him.

"The scriptures say they are messengers from God," Gerbert told Tara.

The girl gaped at him. "They spoke in riddles. One of them called it a mystery."

Alais placed a hand on Tara's shoulder. "What did they say?"

Tara closed her eyes briefly, recalling the words. "*After the fourth comes the fifth seal, the slain souls' home it shall reveal. It lies beneath where they are found, on the holy emperor's sacred ground.*"

As Ciarán listened, he was struck by another reference to the Seven Seals of God. His mind started sifting through the riddle when Pietro jumped on the first clue.

"In Revelation," Pietro began, "when the fifth seal is broken, it reveals the martyrs, the souls who have been slaughtered for following the word of God."

"Slain souls." Gerbert scratched the chin of his ginger beard. "But where are they found?"

Ciarán knew the answer. Years ago at Derry, he illuminated a copy of the book of Revelation, and he remembered drawing the souls of the slain, each one a monk in white robes. But more significantly, he recalled the object above the place where they were revealed to Saint John. Ciarán had decorated the object with golden ink and crowned it with a gilded cross. "They're found under an altar. An altar that must stand on a holy emperor's sacred ground."

"A holy emperor," Pietro mused. "Charlemagne?"

"He was the first Holy Roman Emperor," Gerbert acknowledged. "But I think the clue likely points to a figure closer to antiquity. To Constantine the Great. He was the first Christian emperor, so who could be holier than he? And let's not forget it was Constantine and his mother, Saint Helena, who brought back relics from Jerusalem. One of those was the Testament of Solomon, which helped locate the Key to the Abyss, and who knows what other artifacts he may have discovered. My hunch is that this mystery once more connects Constantine to something that whoever is sending Tara these messages thinks we need."

"Why would we need to find the home of the slain souls?" Alais asked.

Her question sparked a memory in Ciarán. Of something they learned when they discovered Orionde's tower of Rosefleur. It took but another moment to make the connection.

"Suppose the home of the slain is referring to the Otherworld," Ciarán said. "Do you remember Una, the Fae warrior we encountered after entering the gateway to Rosefleur? She called the Otherworld their *purgatory*. In scripture, isn't purgatory, or Sheol, a land of souls? To the Irish, the Otherworld is the home of the Fae, but it's also the land of the dead. And if Dudael lies in the Otherworld, as we all suspect, might this fifth seal show us how to get there?"

Alais drew in a breath. "To find the Cauldron of God."

Pietro blinked in astonishment. "It's been the one thing that's eluded us this entire time."

"And all we needed was the witness to help us find it," Gerbert added. "More importantly, if what the demon told Alais is true, and the pillar that seals the Watchers' prison is indeed weakening, we must get there sooner than we hoped. So it seems this information has come just in the nick of time."

The pope pressed his palms together and tipped them toward Tara. "My dear, we owe a great debt to you and your dreams."

Tara smiled, but it quickly faded. "Have you solved the riddle?"

"Not all of it," Alais said. "What about the holy emperor's sacred ground?"

"It's a place," Gerbert replied, "and I know precisely where it is. If we leave now, we can be there within the hour."

Giovani Bobone, Archpriest of Saint Peter's Basilica, fumbled with the key that unlocked the great doors to the basilica's vestibule.

The pope's sudden arrival, an hour past Compline, had flustered the elderly archpriest, who in turn roused a dozen canons from their beds to attend to the pontiff's every wish. One bleary-eyed canon held an oil lamp so the archpriest could see the keyhole while the rest huddled like a gaggle of black-robed geese in the covered arcade between the atrium and the vestibule.

Ciarán watched from the outdoor atrium known as the Garden of Paradise. Shadows filled the pillared archways that surrounded the rectangular atrium, while a flicker of moonlight glinted off the mosaic of Christ that decorated the basilica's facade beneath the peak of its towering triangular roof. The basilica was the most sacred church in all of Rome. Constantine the Great had built it for Saint Sylvester, the very pope who protected the Testament of Solomon and hid it in a secret vault above the basilica's crossing. So, Ciarán found it fitting that Tara's riddle would lead them back here. But it was the thought of what lay beneath the basilica's altar that intrigued him the most.

It was Alais, who stood in the atrium beside Ciarán and Pietro, who had first asked Gerbert the question. "There's something underneath the basilica?"

"A tomb," Gerbert replied, "nearly a thousand years old, lying directly beneath the altar. The tomb of Saint Peter himself."

That he might soon stand in that holy place sent a chill over Ciarán's skin. Although it was the mystery of what else might lie within that tomb—an artifact, perhaps, which could show them the way to Dudael—that captivated his mind.

Gerbert waited beside Captain Gaido and five of the papal guardsmen who had escorted them to the Leonine City in the dark of night. The archpriest's key caused an audible click, and Gerbert strode toward the great doors. He took the oil lamp from the bleary-eyed cannon and addressed the archpriest. "Giovani, if you and your canons could be so kind as to wait here, we won't be long."

The archpriest stooped his head as if the heavy bags under his pale eyes were weighing it down. "As you wish, Your Holiness."

As the canons opened the great doors, Gerbert gestured for Ciarán, Alais, and Pietro to follow him.

The basilica was the largest church Ciarán had ever set foot in, but he had never done so during nighttime. Gerbert's oil lamp barely pierced the darkness inside the vast nave, and the many shrines and mosaics that adorned the nave's walls were lost within the shadows beyond the towering columns that ran down each side of the central aisle. A hint of incense lingered in the air, and the basilica was deathly quiet, save for their footfalls echoing through the nave.

When they were halfway down the aisle, Gerbert's lamplight caught the twisted columns of gray marble that supported the silver canopy above the altar in the basilica's chancel. Those columns, Ciarán knew, once stood in Solomon's temple before Emperor Constantine brought them from Jerusalem, and their spiraling shape had been mimicked in the ornate scroll case that held the Testament of Solomon. As the lamplight washed over the marble altar, Ciarán wondered if whatever lay beneath it was also one of Solomon's creations.

"How do we get beneath the altar?" Alais asked. "It looks far too massive to move."

"There's a hidden stairwell in the back of the chancel," Gerbert replied. "Saint Peter was martyred in the Circus of Nero at the base of the Vatican Hill. Beneath the hill was a Roman necropolis—a city of the dead—where the early Christians entombed the saint. When Constantine built the basilica in 326, he constructed it on top of the necropolis, immaculately designed so that the altar stood precisely above Saint Peter's tomb. Fortunately, the emperor preserved the entrance to the necropolis, though Pope Sylvester thought it best to conceal it, which is why the tomb was not desecrated by the Visigoths, Huns, and Saracens during the various times they sacked the city."

"The entrance is a closely guarded secret in the Holy See," Pietro added, "much like the hidden door to the papal archives."

Gerbert rounded the raised platform that supported the Solomonic columns and the altar and stopped before a roughly square flagstone about a yard wide.

"The stairway is under here." Gerbert stooped down and reached into a nearly hidden space beneath the altar before removing a slightly curved iron bar as long as a man's arm. "It's a handheld lever to raise the flagstone. Archimedes would be proud."

Gerbert wormed the tip of the bar into the groove between the flagstone, then used it to pry open the flagstone enough for Pietro to slip his hands beneath it. Ciarán knelt to aid him, and together, they slid the flagstone onto the one beside it, revealing a shaft with stone steps descending into the earth.

Stale air rushed to meet him as he followed Gerbert, Alais, and Pietro down the ancient steps. With each step, Ciarán felt anticipation welling within. The steep stairwell plunged more than thirty feet beneath the basilica until it ended on a packed dirt floor and a series of passages that spread in every direction like alleyways of a cramped city street. Gerbert turned down one, clearly familiar with the labyrinthine necropolis. His lamplight brought the eerily quiet catacombs to life. There were frescos on the walls, many of early Christian and biblical imagery, but some images were pagan. Ciarán marveled at one showing Hades dragging a terrified Persephone into the Underworld.

"The necropolis was used by the Romans in antiquity, as well as the first Christians," Pietro explained while Ciarán's gaze lingered on the fresco.

They passed large and small mausoleums until Gerbert turned down another alley leading to a chamber with a yawning hollow hewn into the wall. The face of the stone wall above the man-sized hole was scrawled with ancient graffiti. Ciarán recognized the letters as Greek and read the words aloud:

"PETER IS HERE."

Ciarán felt goosebumps on his arms as he made the sign of the cross.

"This is his tomb?" Alais asked.

"Inside the hollow lies the saint's bones wrapped in a burial shroud," Gerbert said. He, too, made the sign of the cross, and Ciarán had no doubt they stood upon the holiest of ground. "I'd prefer not to disturb the body. I doubt Constantine or Sylvester would have hidden anything under the shroud."

Ciarán peered into the hole. The lamplight illuminated a human form in a dust-encrusted shroud. The only other thing inside the hollow were small pieces of rubble scattered on the tomb's floor. "There's nothing here."

"We may need a different form of light," Gerbert offered. "When Pope Gregory discovered the Testament of Solomon, the scroll case gave off a perceptible glow in my soul light. Whatever we're seeking might be imbued with the same power."

"Let's find out," Alais said. She closed her eyes for a breath and uttered the word. *"Eoh."* Dazzling light burst from her fingertips, dancing across the chamber's walls and flooding the hollow, illumining the remains of Saint Peter.

Ciarán scanned everything her soul light touched. He had used this same trick last year when he discovered the Book of Giants in the vault inside Castel Sant'Angelo. The book had glowed with a faint blue light, like Saint Elmo's fire, and the radiance presaged the ward enchanting the book's cover. But in the tomb of Saint Peter, he saw no such thing.

Pietro began feeling along the wall surrounding the hollow. The wall, however, was made of rock instead of bricks or corbeled stones where one might hide something behind a loose piece of masonry.

Ciarán let out a sigh. "Did Constantine happen to build any other churches in Rome?"

"The Archbasilica of Saint John Lateran," Pietro replied. "But I know that one like the back of my hand. When His Holiness came to the throne, I searched it thoroughly to catalog all the relics. It is full of reliquaries containing the bones of saints, but there were no artifacts like the Testament of Solomon, and certainly nothing that would qualify as a map or device to take us to Dudael."

Alais let her soul light fade, leaving only the glow of Gerbert's oil lamp in the ancient tomb. "What about outside of Rome?" she asked. " Where else did Constantine build churches?"

Gerbert tipped his head and stroked his neck. "Many places. He was the first Christian emperor and a patron of the faith. In the Holy Land, he commissioned the Church of the Nativity in Bethlehem over the place where many believe our Savior lay in the manger, though some attribute that church to the work of his mother, Saint Helena. The same is true of the Church of the Holy

Sepulchre in Jerusalem, built on the hill of Golgotha. As far north as Trier in Germany, he built the Aula Palatina, also known as the Basilica of Constantine. And when he moved his throne to Constantinople, he constructed several churches throughout his new city. It would take a year or more to visit them all."

"If what the demon said is true," Alais said, "the pillar won't last that long."

"We have to be missing something." Ciarán felt sure of it. "Whoever is delivering these messages to Tara knows we need to get to Dudael in time."

"Then perhaps they could be more direct with their messaging," Gerbert said with an edge of frustration.

"If the messenger is anything like Blind Mikkel, that's not how he operates." Ciarán clasped his palms together. "He talks in riddles but always gives enough clues to solve them. We must be overlooking something in the riddle itself." He recited the words Tara had spoken:

> After the fourth comes the fifth seal,
> the slain souls' home it shall reveal.
> It lies beneath where they are found,
> on the holy emperor's sacred ground.

"If we know who the emperor is," Gerbert said, "and we're looking for a clue about one of the many churches he built, that clue must lie within the fifth seal. The seal already revealed the place where the souls are found. But what else does it tell us?"

Ciarán looked to Pietro, who had his fingers pressed against his temples, trying to recollect the verse from Revelation. "When the fifth seal is opened," Pietro recalled, "we see the souls of those who had been slain under the altar. They ask the Lord how long it will be before He avenges their deaths. Then they're each given a white robe and told to wait there longer until their brothers and sisters who will be slain can join them."

"They're given white robes ..." Ciarán muttered. Those words called to mind another memory from when he was at Derry, illuminating a copy of the book of Revelation. He recalled painting white robes, not just on the souls of the slain, but earlier in the book when John of Patmos has a vision of heaven with men seated on twenty-four thrones. "Right before the opening of the Seven Seals of God," Ciarán explained, "John beholds twenty-four elders seated around God's throne. These elders wore golden crowns, but they also wore white robes. So, who are the elders?"

"Scholars have debated that for centuries," Pietro replied. "But throughout the Bible, the elders are men of wisdom. They're the keepers of knowledge, the highest of priests, the wisest of men."

"Is one of Constantine's churches associated with wisdom?" Alais asked.

In the lamplight's glimmer, Gerbert's expression hardened. "The Hagia Sophia, the Church of Holy Wisdom."

Ciarán narrowed his eyes. "I thought that church was built by Emperor Justinian, not Constantine."

"It was," Gerbert said. "But the Hagia Sophia was built atop the ruins of two prior churches. And the first of those was built by Constantine."

Gerbert let out a sigh. "Which means, if you're right, your journey continues beyond Rome, and it ends in Constantinople."

CHAPTER 21

EYES OF THE DRAGON

In the hours past midnight, long after falling asleep following their late-night visit to Saint Peter's tomb, Ciarán found himself suspended in the air, surrounded by a swirling mist. In the vapor, a tall, hooded figure also hovered above the ground. The hood obscured most of his face, but golden irises flared as his eyes met Ciarán's.

A chill crawled up Ciarán's skin. He wanted to run, but his feet no longer touched the ground as the mist coiled around his limbs like gaseous serpents.

"Odamma," the Dragon said in an ominous tone.

The mist encircling Ciarán's right hand sizzled, and the luminescence clinging to his skin seemed to flare as a warmth pressed into his palm. Surrounding him, the swirling mist began its eerie whisper.

Ozam, odamma, cialpor, mir, agrit …

"What are you doing?" Ciarán called to the Dragon.

"Preparing you for the truth."

"Those words? What do they mean?"

For a moment, the Dragon stood silent, and Ciarán could hear the words in the mist brushing past his ears. *Ozam, odamma, cialpor, mir, agrit ...*

Finally, the Dragon spoke. "Mammon told you about the pillar."

Mammon—a demon's name, Ciarán surmised. The one who must have spoken to Alais.

"The fissures crawl up the pillar's shaft, growing longer and deeper by the day," the Dragon continued. "Orcus may have failed to steal the Key, but no matter. The pillar will soon fall on its own. It's only a matter of time, and you're still in Rome, toying with riddles."

How does he know?

"I've already told you, nothing escapes my gaze."

Ciarán grimaced as a terrifying thought stabbed through his gut. *Can the Dragon read my mind?*

"Tonight," the Dragon announced, "I shall move to raise my army, for it is time to gather the nations of Gog and Magog for war. Where is your army, Ciarán mac Tomás?"

He's trying to rattle me, Ciarán told himself. *Don't let it happen.* "There are four fewer soldiers in your army tonight. Orcus, Mammon—the four demons you sent—I destroyed them all."

In the shadow beneath the hood, the Dragon's lips stretched into a grin, revealing perfect white teeth with incisors pointed like a wolf's.

"Demons in your world are incorporeal spirits. Their power is limited by the frail mortal shells they must possess. But the soldiers of my army are flesh and blood, the descendants of my people, the heroes that were of old, the warriors of renown."

"We've defeated them before," Ciarán insisted.

"So you did, but again, at what cost? You lost four of your precious Northmen on the Palatine Hill. Gunnar, Sigarr, Taft, his brother Oddr. And in the theatre, you lost five more, including Magnus, the mightiest of them all."

From the depths of the swirling mists, Ciarán swore he heard Niall's voice call out. *"You're going to let them all die ..."*

Ciarán felt a weight pressing against his temples as if he had dove too deep beneath the surface of a lake. The heat in his right palm grew hotter, and the whispers repeated in the mist.

Ozam, odamma, cialpor, mir, agrit …

"Magnus was always a curious ally," the Dragon went on as if he were oblivious to the sound purring from the vapor. "He hated your shaven men, despised your nailed god. The gods he worshiped were honored by battle and bloodshed. Their heralds are ravens, not docile white doves. Magnus will make a fine servant when he finds his way to me."

"No," Ciarán muttered. "You lie."

"You are the one who believes the lie. You and the others who have died for your cause. Dónall mac Taidg, Isaac ben Ezra, Khalil al-Pârsâ."

"You're going to let them all die!" Niall's voice echoed again from beyond.

Ciarán fought back a scream. He struggled to tear free of the misty coils that held his arms and legs in their preternatural grip.

"And your parents," the Dragon hissed. "They died believing you were the chosen one. Born of Virgo's seed and Charlemagne's line. But they were wrong, and you know it. The bloodline is a myth, and still, they died for that lie. Do you want to see how it happened?"

"No," Ciarán tried to close his eyes, but his lids wouldn't shut.

"You *need* to see the truth." With those words, the figure of the Dragon erupted into flames, and in a breath, any semblance of him had been replaced by the horrible image of two man-sized stakes. Bound to the stakes, above pyres of pitch-coated wood, a man and woman gazed into each other's eyes. The man had long, wild hair, a thick beard, and a gaunt face that may have been handsome once, while the woman was slender, red-haired, and beautiful. *Father and mother,* Ciarán knew, even though he could not remember ever seeing their faces. Tears ran down his mother's cheeks, though his father's steely gaze told her to be brave.

An enormous crowd gathered outside a cathedral to watch the spectacle. Hard-faced guardsmen wearing mail and bearing spears kept the crowd at bay.

Smoke began rising from the pyres, and flames sprouted from the piled wood. The crowd started shouting. "Heretic!" "Witch!" "Let them burn!"

Ciarán's heart hammered in his chest. He wanted to cry out to make them stop, but the mob was working itself into a frenzy.

"Kill the devils!"

"Curse them!"

"Damn their souls!"

As the crowd carried on, a slight monk in a Benedictine habit stabbed a torch into the pyre below Ciarán's mother's bare feet. The flames licked her toes, and she began to scream.

A sadistic smile formed between the monk's ginger beard and mustache as he waved the flaming brand beneath her feet.

When his mother screamed again, Ciarán could not believe his eyes. A cry of terror mixed with rage burst from his lungs.

"Stop, damn you!"

But Ciarán could not move. All he could do was watch in horror as Gerbert of Aurillac lit the fire.

～

"He killed them!" Ciarán cried.

Someone had grabbed his shoulders and was shaking him. Fueled by rage, Ciarán threw his assailant off of him.

"Blessed Sergius!" His attacker flew backward, landing hard on the bed next to Ciarán's.

"Gerbert lit the fires!" Ciarán huffed for breath. "He burned them alive."

"Whatever you're talking about, you're just having a nightmare." Ciarán recognized the voice as Pietro's.

"No, it was real. He showed me. Gerbert lit the fires that killed my parents."

"*Who* showed you?"

Ciarán held his head in his hands. His skull was pounding as hard as his heart. "The Dragon ... he's been visiting my dreams."

"Dear God," Pietro muttered. In the faint moonlight seeping

147

into the chamber, Ciarán saw Pietro make the sign of the cross. "How?"

"He called it the astral plane. It's where he finds me, from the Otherworld, in my dreams."

Pietro shook his head in disbelief. "If it's truly him, you can't believe what he's showing you. Remember the words of Saint John. There's no truth in the Devil. He's the father of lies."

Ciarán gave a long sigh. "It seemed so real."

"If the Dragon *has* found you, we should tell the pope at once."

At the mention of Gerbert, Ciarán balled his fists. "I can't promise I won't hurt him."

"I won't let you," Pietro said, before fumbling to light an oil lamp sitting on the nightstand. As soon as the lit flame flared on the wick, Pietro gasped. "Ciarán, your hair."

"What?"

"It's nearly half gray. Whatever's happening, it's affecting you."

Ciarán jumped out of bed and retrieved a small silver mirror he kept among his meager possessions. As he looked at his reflection in the lamplight, his eyes grew wide. Broad swaths of his hair had turned a silvery gray, as if he were a man twice his age. This was much worse than the silver flecks Alais had observed a few days ago—the day after the first time the Dragon had spoken to him in his dreams.

He scraped his fingers through his graying hair. "We need Alais, too."

"I'll wake them both," Pietro said. "And I'm taking this." He grabbed Caladbolg, which had been hanging in its scabbard from a peg in the wall. "Just in case you were serious about harming the pope."

Ciarán gave him a nod before slumping back in his bed. He pressed his palms into his temples, only realizing then that his right palm was warmer than the left. He stared at his right hand, which looked completely normal, and flexed his fingers. *What is happening?*

He was no closer to an answer by the time Pietro returned with the pope and Alais. As soon as Ciarán set eyes on Gerbert, a newfound anger rushed up the back of his neck.

"I saw you light the fires," he said accusingly.

Gerbert looked at him with a sympathetic gaze. "Pietro told me what's been happening, but I promise you, I did not light the fires that killed your parents. Though I did not stop it from happening either. I had been deceived by Lucien of Saint-Denis, I swear it. If you hate me for what happened, I would understand. But whatever you saw me do in your dream, it wasn't true."

Ciarán shook his head, fists clenched. "It looked so real. How can I trust you?"

"I believe him," Alais said, sitting down beside Ciarán. "When I was to burn at the stake in Selles-sur-Cher, it was not Adémar of Blois who lit the pyre. Nor did Cardinal Bishop Beno light the one intended for Tara. Lighting pyres is a task belonging to henchmen and executioners, not bishops or canons."

Ciarán thought about that. Her words made sense, but he knew what he saw.

With a concerned look, she touched his hair. "It's getting worse."

"Aye," Ciarán admitted.

"Do you think these dreams are causing it?" Alais' hand fell to his arm, and her touch began soothing his Irish temper. So did the look on Gerbert's face; the pope's remorse appeared genuine.

"The first time you noticed the silver in my hair," Ciarán replied, was the day after the Dragon first spoke to me."

Gerbert narrowed his eyes. "If the Dragon has indeed been contacting you from the Otherworld, I can think of nothing more serious. My guess is he's attacking your spirit, trying to weaken you before the final conflict. Maybe even kill you."

Ciarán gritted his teeth. "I fear he can read my mind. When I have thoughts, he knows them."

A look of alarm flashed across Gerbert's face. "If he can read your mind, who knows what information he's gathered during these visions?"

"We have to stop this," Alais said.

Ciarán closed his eyes, recalling his first encounter with the hooded being. "He told me, so long as I dream, I cannot escape him."

"Is there a way we can stop him from dreaming?" Pietro asked.

Gerbert sighed. "There is a draught made of white poppy, which the Greeks call opium. Another, called dwale, is made of hemlock, henbane, vinegar, and wine. Both concoctions will cause a man to lose consciousness. Perhaps such sleep is dreamless, but these elixirs are potent, even poisonous. I shudder to imagine what the effect might be of drinking one before bed every evening."

The last thing Ciarán wanted to do was to drink poison each night to avoid dreaming. "What about a talisman? When the Furies attacked Dónall and me outside Poitiers, he created talismans to ward them off."

"I suspect Dónall constructed them using instructions from the Book of Maugis d'Aygremont," Gerbert speculated. "That book is lost to us now."

Alais' eyes brightened as if Gerbert's words had triggered a thought. "What if he already has a talisman?" Her gaze swept to Caladbolg, still cradled in Pietro's arms. "In the cavern, we both saw how the Dragon looked at that sword. He had seen it before, and he feared it. And we both know how powerful it is. What if the sword —Enoch's device—is all the talisman you need?"

"You want me to sleep holding the sword?" Ciarán asked.

Alais raised an eyebrow. "Do you have a better idea?"

Gerbert smiled. "Once again, it seems Lady Alais has beaten us to it. I can think of no greater weapon against the Dragon than the one forged by God or His archangels to defeat him."

Pietro handed Ciarán the sword. "It's worth a try."

Ciarán took Caladbolg and pressed its scabbard against his chest. The cross-shaped hilt may as well have been a crucifix.

"And perhaps try a little more prayer," Gerbert added. "As Saint Peter wrote in his first book, to resist the Devil, be steadfast in faith."

"You're right," Ciarán admitted. He bade Gerbert and Alais goodnight, then waited for Pietro to extinguish the oil lamp. When the chamber fell into relative darkness, he laid back down, clutching

Caladbolg, and prayed to Saint Columcille for a night of dreamless sleep.

CHAPTER 22

A WARRIOR'S FATE

Ciarán was still tired from his night of fitful rest when the bells sounded for Terce the following morning. With a bit of encouragement from Pietro, he reluctantly dragged himself out of bed and accompanied him to the Archbasilica of Saint John Lateran, where Gerbert said mass for the clergy and laypeople who served the Holy See. Although Jarl Holger had been attending these services since his baptism, he was not among the worshipers this day. Ciarán was not overly concerned at the jarl's absence because he had only been a Christian for a few months. However, the tragedy that had befallen five of *Lindworm's* crew at the theatre the day before—two killed in the theatre's collapse and three slain by the demons—had hit the jarl hard, especially Magnus's death and Breda's injury. So, after the mass ended, Ciarán decided to look for his friend.

After half an hour of searching, he found Holger in the refectory. It was a large room with tables and a small hearth, and only two people were there—Jarl Holger and Strong Bjorn. They were hunched over a table as the scent of wine hung in the air. Judging by the flushed faces of the two men, they must have already consumed a few carafes.

As Ciarán stepped closer to the table, Strong Bjorn, the young giant of a Dane who wore his blonde hair cropped short at the sides, gave him a questioning look. Beside him, Jarl Holger wiped his mouth after a long drink and slammed his cup on the table, knocking over one of the carafes, which spilled what was left of its scarlet contents across the oak tabletop. Holger tilted his head at Ciarán and peered at him with a foggy gaze.

"What happened to your hair?" he questioned, his words slightly slurred.

Ciarán ran his fingers through his graying locks. "I had another dream about the Dragon. He spoke to me again. Alais and Pietro believe the visions are taking a toll, and the hair is part of it."

Holger swore. "Another fine omen."

Across the table, Strong Bjorn stared wide-eyed at Ciarán. "The Dragon?" he muttered.

"Aye," Ciarán said, eliciting a whistle from Strong Bjorn, who wrapped his fingers around the hammer of Thor dangling from his neck.

"I know how you can forget about those dreams," Holger suggested in a gruff voice. "Grab a cup and join us."

As much as Ciarán wished he could forget the dream of the hooded figure and the image of Gerbert lighting the pyres that would burn his parents alive, it was far too early in the morning to start drinking. "Breda was awake at sunrise," Ciarán said, trying to change the subject. "Gerbert says she's completely healed."

Holger's ruddy cheeks brightened with joy. "I know, I saw her! It's a miracle—and all because of Alais!"

Strong Bjorn shook his head as if in awe. "Lifthrasir," he whispered under his breath, using the name Magnus had given her.

Holger filled his cup again, taking a large swallow. "She'll be back soon," he said, his voice breaking slightly. He tipped his cup as if to celebrate the thought.

"She'll be ready for the voyage," Ciarán said.

"What voyage?" Holger asked with a hint of annoyance.

For a moment, Ciarán hesitated, wondering if he should have

chosen a better time to broach this subject. But it was too important to wait. "The one I've come to talk to you about."

Ciarán told Holger about the riddle the four creatures had given Tara in her dreams and their theory that it was pointing them toward something that could show them the way to Dudael. Holger finished his cup and drank another as Ciarán explained their belief that this artifact, or whatever it might be, was hidden beneath the altar of the largest church in Constantinople. "Pietro and I are searching the archives for evidence that Constantine moved treasures or relics to the church. If we can confirm that, we might need to sail for Constantinople by week's end."

"To Miklagard?" Holger snorted a laugh. "Get a cup and drink."

"I need to go back and help Pietro."

Holger's expression darkened before he pounded a fist on the table. "Drink, dammit! It's how we mourn."

Ciarán gave a slow nod. Magnus once warned that Holger had a temper like Thor the Thunderer, and Ciarán could not afford to provoke it now. Besides, he felt for the jarl. Few had lost more in the attack on the theatre than he had. Ciarán took one of the cups atop a cask of ale in the corner of the refectory and sat on the bench across from Holger. The jarl poured him wine until it was about to overflow.

"You want me to set sail for Miklagard?" Holger asked, again using the Danish word for Constantinople. "I've lost nine of my men since arriving in this godforsaken city, five of them yesterday, including my hirdman, my brother. You want me to travel all the way to Miklagard without him?"

"You know why we must do this," Ciarán replied. "You've seen the Dragon, too, and you know we have to stop him."

Holger paused and glanced at Ciarán. He frowned and looked away, lost in thought. "In all the times I have thought about the battle towards which we head—Ragnarok—I've always expected Magnus would fight by my side. Like he has always done. That's how we would be victorious, brothers-in-arms, making one last stand against our foes and reaping their souls with our blades.

Curtana in my hands, Corpse-maker in his. With him at my side, we would have been invincible. But now all that is lost, and I question whether I even care about Ragnarok or the Dragon anymore."

Ciarán took a deep breath, alarmed by Holger's words. The jarl had to go on the voyage—Blind Mikkel was clear about that—and Ciarán knew that without Holger and his Danes, they stood no chance of winning this fight. But Ciarán also realized he would not win a debate with Holger in his current condition. So Ciarán put the cup to his lips and swallowed a mouthful of wine.

"Let us not speak of this now," Ciarán told his friend, handing his cup out for a refill. "Today, let us mourn."

THE FUNERAL TOOK place on Tyr's day, three mornings after the theatre collapsed into ruin. Breda had said Tyr was the god who sacrificed his right hand to bind the monstrous wolf Fenrir, so it was fitting that the sacrifices made by Magnus and the other members of *Lindworm's* crew would be honored on Tyr's day.

They built the pyres atop a hillock a half-mile south of the Porta Asinaria, the gate in the Aurelian Walls closest to the Lateran Palace. All the Danes who had died were pagan, and Gerbert could not allow the funeral to occur within the city's walls.

Dew shimmered on the grassy hillock beneath a pewter sky where Holger led the ceremony, a grim resolve painted on his face. Breda and the fifteen surviving members of *Lindworm's* crew gathered around him to honor the fallen. Ciarán stood with them, between Alais and Tara, while Rosta sat obediently to the girl's left.

The dead lay upon their pyres, each dressed in the mail they had worn in battle, except for Magnus, who wore Ciarán's mail coat. While the Danes believed the dead took their belongings with them into the afterlife, Holger had insisted that Ciarán keep the hauberk of Maugis d'Aygremont that Magnus had been wearing when he died. Before it was taken from Ciarán, the armor had been a gift from Orionde the Fae, and Holger's superstitions would not allow him to bury the armor in a grave.

Lying upon his pyre, Magnus gripped the hilt of his longsword, Corpse-maker, at his chest, just as the other Danes rested with their cold hands touching their blades. "They died with swords in their hands," Holger said reverently. For although the jarl had recently been baptized a Christian, he still clung to his pagan ways. And for a Dane, dying with a sword in his hand meant he would spend the afterlife in Valhalla instead of rotting with the undead in Niflheim.

"Why do they burn their dead?" Tara asked.

"They believe the fire's smoke will carry their souls to the afterlife," Ciarán replied.

Tara looked up at him. "What do you believe?"

Ciarán fell silent for a moment. So many of his friends had died. His best friend Niall, along with his brothers at Derry: Bran and Murchad, Fintan and Senach, and the twins, Áed and Ailil. His mentor Dónall and Rabbi Isaac, and, of course, Khalil, who gave his life to save Ciarán's own. And so many others: Évrard, Brother Remi, Josua's son, Eli, and now Magnus, Fótr, and three more of their crewmates. Ciarán could not suppress Niall's haunting words from his dream. *"You're going to let them all die."* But Niall had not spoken those words on that fateful day in Derry, Ciarán reminded himself. Nor had Niall said them the last time Ciarán saw him, in a vision when he stood at death's door at the pier in Córdoba. That day, he recalled waking in a glen of clover with green hills rising on either side and a bone-chilling mist that lingered in the air. Eli and his fallen brothers at Derry stood there, looking at him. *"We didn't die for nothing,"* Niall had said. *"So bloody wake-up!"*

On that day, Ciarán believed he looked into the afterlife, so he knew what to tell Tara. "The Church teaches of Heaven, and I believe it. There's a place beyond this life. A place our souls go well before our bodies are burned or buried. A place where we'll see our loved ones again."

Alais glanced at them and forced a smile. Her eyes were rimmed red, and Ciarán knew Magnus's death weighed on her conscience. Ciarán carried that burden, too, for he had asked for Magnus's promise to protect Alais from harm, and Magnus had kept that promise with his life. But deep inside, he shuddered, recalling the Dragon's words.

Magnus will make a fine servant when he finds his way to me.

Ciarán tried to expel the memory of the Dragon's words from his mind when Jorundr began chanting a poem.

> *In realm of frost, 'neath moon's cold light,*
> *warriors sailed westward into the night.*
> *On longships borne, with swords in hands,*
> *they sought their fate in distant lands.*
>
> *Valhalla! Valhalla! Their final quest,*
> *for those who fall, eternal rest.*
> *In noble battle, their honor sealed,*
> *by Odin's side, their fate revealed.*
>
> *Die with sword, to the north now soar,*
> *to Valhalla's shores, in the battle's roar.*
> *In death, find life forever grand,*
> *in Valhalla, where the warriors stand.*

When Jorundr had finished, he joined Holger and the other torchbearers. They set fire to the pyres, and as the wood began to smoke and crackle, Breda stepped forth. She wore a black dress with her fiery red hair piled high atop her head and began to sing with a voice like an angel. She sang of the Norns spinning men's fate, for fate belongs to the gods.

> *Norns in shadow, their loom does spin,*
> *crafting the fate of fighting men.*
> *Warriors bleed and bravely strive,*
> *for to the gods, their fate, they give.*
>
> *Valkyries wait for battle's end,*
> *to kin and gods, the fallen send.*
> *Through sea and flame, the pathway trod,*

for their fate is in the hands of the gods.

Odin awaits in vast golden hall,
summoning warriors to his call.
Echoes of glory, in Valhalla applaud,
for their fate is woven by the gods.

Listening to Breda's haunting song, Ciarán could not help but think of the fate that awaited them at Dudael and of all the people who had given their lives on the journey to get there. The thought made him shudder.

For deep inside, he feared that more of his companions would join those fallen souls before they found their way to the Cauldron of God.

CHAPTER 23

DESTINY

L ong after the funeral, Holger lingered by the gravesite, where the scent of smoke and freshly turned soil lingered in the air.

They had buried the ashes of Magnus and the others near the shallow of a sprawling, ancient oak, whose branches cast shadows on the rocks lining the burial mound. They formed the mounds in the shape of longships, a fitting memorial for warriors of the sea.

Holger's head throbbed from the wine he consumed after the funeral, and his muscles burned from digging the graves. The sky above had darkened like his mood. The sun would set soon, and the Romans would be closing the city gates. But he could not bring himself to leave this place. Breda and the others had departed an hour before. She had implored him to join her, but she knew him well enough to know when he needed to be alone.

The pain within him felt like a dull knife buried in his heart, for Magnus, his brother in arms, was dead. It was not supposed to be this way. Magnus should have sailed with him on his voyage to Ragnarok, but the Norns, the three crones who spin men's destiny at the foot of Yggdrasil, had severed that strand of fate. Holger could not help but feel it was because of something he had done. For not only had Magnus fallen, but Breda, too, nearly died in that theatre.

Have I angered the gods?

He glanced up at the sound of beating wings. Two ravens flew in circles before settling on the gnarled branches of the oak. A chill rippled across his skin as he recognized the omen. Had Odin sent his two ravens in disapproval of him turning away from the ancient gods?

"Am I being punished?" Holger asked, feeling a twinge of guilt. "Is that why you are here, because I have turned to the nailed god?"

The ravens stared at him with cold eyes as if they sensed his shame. A rumble of thunder echoed from afar like Thor himself was voicing his displeasure.

Holger reached for the silver crucifix that hung from his leather cord. Even though it felt like a betrayal, he ripped it from his neck and tossed it into the grass.

"You may need that yet," said a familiar voice.

Holger spun around to find a slight figure in a black cloak and hood in the shadows beneath the massive tree. The two ravens flapped their wings, cawing loudly, then flew away as soon as they saw the figure.

The jarl felt a wave of anger wash over him as his eyebrows furrowed. "Do you come in disguise to spy on me?"

"No," Gerbert replied calmly. "I was curious to observe the funeral, but a pope could hardly be seen at a pagan burial." He bent over and plucked the silver cross from the grass. "Are you so quick to abandon your newfound faith?"

Holger set his jaw. "What good has it brought me? My wife nearly died, and my best friend lies in this grave, along with more of my comrades. Magnus was to sail with me to Ragnarok."

"Did Blind Mikkel tell you that?" Gerbert asked, holding out his palms. "Did you see Magnus in the same vision where you saw Ciarán?"

Holger scratched the chin of his beard, thinking back to the vision. They were in *Lindworm*, sailing on a dark river between sheer cliffs while an unending cloud of gloom hung above them. Ciarán with Caladbolg stood at Holger's side. As did Jorundr, decked in his armor and pointed helm, and Strong Bjorn and Freybjorn, too. Magnus had to be there, right? Yet as Holger sifted through those memories, a pain settled in his chest, for as hard as he tried, he could not see his closest friend's face. Holger sighed heavily as he admitted the truth. "No."

"Then, if we believe your visions have a divine origin, it was never meant to be. The act of Magnus saving Alais' life might have been his destiny. For we all know that without her, all will be lost."

Holger clenched his hands into fists. He did not want to believe it could be true that Magnus was supposed to die. "You don't know that for certain."

Gerbert shrugged. "No, it's but a theory. They say the Lord works in mysterious ways."

"But how? How do we even know He's around? What signs does He send?"

"Your visions, for one. But there are others. Tell me, when you took the Holy Lance of Constantine in your hands before you launched it at the Dragon, what did you feel?"

Holger thought for a moment. "That it had power—that it could slay the Dragon."

Gerbert gave a slight grin. "That's what you believed because you had faith. And what happened when the lance hit its mark?"

"It forced the Dragon to shed its skin."

"That was your sign, Jarl Holger. A sign that with faith in God, even a creature as fearsome as the Devil can be defeated."

Holger tipped his chin to the sky and choked back a tear. Then he reached out his right hand.

Gerbert pressed the silver cross into Holger's palm. "Keep this close to your heart, Holger Horiksson, for you are a weapon of God, and your destiny awaits at Dudael."

CHAPTER 24

THE JERUSALEM SCROLLS

"Ciarán, wake up," a voice said. Someone was shaking his shoulder.

Ciarán inhaled a potent scent of vellum and blinked the sleep from his eyes. He found himself surrounded by shelves crammed with books and scrolls, with his head resting on an open book as if it were a pillow. Caladbolg, in its scabbard, rested against his leg. Suddenly, he remembered where he was: the Reading Room in the archives beneath the Lateran Palace.

He and Pietro had been working their third straight night searching for evidence to validate their theory that the Fifth Seal—whatever it might be—had been taken by Constantine to the church he built on the grounds of what now was the Hagia Sophia in Constantinople. So far, their efforts had uncovered nothing. But this morning—*if it even was morning*—Pietro's face was beaming.

"I've found something," Pietro said. "Though I think we can blame Pope Liberius for our troubles. It seems that he, or whoever had my job back then, compiled the writings of all the popes since Pope Fabian in the mid-third century, including the papers of Saint Sylvester. But Liberius, or whoever it was, misfiled a letter to Sylvester among the writings of Pope Eusebius." Pietro shook his head in frustration. "Of course, Liberius *was* thrown into exile by Constantine's son, so maybe all that commotion explains his carelessness."

"You found a letter?" Ciarán asked, rubbing his eyes.

Pietro grinned. "I did. One from Saint Helena, no less." He picked a folded and heavily stained square of parchment off the table.

"What does it say?"

Pietro handed Ciarán the letter. "You should read it for yourself."

Ciarán took the letter. The parchment felt dry and brittle in his hand. He carefully unfolded it. The Latin script was flowing and beautiful.

To Your Holiness, Sylvester, with eternal greetings.

    It is with sincere regret that I must inform you I was unable to change the Emperor's mind about the four scrolls that we, with our Savior's grace, found outside Jerusalem in the sacred place beneath the foul pagan temple built on the site of our Savior's most holy Passion. I tried to persuade him that the scrolls must have come from Solomon's Temple, for their cases were made in replica of the four serpentine pillars we took from there. Therefore, I argued, the scrolls should be placed with the pillars in Saint Peter's Basilica when construction is finished. But my son is stubborn. He believes King Solomon's treasures will bring glory to New Rome and insists on placing them within the Great Church he intends to build beside his new palace. I begged him to reconsider, as you and I had discussed, but his mind is set. Though perhaps because of his devotion to me, he will allow one of the scrolls to remain in Rome, the one titled the Testament of Solomon. He will take the other three, the Lesser Key of Solomon, the Book of Deadly Names, and The War of the Sons of Light Against the Sons of Darkness, to New Rome. I find the first two writings unsettling, and they shall not be missed. The third one is intriguing, but the one saved for Rome is special. A testament of King Solomon himself. Consider it my gift to you.

    Farewell, now and always, with faith in the Lord,
    Helena

Ciarán looked up from the letter, hardly believing his eyes. "This has to be it. Three more scrolls from Solomon. Who could have imagined?"

"It makes perfect sense," Pietro said. "Solomon knew of the prophecy and helped fulfill it two thousand years ago. He created the Testament of Solomon to help future champions find Sirra when the cycle of the prophecy came around again to protect the Key to the Abyss. But we know there's more to the prophecy. Why wouldn't he also preserve the secret to finding Dudael? And if he used his Testament to show the way to the Key, one of these other three scrolls must map a pathway to Dudael. And now we have proof that Emperor Constantine moved the scrolls to his Great Church in Constantinople. It's the confirmation we've been searching for."

All Ciarán could do was nod in agreement. And he already had a theory on which of the three scrolls they'd need. *The War of the Sons of Light Against the Sons of Darkness.* What an apt name for a scroll that would show the way to the battleground for Armageddon—the war between light and darkness. There was only one thing to do now.

Holding the letter, Ciarán rose from his chair. "We have to find Gerbert."

⌇

"WHAT IS IT?" Alais asked.

Ciarán and Pietro had happened upon her while rushing through the palace's marble hallways to find the pope. She looked radiant this morning in a blue damask dress with a like-color veil covering her raven hair.

"We know what Constantine took to the site beneath the Hagia Sophia," Ciarán replied. "I'll explain more when we find His Holiness."

She gave him a curious look.

"We can thank Saint Helena," Pietro said, still beaming.

Her look went from curious to puzzled. "I believe he's with Niccolo in the map room."

The three of them found the pope and archdeacon there hunched over the enormous table with the tapestry-sized map. Niccolo pointed his bony finger at the eastern portion of the Mediterranean Sea while sunlight spilled through the chamber's narrow windows and glinted off the mosaics decorating the walls.

Gerbert looked up. "From the looks on your faces, I take it you've found something."

"Indeed, we did, Your Holiness," Pietro announced. He rubbed his hands together like a man preparing to eat a holiday feast and then recounted the tale of their discovery. He began with Pope Liberius and the misfiled letter. Gerbert listened intently, and his eyes widened with awe when he read Saint Helena's letter. He sucked in a breath before handing it back to Ciarán.

"This does it, then," Gerbert said. "The secret of the Fifth Seal must lie in one of those scrolls. Which confirms the road leads to Constantinople. And if there's any truth to what the demon told Alais about the pillar, there's little time to waste."

The pope glanced at Niccolo, who stood, arms crossed, with a serious expression on his narrow face. "It's a good thing we've been planning for this," Gerbert said.

"Yes, Your Holiness," Niccolo replied with a nod.

"I'll draft a letter to the Patriarch and implore him to give you the scrolls. I suppose I'll have to send a few relics to replace the ones you'll be taking. The Patriarch might fancy himself as the head of the Church, and I'm told he's a proud and stubborn man. But he still must answer to the Bishop of Rome."

Ciarán scratched his head. "Why wouldn't you just order him to give up the scrolls when we get there?"

Gerbert curled his lips. "Because I won't be going with you."

His words struck Ciarán like a blow. "You have to come with us —nothing is more important than this."

"True," Gerbert said, his brow furrowed. "But I am not one of the seven. The prophecy does not demand *my* presence at Dudael. Yet what *is* demanded of me is that I honor my duty to the Church, and to the emperor, and to the world they rule. I've watched over Otto ever since he inherited his throne as a boy just three years old. He's still very young to wear such a heavy crown, and he's not the natural warrior his father and grandfather were. To keep his throne, Otto will need my counsel. And I could never convince him to let me embark on the mission that awaits you. Otto does not believe we stand on the brink of the End of Days. He and his cousin, Pope Gregory, ascribed to the prophecy of Daniel, who prophesied that the end times would not come until four great empires have fallen. The last of those is the Roman Empire, which Otto believes lives on through the Holy Roman Empire he rules today.

"While we're aware of the prophecy etched in the heavens, I've come to realize there may be truth in Daniel's prophecy as well. The Holy Roman Empire brought Europe out of the Dark Ages. The new empire has caused more good than ill, and one reason is its support for the Church. Pope Gregory had become convinced the Church is the true final empire of Daniel's prophecy. After all, *Pontifex Maximus,* the title bestowed on the Roman emperors, now belongs to the popes. The Church is an empire that must be preserved. And I am the head of that empire, which is precisely why I cannot go."

Ciarán glanced sideways at Alais, who looked equally taken aback. He felt heat rush up his neck; he could not believe what Gerbert was telling them.

"If our mission fails," Ciarán said pointedly, "why will any of this matter? The End of Days will be upon us."

Gerbert put his palms together as if in prayer. "Then the people will need a shepherd to lead them through the horrors of the apocalypse until the Day of Judgment. But what if you succeed? What will be left of this empire if I abandon the Holy See? My rule over the Church is tenuous enough, and the events with Cardinal Bishop Beno have imperiled it further. This voyage you'll embark on will not end in Constantinople. It ends in Dudael, in the Otherworld. I cannot try to convince people about the Otherworld and our supernatural cause. Half the priests in Rome will want me tried for heresy or sorcery or both. Nor can I promise them I'll return, for we know how dangerous this mission will be, and there's no guarantee any of you will make it back here.

"Were I to leave Rome and disappear from this world, even for a time, it would be the end of my papacy. A new pope would undoubtedly be installed in my absence, and the Crescentii would likely influence that choice. I hardly need to mention how close the Holy See came to ruin under their rule. I'm worried about what type of civilization would even exist by the next millennium. And who would preserve the secrets of the prophecy for when the cycle comes around again? That mission will lie with the Church, as Saint Sylvester had hoped it would over six hundred years ago."

"But we need you," Ciarán pressed. "There's not a sharper mind in all of Christendom."

"You flatter me, Brother Ciarán, but your mind is razor sharp. And Pietro will go with you, too. On top of that, you have Lady Alais, and we all know that her mind for the prophecy may be the sharpest of them all."

Alais put her hand on Ciarán's arm. "It's alright," she said under her breath.

Ciarán huffed away his next words. He wanted to fight, to persuade Gerbert otherwise, but that was his Irish stubbornness talking. The pope had made up his mind.

The air in the chamber remained tense; then Pietro spoke up: "What about the Dragonslayers, Your Holiness, won't we need those?"

"You will," Gerbert replied. "They may be a key to winning this war. Fortunately, the Archdeacon and I have been planning for this. Niccolo has been recruiting warriors with the strongest of faith among our papal guard and throughout Rome. The type of men who would join a mission like ours, even where there is no promise they'd ever return home. We will train new teams to operate the Dragonslayers and send them in three ships to rendezvous with you after you've completed your business in Constantinople."

"Just three ships full of men?" Ciarán asked incredulously. "That won't be enough."

"It's the best I can do," Gerbert insisted. "The warriors who serve Otto and his lords will not be convinced to join some secret war. These are men with wealth and lands who have much to lose, and there will be no promise of plunder or glory in our battle. If there are men among them of devout faith, perhaps Niccolo can persuade them to join our crews. But that is all we can muster. Besides, foot soldiers will be of little use against the Dragon, as we all know."

"What about the nations of Gog and Magog being gathered for war?" Ciarán asked. "That's what the Dragon told me. He's raising his army—an army of Nephilim."

Gerbert kept his face impassive. "And the last time you fought them, it was Jarl Holger and his warriors who won. But don't think I'm finished asking for help. Through Pietro, I will make a request of Emperor Basil to provide Greek Fire to aid our Holy cause. He believes himself to be the emperor of all of Christendom, and I'll impress upon him that it's his duty to aid the Church. I can think of no weapon more deadly."

Ciarán hung his head. "So that's it then? This is our plan. We sail to Constantinople, tell the Patriarch to give us the scrolls, ask the emperor to give us some Greek Fire, and then figure out what happens next?"

Pietro shrugged. "That's a better plan than we had before today."

"When you arrive in Constantinople," Gerbert told them, "find Severus Synadenos. He's the Syncellus, the Holy See's legate in Constantinople. He has direct access to the patriarch and the emperor and is rumored to be quite shrewd. He should be able to provide whatever you need while you're there."

"Once you've completed your mission in Constantinople," Niccolo added, "you will rendezvous with the ships carrying the Dragonslayers. I've convinced Captain Gaido to lead our holy fleet, which will meet you at the village of Myros, on the southeast coast of the island of Lemnos." He pointed to a small island in the Aegean Sea, west of the channel that led to the Sea of Marmara. At the eastern end of that sea stood Constantinople at the crossroads of the Bosporus and the Golden Horn. "Hopefully, our ships will await you when you arrive."

Niccolo's finger drifted west to the isle of Sicily. "One last thing, Brother Ciarán. Your voyage will take you right past Trapani and the Egadi Islands, where we suspect the Varangian is based. Perhaps you'll find your friends there and learn a thing or two about the whereabouts of Naberus da Roma."

Ciarán felt a sudden swell of hope. Josua and his crew had been enslaved for nearly a year, and this could be a chance to save them. He placed a hand on Caladbolg's pommel. His fingertips brushed against the gemstone. *By Columcille,* he told himself, *I'll save them. And if I learn about Naberus da Roma, all the better.*

He shifted his gaze to Gerbert and swallowed his pride. "You've done enough for us, Your Holiness. I regret my words."

Gerbert's eyes glistened with the mist of a tear. "And I regret everything I had done to you until recently. What happened to your parents was tragic. Brother Lucien had deceived me terribly, and I was too foolish to realize it. But you showed me the truth and added a purpose to my life that I never could have imagined."

Gerbert made the sign of the cross. "Godspeed Brother Ciarán. May the Lord stand with you—and may you fight like the champion I know you are."

CHAPTER 25

HOME

"I'm not going on the voyage!" Tara insisted, tears welling in her eyes.

She had been fretting over the journey to Constantinople since she heard about it at breakfast, and by the time Breda discovered her sulking in the palace vineyards an hour before sunset, her emotions had built up like a flood behind a dam.

Breda wrinkled her nose, as she often did when annoyed. "Stop being such a child," she chided. "Of course you're going. It will be an adventure."

"No, it won't." Tara shook her head. "You don't know about that place."

"Miklagard?" Breda threw up her hands. "It's called 'the Great City.' Some say it's the finest in the world. Who wouldn't want to go there?"

"I don't," Tara said, sniffing back a tear. "It's not … safe."

Breda cocked her head. "Safe? You'll be with all of us. How would you not be safe?"

"You don't understand."

"You're being pigheaded!" Breda snapped, a spark of anger flashing in her green eyes.

Tara stood defiantly, her arms crossed in front of her chest. "I won't go!" she shouted, turning her back on Breda and stomping toward the palace.

Breda's voice floated through the air as she called after Tara. "Be a child then! But I swear to you, two days from now, we will be on that ship, even if I have to carry you onboard myself."

When she returned to her room, Tara crawled into bed and pulled the covers to her chin. She shuddered, struggling to hold back the tears. On his last visit to the convent, Father Michele had told her that one day, she'd go on a voyage in a ship with the head of a dragon. "You'll see things that few people in the world have ever seen," he had promised. "It will take a brave girl to go on that adventure, but I know a brave girl when I see one." The problem was, Tara did not feel brave. And Father Michele had never warned her that her voyage would take her back to Constantinople, the city where her sister and parents had been killed, and the same city where a mysterious woman with a crescent-shaped birthmark wanted to murder her, too. It seemed like a foolish idea, not a brave one.

Even though she had never considered going back there before, the more Tara thought about it, the more the terrible and frightening memories resurfaced. The sound of grappling hooks hitting their boat as the black-clad assassins jumped on board. The flames flickering on the waves. The tall and menacing woman calling out her mother's name.

Hand over the girls, Shirin.

No, Tara told herself, she would never go back there. Not for anything in the world. But what if they tried to make her go? As much as she cared for Lady Breda, Tara knew she wasn't known for speaking idly. Breda was going to carry her aboard the ship, whether Tara liked it or not. *I can't let that happen,* Tara thought. Rome had become her home, even if it wasn't the best home or the kindest one. She thought about Sister Priscilla. The nun had been good to her most of the time. And Tara had friends among the novices. She always imagined that someday she would take her vows as a sister in the convent, and she was sure Sister Priscilla would welcome her back. Maybe they all would. After all, Brother Ciarán had won the trial by combat, proving her innocence. Why couldn't she go home?

The next morning, when the bells of the Archbasilica rang for Terce, Tara threw her cloak around her shoulders and pulled the hood over her head. All around her, people were heading into the sanctuary, but instead of joining them, Tara walked in the opposite direction, toward the city. She was sure no one had seen her leave, but deep down, she felt a pang of guilt as she wondered if she was doing the right thing.

She started down a road paved with flagstones that ran down the shallow valley between the Caelian and Esquiline Hills. A handful of structures dotted the hillsides, which sloped down to vineyards and pastures on either side of the road. Flocks of sheep grazed nearby, tended to by shepherds. Ahead loomed the massive Coliseum where, according to Sister Priscilla, gladiators used to battle to the death. Sister Priscilla had said it was now inhabited by a small community living within its walls, so Tara veered away from it and continued along the old Roman Forum.

Sister Priscilla had warned Tara the Forum was a dangerous place, filled with derelicts and vagrants, wild dogs, and even a wolf or two. She also warned her about evil spirits that haunted the old pagan temples. As Tara passed the Temple of Venus and Roma filled with shadows, she felt a bit of comfort when she saw a basilica standing close to it with its gabled roof and a bell tower topped with a cross. However, the feeling did not last long as she noticed fields full of ruins along both sides of the road and broken columns standing like gravestones covered with weeds and debris.

At the far end of the forum, peddlers led mule-drawn carts into and out of Trajan's Market, where merchant stalls filled the plaza in front of a five-story structure of reddish stone. Tara caught a whiff of baked bread that made her stomach growl as she neared the market-place, alive with the sounds of merchants and shoppers haggling over their wares. Beyond the market stood the large cluster of buildings that made up the city proper. There, the streets would become narrower, more maze-like, and more dangerous. Thieves were known to prowl the cramped alleyways in that part of the city, and Sister Priscilla had often warned it was not safe for a young girl to walk alone. So, Tara stayed close behind one of the peddlers, leading a haggard-looking mule and an onion-packed cart into the city. The cart's wheels creaked as they rolled over the uneven flagstones, marred by a stream of refuse. Tara wrinkled her nose at the rotten stench.

People filled the streets, moving between shops of grocers, tailors, blacksmiths, shoemakers, and other craftsmen. Wooden signs creaked in the breeze while brightly dressed vendors called out to the passers-by. Tara stayed close to the crowd and away from the seedier alleys and side streets, where she glimpsed a group of unkempt young men shooting dice and half-clothed prostitutes already luring customers into the brothels despite the morning hour. When Tara finally spotted the magnificent dome of the Church of Santa Maria Rotunda towering over the clay-tiled rooftops, she felt a swell of hope. But by the time she rounded a corner, entered the modest plaza, and saw the white-faced facade of the Convent of Minerva, her stomach had twisted into a knot. Despite all the times she had been welcomed there, she couldn't be sure if they would accept her back.

Mustering all the courage she could find, Tara took a deep breath and pushed the heavy wooden doors open wide enough for her to slip inside. She was immediately struck by the bitter smell of tallow candles and a choir's song that filled her ears. The prayer service for Terce was still going on, and across the nave, nuns filled the choir stalls as the sisterhood of Minerva joined their voices in a hymn. Tara hesitated to go any deeper into the church. When the service ended, and the nuns began to leave, she watched them file through the cloister doors. But none of them noticed her lingering in the shadows of the vestibule.

When she caught sight of Sister Priscilla among the departing nuns, Tara's heart leaped. She stepped out of the shadows and whispered her name, "Priscilla."

Sister Priscilla turned towards the sound. Then her eyes grew wide, and her hand flew to her lips. A single tear ran down her cheek as her fingers slid away. Her mouth quivered as she murmured, "Tara?"

Without another word, Sister Priscilla pulled away from the line and enveloped Tara in a tight hug. "You came back," she said, beaming.

"I want to come home," Tara confessed as her apprehensions washed away like dried leaves after a rainfall.

"You are home," Sister Priscilla said, brushing away a tear still clinging to Tara's cheek.

"Yes, you are," said another voice with a chill in its tone.

Tara gazed past Sister Priscilla to see the abbess heading their way. The skin of the old woman's face was stretched over her skull, and her lips curved into an unnerving smile. A troop of nuns clustered around the abbess while Tara's pulse quickened. She did not like the expression on the abbess's face.

Worry creased Sister Priscilla's forehead as she turned to face the abbess.

"I saw what you did in the theatre," the abbess said. "Those howling men possessed by devils and the earthquake. Cardinal Bishop Beno told me of your threat. You told him he would die, and then you made it happen!"

Tara felt her heart racing and her mind whirling. She wanted to run, but her feet wouldn't move. "No," she muttered, her voice trembling.

"Don't deny it, child. You may or may not be a witch, but as God is my witness, there's a demon inside you, and it must be purged!"

Tara tried to back away and run when the abbess shouted, "Grab her!"

Before Tara could react, a heavy-set nun named Sister Bertoara grabbed her in a bear hug and lifted her off the floor. Tara screamed as she tried to break away from Sister Bertoara's grip, kicking and thrashing against her. Sister Priscilla rushed forward and clawed at one of Sister Bertoara's arms, but two nuns gripped her shoulders, yanking her away.

The abbess's face contorted into a hateful snarl. "Fetch me some priests! This child needs an exorcism!"

CHAPTER 26
THE LION'S ROAR

Alais' voice was rough and strained from calling out Tara's name, and the unease in her stomach had hardened into a rock. They had searched every room in the palace, as well as the gardens, vineyards, and stables, and yet Tara was nowhere to be found. The one thing Father Michele had asked of Alais was to protect the witness, and now, a day before they were to set sail for Constantinople, they had lost her.

She sat on a soft bench outside the Map Room, her head in her hands as she worried about what could have happened. Her worst fear was that the demons who had attacked the theatre were not the last of their kind in Rome and that one more of them might have come for Tara. Yet how would they know who—or what—she is? Also, at the theatre, the demons weren't looking for Tara; they wanted the Key. But the demons weren't the only threat. Father Michele's message had implied Tara was in danger, and Beno's actions had proven it. Even though Beno was dead, might one of his deranged followers have come for the girl?

Alais was lost in thought when the sound of footsteps on the marble floor made her look up. Ciarán and Pietro were striding down the hallway. Wearing his leather baldric over his scarlet tunic with Caladbolg at his hip, Ciarán just shook his head.

"We searched the entire archbasilica, my lady," Pietro said, holding out his hands. "She's not there."

"We spoke with more than a few guardsmen, too," Ciarán added. "They've seen no sign of an intruder who might have taken her."

"How would they know?" Alais questioned. "If one of Beno's men had abducted her, he might have come here dressed as a priest. Hell, he might even be a priest. Have the guards interrogated every man wearing a black robe?"

"Not likely," Ciarán replied, giving her a sympathetic look. "But they've not seen anyone leave with the girl, either."

Alais looked up at Ciarán. "What do we do now?"

Ciarán grimaced. "Breda and Holger are searching the grounds again outside the palace. Maybe we see what they've learned?"

With a sigh, Alais stood up from the bench and smoothed the skirt of her slate gray dress. "Let's go then."

They were halfway down a hall lined with porphyry columns when they spotted Gaido. The captain of the Papal Guard carried his crested helmet in his left arm, moving toward them with long-legged strides. "My Lady," he called out. "A nun's arrived, asking for you."

Alais tilted her head. "A nun?"

"Her name's Sister Priscilla," Gaido replied. "She's quite distraught."

Alais, Ciarán, and Pietro exchanged glances. "The nun from the Convent of Minerva," Pietro muttered.

Alais' pulse quickened as they hurried with Gaido to the foyer, their footfalls echoing off the high ceiling. Sister Priscilla looked up at their arrival, holding her clasped hands to her lips. Her eyes were red and swollen from tears. At the sight of the nun, Alais' stomach dropped; something was terribly wrong.

"Have you seen Tara?" Alais asked the nun before the woman could utter a word.

The nun's expression was filled with sorrow, confirming Alais' fears. "She returned home," the woman said in a trembling voice. "I welcomed her back. We all would have … but the abbess …"

Alais narrowed her eyes. "What about the abbess?"

"She blames Tara for Cardinal Bishop Beno's death and for what happened at the theatre. She believes Tara has an evil spirit inside her. She's called for a priest and means to purge the demon through exorcism. I don't trust her methods—I fear she'll harm Tara!"

The nun's words sparked a flicker of anger in Alais while Ciarán shot her a look of alarm. "I'll get the horses," he said urgently.

"Find Breda and Holger too," she responded, following on his heels, her anger swelling into fury. They were going to save Tara, even if they had to tear the convent down, brick by brick, to find her.

Tara's chin quivered as another tear streamed down her cheek. She was bound to a sturdy wooden chair, her hands and feet secured with rope that bit into her skin. Out of the corner of her eye, she saw Sister Bertoara, her face smug as she gathered with a dozen or so nuns in the dim, candlelit church. Behind the altar stood the abbess and two priests whom Tara recognized as Cardinal Bishop Beno's men. One was as bone-thin as the abbess and just as old, with a humorless face and tufts of gray hair above his ears. The other was more youthful and burly in his black robes, and he eyed Tara with a lecherous, excited gaze.

The old priest sprinkled the contents of a small pouch into a bowl-shaped brazier atop the altar. The abbess backed away, wrinkling her nose as the brazier flared, casting off whiffs of smoke.

"The fumes will help purge the spirit inside her," the old priest said. He turned to his colleague. "Place it under her nose."

The burly priest flashed an eager grin, revealing a few missing teeth between his plump lips marred by canker sores. From behind the altar, he brought out a strange leather mask with a long curved nose like a heron's beak and pulled it over his head. He glared at Tara through wide eye holes, appearing like some bizarre bird-headed monster. Then he put on a pair of thick gloves and lifted the brazier off the altar. As he stepped closer, his head bobbing like a giant crow, Tara winced. He held out the brazier beneath her chin, filling her nose and lungs with a stench so putrid it made Tara gag.

As she breathed in the fumes, her eyes began to water and bile rose in her throat. She tried to turn her head away from the awful stench, but Sister Bertoara grabbed her by the back of her hair and forced her head closer to the brazier.

"In the name of the Father, the Son, and Holy Spirit," the old priest commanded, approaching Tara with the abbess at his side. "I conjure thee, ye old serpent, Baphomet, who dwells within this child. You spawn of Meridiana, the devil's whore!"

Tara coughed violently, fearing the fumes would suffocate her as the old priest went on. "By the supplication of the angels, and the passions of the saints, and the intercession of Mary, the glorious and ever Virgin, may you be choked, evil one, out of this wretched child, and sent back to the smoking planes of Hell from whence you came!"

Feeling herself choking on the fumes, Tara let out another cough and wretched bile over the burly priest's beak-like mask. He staggered backward, allowing her to catch a breath of less foul air. "I'm not possessed," she sobbed.

"Liar!" screamed the abbess. She lunged at Tara, slapping her face so hard it knocked her head sideways. Tara's cheek throbbed with pain, and she tasted blood in her mouth.

The abbess's face filled with rage. "The fumes don't seem to be working, priest. Take the brand and burn the spirit out of her!"

The old priest frowned. "Very well," he said, turning to the burly priest. "Canon Vero, ready the brand."

"Yes, Father," the burly priest replied with a chuckle, nodding his head in the bird-like mask. He lumbered back to the altar and set the brazier down before removing his mask.

Tara shook, gulping in breaths of air. But her heart pounded in her chest as she wondered what the abbess meant by the brand. When she finally saw it, her heart sunk into her stomach, and she whimpered a word. "No."

The brand was a foot-long iron rod, like a poker used to stir a fire, except at its tip was a palm-sized iron cross. Tara shuddered as the burly priest pushed the cross-shaped tip into the brazier's hot coals.

The old priest raised a finger. "May the heat of this brand sear you, demon, like the word of God Almighty. As it sears her flesh, may its holy purpose burn through thy spirit, in the name of Christ, who conquers all, who cast out demons with but a word spoken with a tongue of fire!"

"Yes," the abbess hissed, clutching her hands.

"Amen," Sister Bertoara crooned.

As the priest recited his prayer again, his voice rising, Tara closed her eyes and clenched her teeth. She wished she could cover her ears, but her wrists were bound tightly to the chair's armrests. Then she felt another stinging slap across her cheek.

"Open your eyes!" the abbess demanded with a sneer. "The brand is almost ready."

When the burly priest pulled the brand from the coals, the cross glowed orange, sending a flutter of fear through Tara's chest. "No," she whimpered again.

The burly priest licked his lips as he stepped forward from the altar, gripping the glowing brand in his gloved hands.

Tara's eyes widened in terror. She felt a sudden lightness in her head as her eyes rolled backward. For an instant, she found herself gazing at the face of the lion, his dark eyes surrounded by golden fur and a blazing mane. *"Defy them!"* the lion roared.

In a blink, the image was gone, and Tara found herself staring at the glowing cross less than a foot from her face. "Stop!" she cried.

A sudden sizzle filled the air around Tara, followed by a whiff of ozone, as the glowing cross burst into flames. The fire surged up the iron shaft onto the burly priest's gloves. The man let out a frightened shriek as the brand fell from his hands and rattled on the floor.

Tara could not believe what had just happened—what *she* might have just done.

Around her, the nuns' voices rose in a gasp

"The demon fights back!" the old priest wailed.

"Pick up the brand!" the abbess screamed hysterically. "Burn it out of her!"

But the burly priest was in no position to pick up the brand, for the flames on his gloves had crawled up the sleeves of his black robes, and the man was flailing toward the altar, howling in pain.

Then, like a booming clap of thunder, Tara heard the church doors thrown open behind her, followed by boots pounding over the stone floor. In a flash, Breda sped past Tara and rammed the butt of her sword into the abbess's face. Blood and teeth flew from the old woman's mouth before she slammed onto the floor and crumpled into a heap. Jarl Holger followed right behind Breda, charging toward the old priest. The man let out a mewing sound as the Danish lord lifted him off his feet with both hands and hurled him over the altar.

Tara could hardly believe her eyes. All around her, the nuns cried out and fled. And amid their screams, Tara heard the lion's voice in her head.

"Be brave, child. Go on the voyage."

Tara gave a faint nod, and the next thing she knew, Alais and Brother Ciarán were by her side, untying her wrists. "We're here now," Alais assured her.

Before Tara could utter a word in response, Brother Ciarán was wrenched backward. Sister Bertoara's meaty hands wrapped around his shoulder as she threw him to the ground.

"There's a demon inside her!" Sister Bertoara yelled, though her words were cut short by a loud thud when the pommel of Breda's sword hammered into the side of her head.

Sister Bertoara dropped like a stone; Brother Ciarán staggered to his feet.

Tara looked at Breda, whose green eyes welled with exhilaration before settling into a more somber gaze. She laid a hand on Tara's shoulder. "Would you rather sail with us," Breda asked, "or stay here with them?" She gestured toward Sister Bertoara, lying unconscious on the stone floor.

With her wrists free of the ropes, Tara threw her arms around Breda. "I'll go," Tara said, sobbing tears of joy. "And I promise, I won't leave you again."

CHAPTER 27

THE HOUSE OF GOGAM

Naberus knelt in the ash-gray sand before the pyramid-like throne at the edge of the ancient harbor. It felt as if the harbor was deep beneath his home of Constantinople, but Naberus knew that through the Gate of Ahriman, they had crossed into the Otherworld where the black waters of the river Acheron flowed into the gloom-filled realm the ancients called *Sheol*.

Behind him knelt his mother, Astarte, and nearly two hundred men and women of their ancestral bloodline. They dressed in fine flowing tunics and long robes of the deepest reds, the darkest blues, and, for some, a classical black silk in honor of their warlock ancestors. They were the members of the House of Gogam, the name they were known by to the people of Byzantium, and they gathered here at midnight to bend their knees before Samyaza.

Naberus breathed in the thick, humid air, awash in the glow of the burning braziers atop the pillars that loomed in a semi-circle around the harbor. The oarsmen from his savior's ship stood like sentries on each side of the throne. Each towered more than seven feet in height, and all were pale-skinned specimens of Gog, shaven, chiseled, and naked save for a loincloth. Lovetar looked out at the assembled crowd from the base of the steps that climbed twenty-

183

seven feet to the enormous high-backed throne, where his master gazed down upon his subjects.

This close, Naberus could feel his master's overwhelming presence, like a Bedouin standing beneath a blazing desert sun. Atop the throne, his master's skin shone the color of fire, reflecting the light from the surrounding braziers.

"My people," his master began, his voice booming through the cavern. "Four thousand years ago, my brethren and I descended from the heavens to conceive a race born of the blood of angels and the daughters of men. We created a world whose glory is the fabric of legends. A time when the gods ruled as kings and your ancestors became the heroes of old, the warriors of renown. Their spirits live in each of you, and once more, I must call on that spirit to aid my divine cause. To restore a world taken from us by those who have since abandoned it, just as they have abandoned the souls in Sheol and subjected your spirits to damnation."

He stood up, nearly eight feet in height. "I SHALL BE YOUR SALVATION!"

Lovetar stepped forward from the base of the lofty throne. "Stand for your god!" she ordered, drawing Naberus and the congregation to its feet.

"Fight for your god!" Lovetar commanded, her voice rising. "Sacrifice for your god—*Samyaza!*"

"Samyaza!" the congregation cried in unison.

"Samyaza!"

"SAMYAZA!"

Their chanting filled Naberus with a powerful feeling of triumph; he had returned to the city of his birth and delivered their people to his master.

Lovetar gestured for Naberus to step aside. He did so as his mother approached the steps that climbed to the throne. Lovetar beckoned her to make the ascent. His mother glanced at him as she started up the stairway. Her once arresting face had grown stately and mature, and strands of gray threaded through her dark hair pulled tightly behind her neck. He could see the pride in her violet eyes, and the crescent-shaped birthmark beneath her left eye shone redder than usual in the light from the brazier's flames.

His grandfather once said her birthmark meant she had been touched by the Old Gods. So he had named her Astarte after an ancient Phoenician goddess, one of their ancestors. When Naberus abandoned his family, making a name for himself in Rome, she had carried out the wishes of her father, the last of the warlocks. In doing so, she had served his master, and now she ascended the steps to receive his divine blessing.

Naberus watched as she stood at the foot of the throne, and Samyaza kissed her forehead. From now on, his mother would serve as Naberus's counselor, and with her league of assassins, any who disobeyed their commands or defied their master's will would meet a swift and brutal end.

When she descended the steps and returned to the congregation, Saleos, the elder who had worn the mask of Hermes, started his climb to the throne. One by one, they would all ascend to Samyaza and swear their eternal loyalty to him and his cause.

Halfway into the ceremony, Naberus felt someone's gaze behind him. He turned to find a woman at the gangplank to Samyaza's ship. She looked like an apparition with her ashen skin, platinum hair, and pale torn dress.

Theodora.

Only months ago, she had been his lover, and before that, she had belonged to Crescentius. Naberus had mistakenly believed that she harbored the Key to the Abyss in her veins and had been prepared to give her to Samyaza. By the time Naberus discovered his master, wounded from the battle beneath Orcus's shrine, he was frantic with fear and wanted to throw her into the river to rid himself of the mistake he had made. That night, however, Samyaza had claimed Theodora as his own, and Naberus had hardly set eyes on her ever since.

He stole away from the ceremony, succumbing to a curious urge to speak with her again. As he approached, he noticed the look of delirium on Theodora's pallid face.

185

Her blue eyes stared at him, dull and listless. "You believe he's your savior?"

Naberus stiffened, surprised by her question. "Do you not witness his glory?"

She answered with a careless laugh. "You see a golden god. But I've seen what he truly is. The burnt and blackened flesh. The sunken eyes. A face more like a beast than a man. He's everything the priests warned us about in the basilicas. And he's no savior."

"Blasphemy," Naberus growled, his anger surging. He reared back his hand to strike her.

She did not flinch. "Let's see how your master takes to a man who would strike his favorite concubine."

Naberus lowered his arm and balled his hands into fists. "He would kill you himself if he heard you now."

She laughed under her breath. "Death would be a gift, though a fleeting one, I suspect. For you and I are damned, Naberus. We conspired to murder a pope. You sent Gregory the Fifth to his grave and, with my aid, through the help of my spy within his palace. That *cannot* be forgiven. Is it any wonder we're condemned?"

"That's what the priests would have you believe, but *he* can change all that."

"Can he? The wound at his side still seeps blood."

"Liar!" he snapped.

"I know the truth."

"You're wrong," he said with a huff. He turned his back to her and strode off toward the congregation.

"Your master's the King of the Damned," she called out as he strode away. "And in the end, the fire that charred his flesh will consume us all!"

A CRISP BREEZE whipped off the Golden Horn, howling over the fortified seawalls of Constantinople. The midmorning sun shining off the water brought little warmth, and Naberus pulled his dark cloak tightly around his shoulders as he made his way up the street that ran along the seawall toward his family's ancestral home.

Although a day had passed, he remained troubled by Theodora's words. They had to be lies, or at least the product of a mind driven mad by exposure to the Otherworld and the splendor of Samyaza. Some mortals, Naberus concluded, were ill-equipped to cope with the existence of the supernatural, and Theodora, despite her cunning back in Rome, must have been one of those. A mortal too fragile to handle the truth.

But her words were not the only thing that bothered him this morning. There was also the message that Lovetar insisted be delivered to his mother. One that concerned an aspect of the prophecy Naberus had been unaware of until now, and he hoped his mother could shed light on it. And then there was the mission Lovetar had given him, the one that came from his master. A mission whose success could ensure victory in this war.

The importance of the mission weighed heavily on Naberus's mind as he arrived at his destination, a walled complex on the Golden Horn a mile northwest of the Sunken Palace. This portion of the city served as a mercantile district where wealthy merchants from Venice, Amalfi, and Pisa lived and worked. Not long after their arrival from Rome, members of his family had established a black market in the district that allowed the less scrupulous merchants to avoid the emperor's oppressive taxes on goods going in and out of the city. His family also sold those merchants protection from the city's rampant crime and thievery. Although unbeknownst to their clientele, his family also controlled the city's thieves' guild, making the arrangement easy to manage and even easier to convince merchants with scruples to consider paying for protection. On top of that, his family controlled a third of the gambling at the Hippodrome and owned some of the city's finest brothels. In the past, it was not unknown for even the emperor to be among their clients. They say Constantinople exceeds all cities in wealth, but also in vice, and for over six hundred years, the House of Gogam had quietly been at the center of it all.

Within the compound's fifteen-foot walls stood four opulent

mansions clustered around a central plaza with a fountain where water splashed around a bronze statue of Poseidon raising his trident. Naberus's family's mansion was the largest of the four, a massive three-story structure, hexagonal in shape and sided with stone, featuring turrets surmounted by roofs of terracotta tiles.

Sturdy double doors opened into a large vestibule with a marble floor and porphyry columns supporting a vaulted ceiling. Naberus's Neapolitan mastiffs, Set and Grimm, lounged near an archway that led to the next chamber. They looked up when their master entered, slapping their tails on the marble tiles. At one time, there had been three of them. They had been Naberus's protectors, three ferocious war hounds who guarded their master like three-headed Cerberus guarded the gates of hell. But Anubis gave his life during the siege of Castel Sant'Angelo, so now Naberus's guardians were down to two. But they remained a fearsome duo. He stooped to scratch each dog's massive head before stepping through the archway.

At the end of a marble hall, his mother waited for him in a sitting chamber where an arcade opened to a terrace overlooking the azure waters of the Golden Horn. She sat at a table sipping a goblet of wine, dressed in a blue silk stola. Above her pale left cheek, her crescent-shaped birthmark shone the same color as her violet eyes.

"Dressed for the races?" he asked, recognizing that her stola was the color of the Blues, one of the city's most famous chariot teams.

"Business must go on," Astarte replied. "The profits from wagers on the races are helping to fund your war." She took a drink of wine. "So, have they told you their plans?"

Naberus nodded. He grabbed a goblet from the side table, took a chair, and poured himself some wine. "Our master leaves tonight to sail for Gog."

"Gog! Gog!" a raven cawed from the terrace. Naberus's lips spread into a smile at the sight of his raven, Hermes, perched on the rail.

"I'm told the Prince of Gog," he said, "has assembled a formidable war band. And he's inflamed with the desire to avenge his brother's death at the battle of Rosefleur."

"Good." Astarte set down her goblet. "But what should we do while they're gone? The longer we sit here, the more time our people have to change their minds about our master's cause. We've already captured one would-be deserter trying to flee the city shortly after midnight."

Naberus grimaced. He feared this might happen. So many in the House of Gogam had lost their faith over the many decades before Samyaza's return, and the reality of deserters both concerned and infuriated him. "Teach them that the price of unfaithfulness is death. You would think they would have learned that lesson by now after seeing the ashes of Malthus and the other unfaithful elders. They must understand that their only hope of survival is to embrace our master and fight for their salvation."

"Fight!" Hermes crowed. *"Fight!"*

"If only they were as loyal as your talkative raven," Astarte said with a dry smile that quickly vanished. "Tell me, how long must we wait?"

"With no time to build ships in the underground harbor and set sail from there, we'll need to sail from here to the other gateway, and we must arrive there by the sabbat at Midsummer when the gate will be open for three days. Once through, we'll traverse the rivers and rendezvous with our master, along with the warships from Gog, and head for Dudael. But, before then, we have matters to attend to. Lovetar had messages for both of us."

Astarte raised a brow. "What possibly could the priestess want of me?"

Naberus took a sip of wine. It was a golden *vinsanto*, sweet with hints of pear and apricot. "Have you ever heard of a prophecy about the Magi's Twins? Lovetar said they are two of the seven."

Astarte sucked in a hiss of breath, then narrowed her eyes. "It was a warning from your grandfather. A prophecy that he and the other warlocks got wind of two decades before I was born. He told me the prophecy came from a leader of a tribe of Zoroastrian Magi in Bukhara who had read the stars. He foretold that the descendant of some woman from Al-Andalus who had joined their sect would give birth to twins in the years leading up to the Millennium.

189

According to the prophecy, these twins would become oracles, holy sisters of the Magi, who would cause great anguish to Ahriman."

Naberus listened intently, beginning to understand Lovetar's concern about this prophecy.

"Before your grandfather passed," Astarte continued, "he made me swear an oath to find the twins and kill them. He believed this sect of Magi had relocated to Constantinople, so he suspected the twins would be born in the city. He was right, of course. And once I learned of their existence, I did what he asked and finished the job."

That was not what Naberus expected to hear. "You're certain of this?"

"My dear son, I was there. We apprehended their ship as they were trying to flee the city. I hurled my dagger into their father's heart as he tried to escape with one of the twins in a rowboat. We sunk the vessel with Greek Fire. The child was in the boat when I saw it disappear beneath the waves. As for the other, the mother was so desperate she jumped into a sea burning with Greek Fire, holding her daughter in her arms. Both of those girls either burned to death in that fiery water or drowned."

"Did you see the bodies?"

Astarte cocked her head. "No, but how could that matter? There is no way those children survived."

"Lovetar said the Magi's twins are alive. That's part of her message to you. The rest is that before you enter the gateway, you must kill them, as you had once vowed."

"They can't be alive," Astarte scoffed. "It would have taken a miracle to save them."

"Then perhaps we live in an age of miracles. But she was quite certain both twins were alive, and I imagine that knowledge came from Samyaza. She's only his messenger."

The color seeped from his mother's already pale face. "She suspects they're here?"

"Perhaps. Or they'll be here soon."

"What do you mean?"

"Lovetar's message to me came from our master. He has foreseen that five of the seven will soon be together in this city. Which means they are coming here. And *she* will be with them."

Astarte raised her eyebrows. "The one who holds the Key to the Abyss?"

Naberus grinned. "Can you imagine what it would mean to steal the power before we even leave for Dudael?"

"We'd hold victory in our grasp." Yet, despite this realization, furrows of concern reappeared on his mother's brow. "She wants you to steal the Key and me to kill the twins. You must speak to her again. Find out what more she knows about the girls."

As she spoke, a look of resolve hardened on Astarte's face. "And tell her, I swear on my life that before Midsummer, the twins will die."

CHAPTER 28

THE NIGHT BEFORE THE VOYAGE

O n the eve of their departure for Constantinople, the pope presided over a lavish feast to honor those embarking on the journey. They gathered in one of the palace's grand banquet halls, its walls adorned with red porphyry columns and lit by the flickering glow of countless candles. Above them, mosaics of Christ sharing bread with His apostles shimmered in the ambient light. The guests sat around three elegantly draped tables, laden with a sumptuous spread that Tara had never imagined possible. Seated beside Breda and her husband at the end of the central table—where the Pope himself dined in an imposing, high-backed chair—Tara marveled at the sheer opulence of the feast before her.

Servants carried out platters of cured ham and bunches of grapes, followed by hot capons that filled the hall with the aroma of roasted meat. Bowls of fresh bread, steaming artichokes, and braised lamb infused with mint and butter followed, along with stuffed pasta resembling tiny purses. Tara relished the soft pasta filled with salty cheese and the succulent lamb and capon. She savored every bite, including the strong white wine—but she made sure not to drink too much. Though everyone else at the tables was drinking plenty. Laughter and tales filled the hall, and Tara felt as if everyone was looking forward to the voyage. Everyone but her.

By the time the dessert course arrived, Tara was ready to return to her room, but the platters full of figs, dates, and nuts surrounding heaps of honey cakes and fruit tarts convinced her to stay.

"It will be fish and salt pork after tomorrow," Breda remarked after quaffing a cup of wine, "so eat up."

Tara nodded and took a bite of a honey cake. She swooned at the sweet taste of vanilla and peach, a flavor so delightful she ate two more cakes, followed by one of the fruit tarts, which hid a custard made of berries. When she was done, she felt as if her stomach might burst. "I think I'll go to my chamber now," she told Breda.

Breda eyed her cautiously. "I'm not going to have to sleep outside your door to make sure you don't run away in the middle of the night, am I?"

"No," Tara replied, "I promise." However, the thought of running away again had briefly crossed her mind. Despite everything that had happened back at the convent, including her vision of the lion telling her to go on the voyage, Tara still dreaded the journey to Constantinople.

By the time she returned to her room and blew out the candle before tucking herself into bed, all she could think about was the evening seven years ago that had altered the course of her life. A nightmare forever etched in her memory. She recalled the fire blazing on the ocean. The black-clad men leaping like devils onto their vessel. The tall woman with a crescent-shaped birthmark below her left eye flipping a dagger into the air and catching it by the hilt. Smoke billowing from the burning sea. Her mother, Shirin, holding her tight and her last words before she jumped overboard. *"Yusuf, forgive me."*

The memory never changed. Each time, a scream caught in Tara's throat as they fell toward the fiery sea. Her mother was speaking again, but this time in a language Tara did not understand. The air sizzled the instant before her blackened staff touched the water. Fire hissed into steam as Tara and her mother plunged beneath the surface.

The cold water stabbed into Tara like a thousand knives, while above, the water's surface glowed with a hellish light. She held her breath. Her mother kicked, swimming as best she could with the staff in one hand and Tara wrapped in her arms. Tara's lungs began to burn; she could not hold her breath any longer. Her mother kicked toward the surface. Where the tip of her staff emerged from the water, the flames dissolved into vapor.

Tara choked in a desperate breath. Through the steam and smoke, she could no longer see the boat. "Hold your breath one more time," her mother begged.

Tara filled her lungs with air and then let her mother take her beneath the waves, each of them kicking with their legs in a frantic attempt to get away from the boat. When they finally burst through the surface, they were free of the burning sea. But just a few yards away, the water still blazed like a lake of fire, and through the smoke, Tara could see the mast and bowsprit of their vessel. Her father and Sara were still on board. Tara wanted to scream, but all she could manage was gasping for air to fill her starving lungs. Her mother clung to her staff, its tip breaking through the surface, but it was not enough to keep them afloat. Tears streamed down Tara's face as her mother kicked farther away from the boat until her mother's breath came in sharp, desperate gasps.

Eventually, her mother came to a stop in the water, her face drained of energy. She glanced towards the western shore, illuminated by a small fishing village's lanterns. "You must be quiet now, my child," she said. "If you make a sound, they'll hear us even from here." Tara sniffled, tears pouring from her eyes. "Hold on to my staff, and don't let go," her mother instructed.

Her mother wrapped Tara's arms around the staff. Tara clung tightly to the slick, wet wooden shaft. Pulling her close, her mother kissed her forehead and held her for a time. It was the most comforting moment that Tara remembered from that night. Then her mother's lips drifted to her ear. "Know always that I love you," she whispered.

Her mother pushed away from the staff. Tara wanted to swim after her, but she remembered her mother's command. She clung to the staff, and it provided enough buoyancy to keep her afloat. Her mother began speaking in a language that was like a song. In her right hand was the small silver cup she usually kept in the pouch at her waist. She splashed it through the water toward Tara, and that's when she felt a strange, warm current wrap itself around her legs. The current carried her through the water, away from her mother.

Tara forced herself not to scream as tears streamed down her face, and her mother slowly disappeared from sight. In the distance, the lake of fire blazed, and her parent's ship vanished in a haze of smoke.

Tara had no recollection of when her grip on the staff had finally loosened, nor when she had washed up on the shore. When she woke, the bright morning sun was blinding her eyes. A man stooped over her. He was dressed in a priest's black robes with a long gray beard and a narrow face weathered with age. Beneath a broad-brimmed hat, he peered at her through kind blue eyes.

"Tara," he said. "I've been expecting you."

She blinked in confusion.

He gave her a gentle smile. "You can call me Father Michele."

CHAPTER 29

INTO THE FIRE

In the palace's grand hall, Ciarán slouched over the table, and his eyes fixated on the last morsel of succulent, braised lamb. A dizzying warmth emanated from the copious wine swirling in his stomach. He was acutely aware that this would be the last lavish meal for some time, yet he felt so sated, almost uncomfortably so; he feared that one more bite might lead him to burst.

Beside Ciarán, Alais rested her head on his shoulder, and Ciarán hoped she would stay there all night. On his left, Pietro sopped up a bowl full of braising liquid with a hunk of bread while across the table, Jarl Holger brought another cup of wine to his lips with his free arm draped around Breda's shoulders. Near Breda, who was laughing and smiling, Jorundr had passed out with his head sideways on his plate with morsels from the feast stuck in his long white-blond hair. Meanwhile, the rest of *Lindworm's* crew were finishing their lamb and capons, gnawing the last vestiges of meat off the bones and polishing off more cups of Falernian wine. Watching it all from the head of the table was Gerbert, clad in his white cassock, patiently sipping from a gilded chalice.

Before long, Gerbert made a twirling gesture, signaling for the servers to clear the table. They did as he commanded, removing the plates and platters until all that was left was a white tablecloth now marred with splotches of braising liquid and meat juice, bread-crumbs, and a myriad of wine stains.

Gerbert stood up from his chair and tipped his chalice. "This tablecloth belonged to Charlemagne," he announced. "It was one of his most remarkable treasures."

"He treasured a tablecloth?" Holger asked, raising a brow.

"Indeed, he did," Gerbert said with a hint of a smile. "After every feast, he would cleanse it by throwing it in the hearth. Would you like to try it, Jarl Holger?"

Ciarán perked up at the pope's dare. The tablecloth appeared woven of an expensive, pale white cloth. He could not imagine ruining it in a fire.

Holger gave Gerbert a quizzical look before getting up from his chair and whisking the stained white cloth off the wooden table. He strode to the large, marble-framed hearth crackling with fire, then hesitated.

"Go ahead," Gerbert urged. "Toss it in."

With a grunt, Holger threw the tablecloth into the hearth. Ciarán joined the others, gathering around the hearth as the flames flared and danced across the tablecloth. The aroma of meat and bread being consumed by fire wafted through the hall, but to Ciarán's astonishment, the tablecloth remained as white as ever as the stains roasted away.

Jarl Holger stepped back. "By the gods," he muttered as gasps of wonder broke out from *Lindworm's* crew.

"Amazing," Alais said under her breath as Ciarán looked on in awe. The tablecloth appeared impervious to the flames.

"Gaido," Gerbert asked the captain of his papal guard standing against the wall with several other crimson-cloaked guardsmen, "can you please retrieve the tablecloth from the hearth?"

Gaido gave the pope a wary look before nodding and unsheathing his sword. He slipped the blade between the white cloth and the burning embers, then used it to pull the cloth free of the fire, stirring up a burst of sparks. People backed away as the table-cloth fell onto the marble floor, as clean and white as before the feast, with not even a thread charred or smoking from the heat. Ciarán could hardly believe his eyes.

"What magic is this?" Holger asked.

"It's not magic at all," Gerbert explained. "Charlemagne's famous tablecloth is woven of a material called Asbestus. Some believe it to be the wool of a salamander or the feathers of a phoenix, but those are just fairy tales. Asbestus is actually a rare white rock so fine in texture that it can be spun into cloth. Fortunately, sometime after Charlemagne's death, his tablecloth ended up in the papal archives, along with our many other relics. I happened upon it around the same time Brother Pietro discovered Saint Helena's letter. Even more fortunate, I learned the ancient Romans used Asbestus to make burial shrouds, and Niccolo managed to locate a storeroom of the rare stone in a vault beneath the Vatican Hill. So, while Charlemagne used the substance to astound his dinner guests, I plan to use it to make cloaks—cloaks that may be resistant to dragonfire."

Ciarán scraped his finger through his hair, marveling at Gerbert's genius. The Dragon's fire was one thing Ciarán feared the most about the coming conflict, and now they just might have a solution to that problem. "When will they be ready?" he asked.

"Not before you set sail on *Lindworm*," Gerbert replied, "but I'll have Gaido bring them aboard the three ships carrying the Dragonslayers. After you find the scrolls in Constantinople, the cloaks will be waiting for you at Myros."

"I can't thank you enough," Ciarán said.

Gerbert gave him a thoughtful smile. "While I may not be able to join you on the incredible voyage that lies ahead, the least I can do is help you survive it."

CIARÁN SETTLED into his bed for what would be the last time before nearly a month at sea. He was full from all the food and wine, with a newfound hope after Gerbert's revelation about the Asbestus cloaks. It had been a better night than Ciarán could have wished for. As he drifted off to sleep, he wrapped his arms around Caladbolg's sheath, embracing the sword's talismanic protection.

But sometime in the hours after he faded into sleep, the Dragon found him.

Ciarán's heart slammed into his stomach as the misty coils lifted him off the ground. Ten feet away, in the billowing, fog-like vapor, hovered the Dragon, his hood pulled low over his face. The golden glow of his irises pierced the shadow.

"You have been hiding from me," the Dragon said. "But you can't escape. Our work here is not done."

The chilling mist wafted across Ciarán's neck, twisting around it like a noose. "What do you want?"

"You'll see." The Dragon lifted his hands. *"Cialpor."* He spoke the word like a command, but Ciarán did not understand its meaning. Near his bare feet, he heard a whoosh, then a sizzle. A spark of electricity kissed his left foot, its heat flowing into his luminescent skin. From the mist swirling around his head came ghostly whispers.

Ozam, odamma, cialpor, mir, agrit …

"Why are you doing this?" Ciarán stammered.

"If we're to be adversaries, we must get to know one another. And I've already learned so much from our conversations."

Ciarán's blood ran cold. Gerbert had feared the Dragon was using these encounters to steal information from Ciarán's mind.

"You've learned about the scrolls." The Dragon's voice held an edge of amusement.

Ciarán tried to close off his thoughts lest he betray anything more to their enemy. Although the only thing he could focus on were the whispers in the mist, repeating that cryptic verse. *Ozam, odamma, cialpor, mir, agrit …*

"Those ancient, dusty writings," the Dragon purred, "drafted two thousand years ago by Solomon the Wise. You believe they can help you. But can they?"

With a hiss, the Dragon sucked in a breath. "For when Solomon was old, his wives turned away his heart after other gods, and his heart was not true to the Lord. For Solomon followed Ashtoreth, the goddess of the Sidonians, and Moloch, the abomination of the Ammonites."

Ciarán had read those words before, in the Book of Kings. The Dragon was quoting scripture.

"So Solomon did what was evil in the sight of the Lord …"

The hooded figure disappeared into the frothing mists. In his place, Ciarán gazed upon a towering statue of a woman, as white as alabaster and utterly naked save for a golden choker around her neck. Long golden rings dangled from the statue's ears as it looked on, with large, black-rimmed eyes set into a face framed by rope-like hair and crowned with a golden crescent moon. The goddess stood in a cavernous temple atop a pedestal before a blazing fire pit. Throughout the temple were women, at least fifty, maybe more, almost all naked like the statue. Some swayed to the rhythm of a chant.

"Ashtoreth, Ashtoreth!"

Others embraced, kissing and stroking, their bodies writhing together to the beat of the chanting.

"Ashtoreth, Ashtoreth!"

Ciarán gaped at the young, supple women as heat filled his loins. In the center of the temple knelt a man with long gray hair and a long gray beard, also naked. A half-dozen women fawned over him, caressing the man, who was well into his later years. His arms were outstretched, and his face seemed lost in delirium. Nearby, several women stood and poured bowls of liquid over their bare breasts. The liquid was ruby red—wine, perhaps. Or blood.

Ciarán's stomach clenched; his arousal turned to dread as another woman, older and dressed in white silks, strode through the crowd holding a screaming infant above her head. The chanting rose to a crescendo.

"Ashtoreth, Ashtoreth!"

The old man seemed oblivious to it all as the priestess stood before the fire pit, holding the infant high in her arms, displaying it for the congregation.

"Ashtoreth, Ashtoreth!"

A primal scream burst from Ciarán's lungs. "Stop, goddamn it!"

As the priestess let go of the child, the image vanished. Ciarán felt himself shaking violently. "Wake up!" Pietro cried.

He shoved something into Ciarán's arms. *Caladbolg.*

"I found it lying on the floor after I heard you cry out," Pietro said. "You must've dropped it in your sleep."

"Solomon can't help us," Ciarán muttered, sitting up and huffing for breath.

"What are you talking about?"

"The Dragon showed me. Solomon and his wives did terrible things. They sacrificed children, for Christ's sake."

"Remember who showed you this," Pietro replied. "The Father of Lies."

"He quoted scripture!"

Pietro clasped his hands together. "That scripture may be true, but Solomon's sins came late in life after taking hundreds of foreign wives. That was not the man who built the temple or wrote the Testament of Solomon. That man was younger, wiser, and closer to God. So, yes, he fell, and the Lord broke up his kingdom as punishment. But that doesn't mean he was not good and just before his fall."

Ciarán pressed his fingers into Caladbolg's scabbard. "What I saw was unforgivable."

"You only saw what *he* wanted you to see. That's part of his deception."

With a heavy sigh, Ciarán handed Pietro the sheathed blade. "Lash the scabbard to my arm. That way, I won't drop it. I can't let this happen again."

As Pietro moved to retrieve a leather belt, Ciarán remembered the Dragon's words. *I've already learned so much from our conversations ...*

So long as the Dragon could infiltrate his thoughts, they would never be safe. Ciarán tried to fall back asleep, but the gnawing dread of what secrets he might have already unwittingly divulged to their enemy left him sickened to his very core.

CHAPTER 30

LINDWORM

For good reasons, Tara hated boats. But now she found herself sitting in the dank hull of a long, narrow ship that Lady Breda called *Lindworm.*

Breda had told her that a lindworm was a sea serpent, which explained the carved dragon head covered in golden scales at the ship's prow. And while Tara had never seen a ship like this, so sleek and low in the water, she had known that one day she would. Father Michele had told her so. Everything the old priest had told her seemed to be coming true, but this voyage was not starting off well.

It began with a queasy feeling in the pit of her stomach as the ship rocked back and forth against the swells as the crew rowed from the river into the Tyrrhenian Sea. She tried to ignore the sensation, focusing instead on the eighteen oarsmen, which included Brother Ciarán, dipping their long oars into the ocean. The men rowed shirtless, and Tara watched the muscles in their arms and back bulge with each stroke. Many of the men had pictures painted on their arms and torso. Some were images of beasts, like wolves, ravens, and stags; others were of serpents or great trees that sprawled up the back to the base of the neck, while several more looked like interlaced ribbons that ended in strange symbols. A few of the men, like Brother Ciarán, had unadorned skin, and the oarsmen glistened with sweat as they drove the ship southward down the Italian coast.

Soon, however, Tara broke into a cold sweat. Although she was doing nothing more rigorous than sitting on the edge of a shallow raised platform in the ship's stern with Rosta snoring by her side. The sweat was followed by a faint, dizzy feeling in her head. She closed her eyes, but that only made the dizziness worse.

"Are you alright?" Alais asked her. Sitting to Tara's left, the beautiful Frenchwoman looked perfectly well, with her bright storm-gray eyes and long raven hair blowing in the salty breeze. She dressed for the voyage similar to Breda in a tight-fitting leather vest over a long-sleeved tunic, with wool hose, high leather boots, and a wool cloak dyed blue like the sea.

"I don't feel great," Tara groaned. The dizziness in her head blurred her vision. At the ship's far end, Brother Pietro looked equally unwell. He huddled near the prow, clutching a leather book satchel to his chest while his pale skin had taken on an almost greenish hue.

Watching Brother Pietro was not helping. When he suddenly lunged over the gunwale and retched overboard, the insides of her stomach rushed into Tara's chest. She barely made it to the side of the boat before spewing her breakfast into the brine-scented sea.

She threw up a second time and then a third and a fourth until her abdomen ached and burned. Breda and Alais held onto Tara's shoulders; someone was rubbing her back. Under her breath, Breda chuckled. "Don't worry," she said, "you'll get used to it. In a few days, you'll be as happy as a Viking riding the waves."

A few days eventually passed, and while Tara did not find herself happy aboard *Lindworm*, at least her adventures with seasickness seemed to have subsided. The Danes, however, appeared over-joyed to be at sea. When they rowed, they often did so to the beat of a song. And when the wind filled the ship's square sail, striped crimson and white, allowing the men to draw in their long oars, the banter in their Danish tongue would fill the hull. Occasionally, two or three men would face off in poetry contests. While Tara could not understand the words, the poems often brought eruptions of laughter or caused the oarsmen to choke up and fight away tears.

The days at sea also affected Lady Breda's handsome husband, Jarl Holger. His expression, so dark in the days after his friend Magnus's death, had lightened considerably. His frost-blue eyes grew bright during the songs and poetry contests, and they took on a loving hue when he was close to Breda.

"The sea gives him life," Breda told Tara on the second day of their voyage. "We stayed too long in Rome."

Another thing that Tara began to notice after several days at sea was that wildlife seemed drawn to *Lindworm*. Seagulls would glide overhead or fly parallel with the sail, and giant fish called dolphins would swim alongside the vessel, their sleek gray bodies cresting out of the water. Jarl Holger insisted these dolphins were not fish but animals because they breathed air through a hole on top of their heads. But they looked like fish to Tara, and their curved dorsal fins were not unlike the shark fins that would occasionally glide along-side *Lindworm's* hull. Occasionally, they even saw whales. Some were slightly larger than the dolphins with blunt heads, while others looked more massive than the longship. Fortunately, Jarl Holger took care to steer clear of those leviathans, easing Tara's fears that she might end up like Jonah in the belly of a whale.

The jarl would often keep the ship just miles from shore, so the coastline was always in view. At times, they would visit cities along the coast to spend the night and replenish supplies, including a forti-fied town named Gaeta and a massive walled city called Naples, with a prominent lighthouse and a formidable castle. Each time, the crew would remove the dragonhead from *Lindworm's* prow before nearing a town or city so as not to alarm the citizenry into believing that Viking raiders had arrived at their shore. Tara was beginning to enjoy these brief visits to the settlements along the Italian coast. But after spending a night at Amalfi, another walled town built on a steep cliffside, Jarl Holger began to keep *Lindworm* farther away from the shore.

One morning, Tara asked Brother Ciarán why they avoided the coastal towns. She spoke with him in the stern while *Lindworm* was at full sail, giving the oarsmen a much-needed break. The salt breeze rustled his hair, now almost entirely gray. It had changed that color in the short time she had known him, and Lady Alais said it was because he was having terrible nightmares. Tara pushed her singular white curl out of her face, a peculiar strand she had always had in her dark hair. Her sister had one just like it, too. Cardinal Bishop Beno had called it a witch's streak, but their mother had called it a blessing and a gift. So had Father Michele, who told her she would become an oracle. But looking at Brother Ciarán, who seemed to be aging in front of her very eyes, she sensed whatever was happening to him was not a blessing at all.

Brother Ciarán gave Tara a thoughtful look and then peered out across the sea, where the land was barely visible on the horizon. "That land out there is the Emirate of Sicily," he said, "and the Saracens won't take kindly to the sight of a Danish longship sailing near their shores."

Tara eyed him suspiciously. "Sister Priscilla said the Saracens are godless heathens who hate Christians."

"I assure you," Brother Ciarán said with a hint of a smile, "many of them are far from godless. They may have a different name for God than we do, but many of their beliefs are not terribly different from our own."

Tara thought about that. While she never told anyone in Rome, she had not been born a Christian, and her mother and father also had a different name for God. But they weren't Saracens, and what Sister Priscilla had told Tara about these Arabic people made her uneasy. "They do hate us, though, don't they?"

"I doubt it's because we're Christians." Brother Ciarán replied. "I've been to the Moorish parts of Spain, and Christians live among the Moors. But when it comes to war, I've found it's usually about land." He pointed to the cliffs far away on the horizon. "That island once belonged to the Roman Empire until the Goths came and took it from them. Eventually, a Greek emperor from Constantinople came and took it from the Goths until the Saracens came and took it from the Greeks. Who knows how soon it will be before someone comes to take it from the Saracens?"

Tara considered everything Brother Ciarán had said, though the thought of Saracens added a new layer of discomfort to the voyage. Even worse, after a day of sailing off the coast of Sicily, Tara got the distinct impression that Brother Ciarán was trying to find some of them. He would stand at the prow searching for other vessels with a fair-haired, beardless Dane named Freybjorn whose eyes, Breda said, were keener than a hawk's. Sometimes, Jarl Holger would join them in their hunt, causing Breda to replace him at the steering oar. On one of those occasions, Tara decided to confirm her suspicions.

"What are they looking for?" she asked Breda.

"Pirates," Breda answered with a broad smile.

"So we can sail away from them, right?"

"No, child. They're on a hunt. About a year ago, a pirate called the Varangian enslaved Ciarán's old crew. The Varangian sails with the Saracens now. So, like a good Dane, Ciarán wants revenge."

Tara gasped. "He wants to fight them?"

"Aye," Breda said with a shrug. "And to take some prisoners. But don't worry. We are Vikings, the lords of the sea. If we find one of these pirate ships, it will not end well for them."

Breda's words only deepened Tara's anxiety about the Saracens, and every morning, she silently hoped that Brother Ciarán would not find what he was searching for.

But then, on their second morning sailing along the north Sicilian coast, Brother Ciarán found them.

CHAPTER 31

A SWARM OF ARROWS

Tara's body tensed as Freybjorn leaned over the dragon-headed prow, shouting out in the Danish tongue as he pointed to something in the distance. Brother Ciarán rushed to the prow, followed by the huge Dane named Jorundr and Jarl Holger. Tara huddled with Breda at the steering oar, along with Alais and Brother Pietro.

"Can you see anything?" Brother Pietro asked, peering at the horizon where the azure sea met the pale blue sky streaked with clouds.

Breda squinted her eyes. "Aye. There's a ship out there."

Tara had to strain her eyes to make out the shape on the horizon —it resembled a small triangle on the edge of the world.

The next thing she knew, Jarl Holger was striding back to the stern, shouting orders to his crew. The men hurriedly reached beneath the rowing benches, pulled out chainmail shirts, dressed in them, and then put on their conical helmets. After that, they returned to their oars, rowing with vigor.

As Brother Ciarán returned to his oar bench, he looked to Alais. "Let's hope it's a pirate ship."

"And if it's not?" Alais asked.

"Then, when we reach her, we'll ask about the Varangian and let them on their way."

Alais nodded at Brother Ciarán, and he resumed his post at the oar, matching the pace of the rowing crew. *Lindworm* gained speed, misting sea spray over the gunwales with each powerful stroke. Before long, Tara's hair and clothes were dripping with brine. Slowly, another long, narrow ship came into view. This one had triangular sails, and its oars moved as if trying to outrun *Lindworm*. Yet with every pull of the Danes' oars, *Lindworm* was gaining on them.

Jarl Holger yelled out more orders in Danish, and the rowers quickened their pace. Tara found it hard to judge distance on the open water, but figured the other ship could not have been more than two hundred yards away. That distance closed further when the wind caught *Lindworm's* sail, aiding the oarsmen and fueling her speed. Then, abruptly, the other ship steered to the left to face perpendicular to *Lindworm*.

"Bastards," Breda cursed, followed by an urgent command from Jarl Holger. The crew scrambled to grab their shields. Breda threw her husband's to him before taking her own. Alais and Brother Pietro grabbed the remaining two.

Tara's heart raced. "What's going on?"

"They're aiming to shoot at us!" Breda exclaimed before raising her shield. Brother Pietro, who was closest to Tara, awkwardly raised his, too.

Tara heard the hiss of the arrows before she saw them, dark in the sky like an oncoming swarm. Fear coursed through her veins as she hurled herself behind Pietro's shield just as the arrows began to fall, a relentless chorus of thuds and thumps raining down on them. One arrow pierced Pietro's shield, and his arm was driven back into his chest by the force of its impact. Alais' shield caught another arrow, while Breda's had two more embedded in its surface.

To Tara's growing alarm, a second volley followed the first. An arrow struck the right side of Pietro's shield with a loud thud, pulling his arm away with the force of the attack. Tara gasped in horror as she found herself exposed as a second arrow flew straight toward her. A scream caught in her throat as an image flashed in her mind—one of golden fur, a fiery mane, and piercing eyes. The lion's booming voice roared a single word: *"BURN!"*

A surge of power raced through Tara's veins like a jolt of lightning, crackling through the air as the streaking arrow exploded into flames. Tara's heart skipped a beat as sparks showered the raised shields of her companions. She turned her head, feeling the heat on her cheek, as the arrowhead clanged onto the deck and its blackened remains scorched her dress.

Brother Pietro's eyes widened in disbelief. "Did you do that?" he asked Alais.

"I can't do that," she replied. Her face mirrored the same shock and awe that Tara felt coursing through her.

"More coming!" Breda cried.

Tara was stunned, unable to process what had happened, when Brother Pietro yanked her beneath his shield. Alais angled her shield to cover Tara an instant before more arrows pounded into the willow boards like a staccato of hammer blows. Suddenly, one of the Danes shouted in agony. To Tara's shock, Hári Grayhair, sitting on the bench across from Brother Ciarán, hollered in pain as an arrow impaled his left thigh. Blood pulsed from the wound.

"Enough of this," Alais muttered. She shifted her shield to her right arm and leaned over the ship's left side until her fingers skimmed the water's surface. Then she began reciting a verse that seemed strangely familiar to Tara—one similar to the words her mother spoke the last time she set eyes on her.

Tara sensed the air sizzle as *Lindworm* pitched to the right. On the left side of the longship, a swell rushed forward from where Alais had touched the water, carrying a faint blue glow beneath the surface. As another volley of arrows rained down on *Lindworm*, the swell grew into a wave, increasing in size as it barreled toward the other ship.

The thudding of arrows was replaced by a chorus of terrified cries as the massive wave of water swept toward the enemy ship like some great whale breaching the surface. A whisper of "Lifthrasir" broke out among *Lindworm's* crew a heartbeat before the enormous wave crashed down on the Saracen vessel. The mast snapped, and the hull rolled over on itself, spilling the archers into the frothing sea. It appeared that the wave had swallowed the ship whole for a moment, but several breaths after the wave broke, the keel bobbed to the surface. All around, men flailed in the water, trying desperately to climb onto the capsized hull.

Tara looked on in awe as Jarl Holger barked another order, and his men traded their shields for oars and began rowing toward the wreckage.

To Tara's surprise, a scrawny man wearing nothing but soaking wet breeches was standing on the capsized hull, wielding an oar like a weapon. As others attempted to clamber on board the boat, he beat them off, cracking the oar to strike their heads or slash the hands of those trying to grasp the slick hull. By the time *Lindworm* reached the vessel, the man stood alone.

He raised his oar in triumph and flashed a disarming smile. "Greetings, my saviors!"

CHAPTER 32

DEMETRIUS

To Ciarán's surprise, the scrawny man standing half-naked on the keel of the capsized vessel spoke Greek.

With his sun-browned skin, shock of black hair, and close-cropped beard, the man could have passed for one of the Saracens, but clearly, this man hailed from Greece. Greek was not Ciarán's strongest language, though Brother Dónall had taught him to speak enough of it when he was an oblate at Derry that he could understand the man.

"Can I come aboard?" the man asked, struggling to keep his balance on the overturned hull rocking aggressively in the frothing sea. The man could not have been much older than Ciarán, and with his bright smile beneath a hooked nose, he did not appear dangerous, despite the violence he had just committed against his shipmates. "I've made sure all the pirates who were shooting arrows at you have drowned. Let their Allah take them now!" He spat into the sea with a look of disgust.

Standing at the prow, Freybjorn and Holger glanced at Ciarán and shrugged. Neither spoke a word of Greek.

"It was a pirate ship, all right," Ciarán explained in Danish. "The man wants to come aboard."

Holger nodded. "Let's see what he knows, but I don't trust him. I'll decide later whether to throw him overboard or hand him over to Hári for that arrow in his leg."

"How do we know you weren't one of the archers?" Ciarán called to the man.

"Because I'm a slave. Those stinking pirates would not give me a weapon. But I could still use this oar. Miserable bastards!"

If the man was indeed a slave, Ciarán thought, that might explain why a Greek was sailing with Saracen pirates. And if that's true, he might know about the Varangian.

Ciarán reached a hand over the prow. The man took it, and Ciarán helped him into the longship. Still dripping wet, the man glanced around at the mail-clad Danes, many of whom were standing at their oar benches. The Danes towered over the seaman.

"A ship full of giants, I see." His gaze settled on Alais and Breda. "And beautiful women, too. How blessed you must be!"

"Who are you?" Ciarán asked. "And whose ship was this?"

"My name is Demetrius, and that ship was called the *Namur Alqarsh*. It's part of a small fleet belonging to the man who enslaved me."

Ciarán crossed his arms. "And who is he?"

"A pirate lord. He serves the emir now, but he started in Constantinople, where I come from. During his last visit there three months ago, he and I had a bit of a …" Demetrius grimaced, holding out his palms. "Misunderstanding."

"He enslaved you over a misunderstanding?"

"It was a game of dice. Perhaps the dice may have been a teensy bit loaded."

"You cheated him?"

Demetrius grimaced again. "He's an evil man. Is it really a crime to steal from evil men? But you can trust me. I have learned my lesson. And now I am saved. Thanks to you and that wave. It came out of nowhere, like a huge whale. What strange luck, eh?"

This man was used to talking his way out of trouble, Ciarán suspected. But now he needed answers. "Your pirate lord, has he ever associated with a man called the Varangian?"

Demetrius's eyes narrowed. "Associated? No. The man who enslaved me *is* the Varangian."

Ciarán could hardly believe his Irish luck. "You serve the Varangian? Then you must know where he keeps his slaves."

"Of course. I live in that shit hole."

With a surge of hope, Ciarán grabbed Demetrius by his shoulders. "Then listen, my friend, we'll give you passage to dry land. But before we do that, you're going to take us to the Varangian."

"I'M GOING WITH YOU," Alais declared, taking a seat on the oar bench beside Ciarán.

He could see she was set on her decision. Ciarán sat shirtless, having stowed his hauberk and tunic beneath the bench. They had been rowing for hours until they arrived at the Egadi Archipelago, where Demetrius said they would find the Varangian's fortress. By late afternoon, however, the wind filled Lindworm's sail, offering a welcome respite from rowing. As they talked, the sun began to set, painting the sky a fiery orange as it slipped behind the horizon.

"You should stay with the ship and the rest of the crew," he argued. We don't know how many ships or men the Varangian has. If our ship is spotted from the fortress or the beach, they could attack. The crew would need your skills."

"And you won't need them in that fortress? You don't know how many men he keeps inside it. If something goes wrong, do you think the six of you will be enough to stop them?"

Ciarán sighed. The plan was to take a small force into the fortress. Just him, Jarl Holger, Jorundr, Freybjorn, and Strong Bjorn, led by Demetrius. "The dungeon's poorly guarded. Demetrius swears to it. I know he's a thief and not one to be trusted, but he hates the Varangian. I believe that. He won't want to be captured again. We'll sneak in through a postern door, which Demetrius will trick them into opening. Then we'll overcome what few men may be down there and free the prisoners. He told me Josua and our other friends were among them not more than three days ago."

Alais crossed her arms. "And if things go awry?"

"I'll have Caladbolg. But if the pirates spot *Lindworm* on the beach, who will protect Tara? You have to stay with her."

"What if Tara can protect herself?" The question came from Pietro, who sat on the opposite rowing bench. Beside him, Hári Grayhair slept soundly against the starboard gunwale, his hand resting on his left leg where Alais had healed the arrow wound.

"What do you mean?" Ciarán asked, scratching his head.

Pietro glanced into the stern, where Tara napped with her arms around a snoring Rosta. "When the arrows came upon us," he began, "one arrow had already hit my shield, pushing me aside. I couldn't stop the next arrow from hitting Tara. But, out of nowhere, it burst into flames and burnt to ashes before it reached her."

Ciarán looked at Alais in disbelief. "Did you see this happen?"

"Yes," she confirmed.

"Did you conjure the fire?"

Alais shook her head. "I can't. The power can control fire, but the fire must already exist. It can't be conjured from thin air, but that's what happened."

Ciarán rubbed the back of his aching neck. "You think Tara did that?

"Unless we witnessed a miracle," Alais replied.

"Perhaps both are true." Pietro removed a leather-bound book from his satchel. It was the copy of the Book of Revelation he had brought for the journey, along with the map of the prophecy and other notes he had tucked away from the Reading Room. Thumbing through the book's velum pages, he stopped halfway through and glanced up. "This is what John of Patmos wrote about the two witnesses: *These are the two olive trees and the two lampstands that stand before the Lord of the earth. And if anyone wants to harm them, fire pours from their mouth and consumes their foes.*'"

Ciarán raised his eyebrows. He had forgotten that passage from Revelation, but what Pietro and Alais claimed to have seen did not truly fit the verse. "The fire didn't come from her mouth, did it?"

"Not exactly," Pietro said. "But the moment before it happened, I heard her utter a word. It sounded like 'burn.'"

"I'll be damned." Ciarán recalled his first conversation with Gerbert about the Book of Revelation. Back then, Gerbert had called Revelation a *metaphora*, but this time, the *metaphora* had been close to the truth. And after seeing the Dragon with his own eyes and learning the true nature of the Key to the Abyss, Ciarán had no reason to doubt Pietro's theory. If Tara was indeed one of the two witnesses foretold in Revelation, why couldn't she wield some miraculous form of the power?

Across from him, a satisfied smile spread across Alais' face. "You see, Tara can look after herself, and she'll have Breda, Rosta, and fifteen Danish warriors to protect her. They won't need me, so I'm coming with you."

Ciarán buried his face in his palms. The logical part of his brain knew he had no chance of changing her mind, however dangerous it would be for her to go with them. But his less rational side was rather pleased that she'd be at his side.

"I'm not going to win this, am I?" he conceded.

"No, you're not," she said, gazing at him with her very determined storm-gray eyes.

As she spoke, her raven hair danced in the salty breeze, and only the vows he had taken at Derry kept him from reaching out and kissing her right then and there.

LYING in *Lindworm's* stern with her arms wrapped around Rosta, Tara kept her eyes closed, pretending to sleep. But she had heard everything Brother Pietro, Brother Ciarán, and Lady Alais had said, and their words sent her mind whirling with thoughts.

Deep down, she could not believe she burned up that arrow or set fire to the exorcist's brand. Each time, she had seen the lion's image and the roar of his voice in her mind. He was one of the creatures who sent her these visions from the boughs of the fiery tree, and like those visions, whatever was happening when the fire appeared must have been his doing, right? But then she thought of her mother and the wonders she could do: quenching the fire burning atop the waves and blasting a ball of flame into one of the woman's assassins. Father Michele had called her mother a magus, and for a moment, Tara wondered if she had those powers, too. But what if those powers were witchcraft, as the abbess and the bishop had believed? How could they be good or holy? Yet then there was Lady Alais. Tara found her powers to be as miraculous as her mother's had been, and all Lady Alais had ever been was kind, while the abbess and the bishop had been only cruel and cunning.

Tara's mind ached. There was so much about what was happening that she did not understand, including the reasons for these visions and how the lion could speak to her in moments when her life was threatened. Then there was what Brother Pietro read about in his book, suggesting these powers were her own, even though that was hard to imagine.

On top of all these questions was why she had to be here in the first place, sailing toward a city where a murderous woman waited to kill her. That was the thought Tara dreaded the most. For if she had to face that woman again, Tara feared there would be no powers to save her.

The only thing she could do to protect herself was run.

CHAPTER 33

AHRIMAN'S GATE

Naberus gazed at the gigantic stone relief of Ahriman plunging a sword into the lion-like Ahura Mazda. It was a symbol of the victory he and his master hoped to achieve, but not yet. For now, he needed to open Ahriman's Gate.

He turned to his sacrifice, held fast by two of his family's black-clad assassins. The deserter struggled in their arms, whimpering. "You can't take me back," he sobbed.

Naberus raised a brow, regarding the deserter for a moment. He was a younger man, a reckless scion of the House of Gogam who found pleasure among the Blues, gambling on the races in the Hippodrome and cavorting with the dancers who entertained the men after the games. He was thin-faced but handsome, with a shock of black hair that hung over his forehead. Though his clothes were expensive, they were dripping wet from their journey through the Sunken Palace. His name was Fidelis, an ironic coincidence given his faithlessness.

"The last time you passed through this gate," Naberus said, "you pledged fealty to our master. To your god. You looked upon his divine form, basked in the glory of his divine presence, and received his divine blessing. Yet still you would betray him?"

The blood drained from Fidelis's face. "I'm no warrior. And surely you have heard the rumors—the last time he came, our entire race nearly met with extinction. He cares *nothing* of our lives."

Naberus felt the anger rising within him. "Without him, your life has no meaning. Your soul is damned, condemned to the Under-world. But *he* can change all of that."

Fidelis shook his head. "This is madness."

From a sheath at his belt, Naberus drew a foot-long dagger and leveled it at Fidelis's throat. "If you will not serve Samyaza in life," Naberus said coldly, "then you will serve him through death."

The deserter's eyes grew wide and desperate. "You know what the priests say about him," he whimpered. "He lies … nothing he says can be trusted. But the priests say there's another way. Reject him and embrace the other—that is the way to salvation."

The man's words sparked a sudden rage. With a violent strike, Naberus scythed the dagger through Fidelis's neck, feeling the spray of blood against his cheek. In his fury, Naberus kept cutting, sawing into the muscle until only Fidelis's spine kept his head attached to his torso.

Naberus let the body fall onto the stone floor. Trying to calm his heavy breathing, he stared at the bloodstained dagger and his blood-splattered clothes. He took several steps back, away from Fidelis lying in a pool of his own blood. Naberus had not felt rage like that since the first time he killed a man, and it was words then too, which ignited his anger. Words from a priest—or, more accurately, a prior. Naberus had never forgotten those words or the savage fury they inspired. Even though the events of that evening had occurred more than a hundred years ago, his memory of that day had never faded.

At the time, he was only twenty-two years old, living at the Monastery of Stoudios, not far from the Sacred Palace. He wore the black habit of a Basilian monk and a shaven tonsure atop his scalp, but he had not yet taken his vows. His mother and grandfather had been enraged at the thought of him choosing a cloistered life in a Christian monastery. They insisted it was a mockery for one of their kind. But Naberus was curious in his youth and wanted to under-stand the Christians and their faith.

Stoudios was the most famous monastery in Byzantium. It had stood for over five hundred years, and its monks illuminated more manuscripts and bound more books than any monastery in Christendom. While Naberus discovered he had a talent for illumination, he spent most of his time in the monastery's vast scriptorium studying religious texts. It was there that he encountered a passage in the book of Genesis that told the story of his ancestors. Though only a few verses long, he became fixated on those words.

When the people began to multiply on the face of the ground, and daughters were born to them, the Sons of God saw that they were fair; and they took wives for themselves of all that they chose. ... The Nephilim were on the earth in those days—and also afterward—when the Sons of God went into the daughters of men, who bore children to them. They were the heroes that were of old, warriors of renown.

Heroes of old ... warriors of renown. The Nephilim of that verse had been his forefathers, and the book called them heroes. So why then had his family and the members of their house been so loathe to even speak of the Christian priests or read their scriptures? Naberus longed for answers, but he found no one among the scholars at Stoudios who wished to discuss the meaning of that passage. It was as if those few verses were forbidden. Tainted. Unworthy of being repeated. Yet why were they in this Bible the monks and priests so revered? A book supposedly filled with words from their God?

Naberus would not give up. When the last of the monks refused to engage with him, he turned to their leader, Prior Symeon. The prior was old for a human, a few years past his sixtieth winter. He was a short, bone-thin man whose tonsure looked like a silver crescent around his bony skull, speckled with the markings of age. The deep creases in his face gave him the look of a wise man, though the constant gleam in his eyes spoke more of cunning than wisdom. The prior was known to spend hours after Compline in the scriptorium reading by candlelight. And that is where Naberus found him on the last night either of them would spend in the monastery.

As large as the naves in many basilicas in Constantinople, the scriptorium was a barrel-vaulted chamber adorned with marble columns and an array of arched windows now closed with heavy wooden shutters to keep out the wind that howled off the Sea of Marmara. Rows of slanted desks ran down the scriptorium, most of which were covered with sheets of vellum and parchment, along with a collection of inkwells, brushes, quill pens, and quill knives— the tools of the scribes and illuminators. When Naberus entered the chamber, the only light came from the glow of a pair of tallow candles at the top of the desk where the prior sat at the end of one of the rows. Hunched over a thick book, the prior carefully turned one of the vellum pages before taking a sip from a pewter cup. Naberus had no doubt the cup contained wine, for the prior's love of books was known to be equaled only by his passion for the fruit of the vine.

Prior Symeon peeled his gaze away from the page when he heard the clap of Naberus's sandals on the stone floor. When the prior turned to look at him, Naberus noticed a redness in the old man's cheeks and the tip of his nose, suggesting the contents of the cup were not his first drink that evening.

The prior raised a bushy eyebrow. "Brother Naberus, shouldn't you be asleep at this hour?"

"How can I sleep, prior, when I have questions no one here will answer?"

"What kind of questions?"

"About a passage in the book of Genesis, when the Sons of God went into the daughter of men."

The prior scowled. "Who told you to read that passage?"

"No one," Naberus replied. "I came across it on my own."

The prior huffed. "You seek dangerous knowledge, Brother Naberus."

Naberus cocked his head. "How can it be dangerous? The book tells of mere history. And it does not speak ill of the offspring of these Sons of God, these Nephilim. It calls them 'heroes' and 'warriors of renown.' Who were these great men?"

"That you interpret the verse of speaking of great men is

precisely why this knowledge is dangerous, particularly to the uneducated mind."

Naberus bristled at the comment. He was hardly uneducated. In fact, he found himself more intelligent and more clever than most of these cloistered monks. How arrogant was this man to believe only he could interpret the verse? "Words mean what they say, do they not?"

The prior set down his cup and stood up from his chair. At his full six-and-a-half feet, Naberus towered over the slight man, who looked up at him indignantly, pointing a bony finger. "In the Bible, the book of Baruch adds clarity to this race of Nephilim. It calls them 'giants, who were famous of old,' and who, because of their great stature, were experts in war. These were the infamous half-men of antiquity, such as Perseus, Orion, and Heracles, born of mortal women and false pagan gods. The men of old saw them as heroes, but they were not. They were pagan abominations. Part of a race cleansed from the face of the Earth when the Lord, God, brought the Great Flood to end their kind!" The prior's face reddened, though his words sent heat coursing up Naberus's neck.

"Abominations?" Naberus questioned, his voice rising. "Old Rome and New Rome were once filled with statues of the heroes you speak of? The Athenians so revered Heracles, they worshiped him as a god."

"A false god," the prior sneered. "And Saint Peter, in his second epistle, tells us what happened to them. For their sin and lust, God did not spare them, but cast them down into the gloomy dungeons of Tartarus to be held until the Day of Judgment."

"Then they have not been finally judged," Naberus pressed. "And what if some still walk among us? Could not they come here and seek salvation, like the rest of the brethren?"

"Still among us?" The prior scoffed. "Nonsense."

"But what if they are?"

The prior's gaze crawled from Naberus's feet to the top of his head, then his face contorted into a mocking expression. "You are delusional. You imagine yourself one of them?"

Naberus gritted his teeth. "Answer my question. Could they not seek salvation here?"

"Never!" the prior spat. "They are beyond salvation, and if you, in your delusions, fancy yourself as one of them, so are you. You and they will burn in the lake of fire for all of eternity!"

Whether it was those words or the contemptuous tone in the man's voice that caused Naberus to snap, he had never been sure. But the words ignited a blinding rage that sent Naberus's left hand slamming into the prior's chest, smashing him against his desk. The impact threw the prior's cup from the table and knocked over the inkwells and jars. With his right hand, Naberus snatched the quill knife from one of the spilled vessels and raised it above the prior's face. A wide-eyed look of horror seized the little man, and words caught in his throat just as Naberus plunged the quill knife into the prior's chest. Naberus hammered the knife, again and again, until he heard bones crack and the prior's black habit filled with blood.

When it was over, Naberus stepped back, huffing breath, aghast at what he had done. The prior's lifeless body slid off the desk, leaving a bloody smear on the pages of the open book he had been reading. His body flopped on the stone floor, lying there dead, just like Fidelis lay on the flagstones in Ahriman's temple.

Lifting his gaze from Fidelis, Naberus turned to the majestic carving of Ahriman on the temple wall. A muscular titan sliding his sword into the belly of the avatar of Ahura Mazda. An image that reminded Naberus how wrong both Prior Symeon and Fidelis had been. For while the Church and their Christ would not offer him salvation, salvation was not beyond him. It would not be denied to him. That is the promise Samyaza had made in Orcus's shrine more than a year ago. On the evening Naberus saw the light.

He grabbed Fidelis by the shoulder and wrenched his body toward the gateway. As he recited the words to open the portal, he watched the deserter's blood fuel the red mist that billowed up the wall.

Then Naberus drew a deep breath and stepped through the gate.

CHAPTER 34
THE VAMPIRE BLADE

Naberus strode onto the ash-gray sand, entering the perpetual gloom of the Otherworldly harbor. The air was warm and humid. In the distance, only one of the great iron braziers atop its towering pillar burned with flames, casting its glow around his master's vessel moored at the harbor.

As Naberus approached, the ship came more clearly into view. The vessel's name was *Mesektet*, the Ship of the Night. It was larger than two Byzantine galleys with a blackened hull that appeared to be built from the spine and ribcage of some titanic sea beast, while scale-like plates filled the spaces between the bones. Down its gunwales ran rows of curved spikes above a score of iron oarlocks fashioned to look like roaring demons. Its bowsprit jutted like the tip of a jagged spear, and a tattered sail hung from its yard with rigging like a spider's web.

As if sensing his arrival, Lovetar sauntered down the ship's gangplank to meet him, followed by two of the hulking oarsmen of Gog. In her supple hands, she carried a sheathed longsword.

Naberus gave her a bow.

"Have you spoken with Astarte?" Lovetar asked. She regarded

him with steel-gray eyes, though the black gem in her forehead seemed like a third eye boring into his soul.

"Yes," Naberus replied, trying to ignore the discomfort he often felt in the priestess's presence. "She was certain she had killed these twins, but if they live, she swears on her life that she'll finish the job."

"They live," Lovetar said without a hint of doubt. "They would be thirteen now. And soon, they will both be in Constantinople."

"How can two thirteen-year-old children pose a threat to our master?"

Lovetar's eyes narrowed. "Like you and I, they are of the seven. They are the descendants of a Moor named Faris al-Basir, one of the companions of Charlemagne, who fought to preserve the secrets of the prophecy and the bloodline of the champion. But the power of the twins comes from a far more dangerous source. From the true enemies of our people, the ones who imprisoned our forefathers. Warn Astarte that they are not to be trifled with. Their end must come swiftly and without mercy."

Naberus could not fathom two children standing against the might of Samyaza, but he had no reason to doubt the Lady of Pain. "It will be done," Naberus promised.

"There is one more thing," Lovetar said. "The sect of magi who protected the twins and their ancestors is alive and well. I suspect they still operate within the city, and I fear they have made contact with Ilat of the Jann. She is as troublesome as Orionde of the Fae had been before she was killed by the warriors of Gog. So beware, the House of Gogam is not the only force lurking in the shadows of Byzantium."

That information surprised him. He could not imagine another force operating in Constantinople without his mother and her spies knowing about it. "I'll beware," he said.

"Good." She held out the sword. It was a narrow blade sheathed in a black scabbard. The hilt was elaborate and graceful, with a cross guard shaped like a dragon. A curved wing protected the grip, and a slender head like a spike aimed toward the blade. The dark metal of the hilt reflected the reddish light of the brazier's flames.

"This is for you," she said, handing him the weapon. "Its name is Murgleis, the Death Brand. Two hundred years ago, a Frankish lord named Ganelon, a devoted servant of the Dragon, nearly stole the Key using this blade. For that is its purpose—it is vampiric in nature. It drinks life but also steals power. And with it, you can seize the Key and end this conflict before it begins."

Naberus took the hilt and drew the double-edged sword from its scabbard. He touched the blade with a finger, and the razor-sharp steel drew a droplet of blood. Naberus winced at the momentary pain; then his eyes widened as he watched the blood disappear as if it had been absorbed into the steel.

Next, she handed him a scroll case made of dark, boiled leather. "Inside is a map to the riverlands of the Otherworld. I have marked the place where you and your ships shall meet us and noted all the landmarks that will guide you there."

"These gifts are more than enough," Naberus replied, bowing his head. "Until we meet again."

"Yes," Lovetar purred. She reached out with a slender finger and touched the disk-shaped amulet hanging at his chest, which she had taken from Malthus before his punishment. "You and I are of the seven," she said, "and together, we shall win this war."

Naberus felt a swell of pride, clutching the deadly gift in his hands. *We will win this war.* "For Samyaza," he said, bringing a thin smile to her lips.

He lingered at the shore long after she had boarded the ship. He watched as the muscular oarsman pulled up the moorings before *Mesektet* drifted away from the harbor. From the demon-shaped oarlocks lining the haunting ship's hull, scores of slender oars dipped into the black waters. They rowed in unison, driving the vessel up the river until it faded beyond sight into the gloom. He knew he would rendezvous with *Mesektet* and his master again, deep within the Otherworld. Without the time to build ships in this ancient harbor, the House of Gogam would have to take a different route, through a gateway less than a week's voyage from the city that would allow their ships to pass into one of the rivers that snaked through the Otherworld on the way to Dudael. The gateway would not open until the Midsummer sabbat, but until then, whatever happened in Constantinople was up to him now.

As he turned toward the gateway, he saw something out of the corner of his eye. Something lying where the black waters met the wet sand. Walking closer, he saw bare feet, long graceful legs, a white shift, and platinum hair matted slickly against a head. He drew a sharp breath.

Theodora's blue eyes stared lifelessly. The side of her lips and left cheek were dark and bruised, and her head was twisted as if she could peer down her spine.

Gazing down at her, Naberus found he felt nothing inside. For a time, she had been his lover, and an extraordinary one at that. She had also been his coconspirator in their plot to kill Pope Gregory, whose sacrifice ultimately freed his master. But Theodora did not turn out to be the woman he had hoped for, the one who carried the Key in her veins. Any feelings he still had for her had died then, so he did not care when his master took her as his own, despite her failings. She should have been honored by that, even grateful. Yet when last they spoke, she had betrayed Samyaza.

"I've seen what he truly is," she had said, *"more like a beast than a man. He's everything the priests warned us about in the basilicas. And he's no savior."*

They were lies—*blasphemous* lies. And if his master had learned of those, as he undoubtedly had, she deserved his wrath.

Naberus turned to leave when he noticed her right hand. It lay limply on the sand, palm opened and covered with some type of luminescent liquid. Naberus crouched down for a closer look. Theodora's palm was slick with faintly glowing blood.

A chill crept up Naberus's neck as he recalled the last thing she had told him: *"The wound at his side still seeps blood."*

He swallowed hard as a chill coursed through his veins. *It can't be*, he told himself, fighting to steady his nerves. *She lies.* But the blood on her palm suggested otherwise.

Naberus shut his eyes, trying to expel the image from his mind. *Samyaza speaks the truth*, he insisted. Samyaza had promised him salvation, and Naberus would not question him now. For without him, they were doomed.

He opened his eyes, feeling clarity in this conclusion. Then he turned his back on the woman's corpse and stormed toward the gateway.

CHAPTER 35

THE SEA GATE

E ven from a mile out at sea, the fortress was a frightening structure.

It stood on a promontory of wave-battered rocks surrounded by a stone curtain wall likely built in Roman times. Behind the wall rose an imposing square keep with crenelated battlements that towered over a natural harbor where a half-dozen ships were moored. Most were similar to the pirate vessel they had overcome, but one was twice its size—the Varangian's drakkar known as *The Reaver*. With that many ships, Ciarán suspected there could be more than two hundred men inside the fortress's walls.

Jarl Holger kept a wide berth around the island as dusk fell over the Strait of Sicily. *Lindworm* curved south, and Ciarán spotted a small cove on the fortress's western face surrounded by cliffs of volcanic rock.

"That's where you will find the Sea Gate," Demetrius told him. "It leads straight into the dungeon."

Anticipation swelled within Ciarán. For nearly a year, he had longed for the day when he might save Josua and the rest of his friends who were captured by Jarl Orn in the English Channel. Orn had sold them to the Varangian, and for months, Ciarán feared for their lives, and that concern lingered like a dull ache in his soul. Yet now, not only had Demetrius confirmed they were alive, but Ciarán was on the verge of saving them. All he had to do was wait for their plan to unfold.

Jarl Holger guided *Lindworm* a mile past the fortress until they found a deserted stretch of beach to make landfall. A new moon was barely visible in the sky, and Ciarán hoped the darkness would shield *Lindworm* from the view of any watchmen in the fortress. Once they were at the beach, it would only be a matter of time.

"The Varangian and his men drink wine like fish breathe water," Demetrius had told them. "No matter that their Allah forbids the fruit of the vine. But the Varangian does not believe in Allah. He is of the Rus and a thing of the Devil. He can drink twice as much as a normal man, but he imbibes like Bacchus himself. Many a night did I have to push those heavy wine barrels up the steps for him from the cellar. Twenty-seven piss-stinking steps! I promise you that well before midnight, most of his men will be so drunk they'll sleep until the morning, when their heads will pound like slave drums. So, the hour before midnight, that is when we should go."

So they waited. Ciarán ate a meal of salted pork and washed it down with watered ale. Others, like Alais, rested, but Ciarán could not imagine sleeping. Instead, he sat on his oar bench listening to the waves, imagining what Josua and the others had gone through, enslaved for nearly a year. When Demetrius signaled it was time, Ciarán jumped to his feet. He slipped on his leather gambeson, followed by the mail hauberk of Maugis d'Aygremont. Over that, he donned his baldric with Caladbolg in its scabbard. He wrapped a dark cloak over his shoulders to prevent even the meager moonlight from catching a gleam of his mail. If there were lookouts on the fortress's walls or atop the keep, they could not afford to be seen.

Ciarán climbed over the side of *Lindworm's* hull and landed ankle-deep in the cold surf. Jarl Holger, Jorundr, Freybjorn, and Strong Bjorn joined him, all dressed for battle beneath their own dark cloaks, followed by Alais and Demetrius. Their guide was still barefoot and bare-chested, and he shivered when he splashed into the hissing tide.

They started up the beach formed of black pebbles instead of sand. When *Lindworm* had faded from view, Jorundr leaned toward Ciarán. "Tell the Greek that if he betrays us, I'll tear his head from his neck."

"Aye," Ciarán said. He relayed the message to a chagrined Demetrius, who earned a merciless glare from the hulking Dane.

"And tell him that after Jorundr removes his head," Strong Bjorn added, "I'll shove his head up the hole in his arse."

Ciarán sighed and passed on the threat.

Demetrius responded with a sheepish grin. "Are they always so violent?"

"Only toward people who make them angry," Ciarán replied. "So don't make them angry."

"Right," he said. He led them along the beach until the top of the fortress peeked over the hilltops. "We are almost there."

Demetrius skulked among the shadows of a shallow cliffside of volcanic rock that marked the edge between the beach and higher ground. Ahead, surf thundered against a natural seawall that protected the cove, spraying clouds of brine each time the waves crashed home. Seawater misted Ciarán's face as he followed Demetrius within the shadows beneath the cliff. Their guide stopped when the cliff wall curved into the cove.

A pool of tidewater filled the cove, save for a narrow pebble beach that rimmed the crescent-shaped cliff on which the fortress stood. The structure appeared to be built into the volcanic rock, and in the darkness, it was hard to tell where the cliffs ended and the gray stone of the fortress began. The fortress's keep loomed sixty feet above the cove.

Where the fortress met the pebble beach, a rusted, iron-bound door had been set into the wall. "That's the Sea Gate," Demetrius said.

Ciarán drew in a deep breath. He reached down to touch the gemstone in Caladbolg's pommel but instead felt Alais' fingers around his hand.

She gave it a gentle squeeze. "Let's go save them."

~

CIARÁN'S MUSCLES tensed as he stood flat against the cliffside, gripping Caladbolg in his right hand. If Demetrius was going to betray them, now would be the time.

The scrawny thief pounded his fist against the Sea Gate; the sound of the blows were drowned out by the roar of the waves crashing against the rocks. Jorundr and Strong Bjorn flanked the gateway.

When the Sea Gate opened, Ciarán tightened his grip around Caladbolg's hilt. A man holding a torch poked his head out of the gate, looking confused. "Demetrius?"

Demetrius held his palms out innocently and shrugged—right before Strong Bjorn yanked the man out of the gateway and slammed him against the cliff wall. The Saracen winced in pain an instant before Strong Bjorn hammered the pommel of his longsword into the man's skull. Strong Bjorn let the man crumple, unconscious, onto the pebble beach.

Demetrius picked up the man's torch and gestured for them to follow him inside the Sea Gate.

When Demetrius disappeared into the gateway, Strong Bjorn ducked in behind him, and Jorundr went in after them. On the other side of the Sea Gate, Holger gestured to Ciarán and Alais, telling them to go next.

As soon as Ciarán stepped inside, the horrid stench of brine and refuse assaulted his senses. Somewhere in the recesses of the chamber, a rat chittered in the darkness.

Demetrius's flickering torchlight illuminated rows of iron bars built into the cave-like chamber. Behind the bars, a host of men slept on the floor, their snores mixing with the pounding surf. *He keeps them like dogs in these filthy cages,* Ciarán realized. He clenched his jaw, glancing around the dank chamber. There were no other guards, but outside Demetrius's torchlight, dark shadows filled the hollows. While he searched for Josua among the sleeping men, he felt Alais' hand on his shoulder.

Demetrius crept up to one of the larger cells, holding his torch and a ring of iron keys he had snatched from a peg on the wall. *"In this one,"* he mouthed to Ciarán. He turned the key in the lock and slowly opened the cell door, daring the rusted hinges to creak. He left the key in the lock and looked around before tiptoeing up to one of the sleeping men.

Ciarán held his breath.

Demetrius shook the sleeping man's shoulder. The man bolted awake. Demetrius slapped a hand over the man's mouth and whispered something into his ear.

Beneath a mane of long, curly hair, the man stared at Ciarán and Alais with a stunned look. Ciarán felt a surge of hope. The eyes were Josua's.

Demetrius removed his hand from around Josua's mouth. His jaw fell open, dropping his scraggly beard to the base of his neck. Josua stood up, shirtless and dirt-caked, with sores marking his chest and arms. He staggered out of the cell, where Alais rushed to meet him, wrapping him in an embrace.

"How is this possible?" Josua muttered. "He said you were dead."

"You're safe now," she told him, her eyes welling with tears. Josua began to sob. "You can go home to Aster and your children."

Fighting back a tear, Ciarán put a hand on Josua's shoulder. "Who else is with you?"

"Only three. Mordechai, Lucas, and Oliver." Josua blinked hard. "How are you alive?"

"Khalil and I were captured by the Danes."

"Is he here too?"

Ciarán closed his eyes and shook his head. "He's with Dónall and Isaac now."

Pain filled Josua's expression.

Alais laid a hand on his cheek. "Find Mordechai and the others. We need to get you out of here."

Josua nodded while casting a wary glance at Holger and the other three Danes.

"They're friends," Alais assured him.

In the cell, Demetrius had woken Mordechai. The strapping

young sailor's hair had grown so long it spilled over his forehead and shoulders, while a thick beard covered everything below his strong, hooked nose. He gazed at them with a look of disbelief before pure elation spread across his face.

Next, they roused Lucas and Oliver from their sleep. The two seamen looked equally awed to lay eyes on Ciarán and Alais.

Ciarán asked Freybjorn to get them back to *Lindworm*. Josua and his crewmates appeared hesitant to follow the Northman, but Ciarán promised he was an ally. "Our ship is waiting a mile down the beach. You'll be safe there. But we have unfinished business here."

As Ciarán completed his explanation, a look of alarm flashed across Demetrius's face. "Aren't we all going back? You have what you came for?"

"Not everything," Ciarán said, leveling his gaze on the scrawny thief. "I still need to speak with the Varangian."

CHAPTER 36
THE VARANGIAN

A dank stairway curved upward from the dungeon to the fortress's great hall. Holding the torch, Demetrius reluctantly led the way.

Ciarán followed behind him, gripping Caladbolg. As they neared the archway that led into the great hall, the air became thick with a scent of smoke, stale wine, and vomit.

When they reached the hall, Ciarán gazed upon the aftermath of what must have been a celebration of pure debauchery. At least a score of half-naked women lay sleeping on a rush-covered floor, where more than twice that many men passed out in various stages of undress, all bathed in the dim light of a dying hearth at the far end of the hall. A legion of cups and goblets were strewn across the darkly stained rushes, while the remnants of a feast littered a long trestle table where a host of rats were cleaning up the scraps.

"Dear God," Alais said under her breath.

Ciarán turned to respond, but Demetrius held a finger to his lips. He pointed across the hall toward a shadowy archway to the right of the hearth. *"We go there,"* he mouthed.

Demetrius started into the hall, tiptoeing like a dancer around the maze of unconscious women and pirates. Ciarán followed, breathing slowly as he padded around the bodies. The thick rushes on the floor muffled his footfalls, but with each step, he feared someone might awake. And, despite their stupor, the sleeping men appeared to be a dangerous lot. Most were rugged, muscular men with sun-browned skin and stern, angular faces. Some, like Jorundr, had wild patterns or images of beasts drawn into their flesh with oak gall ink; others had shaved heads and wore jewelry in their ears. Sword belts with curved Moorish blades lay strewn near the cups and goblets, along with tunics, breeches, and boots, depending on the pirate's state of undress. The women among them were dark-haired, olive-skinned, and often beautiful, and Ciarán had to pull his gaze from their naked breasts or bare hips and the spaces in between.

When their party had reached the far end of the hall, Demetrius led them up another series of stairs that climbed to the keep's upper stories. Fading rushlights burned from brackets in the stairwell, filling the space with the stench of melted tallow. The stairway led to an antechamber with an iron-bound door in the far wall. "That's the door to his chambers," Demetrius whispered. "I doubt it will be locked. Are you sure you want to go in there? He's a monster."

"Who has information we need," Ciarán answered under his breath.

"We enter on my signal," Holger told them. "Jorundr, get the door. Strong Bjorn, if there's a woman in there, don't let her scream."

The brawny young Dane nodded back. Holger drew Curtana from his scabbard and glanced at Demetrius. "Follow us with that torch," he told the thief in stilted Latin. "I don't want to be surprised by anything in the dark."

"Right," Demetrius said, clearly familiar with the language.

As he waited for Holger to give the signal, Ciarán felt Alais' fingers squeeze his left hand. He squeezed hers back, then drew a sharp breath. Holger gave the signal, and Jorundr threw open the door.

The Danes stormed in first. Ciarán and Demetrius charged in behind them, catching a breath of sweat and musk. From a four-post bed against the far wall, Strong Bjorn grabbed a plump, naked woman and slapped his massive hand over her mouth. She fought back, kicking her heels into his shins, but she was no match for his strength. However, the man who sat up in the bed was another story.

As tall as Strong Bjorn with even broader shoulders, the Varangian sat unmoving, staring down the blades of Curtana and Jorundr's sword, their tips pricking his neck. Tattoos covered the Varangian's shaven head, the entire left side of which was scarred and discolored as if it had once been set on fire. A jagged black scar from a knife or sword cut stretched from his forehead to his burned left cheek before it was lost in a thick, graying beard. Along with the scars, the man's prominent nose and hate-filled eyes gave the Varangian a visage that fit Demetrius's description. Ciarán had never seen a man so savage and monstrous.

The Varangian's gaze shifted to the right side of the bed, where his sword belt lay beyond reach on the floor beside the woman's dress. On the other side of the bed, a small wooden table held a carafe of wine. His eyes returned to his attackers with a spark of recognition in his gaze.

"Jarl Holger," the Varangian said, his mouth twitching into a subtle grin. "It seems we're no longer allies."

"We were never allies," Holger growled.

The Varangian turned to Ciarán. "You're the Irishman. The one he paid us to kill. You and the Moor. But I don't see that one."

Ciarán's anger flared. He leveled Caladbolg at the Varangian's neck. "Where's the man who paid you to kill me?"

"Ah, Naberus da Roma," the Varangian said through a grimace. "The alchemist, the astrologer, the *consigliere*." The Varangian chuckled under his breath.

That's when Ciarán noticed the chains. Five of them, worn around the Varangian's neck and over his hairy, tattooed chest. Four were silver. One featured a hammer of Thor, while the other three were adorned with crude pendants: a shark's tooth, a bear's claw, and a seashell. But it was the golden chain with a circular medallion that caught Ciarán's eye. A disk with a seven-pointed star and a dragon's head shaped like an inverted pentagram in its center.

Ciarán tapped the medallion with the tip of Caladbolg's blade. "Where did you get that?"

"It was a gift for being such a loyal ally."

"Let me see it," Ciarán said.

With his free hand, Holger reached over and tore the golden chain from the Varangian's neck. He handed it to Ciarán.

Ciarán studied the medallion. It was similar to the amulet Gerbert had found on one of the Nephilim who had attacked them on the Palatine Hill. A crown tipped each of the points of the heptagram; however, unlike the one Gerbert found, this one had a series of letters in the spaces between the pentagram-shaped dragon.

Together, the letters spelled a word:

G-O-G-A-M

"Gogam?" Ciarán asked. He narrowed his gaze on the Varangian. "What does it mean?"

"The House of Gogam," the Varangian replied. "It is his family's name. You know him as Naberus of Old Rome, but he hails from *Nova Roma*—Constantinople. Some say his family is ancient, so old they came from Old Rome with Emperor Constantine to found his new city. A few believe the family gained its wealth and power through a deal with the Devil himself. But now they rule the shadows of New Rome. Smuggling, gambling, brothels—they all belong to the House of Gogam. And no one lives long who gets in their way, which is why it is good to be one of their favored allies." The Varangian's grimace spread into a cruel smile.

Ciarán had not expected that Naberus da Roma had a connection to the city where they were headed. And somehow, Naberus's family had come to embrace the same seven-pointed symbol that Gerbert equated with the Dragon. Perhaps through a deal with the Devil himself, if anything the Varangian said could be trusted. "When was the last time you saw him?" Ciarán demanded.

"When I ferried him and his warriors to Old Rome several weeks before the pope's death."

His warriors? Ciarán wondered if the Varangian spoke of the Nephilim they had fought on the Palatine Hill, which would explain the similarity between the medallions. However, Ciarán and Gerbert had always assumed Naberus brought the Nephilim up from the Otherworld through the gateway in the Etruscan shrine. How would he bring them from Constantinople?

"I've not seen the *consigliere* since," the Varangian said. "And now I serve the Sword of the Faith. He pays just as well. But I can see that's not enough for you." His gaze shifted from Ciarán to Holger. "Will you give me my sword?"

"Why would we do that?" Ciarán snapped.

"Because a man knows when he's going to die." The Varangian jerked his head toward Holger. "I can see it in his eyes. He is a Danish lord, and he knows it is unwise to let one's enemies live. Let me die with a sword in my hand so I might see Valhalla."

Holger regarded the Varangian for a moment before turning to Jorundr. "Give it to him."

"We don't have to kill him!" Ciarán objected. "My lord, you're a Christian now."

Holger glared at Ciarán, then glanced at Jorundr. "Get him his sword."

Ciarán's mouth hung open as Jorundr nodded grimly. The hulking Dane sheathed his blade, then reached for the Varangian's sword belt, but it was no longer on the floor. Demetrius held it in his hands.

"No," Demetrius snarled. He tore the Varangian's sword from its scabbard.

Alais gasped.

Ciarán's eyes flew wide as Jorundr tried to grab Demetrius, but the scrawny man was too quick. In a fury of rage, he stabbed the blade into the Varangian's neck.

The Varangian choked on his scream.

"Die, you miserable bastard!" Demetrius said through gritted teeth as he ripped out the sword and plunged it back into the gaping wound.

Ciarán staggered back. Jorundr wrapped Demetrius in a bear hug, pulling him off the Varangian, whose massive right hand slapped his chest as if searching for the blade. Holger grabbed the Varangian's hand and brought it to the sword's hilt jutting from his neck. The pirate's fingers brushed the pommel before his hand fell limp onto the bedsheets.

During the commotion, Strong Bjorn must have taken his hand from the woman's mouth, for right then, she let out a blood-curdling scream.

She wailed a second time before Strong Bjorn shut her mouth, only to hear Jorundr yowl in pain. Demetrius was biting his arm, struggling to get free, until Jorundr ripped out his own sword and smashed its pommel into the thief's skull. Demetrius's head fell limp. Meanwhile, a chorus of alarmed cries came from the stairwell, while there was a whoosh of fire in the chamber. In his rage, Demetrius had dropped the torch. Flames were crawling across the bed, filling the chamber with smoke.

Ciarán could hear men pounding up the stairs, crying out in Arabic.

Alais shot him a worried look.

"Something just went awry," he conceded.

"Yes, it has," she replied, rolling her eyes.

Ciarán felt a thrum in the air as she began reciting words of power, gesturing toward the burning bed. The flames roared as if fueled by her power, turning the bed into a blazing funeral pyre for the Varangian.

"Alais?" Holger asked warily, backing away from the burning bed, which was throwing off heat like a bonfire. Strong Bjorn, looking just as wary, let go of the woman, who began screaming hysterically.

Alais motioned for them to get against the wall before moving her right arm in a circulating motion. The flames surged, gathering into a round shape until she threw her arm forward, hurling the enormous ball of fire out of the chamber and into the stairwell.

With a thunderous boom, the fireball exploded down the stairs, drowning out the yells of men and shaking the wooden floor beneath their feet.

Ciarán felt the pulse from the blast in his bones, followed by a surge of relief.

"That should clear out the stairwell," she said.

Ciarán nodded, still in awe. But then, a new roar echoed from the floors below—a cacophony of men, desperate and alarmed.

"You cleared the stairwell all right," Holger said irritably. "But you've woken the entire bloody fortress."

CHAPTER 37

IN THE BELLY OF THE BEAST

E very nerve in Alais' body tingled as the cries erupted from the chambers below them.

A moment ago, Ciarán had imbued his soul light into the gemstone within Caladbolg's pommel, and now the weapon's blade blazed with white fire as he led the charge down the stairwell through a lingering haze of smoke. She knew that the weapon in all of its fearsome glory would terrify most of their would-be attackers and send them fleeing like rats from a burning ship. But some would stay and fight, and Alais knew their numbers could still overwhelm her, Ciarán, and the three Danes.

"Columcille!" Ciarán yelled the name of his patron saint as he bound down the stairs. Holger and Strong Bjorn roared behind him while Jorundr trailed after them, having slung the unconscious Demetrius over his broad left shoulder. Alais followed Jorundr, skipping around the bodies of Arab pirates. Whether they lay dead or unconscious from the fireball, Alais could not tell, although their skin was red and swollen from the heat of the blast.

Ciarán reached the hall first, and the screams that followed confirmed that the power of Enoch's device had struck fear into the pirates' hearts. Behind the Danes, Alais burst from their stairwell into the hall. The drunken revelers who had been sleeping in a stupor had woken now, and they had been joined by a horde of their comrades spilling into the hall from an adjacent antechamber that must have led to the barracks. There were four or five dozen pirates bathed in the hearth light and the glow from the white fire blazing from Caladbolg. At least half of them had dropped their curved swords and were clawing past the rushing horde to escape the terror brought on by Caladbolg's fiery blade. Though more than a dozen were raising their scimitars and hollering in Arabic, pressing toward Ciarán and the Danes.

Swinging Caladbolg in a wide arc, Ciarán cleaved through the initial wave of attackers. Men screamed as the fiery blade shattered scimitars and seared through flesh and bone. Curtana punched through the chest of another raving attacker while Strong Bjorn bloodied two more of the much smaller men with his longsword. A thick-bearded pirate rushed past Jorundr, driving his curved blade toward Alais. She darted back and, barely thinking, summoned the full force of her soul light through the palm of her outstretched hand. The burst of light lanced into the face of the rushing pirate, blinding him instantly and allowing Jorundr to hammer a sword blow across the man's naked back. The pirate collapsed at Alais' feet, dying from his wound.

Alais felt a surge of energy and a sense of clarity. She knew the spirit inside her had survived countless battles, and she let her instincts take over. As Ciarán and the Danes cleaved their way through the onslaught of pirates, Alais used her soul light with devastating precision, blinding attackers on all sides. When a new wave of pirates flooded the hall from the antechamber, Alais whispered words of power to summon a fierce blast of wind that toppled the trestle table and sent its contents—cups, goblets, knives, and rats —hurling into the new arrivals. The stunned pirates proved no match for Ciarán and the Danes, wielding their blades with a deadly effect.

"Columcille!" Ciarán repeated as he fought.

"*Odi-i-i-n-n-n!*" Jorundr hollered.

"*Lifthrasir!*" Strong Bjorn cried.

Around them, a dozen or more pirates barked Arabic curses as they charged into the hall. One leaped through the air at Ciarán, only to be impaled by Caladbolg, whose fire rushed into the wound and burst like a torch's flame from the dying man's mouth. The screams of three more pirates were silenced by the hiss of Danish blades. When the pirates' swords struck home, the blades glanced off mail coats or Ciarán's hauberk. The bare-chested pirates, however, had no such armor to protect against the Danes' deadly strikes, and within a breath, four more of the pirates met their end as Ciarán and the Danes pressed on toward the stairwell that led down to the dungeon.

By the time Alais reached the archway that led to the stairwell, at least twenty-five bodies lay sprawled on the bloodstained rushes, and the air stank of sweat and blood. The several pirates still standing were backing away into the antechamber while Ciarán motioned for Alais. "Head for the Sea Gate," he said, huffing for breath.

She hurried down the stairs only to find the dungeon alive, with men hollering and banging on the bars of their cages. The cage that held Josua and Mordechai was empty, and the sea gate stood open. Alais estimated the slaves numbered two score across three cells. She recalled the image of Josua and his crewmates wasting away in this dungeon and knew what she needed to do. She searched for the ring of keys and found them still hanging from the lock in the empty cage. After rushing to grab it, she began opening the three cells.

Strong Bjorn emerged from the stairwell. "What are you doing?" he asked hurriedly.

"Freeing these men," she told him.

The caged men gazed at Alais as if she were some angel who had come down from heaven as she unlocked the cells. Some stormed right past her toward the sea gate, while others clasped their hands in gestures of gratitude, tears welling in their eyes. Ciarán and Holger helped usher the freed slaves out of the gateway.

Jorundr nodded toward Demetrius, slumped unconsciously over his shoulder. "Can I leave the bastard here?" Jorundr growled.

Ciarán shook his head. "No, we owe him more than that."

243

Jorundr grimaced before carrying the unconscious thief through the Sea Gate. Alais followed him into the briny night air. Waves boomed against the seawall surrounding the cove. Ciarán trailed behind her, sheathing Caladbolg at his side. In a breath, Holger and Strong Bjorn joined them.

Ahead, in the moonlight, the forty or so freed slaves were splashing through the cove as they fled the fortress. Jorundr followed them but stayed along the narrow pebble beach beneath the cliff wall. Alais trailed close behind him, with Ciarán, Holger, and Strong Bjorn on her heels. Through the thunder of the waves, something whizzed past her ear. Suddenly, the slaves in front of her began to stumble and plunge face-first into the cove. Alais' eyes flew wide as she saw arrow shafts jutting from their backs. The slaves started screaming as more and more fell to the thudding rain of arrows. An instant later, Strong Bjorn cried out. An arrow sunk deep into his right shoulder.

Alais glanced behind her and felt a surge of fear. The fortress walls had come alive with torchlight, casting an orangish glow on scores of archers leaning over the battlements.

Jorundr dove beneath a curve in the cliff wall, throwing the unconscious Demetrius onto the rocky beach, where he landed with a moan. Her heart pounding, Alais lunged toward Jorundr as an arrow shaft exploded into the volcanic rock above her head. The curve in the cliff, less than ten feet wide, acted as a shield against the storm of arrows, but it did nothing to aid the fleeing slaves, who continued to fall beneath the deadly barrage.

Holger and Ciarán pulled Strong Bjorn beneath the cliff. Blood was pooling through the mail covering his shoulder where the arrowhead was buried. Holger grabbed the arrow shaft. "This will hurt," he told Strong Bjorn. He yanked the arrow, but it did not budge. Strong Bjorn roared in pain.

Alais' gaze fell to a broken arrow tip on the wet pebbles. The arrowhead was barbed. "You're going to need to cut it out," she said. "When you do, I can stop the bleeding."

Holger gave a grim nod. He broke the arrow shaft, shortening it considerably, and then he and Ciarán helped lift Strong Bjorn's mail coat over his head. Strong Bjorn clenched his jaw while the tears in his eyes betrayed his pain.

Alais handed him a shard of driftwood, one of many washed ashore. "Bite down on this."

He did as she told while Holger pulled a knife from his belt. Arrows continued to pelt the volcanic rock atop the cliffside; others rammed into the pebble beach less than a yard from where Alais pressed herself against the cliff wall.

"Be quick about this," Jorundr said urgently. "Once they realize they have us pinned behind this wall, they'll send men out the sea gate to hunt us down!"

"I'm working as fast as I can!" Holger shouted.

Alais' muscles tensed as Holger cut into Strong Bjorn's bare shoulder. Blood pulsed from the cut. Strong Bjorn grunted in agony, biting down on the driftwood shard as Holger dug out the barbed arrow tip. As soon as she saw the metal free of the wound, her hand was on Strong Bjorn's shoulder with a verse flowing from her lips born from the language of creation. She felt the thrum in the air as the power took hold of the Dane's flesh. She imagined weaving together the severed strands of muscle as she recited the words, recalling her teaching from Gerbert and drawing upon the innate knowledge residing within her spirit. That knowledge had come to her so effortlessly since her mind was awakened months ago in the Temple of Venus and Roma, and she watched now as the blood receded and the wound began to close under the power of the ancient verse uttered beneath her breath. When it was done, Strong Bjorn closed his eyes and breathed a relieved sigh. He would need rest, she thought, before realizing that the hammering of arrow strikes had stopped. All she could hear were the waves.

"They'll be coming out the gate!" Jorundr warned.

"We can't move," Ciarán said sharply. "As soon as we leave this position, those archers will have a clear shot."

Alais knew Ciarán was right—they were trapped here. Her gaze drifted across the bodies of slaves lying face down in the cove with arrows in their backs. Men whose lives had been stolen by these pirates and who died without mercy only moments after tasting freedom. Murdered by the men who would be storming from the sea gate to kill them all. A fierce determination welled within her as she recalled the voice that had screamed inside her head at the Theatre of Pompey. *"You are Sirra!"*

She peered around the curve of the cliff wall. Fifty yards across the cove, the sea gate stood open in the fortress wall. The fortress was much larger than the theatre had been, but it was still made of stone. She drew a deep breath and placed her hand on the volcanic rock. *I am Sirra,* she told herself before speaking the words of power to crack the earth. As the verse rolled off her tongue, the air began to sizzle, and the cliffside started to shake, followed by the ground beneath her feet.

"What are you doing?" Holger asked with alarm.

Alais ignored him, focusing on the verse and creating a fissure that traveled along the cliff wall. The cliff quaked violently, and as the tremor spread, it began to collapse, dropping tons of rock into the cove.

"Leave her be," she heard Ciarán tell Holger as the fault line spread along the cliff until it reached the foundation of the fortress.

The structure began to shake, and soon the rumbling of the tremor drowned out the crashing of the waves. Men cried out from the battlements while others stepped warily away from the Sea Gate. The water in the cove was frothing like a cauldron as the earthquake spread. On the side of the fortress wall, a crack formed in the stone, crawling upward and branching out like a leaf-bare oak. Stone bricks were shaken from the battlements, and the keep looming above the fortress walls began to sway. Alais repeated the verse, each time with more vigor, throwing all of her energy into the effort. Ahead, the rest of the cliff crumbled into the cove as the tremor roared louder, only to be joined by a thunderous crack from the fortress. The keep's foundation gave way. A hail of stone and dust rained down on the archers as the structure caved in. The ramparts split, spilling more men into the imploding heap of stone and debris. A massive piece of the curtain wall gave way and plunged into the cove, blasting water into the air and mixing with billowing dust as the Varangian's fortress collapsed into a mountain of rubble.

It took several minutes for the ground to stop shaking. And when it did, Alais found Ciarán and the Danes gaping at her in awe.

She looked at Ciarán. "Aren't you glad I came along?"

Still staring, he gave a faint nod. Then he reached out and wrapped her in an embrace.

CIARÁN AND HOLGER helped Strong Bjorn to the beach, where *Lindworm's* crew waited beneath the moonlight.

Freybjorn and Hári Grayhair rushed to the aid of their crewmate, while Breda threw her arms around Holger.

"Was that an earthquake?" Freybjorn asked Ciarán. The beardless Dane had a bewildered look on his face.

"Aye," Ciarán replied. "But it was one of Alais' making. She took down the fortress and saved our lives."

"*Lífthrasir,*" Freybjorn muttered reverently, wrapping his hand around the pendant of Thor's hammer hanging around his neck.

Ciarán glanced at Alais, and she gave him a warm smile. His mind was still in a haze from the moment they had shared. If only he had reached out and kissed her. But his vows had held that instinct in check.

"Get aboard the ship," Holger called out. "We'll row by moonlight until we're away from this place."

The crew followed the jarl's orders, scrambling aboard the ship while others pushed the vessel into the lapping tide.

Alais took Ciarán's hand as he helped her aboard. They found Josua, Mordechai, Oliver, and Lucas huddled in the stern with Pietro and Tara. Josua sipped on a cup of ale, a grateful expression on his face. "You came back for us," he said. "I never thought it possible."

"I only wish we could have saved you sooner," Ciarán admitted.

"Brother Ciarán never ceased planning for this day," Pietro added.

"It wasn't all me," Ciarán said with a shrug. "There's a priest named Niccolo you'll need to thank if you ever return to Rome.

Without his efforts, we might have never found the Varangian's lair."

Josua grimaced at the mention of the pirate lord's name.

Alais placed a hand on Josua's shoulder. "He's gone," she told him gently. "He won't be terrorizing anyone ever again."

"I hope he rots in Sheol," Mordechai said. You know, we almost escaped from the devil once in Rome when he brought Naberus da Roma and those men back to the city."

Ciarán raised a brow. "You were on that voyage?" The Varangian had mentioned it too. "What do you remember about those men?"

"They were warriors who served Naberus. And they were large men, as tall as the Varangian. Some even taller."

"And there was one more," Josua said. "A giant brute who never removed his helmet. He must have stood eight feet tall. I wonder if he was even a man like us."

None of them were, Ciarán thought. He remembered the medallion Gerbert had taken from one of those men on the Palatine Hill. The one that looked similar to the medallion he had taken from the Varangian. Ciarán removed it from his belt pouch. "Did one of those men wear a medallion like this?"

Josua took the medallion, studying it. "I believe so."

"Did you hear them speak about something called the House of Gogam?"

"Maybe," Mordechai replied. "It's a place in Constantinople, I think, where they came from."

Josua shook his head. "But there was another name that they called it. It reminded me of a Hebrew word. One I'd heard my Uncle Isaac and Brother Dónall speak of during our voyage to Córdoba. But I can't think of it now."

"A Hebrew word?" Ciarán said, surprised. *And one Dónall and Isaac had spoken of?* Ciarán took back the medallion and focused on the words surrounding the image of the dragon. Ciarán felt fairly certain Gogam was not a Hebrew word.

"Can I see it?" Pietro asked. Ciarán handed him the medallion. After a moment, Pietro's eyes grew wide.

"What is it?" Alais asked.

Pietro held out the medallion. "Unlike Latin, which is read from left to right. Hebrew is read from right to left."

As Ciarán read the word backward, a chill washed over his skin. Read from right to left, the meaning of the letters was unmistakable.

M-A-G-O-G

Ciarán spoke the word out loud.

"That's the one," Josua said. "The House of Magog."

"Blessed Sergius," Pietro muttered.

"What does it mean?" Mordechai asked.

Ciarán swallowed hard. Suddenly, everything he learned from the Varangian took on a new and terrifying meaning. *An ancient family ... who made a deal with the Devil ... who now rules the shadows of New Rome.*

He glanced at Alais and could tell from the look in her eyes that she had reached the same conclusion. He rubbed a hand across his face. "It means that the Nephilim—the race of Magog—haven't been trapped in the Otherworld like we thought. Instead, they've been living in secret among us. And since the reign of Constantine, they've made their home in Constantinople."

"Which means," Alais said gravely, "we're sailing straight into the arms of our enemies."

PART THREE

When he opened the fifth seal, I saw under the altar the souls of those who had been slaughtered for the word of God and for the testimony they had given ...

— Revelation 6:9

CHAPTER 38

SAILING TO BYZANTIUM

Twelve days after their assault on the Varangian's fortress, *Lindworm* arrived at the port of Sithines in the land of Greece.

The massive port consisted of three harbors, each crammed with merchants' cogs, sailing ships, and fishing boats, while seagulls hovered above the planks where the fishmongers gutted their daily catch. Beyond the harbor, a town crawled up a rocky peninsula, and behind it, atop the distant hills, stood the ancient city of Athens. Ciarán marveled at the sight. The midday sun shone off a columned citadel crowning the highest hill. At the foot of the crag rose stone buildings with grand archways older than those of Rome standing amid pillar-like cypress trees and sprawling gardens. It was a city of legend. The place where Socrates once roamed the plazas, where Plato had written his philosophy, and where Aristotle had tutored Alexander the Great. Ciarán longed to walk through its fabled streets, but knew he must forgo any hope of seeing that glorious place. For their mission remained urgent. And today was the day Josua would leave them.

His friend had announced his intentions the day after being freed. "I have given too much for your cause," Josua told him. "My oldest boy is gone, and I have not seen my wife or my daughters or my youngest son—my only son, now—for more than a year. I feared I would never see them again, and I wept for them every day in that cell until the tears stopped coming. You convinced me once of the importance of your cause. And the fact that you still pursue it with such fervor tells me you still believe it to be true. But if it is, and the world might end were your mission to fail, as you Christians believe, I would rather spend the End of Days with my wife and children in my arms. So I cannot go with you. I have to return to Bordeaux."

Alais had wept at Josua's words. Ciarán knew she still carried guilt for the death of Eli, Josua's oldest son. He had died in Córdoba trying to save her from a Moorish arrow. So, Ciarán could not blame Josua. He knew now what love felt like, and had it been Alais waiting for him halfway across the world, he wondered if he, too, might make the same choice.

Josua told them the port of Sithines was the largest in Greece and was popular with Venetian merchants. Not long after they had arrived, Pietro used some of the silver coins the pope had provisioned them with to buy Josua passage on a merchant's cog bound for Venice. Lucas and Oliver chose to go with him. Their families were in Bordeaux, too, and the two crewmen shared Josua's longing for home. Only Mordechai elected to stay. Ciarán knew Mordechai harbored a fondness for Alais, and perhaps that is why he decided to remain with *Lindworm's* crew. But Ciarán also knew that Mordechai was brave and strong and an expert with a bow and arrow. They could use a man like him on this voyage.

Lindworm set sail from Sithines on the sixth day of June. Mordechai and Demetrius took their places on the oar benches, adding to the longship's depleted crew. After leaving the Varangian's island, Demetrius begged them to take him home to Constantinople. Jorundr argued vociferously against this, hoping to throw the scrawny thief overboard into the Mediterranean Sea. But Ciarán believed Demetrius's knowledge of the city might prove helpful, particularly now that they knew the disturbing truth about the House of Gogam. So Holger had overruled his old friend, and Demetrius eagerly embraced his role as an oarsman.

Within a day, they were sailing in the bright blue waters of the Aegean Sea through the legendary Greek Isles. Ciarán remembered reading Homer's *Odyssey*, and he wondered now if they were sailing around the same islands where Odysseus defeated the Cyclops or Circe turned Odysseus's crew into swine. He imagined the nymph Calypso might have seduced Odysseus on one of these rocky isles, and questioned how close they might be to the straight of Scylla and Charybdis when the ship passed between two of the smaller islands.

Several days later, they moored in Myros on the island of Lemnos. The small Greek fishing village, which had stood on the isle since before the time of Herodotus, is where they would rendezvous with Gerbert's ships carrying the Dragonslayers after they had recovered the scrolls in Constantinople. They stayed the night in Myros, but before they left, Pietro delivered a message from the pope to the parish priest asking him to await the arrival of the papal vessels and provision them with food and drink. The old priest protested at first, claiming his parish was poor and the fishing had not been good this year. But when Pietro handed the priest a purse full of silver coins, it changed his attitude and brought a half-toothed grin to his age-worn face.

The day they departed Myros, *Lindworm* passed through a narrow strait flanked by sandstone cliffs into the Sea of Marmara. The following afternoon, a storm rolled into the inland sea, forcing the longship to make landfall at a beach on the western shore. According to the map Pietro had brought on the voyage, they would arrive at Constantinople tomorrow. "Get a good night's sleep, "Pietro said. "We'll have much to do tomorrow once we find the Syncellus. "

"Aye," Ciarán replied. Ever since he began lashing Caladbolg to his arm with a leather belt, the Dragon had not invaded his dreams, and after weeks of hard rowing, Ciarán welcomed sleep whenever he could get it. But first, he wanted to see if his theory about Demetrius's usefulness might bear fruit.

He found the Greek warming himself around one of the several campfires built by *Lindworm's* crew. Demetrius was clad now in a proper wool cloak and a linen tunic with homespun breeches and leather boots, part of the clothing that Pietro had procured for him and the other freed slaves on the Greek isle of Kythira. Although, like everyone on *Lindworm*, Demetrius's clothes were damp from the earlier storm. Around the far side of the campfire, Strong Bjorn and several of the younger Danes ignored Demetrius, drinking ale and laughing at whatever stories they shared.

Ciarán sat down beside Demetrius as an ember cracked in the fire. "Tomorrow, you'll be home," Ciarán said.

Demetrius flashed a smile of bright white teeth. "I've longed to return there. I suspect some of my guildmates have missed me."

"Guildmates?" Ciarán had never heard the word.

"A guild is an association among craftsmen that looks out for its members' interests and prevents nonmembers from operating within the city. Almost every trade has a guild in New Rome. There is a bakers' guild, a candlemakers' guild, an innkeepers' guild, a leather cutters' guild, and even an alchemists' guild. And there is a guild for my trade, too."

"A thieves' guild?"

"We prefer to call it the procurers' guild," Demetrius said with a sheepish expression. "For that is why the wealthy in New Rome tend to hire us. Procuring things they covet from their rivals."

"In your trade, have you ever come across a wealthy family that calls themselves the House of Gogam?"

Demetrius gave him a knowing look. "They say New Rome is the wealthiest city in all the world, but with that comes scheming and assassinations. And where *that* is concerned, chances are the House of Gogam is behind the murder. They are dangerous people; I can assure you of that."

"I have no doubt. But I want to know how to spot them. How to avoid them."

Demetrius chuckled under his breath. "I've spent my entire career trying to avoid them. It's easier said than done. Their homes are walled palaces on the Golden Horn, near the Venetian ward. No one in my guild would dare procure anything from them. If you are worried about them, stay far away from their palaces, and I would stay away from the brothels and the gambling dens, too. But you don't look like the type who would enjoy such places. It's said they avoid the emperor's court, so you will not find them near the Imperial Precinct unless it's a racing day, of course."

"Racing day?"

"The chariot races. Do they no longer have those in Old Rome? Well, they are huge in New Rome. They take place in the Hippodrome, where the greatest charioteers in the world compete before the emperor and sixty-thousand screaming fans."

The number made Ciarán's jaw drop. "That's more people than all of Rome!"

"All of *Old* Rome. They say New Rome has over four hundred thousand people within her walls."

Ciarán could hardly believe his ears. That would mean Constantinople rivaled Córdoba in size. And he did not think there was another city as massive as Córdoba in all the world.

"Trust me," Demetrius went on, "in a city that large, it's easy to operate in the shadows, as the House of Gogam does. Outside their palaces, they are hard to find. But if they want to find you, they will. They say no one escapes their reach."

Demetrius's words roiled Ciarán's stomach, for what if the House of Gogam knew he and Alais were headed to Constantinople? Ciarán did not recall mentioning the city in his last encounter with the Dragon, but he remained concerned the Dragon could have stolen that knowledge from his mind. But even so, Ciarán reasoned, the Dragon had not visited him since their voyage began, so how would he know when they would arrive? It was the only thought he could take comfort in.

"Let's hope they're not looking for us," Ciarán said.

Demetrius frowned. "Why would they be?"

"No reason," Ciarán lied. "I should get some sleep."

Ciarán left Demetrius by the campfire and climbed aboard *Lindworm*. He found Alais dozing in the stern next to Tara and Pietro, who had curled up beside the iron-bound chest that contained their coins and the relics the pope sent as gifts to the Patriarch of Constantinople. Tara and Pietro were sound asleep, but Alais opened her eyes as Ciarán approached.

"You look troubled," she said.

"It's nothing," he replied, sitting down beside her.

She closed her eyes and rested her cheek on his shoulder. He welcomed her touch while his thoughts drifted back to what Demetrius had told him. He prayed they could get in and out of Constantinople without attracting the attention of Naberus or his family. But what if the House of Magog knew they were coming? He shuddered at the thought, unable to shake the feeling of how dangerous this mission had become.

ON THE DAY they would arrive in Constantinople, Ciarán took the oar bench closest to the stern, across from Demetrius. Following the storm the night before, the Sea of Marmara was thick with swells, rocking *Lindworm* from side to side as the crew rowed through the dark blue waters. Jarl Holger had removed the dragon head from *Lindworm's* prow, as he had done each time they approached a foreign port. After all, the last thing most people wanted to see was a dragon-prowed longship nearing their shores.

By late morning, the city came into view. Ciarán stared in awe at its size: a metropolis as spectacular as Córdoba, sitting atop a rocky promontory where stone walls rose from the very sea itself. Above those walls towered domes, pillars, and hundreds of buildings that climbed the city's hills. Among them were countless churches with round spires and domed roofs clustered near mansions and houses three stories high, along with arched aqueducts and towering columns. Near the promontory's eastern end sat a sprawling palace with golden domes and a lighthouse alongside tree-filled gardens. Behind the palace stood a hulking edifice of white marble topped with a massive dome, gilded along its rim and at its peak, reflecting the sun as if it were a brilliant jewel crowning Constantinople.

Up and down the rowing benches, the Danes uttered in amazement as they gazed upon the glory of the city they called Miklagard. Ciarán imagined that, in all their travels from Scandinavia to England and France, they had never seen such a marvelous place. And outside of Córdoba, Ciarán doubted a more magnificent city existed anywhere in the world.

"What's that?" Ciarán asked Demetrius, pointing to the enormous domed structure.

"That is Hagia Sophia," Demetrius replied, "the church of Holy Wisdom."

Even from this distance, Ciarán marveled at the structure, which looked larger than even Saint Peter's Basilica in Rome. Hagia Sophia is where they would find the Fifth Seal among the Jerusalem Scrolls, and for the first time on this voyage, their mission's goal seemed nearly within reach.

Demetrius gestured toward a sprawling palace in front of the Hagia Sophia and the curved facade of a titanic arena. "That is the Sacred Palace, where the emperor lives, and behind it is the Hippodrome, where the chariots race. The emperor has a secret passageway that leads from the Kathisma, where he watches the races, to the palace. He has a similar passageway into Hagia Sophia."

"How do you know?"

Demetrius gave him a little smile. "I may have used it once."

"You broke into the emperor's palace?" Ciarán asked incredulously.

"No," Demetrius shook his head. "I *broke* into Hagia Sophia and then *snuck* into the emperor's palace. Her name was Maria. She was one of the emperor's serving girls, as beautiful as Cleopatra. We made love in the garden under the stars. But alas, only once. For the emperor married her off to one of his soldiers."

"You snuck into the palace for a woman? I thought you were going to tell me you stole something from the emperor."

Demetris wrinkled his face. "Do you think I'm crazy, stealing from the emperor? No, this was a labor of love. But I *did* break into Hagia Sophia. I'm very good at my job."

Ciarán just shook his head. However, he was beginning to appreciate the lengths one might go to for love.

"Besides," Demetrius added, "I've found another, almost as

beautiful. With luck, she'll be waiting for me." He punctuated his words with a wink.

As *Lindworm* neared the enormous seawalls, the Hagia Sophia became even more awe-inspiring. Thick buttresses on the church supported archways and half-domes, climbing like giant steps to a circular arcade upon which stood the spectacular gilded dome. Trees surrounded the structure, flowing westward into the Sacred Palace, where more gardens decorated the spaces between what looked like a half-dozen smaller palaces, halls, and churches as if the emperor's abode was a small walled city attached to the larger metropolis. Orchards and flower gardens meandered down the hillside, framing a flat green field before the seawalls eclipsed the rest of the view.

"What's that meadow in front of the palace?" Ciarán asked.

"It's a polo field," Demetrius said. "They play a game there on horseback with mallets and a little ball. The Arabs invented it, I think. But they say the emperors have been playing it for hundreds of years."

Ciarán shook his head in awe. In all his life, the only sight to rival the Sacred Palace had been the caliph's palace of Medinat al-Zahra outside of Córdoba, where giraffes and gazelles had grazed in gardens of lavender and palm trees.

Lindworm followed the curve of the promontory, giving Ciarán a view of the eastern face of the Hagia Sophia. He got the sense the Church of Holy Wisdom was square, like the Church of Santa Maria Rotunda, instead of cross-shaped like most of the basilicas throughout Rome and the cathedrals in France.

"We're entering the Bosporus," Demetrius said, referring to the narrow straight between the city and the rocky cliffs on the eastern side of the waterway.

Fishing boats and trading vessels sailed the strait where gulls soared in the pale blue sky, occasionally diving into the Bosporus, hunting for fish. As *Lindworm's* crew rowed northward, the promontory curved to the west, where a fortified tower stood like a sentinel. Here, the strait forked where another rocky promontory emerged from the sea with a similar fortified tower adjoined to another walled settlement. "Demetrius gestured to the nearest of the forti-fied towers. That is the Kentenarion Tower, and across the way is the Kastellion Tower. Behind it is Galata, where the Jews live. The towers guard the entrance to the Golden Horn. Look, we are coming up on the chain."

From each of the towers, a gargantuan chain three times the size of the chains that can block the Tiber in Rome dipped into the water. Ciarán could see wooden floats beneath the titanic links, keeping the chain near the surface. When pulled tight, Ciarán imag-ined the chain could block the entire channel, nearly a thousand feet wide, preventing any vessel larger than a rowboat from passing into the Golden Horn.

Lindworm entered the channel into the crowded harbor that rivaled that of Sithines. In fact, there appeared to be four harbors along the Golden Horn compared to Sithines's three. In the nearest harbor, more than a hundred vessels packed the harbor and the waters up to the stone and timber wharves. Many were stout merchant cogs and trading galleys with sails but no oars, although there were sleeker vessels with triangular sails and oarlocks similar to the Saracen ship they had encountered off the Sicilian coast. Among these were sloops and fishing boats, along with a flotilla of smaller craft, some with square sails and others mere rowboats moving about the busy harbor where the cries of gulls filled the air.

Holger called to his crew, ordering them to slow their pace as he tried to steer *Lindworm* through the tumultuous crowd of vessels. Not long after, a thick-hulled, pot-bellied craft that looked to Ciarán like a small cog bobbed through the choppy water, nearing *Lindworm*. The vessel's eight-man crew wore bronze helmets and crimson cloaks and carried round shields and spears. "Who are they?" Ciarán asked Demetrius.

"Tax collectors," Demetrius said. "They work for the Harbor Master."

Having handed the steering oar to Breda, Holger strode toward the prow, his hand on Curtana's hilt.

"I'd better go," Ciarán groaned. He leaped up from his oar bench and hurried after Holger, who was yelling at the men in the vessel. Its hull bumped against *Lindworm's* prow, and one of the burly, bearded guardsmen tried to board the longship, but Jorundr blocked his path. The hulking Dane shoved the man into his ship, where he staggered backward into two of the spearmen. The man's face flushed with rage. "How dare you! I am captain here, and by the authority of the Harbor Master, you shall let me board! And you'll pay for laying a hand upon me, barbarian!"

Pietro pushed his way in front of Jorundr. "He meant nothing," Pietro stammered. "He's not used to letting strangers board his ship, that's all."

"Stupid barbarian," the captain snarled. For the first time, Ciarán was grateful the Danes did not understand Greek. "Let me board," the man demanded. "You must pay the *Kommerkion.*"

"Pardon?" Pietro asked.

The captain huffed. "The customs tax on all goods you're bringing to the city. I also need to document your names and your cargo. And you must pay a fee for a berth in the quay, not to mention a heavy fine for that barbarian's insolence." Not a drop of anger had drained from the captain's reddened face; Ciarán did not like where this was heading.

"We come on authority of His Holiness, the pope," Ciarán announced.

"Ha!" the captain scoffed. "You are barbarians, save for this monk. The pope sending barbarians—do you think I'm an idiot?"

Ciarán suddenly became aware of his own appearance. He stood there bare-chested, his skin slick with sweat from rowing. His beard had thickened during the voyage, and his hair had grown to his shoulders. Around him gathered the Danes, many inked flesh and arm rings, with some wearing the hammer of Thor around their necks. No wonder the captain did not believe them.

"Who does this fool bastard think he is?" Holger growled.

"Calm down, everyone!" Pietro snapped in Latin. "Let this man board, and let me handle it."

Ciarán instructed the Danes to let the man aboard while Pietro pushed his way toward the stern through the mass of curious Northmen. They let the captain climb aboard the ship, though Ciarán kept a wary eye on Jorundr in case he decided to throw the man into the water. The captain was stout and muscular, but he would be no match for Jorundr or Strong Bjorn, who peered menacingly at the tax collector.

"I don't like this one damn bit," Holger told Ciarán under his breath.

"Pietro will take care of it," Ciarán insisted.

A few moments later, Pietro returned from the stern, waving a letter bearing the papal seal. He handed it to the captain. "A letter of transit from His Holiness Pope Sylvester the Second."

The captain eyed the letter skeptically. He opened it, and his lips moved while he read it to himself. When he looked back up, the redness had faded from his sun-bronzed face. "If this is a forgery, you'll hang for this."

"It's genuine, I assure you," Pietro insisted. "What will the patriarch do to a man like you when he learns you've held up the pope's emissaries from Rome?"

The captain scratched the chin of his beard as his lips twisted into a grimace. "I'll have to take this up with the Harbor Master." He held out his palm. "You must still pay a fee to berth your vessel. Even the pope would honor such a standard request. Pay it, and for now, at least, I'll forgive the actions of the barbarian who laid hands on me when I tried to board."

"How much?" Pietro demanded.

The captain told him, and Pietro paid the price with coins from the small purse tied to his belt. "We'll follow his boat to our berth," he told Holger.

Grateful they had avoided what might have been a disaster, Ciarán headed back to his rowing bench. Demetrius hunched over on his bench as if he had been hiding behind the group of Danes. He shrugged as Ciarán approached. "What? I've found avoiding interaction with the authorities leads to a healthier life in my line of work."

Ciarán shook his head. Then his gaze fell on Alais. She had both arms around Tara, who held her head in her hands. Rosta was licking her forearm.

Alais looked up at Ciarán.

"Is something wrong?" he asked.

Alais whispered something to Tara, then stood up and guided Ciarán toward the other side of the ship. "This place is bringing back bad memories. Remember what happened to her family here."

"Aye," Ciarán said. "I should have known." Recalling what Alais had told him about Tara's family reminded him of what Demetrius had said about the assassins of Constantinople. A thought sprung to mind. "Is it possible?"

"That the House of Magog suspected Tara was one of the two witnesses?" Alais finished his sentence.

"So they tried to kill her." Ciarán rubbed his forehead.

"I have to believe that's true," Alais said firmly. "But this time, she has us. And heaven help the first one of them who tries to lay a hand on her."

CHAPTER 39

THE GOLDEN HORN

W hen Tara first laid eyes on the city, the memories rushed home like a flood.

The grapplings slamming into the deck. The boat lurching violently, and her sister's grip coming free of her hands. Their father frantically picking Sara off the deck moments before the other ship crashed into their vessel's stern, and the black-clad assassins flying onto the ship before plunging their long knives into the crewmen. The tall woman with the moon-shaped birthmark and the cold way she spoke to their mother. *"Hand them over, Shirin."*

Tara could hardly believe she was back in those waters, which that night burned with flames. Never had she imagined returning to this place, and nothing Father Michele had told her about a voyage on a ship that looked like a dragon had prepared her for this moment. A feeling of dread weighed on her shoulders. She wanted to hide, but on *Lindworm*, there was nowhere to go, and with each stroke of the oars, the vessel moved closer to the place where those assassins came from.

The dread within her threatened to burst into panic before Lady Alais recognized her distress and tried to comfort her. "It'll be alright," Alais assured her. "Seven years have passed. No one would remember you now, and I suspect no one thought you'd ever return to Constantinople. If they even believed you survived what had happened at sea."

Tara prayed she was right—she had to be right. *Be brave,* Tara told herself. If only it were working.

She did, however, take some small comfort in being surrounded by *Lindworm's* crew, particularly as they pulled on their tunics, leather vests, and chainmail coats once the longship moored at a berth in the crowded harbor. Seven years ago, her family had not been accompanied by warriors like these or Lady Breda and Brother Ciarán. Waiting in the stern, Tara dug her fingers into Rosta's coarse fur. He had remained by her side for most of the voyage, and she reminded herself that on that night, there had been no boarhound to protect them either.

Tara watched as Brother Ciarán, Brother Pietro, and Jarl Holger disembarked the ship and followed the red-cloaked captain and his tax collectors into the noisy, bustling wharves. Dockworkers, fishermen, merchants, and seamen thronged the wharf, moving crates, sacks, and chests onto and off of ships of every shape and size, hollering back and forth between the men on board and those on the piers. Mixing with these sounds were the cries of seagulls feasting off the remains of fish cleaned by fishermen right on the docks while other seabirds hovered above the chaos, squawking incessantly. Around the piers, the air smelled of fish and brine, along with a hint of refuse from the sewage floating at this end of the harbor. Tara wrinkled her nose at the stench.

"Time to go," Breda said, stretching her limbs.

Alais placed a comforting hand on Tara's shoulder. "You're safe with us."

Tara gave her a wary nod.

Freybjorn helped Alais onto the wooden pier, followed by Tara. After Breda joined them, Rosta stood up to go next. "No Rosta," Breda said. "Stay on *Lindworm* and guard the ship."

The boarhound answered with a disappointed look and slumped down on the deck planks with a long sigh.

"Where will we go from here?" Tara asked.

"To the house of some priest who works for the pope," Breda explained. "He will take Ciarán and Pietro to the people they need to see."

"I've heard the priest lives in a palace," Alais added.

Breda rolled her eyes. "I lost count of how many palaces I saw on the way in. They say Miklagard is the richest city in the world. You'd think everyone here lives in a palace."

Tara did not remember growing up in any palace. What pieces of memory she could conjure from her childhood were of a small but comfortable home with a warm hearth. She recalled the aroma of basil and tarragon lingering in the air, along with the scent of stewed lamb and a spicy paste called harissa. And she remembered the banter. During the daytime, it filled the house and the homes on their narrow street. Their neighbors were friendly people, just like her family. Not Greek, but Persian. She wondered where in this massive city her old neighborhood might be if it was still here at all.

They waited on the pier with the Danes, Demetrius, and the handsome young man named Mordechai, whom they freed on the pirate isle. Whatever the red-cloaked captain was doing with Brother Ciarán, Jarl Holder, and Brother Pietro was taking an awfully long time. Tara was beginning to sweat beneath her cloak in the noonday sun when she felt a strange feeling, like they were being watched.

She scanned the busy wharf. *Lindworm's* crew was earning its fair share of glances from the dockworkers and sailors, but while some of those glances lingered for a time, none were outright staring at them. Except for a man sitting on a large crate about a quarter of the way from the piers to the towering city walls. He was dressed in a flowing, long-sleeved tunic, with his legs hanging over the side of the crate and what looked like slippers on his feet. Young and clean-shaven, he wore a floppy hat that matched the dark-blue color of his tunic. He was chewing something, and Tara saw him spit out a nutshell. When her eyes met his, the man did not look away. Instead, he winked at her.

Tara's muscles tensed; she tugged Breda's arm.

"What's wrong?" Breda's eyes narrowed.

"There's a man watching us."

"Where?"

Tara nodded in the man's direction. Though now he had turned away from them and was talking to a very tall, broad-shouldered man with a scraggly black beard. The tall man, who looked much older than the man sitting on the crate, was leaning on a thick wooden staff knocked with lines up and down its shaft.

"Them?" Breda asked. "They look like merchants. That staff is a measuring stick. I wouldn't worry about them. Besides, I doubt they've ever seen a longship as fine as *Lindworm*. And maybe they've never seen a Dane in their lives."

"But he was staring at *me*," Tara insisted.

Breda twisted her lips. "They look like they're talking business."

Before Tara could say another word, she heard Jarl Holger returning to the pier. He was complaining in Danish, but Tara had picked up enough of their language on the voyage from Rome to understand what he was saying.

"These Miklagardians are brazen thieves!" the jarl ranted. "They want to tax anything that enters the city—everything but our shoes and clothes. I've never encountered greedier men in all my life. There's even a fee to enter the city gates!" He balled his hands into fists. "And the documents. They wanted each of our names, where we were from, and why we're here. No man should stand for this."

"Did they know you are a jarl, my love?" Breda asked.

"They did not care," Jarl Holger replied through gritted teeth.

"I will say," Brother Ciarán added, shaking his head, "there's a certain arrogance about this place. And they wanted all of this in writing. What a waste of good parchment."

"Why not grab our shields and spears and go take our money back?" Strong Bjorn suggested. "We can show them the Danish way of things."

"There will be none of that!" Brother Pietro insisted, albeit clumsily in the Danish tongue. "Give unto Caesar what is Caesar's, and give unto God what is God's. And *that's* whose work we're here to do. So put aside any talk of armed resistance, and let's find the Syncellus."

Tara imagined this Syncellus was the priest they were going to see. Demetrius claimed he knew where the man lived and offered to take them there. In the meantime, Tara kept sneaking glances at the man in the floppy hat. He was still talking to the very tall man with the staff, but every once in a while, he would look back their way. The sight of his gaze sent a chill down the back of her neck.

Someone tapped her on the shoulder. "Let's go," Alais said.

The party that set out to find the Syncellus consisted of Brother Pietro, Brother Ciarán, Alais, Mordechai, and Tara, along with Jarl Holger, Breda, and two more of the Danes: Jorundr and Strong Bjorn, who carried the iron-bound chest containing the holy relics Brother Pietro had brought from Rome. Demetrius guided them through the congested wharf toward the enormous double gates that led into the city. Tara looked up to admire the walls of white stone, which had to be at least forty feet tall. Twin towers, ten feet taller than the walls, flanked the gateway, topped by battlements crowned in reddish brick similar to that decorating the crenelations on the walls. *I remember these,* Tara thought.

After climbing a series of broad stone steps, they reached the gateway, where they were stopped by a quartet of red-cloaked guardsmen. Brother Pietro, however, showed them something written on a square piece of parchment, and the guards waved them through.

When they had passed beneath the gateway through a fifteen-foot-long tunnel, Demetrius turned to them and stretched out his arms. "Welcome, my friends, to Nova Roma, the greatest city in all the world!"

Tara had little doubt Demetrius's boast was true once she saw the city that awaited them. A broad avenue ran between rows of shops and houses two and three stories high, many of which had colonnaded porticos like the finest buildings in Rome. In the distance stood a plaza dominated by a soaring obelisk and a statue of an emperor on horseback. People filled the lively corridor, including merchants pulling carts and guiding mules and horses piled high with goods; men and women dressed in colorful, flowing tunics and cloaks; and simply clad porters carrying ornately carved litters. Flagstones paved the avenue, which, to Tara's astonishment, was completely free of the mud and refuse that forever plagued the old Roman streets around the Convent of Minerva.

When they reached the plaza, Tara found it was as large as any she had ever seen. Columns with hanging golden banners outlined the vast rectangular space, which on the outskirts harbored tents and stalls for a sprawling marketplace, while near the obelisk, a pair of jugglers performed before an expectant crowd. The market was full of noise and people bustling about. From a quick glance, it looked as if someone could purchase anything here. There were merchants selling perfume, olives, spices, cloth, pottery, and vegetables of every kind. Others offered candles, leather, jewelry, fur, and even live birds of brilliant green, yellow, and red. As they entered the market, the aroma of baked bread and sizzling meat wafted from the stalls, making Tara's mouth water after weeks of eating fish and salted pork.

"It's amazing," Breda remarked, eying a merchant's stall displaying rolls of blue silk interwoven with gold and silver thread.

"Only in Córdoba have I seen anything like it," Alais said.

"It's just like the bazaars in Córdoba," Mordechai added with a wide-eyed expression. "Évrard and Josua would have loved this place."

Alais gave Mordechai a warm smile while Breda wandered over to the silk merchant's stall.

"We don't have time for this," Brother Pietro protested. "The pope was very clear. Our first mission is to find the Syncellus."

"This won't take but a moment," Breda said, waving Pietro off.

Alais followed Breda, and Tara joined them. The silk merchant displayed racks of fabric in an array of colors as wondrous as Tara had ever seen. Breda ran a yard of blue silk through her fingers before turning to Tara. "Ask what this is."

Tara asked the silk merchant, a woman in her middle years with a bright face browned by the sun. She wore long, dark hair in intricate braids that joined behind her head. "It's called samite," the merchant said. "Tell your mistress it would look splendid on her."

"Am I talking to myself?" Brother Pietro held out his palms. The rest of their party had joined the women around the silk merchant's stall while the monk's face wrinkled into an annoyed expression. "We have to get to the Syncellus," he insisted.

A minute later, Pietro sniffed the air, and his expression melted. Tara caught it, too: a delectable whiff of warm honey.

"What do we have here?" Brother Pietro asked, raising a brow. He looked down the row from the silk merchant's stall. Past the tent of a craftsman displaying elaborately painted bowls of various shapes and sizes stood a baker's stall selling palm-sized honey cakes. "I suppose the Syncellus could wait a few moments for some of those."

"I suspect we all could use one," Brother Ciarán said.

Tara felt overjoyed when Brother Ciarán and Mordechai returned with handfuls of the sweet-smelling cakes. Mordechai offered her one. "It smells delightful," he said, flashing a grin.

She thanked him and took a bite. The flavor nearly caused her to swoon: rich honey mixed with warm, spicy cake. She could not remember eating anything so magnificent in all her life.

After devouring the cake and licking the honey off her fingers, Tara's gaze drifted to the stall to her right, where a man with a thick mustache was selling necklaces beneath a rich, woven canopy. The jewelry dangled from gracefully carved wooden racks. She began admiring one necklace made of beautiful amber beads when she felt eyes on the back of her neck.

Slowly, Tara glanced over her shoulder. Six stalls down stood the young man with the floppy hat. He stared at her intently, sending a prickle down her skin. The man was taller than he had looked sitting on the crate, so tall he could see over the heads of everyone in the crowd.

"Lady Breda!" Tara whispered.

"What, child?" Breda asked, stepping near her.

"The man from the wharf. He *followed* us."

Breda narrowed her gaze. "*Veslingr!*" she swore. Her left hand clutched the hilt of her sword. "Wait here—I'll find out what he's up to."

Breda started pushing her way through the crowd.

When the man spotted her, he bolted into a gap between two stalls.

"*Veslingr!*" Breda yelled. Then she tore off after him.

"WHAT IN THE name of the gods?" Holger swore under his breath.

He had no idea why his wife called some stranger a *Veslingr*—an annoying coward—and went after him. The man, who was tall, maybe even taller than Holger, darted into the gap between two merchant stalls. Breda ran after him with her hand on the hilt of her sword. If the man had done anything to offend her, Holger might kill the man himself. But the last thing he expected to do after arriving in Miklagard was murder one of its citizens. Yet judging from the look in Breda's eyes, that's exactly what might happen if Holger didn't stop her.

Without a glance at his companions, Holger barreled into the pathway Breda had carved through the stunned crowd. He dashed into the gap between the stalls, his broad shoulders knocking against one of the tentpoles. The merchant cried an angry protest, but by then, Holger had emerged from the market into a narrow street framed by stone and timber buildings. Twenty strides away, he glimpsed his wife's fiery red hair as she sprinted into an alleyway on the left.

"*Vámr!*" Her voice rang out as she hurled another curse at the man.

Holger turned into the alley, his heart pounding. "Breda!" he hollered, but she veered down another narrow street.

This place is a gods-forsaken maze! Holger thought, chasing after her.

The street ran between rows of shops and houses with brick facades. Twenty paces ahead, Breda charged down the street, weaving her way between a heavyset peddler pulling a cart and a small crowd gathered around a bread stand outside a bakery. Moving swiftly, the lanky man with the floppy hat was another twenty paces ahead of Breda. He veered into another alley, nearly toppling the stand of a startled fruitmonger.

"Breda!" Holger cried again.

This time, his wife glanced over her shoulder.

"Husband," she said, not slowing down. "Help me catch him!"

"Who is he?"

"He's been watching us since we arrived!"

Holger muscled his way past the large man with the cart and followed her down the alleyway. *How does this man even know who we are?*

The alley was narrower than the others, twisting left, then right between buildings so close together their roofs all but covered up the sun. Breda slowed down, allowing Holger to reach her. Up ahead, the lanky man slowed his pace. He gave them a mocking wave of his hands before skipping beneath an archway that bridged the buildings on either side.

"He's taunting us," Holger growled.

"*Veslingr,*" she cursed again.

Holger and Breda strode after the man—until a figure stepped into their path beneath the archway. The stranger was a towering man, taller even than Strong Bjorn, and built just as broad. A scraggly black beard dripped from a cruel face over a long gray tunic. In his huge hands, he clutched a thick staff, wielding it like a weapon.

As he eyed Holger and Breda, his lips spread into a fiendish grin.

CHAPTER 40
JÖTUNN

Everything happened so fast. One moment, Ciarán was enjoying a delightful honey cake outside a silk merchant's stall, then a breath later, Breda was yelling at a man six stalls down before darting after him with her hand on the grip of her sword.

Holger charged after her, drawing gasps from the stunned crowd. Both he and Breda disappeared between two tents, as did the man they were chasing, whoever he was.

Ciarán's hand flew to Caladbolg's hilt. "What just happened?"

Alais turned toward him, concern etched on her face. She had her arms around Tara. The girl looked scared.

"She said a man followed us from the wharf," Alais told him.

A stab of alarm struck Ciarán hard. He already feared the Dragon might have discovered their intentions, but the possibility he had spies waiting for them in the harbor made that fear all too real.

"What in the name of Blessed Sergius is going on?" Pietro asked, with crumbs stuck on the chin of his beard. Beside him, holding the chest full of relics, Strong Bjorn looked equally confused.

Demetrius cocked his head. "Was it a pickpocket?"

"No," Alais said urgently. "Someone's been following us since the harbor."

"Should we go after them?" Mordechai asked.

"Absolutely not!" Pietro exclaimed. "We have to find the Syncellus."

"So you'd have us leave them?" Ciarán snapped.

Pietro's expression hardened. "Jarl Holger and Breda are more than capable of taking care of themselves. But what we cannot do is risk getting lost in a city this large playing some game of cat and mouse when we have a mission to complete. We need the Syncellus to get to the patriarch, not to mention the emperor. How else do you hope to get your hands on those scrolls?"

The alarm rising within Ciarán edged toward dread. "What if the House of Magog knows we're here?"

"And if they do," Pietro said firmly, "the one who needs protecting is right here with us." He cast a sideways glance toward Tara.

Ciarán let out a frustrated sigh, but Pietro was right.

"I'll follow them," Jorundr said with a look of grim determination.

"Good," Pietro replied. "Find us at the Palace of Antiochos. That's where the Syncellus lives."

With a nod, Jorundr stormed through the crowd, heading for the tent behind which Holger and Breda had disappeared.

Watching Jorundr go after them eased some of Ciarán's concerns. They're warriors, he reminded himself, and they've fought Nephilim before. But he needed to stay with Tara and Alais. For if the House of Magog had indeed learned of their arrival, protecting the two of them was more important than anything in the world.

HOLGER PLACED his hand on Curtana's pommel. The towering man with the scraggly black beard clutched his quarterstaff in both hands, watching them with a wolfish gaze.

"Move aside!" Breda commanded in broken Latin.

The man did not move. Instead, he chuckled under his breath.

Holger glanced sideways at Breda. She gave him a subtle nod before ripping her sword from its sheath. Holger pulled his own blade free of its scabbard. This interloper was no battle-hardened Northman, so Holger expected to make quick work of this fool. With a nod toward Breda, they charged.

The tall man backpedaled into a small courtyard between two buildings with closed doors and shuttered windows. With a furious roar, Holger swung his blade in a downward arc, aiming for the man's shoulder, while Breda lunged low, stabbing at the man's thigh. Moving faster than a person this large should, the man caught Curtana with the right end of his staff before dropping the left end to knock away Breda's sword. He jerked forward, stabbing the butt of his staff into Breda's stomach, knocking her on her rear.

Holger responded with a high backhanded strike that should have cleaved into the man's neck, but the man parried the attack hard, throwing Holger off balance. The next thing he felt was the quarterstaff slamming into his ribs. Holger grimaced as he crashed into one of the building's brick facades. The last time he had taken a blow that hard was when they fought the jötnar on the Palatine Hill, on the night Naberus da Roma freed the Dragon. Holger found the thought of a jötunn in the heart of Miklagard hard to believe, but the threat this giant of a man posed was all too real.

Breda jumped to her feet, hollering her own battle cry. But the man was ready for the attack. His quarterstaff met her blade so hard it tore the weapon from her grasp. Holger responded with a flurry of sword strikes. The man jerked his staff back and forth, blocking each one as the clack, clack, clack of Curtana's steel on the hardwood shaft filled the courtyard. Having retrieved her sword, Breda swung low at the man's left shin, but with surprising agility, he raised his leg, and her blade passed harmlessly beneath his sandal. In the same breath, he kicked his foot into Breda's chest, sending her flying backward.

Holger saw his chance. With the man balanced on one leg, he sliced Curtana sideways. This time, the razor-sharp blade scraped across the man's ribs, tearing through his tunic into his flesh.

Roaring in pain, the man spun away, quickly regaining his balance. Holger lunged, thrusting with his sword, but the man whipped the staff upward, stopping Holger's blade. Then the man kicked out with his right leg, catching Holger in his exposed gut. The force of the blow knocked the wind from Holger's lungs. He staggered back as Breda rushed the man, landing a slash across his thigh.

The man roared with rage. He rammed the butt of his staff into her shoulder, spinning her around. Then the top of his staff, swung in a vicious arc, slammed into her cheek. A scream caught in Holger's throat as he saw Breda's head whip backward before she collapsed onto the flagstones.

As he struggled to regain his breath, a sudden coldness struck Holger in his core. Breda was lying on the ground, unmoving.

Standing over her body, the man chuckled again under his breath. "I thought you'd be a worthier foe after what you did to our brethren in Rome," the man said in a deep voice, speaking fluent Latin.

Holger narrowed his gaze. This *is* a *jötunn*.

"Your bitch of a woman," the man continued, "was easy to put down. So now I kill you in the name of Samyaza."

Holger knew that name, for Ciarán had mentioned it. *It was the name of the Dragon.*

He readied Curtana, glimpsing the runes running down its steel blade. They reminded him of the day Blind Mikkel had translated them. *"It says, 'My name is Curtana, of the same steel and temper as Joyeuse and Durandal.'"* According to Ciarán, they were three legendary blades forged by Orionde the Fae. One of the Vanir in the language of his people. *What better weapon to slay a jötunn?*

He drew the sword closer to his lips. "Curtana," he whispered, "I need all of your magic now."

Gripping his sword with both hands, he raised it above his head and bellowed a new battle cry. *"Curtana!"*

With all of his strength, Holger swung the sword. The man lifted his staff to parry the blow, but Curtana struck the hardwood with a sound like a peal of thunder. Against the might of the Fae blade, the hardwood splintered, shattering the staff in two. The man gaped at his broken weapon as Holger struck again, like a woodsman chopping a log. Curtana buried its blade in the man's chest.

The wheezing sound of a final breath hissed from the man's lips as Holger wrenched the sword free. The man stared unblinking before toppling backward like a felled tree, landing hard on the flagstones. Not bothering to clean the blood from the blade, Holger slid Curtana into its scabbard and rushed to Breda's side.

Her beautiful face was red on one side and beginning to swell. He put a hand under her head; her eyelids fluttered, and she groaned.

Holger's spirits soared. *She's alive.*

He lifted her off the ground and carried her in his arms, only to see Jorundr running toward him.

"What happened?" Jorundr asked in alarm.

"We were attacked," Holger replied grimly. "The jötnar we encountered in Rome are in Miklagard, too."

Jorundr blinked in astonishment.

Holger grimaced fiercely. "And seeing you here tells me they've succeeded in dividing us."

CHAPTER 41

THE SYNCELLUS

Tara kept peering over her shoulder, unable to shake the feeling she was still being watched.

Her worry for Lady Breda only made the feeling worse. Jarl Holger and Jorundr had gone after her, but none of them had returned, and Tara could not help but wonder if the man with the floppy hat had somehow eluded them.

Tara held hands with Lady Alais as they made their way up the broad avenue, heading toward the home of this important priest called the Syncellus. Demetrius, Brother Pietro, and Strong Bjorn led the way past enormous mansions, magnificent monasteries, and churches with domed roofs. Mordechai took up the rear along with Brother Ciarán, who looked tense, eying everyone they passed with his hand resting on the pommel of his sword, Caladbolg. Crowds of people dressed in colorful cloaks and flowing tunics moved up and down the avenue. Many shuffled between storefronts, cookshops, and fruit stands along the street while a tide of peddlers and merchants guided carts and pack animals to and from the harbor, alongside the occasional litter born by teams of slaves or servants. Somewhere in that throng of humanity, Tara feared, the man with the floppy hat had his eyes on her, observing her every move.

The deeper they journeyed into the city, however, the less crowded the streets became. Many shops and storefronts looked closed, and the fruit and vegetable stands that had lined the avenue mere blocks away were nowhere to be seen. The din of a hundred private conversations gave way to a new yet unexpected sound: trumpets and horns blaring in the distance.

"What is that?" Alais asked.

Demetrius turned toward her and spread out his palms. "We're nearing the Hippodrome. The afternoon races must have started."

Tara could not remember what the Hippodrome was, but she understood quickly once Demetrius led them down another wide street perpendicular to the main avenue. At the far end of the street loomed a colossal structure. It reminded her of Rome's Colosseum with its pillared arcades, but this Hippodrome was much larger and more rectangular in shape, as if it stretched for blocks on end. The sound of trumpets and horns mixed with cheers and applause.

"That's where they race the chariots?" Mordechai asked.

"They do," Demetrius replied. "It's home of the Blues and the Greens, the finest charioteers in the world. That's why the shops here are all closed. Everyone goes to watch the races. I'm partial to the Greens, myself. They have the boldest drivers and the prettiest dancers."

"Can we stick to the task at hand?" Brother Pietro groused. "We're not here to see a chariot race; we're here to find the Syncellus. Are we anywhere near his palace?"

"We're getting there," Demetrius said with a hint of annoyance. "It so happens his palace stands in the shadow of the Hippodrome."

Demetrius was not lying. Turning down another street, they found a pair of palaces with a church in between them. Each of the structures was hexagonal in shape, surrounded by circular turrets with domed or half-domed roofs. The top of the tallest dome must have stood forty feet high, but that paled compared to the massive Hippodrome, which towered another twenty feet behind the palaces. Groves of trees and manicured gardens nestled around the palaces and the church, and Tara might have heard birds singing in the branches if their song had not been overwhelmed by the thunderous roars erupting inside the massive stadium.

"Which one is the Palace of Antiochos?" Brother Pietro asked.

Demetrius pointed to the farther of the two palaces. "That one, attached to the Church of Hagia Euphemia."

After passing the church, Demetrius escorted their party around a semicircular portico lined with pillars that reminded Tara a bit of the cloister at the Convent of Minerva. The portico opened into another garden with column-like cypress trees and beds of purple violets, green herbs, and yellow chrysanthemums. A pathway cut through the garden, ending in stone steps that led to a pair of imposing bronze doors.

"Finally," Brother Pietro huffed. He smoothed out the wrinkles of his black habit and wiped the sweat from his bearded jowls. "Strong Bjorn," he announced, "join me with the relics."

The giant Dane nodded, looking eager to be rid of the heavy chest he had hauled all the way from the harbor. He followed Brother Pietro to the doors while Tara and the rest of their party waited at the base of the steps. No other people were in the garden, and the few on the street they just left appeared to be heading to the Hippodrome. For the first time since their arrival, Tara felt as if they had escaped whoever had been spying on them. She hoped that once they were inside the Syncellus's palace, she would feel even safer.

Pietro rapped on the doors, and a moment later, they opened, revealing a large, thick-bearded priest wearing black robes and a square-shaped hat. "Can I help you?" the priest asked. The burly priest spoke Greek and had a deep voice, so Tara could hear him well enough over the occasional roars flaring up from the nearby stadium.

Brother Pietro held up the letter bearing the pope's seal. "I am Brother Pietro of Rome, Papal Librarian to the Holy See, on a mission for His Holiness, Pope Sylvester the Second. I've come to speak with the Syncellus, Severus Synadenos."

The priest gave him an amused look. "We've had no notice of a papal emissary. But that seal looks real enough. Unfortunately, you'll have to wait."

"Wait?" Brother Pietro scoffed. "I was sent by the pope. His Holiness's mission cannot be delayed."

"Well, His Holiness the pope should not have sent you on racing day," the priest said. "The Syncellus is with the emperor and the patriarch in the Kathisma. It's well-known that His Eminence, the Syncellus, is an enormous fan of Scortius of the Greens. He never misses a race."

"Blessed Sergius!" Brother Pietro threw up his hands. "How long will that last?"

The race will be over before sunset," the priest replied, still amused. "But afterward, His Eminence will join the emperor at a banquet in the Sacred Palace. Those tend to last a while."

"For the love of God, we can't wait for banquets! Or races, for that matter. I'll go find him myself."

The priest raised a bushy brow. "Do what you must. Though best of luck getting past the Imperial Guard."

Tara did not like where this was heading. This priest seemed far from deferential to the wishes of a pope, and she could sense Brother Pietro growing more frustrated by the minute.

"Even emperors must honor requests from the pope," Brother Pietro said with a huff. He glanced at the iron-bound chest clutched in Strong Bjorn's massive hands. "May we leave this chest in your care? It contains gifts from the pope to the patriarch. It's not to be opened under any circumstances. Understood?"

The priest wrinkled his nose. "The pope's gifts will be safe here."

As Strong Bjorn entered the palace to set down the chest, Brother Pietro stormed back to their party. "Demetrius, can you show me the way into that stadium?"

Demetrius ran his fingers over the chin of his beard. "You want to get inside the Kathisma while the emperor is there?"

"Do you think that's wise?" Brother Ciarán asked. Tara had been wondering the same thing. She had never stood in the presence of an emperor or a king and could not imagine doing so now.

Brother Pietro sighed. "Can you think of a better option? If your suspicions are correct about our enemies lurking in this city, we may not be the only ones looking for the Fifth Seal. And I don't want to think of the consequences should *they* find it first. The sooner that scroll's in our hands, the better."

The mention of enemies in the city sent a flutter through Tara's stomach. Alais put a hand on her shoulder. "It will be alright," she said under her breath.

"Can you do it?" Brother Pietro asked Demetrius.

Demetrius gestured toward the purse tied to Brother Pietro's belt. "I have friends among the Greens. If there's enough coin in that purse, I can make it happen."

Brother Pietro clapped his hands. "Very well, then."

Once Strong Bjorn returned, they headed toward the street, and Tara tried to stanch her growing unease at the thought of venturing back into the city. From inside the stadium, trumpets sounded a triumphant tune mixed with a wave of raucous applause. "Another race is starting," Demetrius said.

Within a half block, a row of taverns led toward one of the Hippodrome's towering gates, and the smell of cookfires filled the air. Young women, who were far less modestly dressed than those Tara had previously seen in the city, lingered outside the establishments alongside small gaggles of shifty-looking men. One of the men, a short fellow with a weasel-like face, scurried up to their party as they neared the gate.

"Care to place a wager?" the man asked with a smile full of rotting teeth. "The Blues are favored in the next race, but there's good money to be had on the Greens!"

"Not today," Demetrius replied tersely.

"How about you, young man?" the weasel-faced man grabbed Mordechai by the sleeve of his tunic. "You never know when Lady Fortuna will favor you?"

Tara's muscles tensed as Mordechai jerked his arm free. She was afraid the man might harass her next when she noticed another group of people hurrying toward the gate. There were six of them, more than a hundred paces away, but moving fast. When she saw the floppy hat on one of the men, Tara's blood froze.

With him were four other men, tall and lean, wearing dark blue tunics and flowing blue cloaks. A woman joined them, nearly as tall as the men, dressed in a long, blue stola. Her long dark hair was pulled tight behind her head, and though Tara could not see it from this distance, she knew the woman had a crescent-shaped birthmark beneath her left eye.

For after seven years, the woman who murdered Tara's family had found her.

CHAPTER 42

INTO THE HIPPODROME

Tara grabbed Alais' arm hard; the girl's face looked ashen. "They're here," she said in a worried tone.

Alais spotted the six figures, a woman and five men, including the man from the harbor. All six were tall and lithe, and Alais had little doubt Tara was right.

"We have to run!" Alais exclaimed.

Demetrius and Pietro shot her puzzled looks while Ciarán locked eyes on the six figures. "Gogam assassins," he said urgently to Demetrius.

The thief's eyes widened. His gaze darted in every direction.

The six figures were less than eighty paces away, moving fast with long strides.

With catlike speed, Demetrius snatched Pietro's purse from his belt. "Follow me!" Then he bolted toward the gateway to the Hippodrome.

Holding Tara by the hand, Alais hurried after him with no time to consider whether entering the gigantic stadium was a wise move.

"Stop them!" Alais heard the woman cry in Latin as the six figures broke into a run.

"Kópste tachýtita!" A large man in a bright yellow tunic called out

in Greek. He rushed into the open gateway, waving his hands. *"Prépei na pliróseis!"*

Behind him, two guardsmen in bronze helmets and scarlet cloaks jumped to attention. Their eyes flew wide at Demetrius and the rest of their party charging toward the gate.

Demetrius ripped open the purse. He flung it toward the man and the guards, unleashing a hail of silver coins. The man in the yellow tunic dove for the loot clattering on the flagstones, as did one of the guards. But the other guardsman stepped into the path, raising his arms and bellowing a string of foreign words: *"Den epitrépontai ópla ston Ippódromo!"*

Strong Bjorn hurled a fist into the guard's chin. The blow sent the guard reeling, clearing their way into the stadium.

"Get the girl!" the woman screamed, her voice closer now.

Alais pulled Tara through the towering gateway. They found themselves in a cavernous yet deserted entry hall with a vaulted ceiling and three exits. Torches burned from brackets on the walls. Ahead, a stone stairway branched left and right, climbing to the stands where sunlight spilled through the archways. From inside the stadium came a flourish of horns, cymbals, and drums.

"This way!" Demetrius urged, bounding up the stairway, branching right.

Still holding Tara's hand, Alais climbed the steps along with Ciarán, Mordechai, and Strong Bjorn. Behind her, she heard Pietro's huffing breath, followed by the woman's voice booming through the gateway.

"There they are!"

At the archway, Alais pushed Tara into Ciarán's arms. The girl looked terrified. "Protect her," Alais said as a raucous roar erupted in the stadium.

"Aye," he replied with a nod.

Before stepping through the archway, Alais glanced behind her. The woman and the five men had reached the gateway. Her sharp gaze caught Alais'. The woman had a hard but stately face and a ruthless glare in her eyes. And just like Tara had mentioned, a crescent-shaped birthmark above her left cheek.

Alais drew in a breath. *Remember, you are Sirra.*

She followed Pietro through the archway into a scene more overwhelming than she ever could have imagined. At least fifty or sixty thousand people filled the titanic stadium—more than the population of Poitiers or all of Rome. Most were clad in tunics of blue or green, though a small minority wore red or white, all cheering at the top of their lungs as eight chariots raced around the U-shaped track. The charioteers, also dressed in tunics of green, blue, red, or white, whipped their teams of four horses, stirring up storms of sand and dust. Down the center of the track rose an Egyptian obelisk a hundred feet tall, along with bronze statues of stallions and heroes. One appeared to be Hercules, while two others near a giant she-wolf must have been Romulus and Remus. Alais felt dizzy at the sight of it all.

She grabbed hold of Ciarán's cloak to steady herself. They were in an aisle that ran more than a hundred yards down the stadium. Men wearing blue or green tunics crowded the aisle, standing and cheering on the charioteers. In fact, everyone in the stadium appeared to be standing, from the horde of people on the marble stands that descended toward the racetrack to the mob of fans in the stands that climbed twenty or more rows to the top of the stadium. The benches in the stands above the aisle were wooden instead of marble, and judging from the ragged tunics of many in the higher rows, their inhabitants were poorer than those in the marble stands closer to the track. Most were men, although Alais spied women and children among the crowd in the top rows.

Ahead, Demetrius was using Strong Bjorn to press his way through the people cramming the aisle. The Dane towered over most in the crowd, and with his broad shoulders clad in his mail shirt, he met little resistance. Mordechai followed Demetrius, protecting Tara and Pietro behind him. Ciarán still held the girl's hand, and Alais kept a grip on his cloak.

Slowly, they worked their way through the crowd. Too slowly, Alais feared. By coming here, Demetrius must have thought the mass of people would offer some protection. Yet that assumed their pursuers were unwilling to commit murder in front of so many people, including the emperor, who must have been watching the race from the massive, ornately decorated box on the other side of the Hippodrome. Though, in truth, Alais did not know what these people were capable of.

She kept glancing back at the archway. Before they had trudged barely twenty yards down the aisle, the woman emerged with the man in the floppy hat and two of the blue-cloaked assassins. Violently, they began pushing people out of their way, drawing gasps from nearby members of the crowd. Sunlight glinted off a long steel dagger in one of the assassin's hands. At that moment, Alais understood these people would risk anything to get their hands on Tara.

"They're coming!" Alais warned.

Ciarán glanced back. "Demetrius, move faster!"

"Yes, faster!" Pietro urged.

But the crowd was too dense. Unless Strong Bjorn began hurling people into the stands, Alais knew they would never outrun their pursuers. And they appeared to have no qualms about knocking people into benches or shoving them to the ground. Even worse, some in the crowd seemed to recognize their pursuers and moved out of the way to let them pass.

We won't escape them, Alais realized.

On the track below, a trio of chariots roared down the raceway, with two others close behind. The air was filled with cheers from the crowd and the stampede of hooves as the chariots whipped up clouds of sand and dust in their wake. That gave Alais an idea. She sucked in a breath, feeling a tingle of power in her veins, and began reciting the words to summon the wind. She felt a sizzle in the air around her and sensed the wind whistling around the track. Focusing on the cloud of sand and dust, she uttered more words to give the wind strength and watched as her growing gale carried up the sandy cloud. She flung her hand at the assassins, guiding the wind straight toward them. Cries rose from the crowd below as the cloud of sand, like a swarm of hornets, whizzed overhead. The angry cloud struck the woman and her assassins with the power of a storm. Hands flew to their faces as sand stung their eyes, and the force of the wind lifted them off their feet, sending them crashing into the row above the aisle.

Alais knew this move had only bought them a few moments. "We have to move!"

Many in the crowded aisle were gaping at the commotion Alais had created in the stands and started moving in that direction. With Mordechai's help, Strong Bjorn began pushing the oncoming tide of people out of the way, clearing a path. Pietro followed Demetrius with Ciarán right behind them, pulling Tara through the crowd. Alais tried to stay on their heels but gasped when she saw the other two blue-cloaked assassins emerge from an archway twenty yards ahead.

The assassins barreled through the crowd with long daggers in their grip. Spectators leaped to get out of their way, and in a heartbeat, the first of the two lunged, thrusting his dagger at Strong Bjorn. The Dane spun away, and the dagger's blade scraped against the chainmail covering his rib. But in the same motion, he reached around and grabbed the assassin's shoulders with his enormous hands. With a grunt, he used the assassin's momentum against him and launched the man into the stands. The assassin slammed into a gaggle of green-clad supporters, who, seeing the blue cloak, began walloping on the man.

The second assassin, however, ran straight past Demetrius and knocked Pietro and Mordechai aside with sharp blows of his elbows. The assassin raised his dagger, his eyes locked on Tara. Alais reacted with a sudden rage. *"Eoh!"* A searing ray of soul light blasted from her palm into the assassin's eyes. The dagger fell from his grip as he clawed at his face. Then Mordechai threw his whole body onto the man's back, knocking him to the ground. Ciarán and Tara darted past the assassin while Demetrius waived them toward the archway. Mordechai climbed to his feet just as Strong Bjorn kicked the prone assassin in the head. The man's neck snapped back, spraying blood and teeth into the stands.

Alais rushed past him. In a breath, she was in the stairwell, hurrying down the steps into the cavernous bowels of the Hippodrome.

Over the roar of the crowd, Alais swore she heard the woman screaming a command. *We only slowed them,* Alais thought. *They're still coming.*

At the bottom of the stairs, Demetrius nearly collided with a troupe of green-clad performers.

A slender young woman whose scant green clothes barely covered her smooth olive skin let out a gasp. A look of utter surprise filled her otherwise pretty face, framed by flowing black hair.

Beside her, a bare-chested juggler, judging from the burning firebrands gripped in his hands, appeared equally stunned to see Demetrius. Two more short but muscular young men who might have been acrobats and a heavyset man holding a pair of cymbals also seemed to recognize their guide.

"Anastasia!" Demetrius said in a grateful tone.

The woman, who Alais suspected was a dancer, shook her head, tears welling in her eyes. She spoke to him in Greek, and he replied in a hurried voice. Her expression changed from surprised to overwhelmed. She asked him a question.

All Alais could glean from his answer was the word "Gogam."

A look of sudden concern flashed across the dancer's face. She spoke rapidly to Demetrius before he turned to their group with eyes full of hope.

"They're friends," he said. "And they'll help us."

CHAPTER 43

FRIENDS IN LOW PLACES

A s Ciarán witnessed the exchange between Demetrius and the dancer, everything suddenly made sense.

Demetrius had found another almost as beautiful as the woman he once broke into the palace to make love with. And he favored the Greens over the Blues because they had the prettiest dancers. *That's* why he had led them into the Hippodrome. Because he had friends here.

And the dancer, Anastasia, was clearly more than a friend. By her words, she knew of Demetrius's abduction by the Varangian and feared he was dead. She cried tears of joy when she saw him alive, and now she and her troupe of fellow performers were leading them hurriedly through a maze of chambers inside the Hippodrome.

In the distance, a shrill woman's voice sounded from one of the passageways. "Find them!"

Ciarán's heart was pounding from the harrowing escape through the crowded stands, but the sound of the woman's voice caused his heartbeat to quicken. Tara clung to his hand with a fierce grip, her eyes welling with fear.

Anastasia rushed them through a chapel to what looked like a drinking hall that reeked of stale wine and ale, into an enormous pantry, and out again into a sprawling stable decorated in Green. Torches or candles lit every chamber, and Ciarán was beginning to wonder if a veritable city existed within the Hippodrome.

From the stables, she took them into a barracks or dormitory with rows of beds. A score of green cloaks hung from pegs on the wall. "Put these on," she said hastily.

Ciarán snatched a cloak and handed it to Alais. "She wants us to wear these." He gave Tara a cloak and then donned one of his own. The cloaks had hoods, and Ciarán followed Demetrius's lead by pulling the hood over his head.

Dressed like members of the Greens, they followed Anastasia into a chamber with cots and racks of clay jars, which Ciarán assumed was an infirmary, and then into another drinking hall that sported long green banners hanging from the walls. One of the acrobats pulled aside a banner, revealing a sturdy wooden door. Anastasia unlatched it. "Follow me," she said.

The door opened into a dark stairwell, descending to what Ciarán could only imagine was somewhere beneath the city streets. The juggler stepped in first, using his firebrands to illuminate the stairs.

The stairwell was narrow, spiraling deep below ground. Judging by the number of steps, Ciarán estimated they were fifty or sixty feet beneath the stadium.

"I don't hear them anymore," Alais said softly.

"Are we safe?" Tara asked.

"Aye," Ciarán replied. "I think so."

The stairway ended in a vaulted passageway. "Where are we going?" Pietro asked.

"To the compound of the Greens," Demetrius said from up ahead. "It's across from the stadium, but Anastasia says members of the House of Gogam would never go there. They are partial to the Blues, and no one of the Blues would dare break into the home of the Greens unless they wanted to start a riot. Not even the emperor's soldiers would invade the house of the Greens."

Ciarán could hardly imagine the kind of society where fans of chariot racers wielded such power in a city. But he also was not sure Anastasia's assumption was correct. After what the assassins were willing to do in front of thousands of spectators in the Hippodrome, perhaps they *would* risk a riot to get their hands on Tara. The only comforting thought was that the assassins had not seen them with the dancer and her fellow performers, so they would not know the Greens had come to their aid.

When the passageway ended in a sturdy, iron-bound door, Anastasia knocked on it six times in a particular rhythm that led Ciarán to believe it was a code. A moment later, the door was opened by a heavyset, bearded man wearing a green tunic. A short sword hung on his hip.

The doorman gave Anastasia a bewildered look. "Shouldn't you be performing about now?"

"Demetrius has returned," she said. "He's well, but needs our help."

The doorman raised a thick brow. "Demetrius?"

The thief waved at the doorman.

"Come in," the doorman said.

They entered a cellar with enormous barrels lining the stone walls and a scent of aged wine hanging in the air. As soon as they were all inside, Anastasia threw her arms around Demetrius and gave him the most passionate kiss Ciarán had ever seen. Beside him, Tara blushed. Pietro looked so uncomfortable he had to avert his eyes.

"They're lovers," Alais whispered to Ciarán with a smile.

"It appears so."

When the pair had finished their kiss, an obviously aroused Demetrius took Anastasia by the hand and led her deeper into the cellar. For an instant, Ciarán wondered if they planned to consummate their reunion in front of them, but the two simply spoke quietly. When they were done, Demetrius sidled up to Ciarán and Pietro.

"Anastasia knows your Syncellus," Demetrius said. "She's willing to find him and see if he'll come here."

Pietro glanced at Ciarán with a look of hope. From a pocket in his habit, Pietro pulled out the letter bearing the papal seal.

"Tell her to give this to the Syncellus," Pietro said. "And let's pray to God it persuades him."

～

ANASTASIA of the Greens helped answer Pietro's prayers.

Ciarán and his companions sat at a trestle table in a comfortable chamber between the largest kitchen he had ever seen and an enormous banquet hall with marble walls and columns hung with long green banners and adorned with bronze statues of famous charioteers. One of the cooks had provided a meal of clam soup, stuffed grape leaves, warm bread, and a carafe of pale golden wine. Tara ate heartily, no longer looking afraid, and so did Ciarán, who thought this was the most delicious food they had eaten since leaving Rome. He was sipping the tangy broth from this bowl when Anastasia entered the chamber with a man who must have been Severus Synadenos, the Syncellus of Constantinople. And, to Ciarán's surprise, the thick-bearded priest from the Palace of Antiochos and Jarl Holger were with them.

The Syncellus looked annoyed. His clean-shaven face already bore a haughty expression, and his bulbous nose was a shade of red, probably from too much wine. His robes were scarlet embroidered with rich golden thread, much like an archbishop might wear, bulging at his paunch above a golden belt. A scarlet square-shaped hat similar to the black version worn by the priest crowned his head, and the dark, short-cropped hair above his ears was flecked with silver. A gaudy golden crucifix hung at his chest. Beside him, the thick-bearded priest looked equally annoyed, even offended, while Holger appeared grateful to have found them. But Ciarán sensed the anger simmering within his friend, and his left cheek was reddened and scraped.

Ciarán and his companions rose from the table when Anastasia entered with the men.

"Who among you is Brother Pietro?" the Syncellus asked in a

haughty tone that matched his expression. Like everyone they had encountered in Constantinople, he spoke in Greek.

"I am, Your Eminence," Pietro said.

"Then can you explain why this northern barbarian went to my palace and abducted my vicar?" the Syncellus asked pointedly. "After receiving your letter from dear Anastasia, I left the emperor's presence only to find this barbarian practically dragging Vicar Eufasius through the streets. Why on earth are supposed emissaries of our new pope cavorting with such a man?"

Once again, Ciarán was grateful Holger did not understand Greek. "Let me speak with him, Your Eminence," Ciarán said.

"And who are you?" the Syncellus asked.

Pietro answered. "That is Captain Ciarán of the Papal Guard." It was the title Gerbert had given Ciarán before they departed. The title was purely honorific, imposed solely because the pope thought a higher station might make powerful men like the Syncellus more willing to speak with Ciarán.

"And with us also," Pietro continued, "is Alais, the Lady of Selles-sur-Cher and cousin to the Duke of Aquitaine. The barbarian you speak of is Jarl Holger of Denmark, a descendant of kings and a baptized Christian. They are all devoted servants and allies of His Holiness, the pope."

The Syncellus wrinkled his reddened nose. "Do speak with him," he said to Ciarán, "and straighten out this indignation. In the meantime, Anastasia dear, could you fetch me more wine?"

Anastasia scurried off to please the Syncellus while Ciarán gestured for Holger to join him away from the others.

"What happened?" Ciarán asked in Danish. He could smell the sweat beneath the jarl's mail.

"We were lured into a trap," Holger replied with lingering rage. "We were attacked, I swear, by one of the jötnar, like the ones we fought back in Rome. I killed him, but Breda barely escaped with her life."

The news about Breda sent a pang of dread through Ciarán's chest. "Does she need Alais' help?"

Holger shook his head. "She was knocked unconscious, but she's come to. Jorundr carried her back to *Lindworm*."

Ciarán gave a relieved sigh. "We were attacked as well. There were six of them. Demetrius took us into the stadium to try to escape, and Alais slowed them down a bit, but we couldn't stop them. Fortunately, this dancer, Anastasia, gave us aid and took us here. The enemy knew we were coming."

"So it seems," Holger agreed. "I believe the jötnar intended to divide us."

Ciarán clenched his teeth. He had been afraid of that. Even more, while they may have avoided the House of Magog for now, there was little doubt their adversaries would make another attempt on their lives. "You need to take *Lindworm* out to sea. She's not safe in the harbor, and neither is the crew."

Holger nodded grimly. "That would be wise."

"Let me speak with the Syncellus," Ciarán said, putting a hand on Holger's shoulder. "Then we'll decide who goes with you." He gave a sideways glance to Vicar Eufasius. "What happened with this priest, by the way?"

"Jorundr told me the name of the palace you were going to. I found it, but this fool of a man would not have words with me. Nor would he tell me where you'd gone. So Curtana and I made him an offer—either take me to you or prepare to meet God in Heaven."

Ciarán curled his lips. "Not a very Christian thing to do."

Holger simply grunted.

When Ciarán rejoined the group, Pietro was conversing with the Syncellus, who was sipping from a goblet of red wine and eating bread from the table. He casually dipped a piece into Pietro's bowl and stuffed it in his mouth.

"I apologize for Jarl Holger, Your Eminence," Ciarán said. "He and his wife were attacked by a man near the market, so he was desperate to find us."

"Is that so?" the Syncellus asked between bites. "I could have the barbarian brought up on charges, you know? It's a serious crime to assault me or my staff, and were the emperor to hear of it ..." He paused. "Let's just say he would not be pleased. But from what

Anastasia told me, and Brother Pietro just confirmed, you've met with your own troubles. For the life of me, I can't understand how a delegation from the Holy See would attract such unsavory types so quickly after arriving in the city. Especially when no one knew you were coming. I had not a word of it before Anastasia found me at the Kathisma."

"We believe they're members of the House of Gogam," Ciarán explained, "if you've heard of them."

"Gogam?" The Syncellus wrinkled his nose. "They're an old family. Some of their members have long been generous donors to the Church. Very generous, as I recall. There were always nasty rumors, but …"

"Sometimes rumors are true," Pietro interjected.

"Did these pursuers of yours announce that they were of the House of Gogam?" the Syncellus asked.

"No," Pietro conceded.

"Then it's pure speculation. The real question, however, is why anyone would want to harm you."

Ciarán knew he could not trust this man with the truth about the prophecy or Tara's connection to the witnesses of Revelation. The man would not believe it anyway. Though he did not have to lie. "The girl who's with us. We think she may have a price on her head."

The Syncellus lifted an eyebrow. "The girl can't be more than thirteen. Who on earth would hire assassins to kill her?"

"She's from here. We believe it may be a vendetta against her family. They were murdered here seven years ago."

Ciarán knew Tara could understand what they were saying. He glanced at her, and the look she returned told him she was being strong.

The Syncellus set down his wine and sighed. "I wish I could say family vendettas were unusual in this city, but I also wish it would rain less in the fall." He wiped his mouth with his gold-embroidered sleeve. "In his letter, the pope asked me to arrange an audience with the patriarch and the emperor. I will see them both tonight, and I'll explore what I can do. In the meantime, since you are papal emissaries, I can arrange accommodations within the Sacred Palace. I doubt whatever trouble you've found yourself in would dare follow you inside those walls."

Pietro's expression brightened. "That would be gracious of you."

"I suppose it's the least I can do," the Syncellus replied. "Of course, the barbarians will be unwelcome. And ..." His gaze shifted to Mordechai. "Is that one a Jew?"

Pietro gave a reluctant nod.

"I won't even ask why you are traveling with one of them, but I will not advocate for a Jew taking lodgings in the Sacred Palace, so he, too, is unwelcome."

Ciarán bit his tongue. He did not like this man and would not trust him.

"Also," the Syncellus said, eying Caladbolg, "there are no weapons or armor allowed within the palace walls. I can offer to keep that sword and your hauberk at my residence. But you'll need to surrender them."

Ciarán gave Pietro a subtle shake of his head. He could never risk surrendering Caladbolg—the weapon the enemy most fears—into the hands of this man. After losing the blade once, he could not fathom losing it again.

"We can entrust our belongings with Jarl Holger," Pietro said.

The Syncellus frowned. "Do as you wish." He took a long drink of wine, emptying his goblet. "Once I've made your arrangements, I'll send Vicar Eufasius to let you into the palace."

With that, the Syncellus spun on his heel and left the chamber. When he was gone, Ciarán explained what had transpired to Alais and the others. Alais grew concerned at the news of Breda's injury and even more troubled when she learned Holger would have to take *Lindworm* and Caladbolg out to sea.

"Caladbolg is your talisman," Alais said. "Are you sure you want to do this?"

"We've no other choice." Ciarán pulled off his baldric attached to the scabbard where Caladbolg remained sheathed and handed it to Holger. "Keep it safe."

Holger took the sword. "I'll guard it with my life."

Next, he removed the hauberk that once belonged to Maugis d'Aygremont and gave it to Strong Bjorn before the group discussed their plan. They decided *Lindworm* should sail to Myros and await the arrival of Gerbert's ships. Somehow, either through the Syncellus or by simply booking passage on a vessel, Ciarán, Alais, Tara, and Pietro would find a way to rendezvous there. Until then, the four of them would make do. They would speak with the emperor and patriarch, obtain the Fifth Seal, and get out of Constantinople as fast as a ship could take them.

As Strong Bjorn, Mordechai, and Holger set off with Caladbolg and his hauberk, Ciarán knew full well he would have nothing to protect his dreams from the Dragon.

And if the House of Magog were to find them again, they would have only Alais and her power to protect them.

CHAPTER 44

THE SACRED PALACE

I nside the House of the Greens, Tara wished she could have left with Jarl Holger. She wanted to be away from this city; the thought of going back outside where that woman and her henchmen awaited sent a shiver down her spine.

"We'll be safe in the palace," Alais told her.

Those words did little to console Tara. Could they really trust that their pursuers wouldn't have spies in the palace? The menacing woman who knew her mother's name and had murdered her father and sister seemed determined to finish what she began seven years ago.

When the vicar finally returned, Tara's stomach was in knots. He had two young priests with him, each holding a handle of Brother Pietro's heavy chest containing the holy relics he brought from Rome. The two guardsmen accompanying them in their red cloaks provided some measure of relief, but Tara wasn't convinced it would be enough. She could feel in her bones that the woman and her assassins would find her again, and so long as she was in this city, she would never be safe.

"To be prudent," the vicar told them, "you may want to keep those green hoods and cloaks on, at least until we get there. It's a good disguise. Upstanding members of the Greens and the Blues are frequent guests in the palace."

Tara drew the hood of her green cloak over her head. Lady Alais, Brother Ciarán, and Brother Pietro did the same, but Demetrius had taken off his cloak. That's when Tara realized he wasn't coming with them.

"We owe you our lives," Brother Ciarán said to Demetrius. "There's no way we can repay you."

Demetrius grinned. "You freed me from slavery, and now I can be with Anastasia. You owe me nothing. But if you need me again, ask for me at Zosimo's. It's a tavern just three blocks away from here."

Brother Ciarán nodded. "Take care, Demetrius. And try to stay out of trouble."

"Can a tuna stay out of the sea?" Demetrius replied with a slight shrug. He gave them a wink, then turned to join Anastasia. "Keep safe, friends!"

As Demetrius walked away, Tara wondered how much she would miss him. She had grown to appreciate his carefree attitude, and without his daring, they would have never escaped from the Hippodrome. Tara decided Demetrius had a good soul—and she would miss him. But she pushed these thoughts away as they prepared to go out into the streets, where danger awaited.

The vicar and his guardsmen led Tara and her party out of the House of the Greens into a street that curved around the semi-circular end of the Hippodrome. A crenelated brick wall ran along the other side of the street. Tara felt a tingle of apprehension as her gaze darted down a perpendicular street running north, searching for the blue-clad woman and her assassins. Tara saw no sign of them as a thunderous roar erupted from the stadium. Another race must be underway.

Alais held tightly to Tara's hand as their party hastened down the street, passing the towering archways of the Hippodrome. After they rounded the turn, the street became narrower and tucked away between the stadium and a magnificent brick wall that curved around to the north. All the while, Tara kept looking back in case she saw the woman and her followers somewhere close behind her.

"We'll enter the palace through the Gate of the Snail," she heard the vicar say up ahead. "It's a discrete entrance."

To Tara's relief, they arrived safely at a gatehouse halfway down the length of the Hippodrome. Six more red-cloaked guardsmen with bronze helmets and long spears guarded a pair of tall bronze doors set into the gatehouse. When the guardsmen saw the vicar, two of them pulled open the doors.

"The Gate of the Snail," Brother Pietro remarked as they entered the gatehouse, "how clever."

Inside the gatehouse was a staircase made of polished porphyry and white marble. Sunlight streaming through the narrow windows threw reflections onto the glimmering stairs, winding upward like a snail's shell. Tara found a sense of relief when the guardsmen barred the entrance shut behind them.

The circular stairway climbed to a broad archway that opened into a wide hallway lined with marble columns. Colorful mosaics depicting emperors charging into battle decorated the walls. The small pieces of glass and stone that made up the mosaics glittered in the sunlight that spilled into the hallway from arched windows high above the floor.

A trio of young men clad in yellow silk robes glanced at their party as they entered the hallway. The men were completely bald and beardless, with pale, soft-looking skin.

"They're eunuchs," Alais said under her breath.

Tara shook her head. She had never heard of a eunuch.

"They're missing a few pieces below the waist," Alais explained, causing Tara to blush.

They followed the vicar past the eunuchs and down an intersecting hallway where twin doors opened into a garden. Tara's mouth fell open when she stepped outdoors. An elaborate fountain sprayed water into the air, while in the trees, small birds sang with voices like flutes. Their feathers were made of gleaming silver and gold, and it took a moment for Tara to realize they were not real, though somehow they sang a tune that carried over the splashing fountain. Several more fountains with dancing plumes of water were spread throughout the garden, where bronze statues of horses, lions, and a three-headed serpent stood among beds of yellow, white, and violet flowers. A gentle breeze carried the scent of jasmine. At least three more palaces with pavilions, terraces, and high domed roofs of terracotta tile surrounded the garden. One was built of yellow stone, while the other two had white marble facades and pillared arcades. There was a church, too, with its own domed roof, and behind it, a towering lighthouse. Amid the chirping of the metal birds and the soothing sound of falling water, Tara was at a loss for words.

"It's unbelievable," Alais muttered in awe as she released Tara's hand and walked towards one of the trees with the metal birds. The vicar smiled and paused, allowing them to take in the sight.

"Never in all my years," Brother Pietro muttered.

"Only in Córdoba have I seen anything to rival it," Brother Ciarán remarked.

Tara had never been to Córdoba, but she could not imagine a more wonderful place in the world. She had almost forgotten the situation that brought them here when she noticed all the people moving between the palaces. Many looked like eunuchs, though others were women dressed in plain-looking clothes carrying baskets, and Tara imagined they were servants working in the palace. However, one group of six women, walking toward the nearest palace, wore more colorful, luxurious garments. Tara's body tensed when she spotted one wearing a long blue shawl—it was only after a moment that the woman's small stature made Tara realize it couldn't have been her pursuer. As Tara got a better glimpse of the group, her eyes widened. The woman with the blue shawl was a girl of Tara's age with dark hair, just like hers, and a single lock of white cascading down her forehead. Tara stood stunned, as if she were looking at a ghost.

Before she could utter a sound, the girl and her companions had already slipped through the entrance to one of the palaces. Tara barely choked out the name—"*Sara?*"

CHAPTER 45

SHIELDS AND CROSSBOWS

"Row, dammit!" Holger yelled to his crew.

Lindworm rocked in the choppy harbor as the Danes pushed her off from the docks, seawater slapping against her hull. The Danes pulled their oars, trying to get the vessel away from the pier.

"Hurry!" Holger barked, craning his neck to watch the horde of jötnar flooding through the gateway to the wharves. Thirty or so in number, they towered in height. Many slung huge wooden crossbows over their broad shoulders. Others carried firebrands with dark smoke wafting skyward. Fishermen and sailors hurried away from their path, and the red-cloaked guardsmen were nowhere to be seen.

The jötnar muscled their way past anyone standing in their path, rushing toward the piers. With their huge strides, they would reach the edge of the wharf in no time.

Holger's muscles tensed as he tugged on the steering oar. "Row!"

Lindworm struggled to push through the swelling sea, grazing the hulls of other ships in the crowded harbor, making it difficult for the oarsmen to do their job. The longship had traveled barely twenty yards since pushing off from the pier.

"We won't escape those crossbows!" Breda said urgently.

"Shields to the aft!" Holger ordered.

The Danes closest to the aft dropped their oars and tore shields from the strakes on the gunwales. Hári Grayhair was the first to reach the aft, raising his shield bearing a snarling wolf painted on its face. Breda grabbed her own shield, using it to protect Holger at the steering oar, while Birghir, Ormr, and Askil crowded the stern, their shields overlapping to create a wall.

Breda cried out as a bolt slammed into her shield. Its steel tip pierced the willow boards, nearly slicing her arm, but Breda kept her shield firm. Holger was already amazed at how quickly she recovered from her fight in the alleyway, and right now, she looked as fierce as ever. It was one of the things he loved about her the most. She may not be Danish, but by the gods, she was a shieldmaiden.

More bolts pounded into the shield wall. Birghir cursed as the tip of a bolt punched through his shield and sliced into his arm. Others thudded into *Lindworm's* stern or splashed into the nearby water. A second volley followed, hammering their shields and smashing through the wood.

"Those goddamned crossbows are powerful," Hári growled. "They're ripping through our shields like they're made of bloody sailcloth!"

Another volley battered the shields. This time, Askill yowled as a bolt pierced clean through to his forearm.

The tall, young man named Mordechai joined them in the aft, clutching a bow and a quiver of arrows. "Let me take a shot."

"Lower the shields," Holger replied with a nod. "Let him try."

Mordechai nocked an arrow, drew back his bowstring, and let it fly.

Peering through a gap between Hári and Breda's shields, Holger watched as the arrow landed in the neck of one of the jötunn cross-bowmen. A second shaft embedded itself in the chest of the next jötunn. The man's hands flew to the arrow as he tumbled over the edge of the pier into the harbor.

"The lad can shoot!" Holger said with a grin.

Mordechai ducked behind the shield wall as another flurry of crossbow bolts slammed into the barrier. But as soon as they did, he sprang back up and loosed two more arrows. Both hit their mark, one dead in the heart, another straight through an eye socket, knocking out two more crossbowmen. Meanwhile, *Lindworm* had cleared most of the ships and boats crowding the area near the harbor, and with her oars splashing and her sleek prow knifing through the sea, she was putting distance between her and the wharves.

The next volley brought fewer bolts as Holger saw several of the jötnar running for cover. Still, he watched in awe as Mordechai dropped two more crossbowmen.

"Six of them have boarded a skiff," Mordechai hollered. "They're rowing after us."

"They won't catch *Lindworm,*" Holger said.

"They have crossbows," Mordechai replied.

"Then take them out, lad."

Lindworm was now gliding through the water, propelled by the oarsmen, nearing the mouth of the Golden Horn. Mordechai put arrows into two of the jötnar in the front of the boat, causing the rest to think better about rowing after the speeding longship.

Only one more crossbow bolt struck their shield wall before *Lindworm* reached the gigantic chain dripping from the two towers into the sea.

CHAPTER 46
THE PRICE OF FAILURE

N aberus could barely contain his fury.

The target of that anger sat in a heavy wooden chair in the center of a high-ceilinged cellar with wine barrels stacked against the stone wall. The man's arms had been pulled behind his back and bound at the wrists. His ankles were bound to the chair's legs.

Torchlight flickered against the man's pale, beardless face. Blood caked around a swollen lip, and fear welled within his wide-open eyes. The man, named Dantalion, was young for their kind, perhaps sixty or sixty-two, though to the humans of Constantinople, he looked no older than his early twenties. A third cousin of Naberus, he shook nervously in his bonds while urine pooled at his feet around a floppy, dark-blue hat.

From the chamber's shadows, a low growl rumbled from one of Naberus's mastiffs. *The dog can smell the man's fear.*

Two others in the chamber regarded Dantalion sternly. Astarte stood with her arms crossed; the birthmark above her left cheek appeared more red than violet in the torchlight. Meanwhile, Saleos prowled the chamber like a panther, dressed similarly to one of her assassins in a blue cloak with the hood hanging behind his neck. He was a hard-looking man with a shaven head and a deeply lined face, one of the four surviving elders of the House of Magog.

"We found Flauros," Astarte said icily. "Dead in the streets with a sword wound in his chest."

Dantalion grimaced at the news.

This man is weak, Naberus thought, trying to control his rage. He had spent a lifetime mastering his emotions and learning to keep his anger in check. As consigliere to the Crescentii and corrupt popes, he had to be a voice of reason, controlling the passions that ruled these powerful and ambitious men. But that was before Samyaza. Naberus had witnessed his master's vengeance, and the price of failure was fire and death. Even more, Lovetar had put *him* in charge of the House of Magog, and Naberus would not let them fail his master. His life—*and his salvation*—depended on it. Yet Dantalion's foolishness had put all of this at risk, and now anger burned within Naberus like a blacksmith's forge.

"He was with you at the wharves, was he not?" Saleos asked.

"Yes," Dantalion stammered.

"And you saw the girl?" Naberus already knew the answer. "And there was a raven-haired woman with her, too?"

Dantalion gave a feeble nod.

Naberus clenched his hands into fists. "So there were two of you at the wharves when you saw the girl? All it would have taken was for one of you to pounce on her and ram a dagger through her heart. Had you killed the woman, too, this war would already be over."

"They were with a crew of barbarians," Dantalion said. "They were Northmen. Nearly twenty of them, and they were heavily armed. They would have killed us."

"And here you are alive," Naberus said through clenched teeth. "But so is the girl. I would sacrifice a hundred of your lives for hers."

Dantalion's face grew ashen. "We thought it would be better to tell you of their arrival and return when we had enough numbers to face them. I had my eye on her the entire time, I swear."

Naberus snapped. He ripped his slender blade, Murgleis, from his scabbard and pressed it against Dantalion's throat. "Your job was to kill a defenseless girl. And yet you never made an attempt on her life between the wharves and the Hippodrome?"

"There were too many of them." Dantalion nearly choked on the words. "One of them had the device—the sword."

"Another thing you let get away!" Naberus pressed harder, and the razor-sharp blade broke the skin of Dantalion's neck. Naberus watched as the red blood disappeared into the blade, and this time, he sensed it. A surge of energy pulsed from Murgleis, up his arm, and into his chest and lungs. He gazed in amazement at the blade. *What if . . .*

"Cousin," Naberus hissed, "it's time you learned the price of failure."

Dantalion whimpered as Naberus lowered the sword—before plunging it through the man's ribs. He thrust the blade as deep as it could go, then cried out as energy flooded into his veins.

The prisoner wailed in horror. Naberus felt the man's life force pulsing inside him, a sensation of heat and light, of vigor and sheer strength, like nothing he had ever known. The muscles in his chest and arms pressed against the woolen cloth of his cassock as if they wanted to rip through the fabric.

He let Murgleis fall from his grasp and grabbed Dantalion's head with both hands. Then he squeezed. He felt the bones in Dantalion's skull shift. He lifted Dantalion off the ground, chair and all, and raised him to eye level. The man and chair must have weighed over two hundred pounds, but to Naberus, he was no heavier than a bucket full of water. The spark had gone from Dantalion's eyes. Naberus dug his fingers deeper into the man's head. He squeezed harder, gritting his teeth, until Dantalion's skull cracked like a goose egg.

Naberus let go. The hardwood chair splintered upon striking the stone floor, leaving Dantalion's corpse in its wreckage. Saleos stared at Naberus with wide eyes, while Astarte gaped at him with a look of awe.

Glancing back at the corpse, Naberus snapped his fingers. "Set, Grimm, he's yours."

Out of the shadows bound the two mastiffs. They tore into Dantalion with ravenous growls.

Naberus did not stay to watch. He picked up Murgleis, its blade clean of blood, and re-sheathed the sword. Then he gestured for his mother and Saleos to join him on the other side of the cellar.

"We cannot let the girl and the woman leave the city," Naberus told them.

"Their ship is gone," Astarte said. "The Northmen fled and killed six of ours during their escape. Two more were left badly wounded."

This news drew a frustrated sigh from Naberus. These Northmen were becoming a problem. "Tell me the woman and the girl weren't with them."

"They weren't," Astarte replied. "I have spies at all the gates and throughout the harbor. They won't be able to leave the city."

"Good." Naberus crossed his arms. "Now, how do we find them?"

"In the Hippodrome," Saleos said, "I recognized one of the men with them. I don't know him personally, but I'll see what I can learn."

From a pocket in his cloak, Saleos pulled out a golden mask and placed it over his face—a mask bearing the image of Hermes, the herald of Olympus and the god of thieves.

CHAPTER 47

THE BASILEUS

Pietro and Ciarán shared a lavish guest room in one of the palaces across the hall from Tara and Alais' chamber. Ciarán let out a groan of relief as he sunk into the feather mattress of his finely carved, four-post bed piled high with silk blankets and pillows stuffed with goose feathers. Atop a small table burned a brass oil lamp that gave off a scent of jasmine. He had never known luxury like this, and after nearly a month of sleeping on *Lindworm's* deck planks or damp beaches around a campfire, he had to fight the urge to collapse and fall fast asleep.

Tara's news from early in the day had sent his mind whirling. The thought that her twin sister might not only be alive but also living in the Sacred Palace added an entirely new dimension to their mission. Pietro quickly pointed out that since the girls are twins, just like the twins of Gemini, Sara may be the second witness. If that was true, they had to find a way to see her again and make contact. Ciarán did not know how they would explain to this girl, who somehow lived in the wealthiest palace in the world, that she would need to join them on a quest to the Otherworld to fight the Dragon. But he had time to figure that out. Now, he had to prepare himself for what might happen once he shut his eyes and fell asleep.

Ciarán said a quiet prayer to Saint Columcille for protection and another to Saint Mary to watch over him as he slept. Then he reached over to extinguish the brass lamp.

"Are you sure you want to do that?" Pietro asked, already covered in one of the silk blankets.

"We can't very well stay up all night. We'll look like hell when we meet the emperor and the patriarch. That's what really matters, right? Getting the scroll."

"I won't argue with you," Pietro said with a yawn. "But I'm waking you up the first time you let out a cry."

"Fair enough." Ciarán sucked in a breath, then snuffed out the lamp, knowing that as soon as his mind drifted into sleep, the Dragon might find him.

And so the Dragon did.

Ciarán could not tell how long he had slept before he found himself surrounded by the swirling mists, his arms and legs outstretched, hovering above the ground. Across from him, the Dragon's golden eyes glared from the shadows of his hood.

A strange word thundered from his lips. *"Mir!"*

The sound of the word pulsed into Ciarán's forehead, followed by a wave of heat. His brain pounded in his skull. Ciarán gritted his teeth, hoping the headache would end, as the whispers from the flowing mist began repeating those five alien words.

Ozam, odamma, cialpor, mir, agrit ...

"You have found your way to Byzantium," the Dragon said in a threatening tone. "It's only a matter of time before my servants there find you."

Ciarán closed his eyes, focusing on those five strange words, trying desperately to avoid any thoughts of where he was or what he had planned, lest he betray those thoughts to the Dragon.

"I already know your plans," the Dragon hissed as if he could still read Ciarán's mind. "You seek aid from the Patriarch of Constantinople and the illustrious emperor, Basil the Second."

"Holy mother of God," Ciarán muttered as a chill rushed down his limbs. *He knows everything,* Ciarán thought amid the pounding in his skull.

"Basil the Bulgar-slayer, the Basileus, the Imperator and Caesar of New Rome, a man more content to wage war than serve as the ruler of Christendom. Do you truly think he can help you? A man who worships me more than he does his own God?"

"You're lying," Ciarán said. "The emperor's a patron of the Church. He'd never worship you."

"All men of war worship me. War is chaos, and darkness, and death, revealing the true nature of God's creation. Every time a battle is fought, men are slaughtered for the ambition of those who rule them, their corpses left as feasts for crows. And warriors are cruel. Pillaging villages, burning homes, raping women, slaying children. The sounds of battle—the clang of swords, the hiss of arrows, the screams of the dying—those are the hymns sung by warriors whose deeds bring glory to the one who inspired it all. The very first rebel, when war broke out in Heaven."

The Dragon raised his arms. "Behold, your holy emperor Basil."

The mist enveloped the Dragon, and in a breath, both it and he were gone, replaced by a vision of a barren valley flanked by towering, snow-capped mountains. Thousands of men dressed only in stained tunics and breeches knelt on the ground, their hands tied behind their backs. Most were young, dark-haired, and strong-jawed, while others were more senior, with flecks of gray in their beards. Their captors also numbered in the thousands, wearing chainmail with breastplates and conical helmets, many of which were topped with horsehair plumes. Some held kite-shaped shields decorated with an array of colorful patterns. Their leader paced slowly, surveying the prisoners. He was shorter than many of the warriors, but stocky and broad-shouldered, clad in shining polished mail. His face was hard, almost cruel, with arched eyebrows, piercing blue eyes, and a strong nose above a mustache and beard beginning to gray. A sleek golden crown and flowing purple cloak marked him as a king. An emperor. Basil the Second.

The emperor gave a command, and soldiers emerged from the ranks of captors holding small braziers by the handles. Others placed sharpened sticks into the hot coals. Soon, there were scores of men carrying braziers and even more wielding smoking hot rods.

The emperor gave another command, and suddenly, the soldiers turned on the prisoners, plunging the hot pokers into their eyes. Prisoners screamed and wailed, their cries filling the valley in a chorus of agony. The soldiers went from prisoner to prisoner, taking both eyes each time, leaving sobs of anguish and tears of blood.

"Fifteen thousand," came the Dragon's voice from somewhere beyond the vision. "That is how many he blinded, leaving only one of every hundred with one good eye so they could lead the legions of defeated Bulgarians back home. All this done by the will of your holy Christian emperor."

A knot coiled in Ciarán's stomach while bile rose in his throat. He heaved, about to wretch, when the image faded, and he felt someone shaking him.

"Time to wake up!" Pietro said.

Ciarán sat up in bed, still feeling like he might vomit.

A hint of moonlight through a window revealed the concern on Pietro's face. "Whatever he showed you was a lie."

"No." Ciarán shook his head; the sour taste of bile lingered in his throat. "This was too real. The emperor …" A shudder crawled from his stomach to the base of his throat.

"What about the emperor?"

Ciarán swallowed hard. "The man we're here to see may be as evil as the Devil himself."

CHAPTER 48

THE GOLDEN THRONE

I n the morning, the eunuchs arrived.

They met Ciarán and Pietro at their chamber, three perfumed men dressed in long-sleeved golden robes and slippers. All three had smooth, soft-looking skin with nary a blemish, and their heads were completely hairless. Even their eyebrows were painted on. Two were tall and long-limbed, one skinny and the other tautly muscled, while the leader was shorter with a rotund belly and a cherubic face. Their perfume carried the scent of lavender.

The lead eunuch eyed Ciarán from head to toe before raising one of his painted eyebrows and addressing him with a high-pitched voice. "I am Eutropius, Chancellor of the Imperial Palace. I'm here to advise you that the emperor and patriarch will see you after Sext. The Syncellus will meet you beforehand. We were told that your appearance was entirely unpresentable. Aetius and Lausus are here to remedy that."

The tall, skinny eunuch touched his chin with an extended index finger. "I question whether we have enough time. They are horribly unpresentable."

The muscular eunuch leaned in to sniff Ciarán, then puckered his mouth and wrinkled his nose. "Ghastly."

Ciarán glared at the eunuch, though he imagined he smelled less than pleasant after so many weeks at sea.

"What happened here?" asked the skinny eunuch as he reached out to touch Ciarán's hair.

Pietro gave Ciarán a knowing look. After last night's dream, Ciarán's already gray hair was beginning to turn white.

"How curious," the muscular eunuch said. "He has the face of a man in his twenties and the hair of a grandfather in his sixties."

"You talk as if I'm not standing right here," Ciarán said. "Let's just say I've seen some things lately that would turn many a man's hair gray. Though I suppose you would not have that problem."

The muscular eunuch gave him a smirk.

"Chancellor," Pietro interrupted. "I'm certain we can make ourselves presentable on our own, thank you."

A snide grin spread between Eutropius's ample cheeks. "*Not* if you want to see the emperor. Aetius and Lausus will escort you to the baths."

"I fear for the bathwater," the skinny eunuch sighed.

"Oh, one more item," Eutropius announced, raising a pudgy finger. "The Syncellus told us you have letters for the emperor and patriarch from His Holiness, the pope. I am here to retrieve them."

Pietro had planned on delivering the letters personally, but after some grumbling, he acquiesced to Eutropius's wishes and handed over the letters.

"One last thing, Chancellor," Ciarán said before the eunuchs took them to the baths. "There are two ladies in the chamber across the hall who I am sure would enjoy a warm bath, too."

"I'll have that arranged," Eutropius said, clutching the folded letters with the wax papal seals.

When Eutropius left, the muscular eunuch, Aetius, and the skinny one, Lausus, escorted Ciarán and Pietro to the bathhouse where they were bathed, enduring occasional insults from the two eunuchs. The bathwater was as refreshing as anything Ciarán could remember, and he felt as if he could soak in it all morning. Also,

Lausus was a proficient barber, and Ciarán did not mind when the eunuch trimmed his beard close and cut his hair short in the Roman style. Meanwhile, Aetius shaved Pietro a new tonsure, then presented him with a clean, black Benedictine habit and a new pair of sandals. Lausus brought Ciarán a tunic of white silk trimmed in gold, a clean pair of breeches, new leather boots, and a gold-trimmed crimson cloak. When Ciarán looked at himself in a silver mirror hanging in the marble-walled bathhouse, he beheld a handsome man dressed like a lord, albeit one with well-trimmed hair and a close-cropped beard turning as white as an elderly scholar's.

After the eunuchs departed, Ciarán and Pietro waited for the Syncellus under a garden pavilion while a trio of servants brought them a meal of salty cheese, warm flatbread, and delicious purple olives. As Ciarán enjoyed the food, he thought about the emperor and the atrocities he saw him commit in last night's vision. He dreaded meeting that man, but knew this would be a critical moment in their mission. For not only did they need the scroll containing the Fifth Seal, but also the deadly weapon called Greek Fire. Ciarán had seen what that weapon could do outside the Temple of Venus and Roma, and he could only imagine how valuable it might be against an army of Nephilim.

His Eminence, Severus Synadenos, the Syncellus of Constantinople, joined them after breakfast. Despite the late morning hour, he already reeked of wine, and Ciarán noticed a few dark red stains on the sleeve of his scarlet robe. "You are fortunate," the Syncellus said, "that I arranged an audience so quickly and even more fortunate that both the patriarch and emperor had already planned to visit this afternoon."

"We are grateful, Your Eminence," Pietro replied.

The Syncellus gave them a satisfied smile. "You should be. Now, let's go over the ritual that will occur when you enter the throne room. The emperor will address you first, and only when he's done will you speak to the patriarch. But if you want to talk to them at all, you will do precisely as I will instruct you this morning. The emperor will not care if the pope sent you if you disrespect our customs in New Rome."

Ciarán could only imagine what this ritual entailed, and he loathed the idea of showing this atrocious emperor any courtesy, but first, he had a question. "Your Eminence, I want to ask the emperor about a girl living in the palace. We believe she may be the sister of Tara, the girl we're traveling with."

The Syncellus looked at Ciarán like he had two heads. "You'll do no such thing. The emperor has the pope's letter and will tell you his wishes. You will speak only if asked a question, and you most certainly will not waste his time on something so trivial as a girl."

Pietro glanced at Ciarán, who drew a slow breath to still the anger rising inside him. "This is no trivial matter."

"It is to an emperor who rules half the world."

"If this girl is Tara's sister," Ciarán pressed, "she's important to the pope, too."

The Syncellus chuckled under his breath. "I think you'll find that the new Frankish pope is less popular in the eastern empire than in the west. As you know, the emperor and patriarch were very fond of the papacy of John Philagathos, whom the boy king in Old Rome defrocked and humiliated after cutting off his nose and ears and taking both of his eyes. All at the hands of the same boy king who appointed the current pope."

Pietro's face flushed red. "Your Eminence, that boy-king is the Holy Roman Emperor. He's also the only son of Queen Theophano, one of the emperor's cousins."

"Theophano was not purple born," the Syncellus said, feigning a yawn. "And she and the emperor are not cousins. Theophano's uncle, Emperor John the First, became a paramour of the emperor's royal mother long after the emperor's father passed away. The emperor never cared for Theophano before she married that crude German king who sired the child now sitting on the western throne."

As Ciarán listened, a wave of unease washed through his stomach. He had known there were tensions between the Eastern and Western empires, but listening to the Syncellus, he was beginning to appreciate how deep the animosity between them must run.

"Captain Ciarán, you're looking a bit green," the Syncellus said.

"It's not my wish to upset you before you meet the emperor. When our audience is finished, I will look into the whereabouts of this girl you speak of."

The promise lifted Ciarán's spirits. "Thank you, Your Eminence."

"You're welcome," the Syncellus said, raising his index finger. "Now, listen carefully to what I'm about to tell you, and don't deviate one iota from these instructions. Unless, of course, you want to be thrown out of the Sacred Palace before the emperor says a single word."

CIARÁN AND PIETRO followed the Syncellus down a high-ceilinged passageway decorated with mosaics of exotic lions, peacocks, and eagles that ended in a pair of towering bronze doors. A guardsman dressed in a bronze helmet, gold tunic, and red cloak waited at the doors holding a golden staff topped with a double-headed eagle. According to the Syncellus, he was the herald who would announce their arrival.

"Remember everything I told you," the Syncellus said under his breath.

Ciarán nodded, focusing on the ceremonial ritual as the herald opened the bronze doors. The herald rapped the butt of his staff on the marble floor. "Brother Pietro Martino," he announced in a booming voice, "Chief Librarian to His Holiness, Sylvester the Second, and Ciarán mac Tomás, captain of His Holiness's papal guard."

Before the ceremony began, Ciarán caught but a glimpse of the octagon-shaped throne room awash in shimmering gold. Light from hanging oil lamps mixed with sunlight spilled through an arcade of tall windows, glinting off golden walls. On the right and left sides of the chamber stood two artificial trees of gold and enamel, and at the far end sat a porphyry dais like a distant island in a sea of white marble laced with veins of gold. On the platform rose a massive golden throne with armrests shaped like lions where the man from

Ciarán's vision sat. A second man in clerical vestments sat to his right in a less elaborate but gilded chair while armored guardsmen flanked each throne, the chamber's golden hue reflecting off their polished chainmail.

As Ciarán and Pietro began the ceremony by kneeling and lowering their heads until their foreheads nearly touched the cool marble floor, a chorus of metal bejeweled birds in the golden trees burst into a triumphant song. Trying to suppress his wonder at the singing metal birds, Ciarán counted to ten, then stood. With Pietro mimicking the same moves, Ciarán advanced three paces and knelt again, lowering his head as before. This time, the emperor's lion-shaped armrests began to roar. As the roaring filled the chamber, Ciarán rose again, took three more steps, and knelt one last time. He kept his forehead on the floor, knowing he could not stand until spoken to. The wait lasted until the birds finished their anthem and the lions ceased their roars. Eventually, Ciarán heard Eutropius's voice. "You may stand now."

Ciarán rose to his feet, only to realize the portly eunuch was standing next to an empty space where the emperor's throne had been. Beside Ciarán, Pietro gasped. The golden throne floated twenty feet above the porphyry dais as the emperor looked down, gripping his lion-shaped armrests. Sucking in a breath, Ciarán reached out and grabbed Pietro's sleeve. Ciarán had seen real magic before in the power wielded by Dónall and Alais. Though around the throne and along the golden drapes, there were no telltale signs of its use, such as a faint glow like Saint Elmo's Fire or a thrum or sizzle in the air. Whatever this trick was, it was not magic, but its purpose was unmistakable—to show that the Byzantine emperor ruled above all.

Staring down from his golden throne, Basil the Second looked younger than the man from Ciarán's vision. Less gray stained his beard, but his sun-browned face held the same hard look, his blue eyes peering out beneath sharp, arched eyebrows. A chainmail vest covered his broad chest, a symbol that Basil the Second was a seasoned warrior but also an emperor, marked by a golden medal-

THE CAULDRON OF GOD

lion shaped like a two-headed eagle, his purple imperial cloak, and the golden crown atop his head.

In the chair beside him, Sergius the Second, Patriarch of Constantinople, looked amused. He was a thin man as old as Gerbert, with a high forehead and bronzed skin that contrasted with his white and gold clerical vestments. A wry smile curled at the edges of his lips between a closely trimmed mustache and beard. To his right and Eutropius's left stood a dozen of the fabled Varangian Guard. Most were Rus or Norsemen, each as tall as *Lindworm's* Danes and as formidably dressed as a Viking war band in chainmail coats, and round, plumed helmets, holding long-handled battle axes at the ready. The Varangian himself once hailed from their ranks, and Ciarán could see the resemblance between that man and those protecting the Byzantine emperor.

As the emperor's throne lowered back onto the dais, Ciarán noticed a flutter in the long golden curtains that ran from the base of the high-domed ceiling to the marble floor. Behind those curtains, he imagined, must have been the contraption that raised and lowered the golden throne. Though he had no time to ponder how such a contraption might work, for in the emperor's stern expression, Ciarán had a feeling the man had already reached a decision on the request in Gerbert's letter. All Ciarán could do now was hope the emperor made the right choice.

When it had come time to write the letter, both Ciarán and Gerbert knew it would have been pure folly to try to convince the Byzantine emperor about the truth behind their mission. So, instead, the pope invented a new reason to request Greek Fire. And while his plea was a mere pretext, it had enough grounding in reality to make it believable, if not compelling. In his letter, Gerbert sought to convince the emperor that the Saracens of Sicily were growing bolder under their emir, the Sword of the Faith. A century ago, the Saracens sacked the Leonine City and nearly burned Saint Peter's basilica to the ground. It could happen again, and this time, the danger came not only from the Saracens in the South, but also from the Moors in the West. In Spain, Al-Mansor was waging a holy war against Christendom. Two years ago, he laid waste to the most sacred sanctuary in Spain, Santiago de Compostela and the tomb of Saint John. All he would need is a fleet of ships to do the same to Saint Peter's, for other than its walls, the Leonine City was defenseless. But Constantinople was not. Twice when the Saracen fleets came for the city, Greek Fire turned their ships into infernos. So, Gerbert implored, if Basil wished to be the greatest emperor in Christendom, he should provide the same defense to the Holy See. Ciarán did not know if the message would appeal more to the emperor's vanity or his Christian sense of duty, but either way, he prayed it would be successful as he looked into the emperor's cold blue eyes, awaiting his verdict.

When the emperor finally spoke, his strong, measured voice filled the throne room. "So the pope wants Greek Fire, our greatest weapon." The emperor tilted his head to the right, tugging on his side whiskers. "Captain Ciarán, do you know why no one other than New Rome possesses this weapon?"

Ciarán swallowed hard. The last man he had encountered as imposing as the emperor was Al-Mansor himself. "No, Your Majesty."

"It is because Greek Fire is also our greatest secret. My grandfather, Constantine Porphyrogennetos, admonished my father never to reveal its secret and never to provide the weapon to anyone who could decipher how to create it. Some say our new pope possesses the most brilliant mind in all of Christendom. I've heard stories of his fantastic inventions—the water clocks, the abacus, the golden head that talks. I think if any man in the world could deduce the secret of Greek Fire, it would be him. And if he did, then the young German king would possess the greatest weapon on Earth. Need I remind you that his red-bearded father waged war against our lands in Italy? Imagine if he had possessed Greek Fire."

A lump hardened in Ciarán's stomach. "Your Majesty, I swear on my life those are not the pope's intentions. The threat posed by the Saracens and the Moors is real. I have looked Al-Mansor in the eyes, and though I lived to tell about it, I can assure you that if the great hajib of Córdoba sets his sights on the Holy See, nothing will stop him."

322

The emperor narrowed his gaze. "I have heard Al-Mansor is a dangerous foe, so I suggest the young German king put more of his Saxon and Bavarian troops on the Leonine Walls. But, Captain Ciarán, my decision is final. I will not betray the oath my father made to my grandfather, even for the Holy See. I am sorry you traveled so far to receive this news, but perhaps the pope's request to the patriarch will be more favorably received."

The emperor nodded to the patriarch as Ciarán's spirits sank into his stomach. He wanted to tell the emperor that the real threat was not Al-Mansor but the Devil himself. Though from the steel-hard look in the emperor's eyes, he knew there would be no changing the man's mind.

In the gilded chair beside the emperor's golden throne, the patriarch steepled his fingers. "His Holiness, the pope, offers gifts of relics in exchange for one of our own. Brother Pietro, tell us of these wondrous gifts."

Pietro cleared his throat. "His Holiness offers the Girdle of Saint Thomas in a gold and jewel-encrusted reliquary, as well as the sword of Saint Peter that cut off the servant's ear in the Garden of Geth-semane. These are two of the Holy See's most precious relics, and they will be a worthy replacement for the one the pope seeks from Your Beatitude."

Just say yes, Ciarán prayed silently, waiting for the patriarch's reply.

The patriarch sighed. "I would very much have enjoyed such relics in Hagia Sophia, but I cannot accept them."

"Why not, Your Beatitude," Pietro asked. "The pope was quite insistent."

"Because, Brother Pietro, I cannot fulfill my end of the bargain. There is no reference to the scroll His Holiness seeks in our records. I have personally never laid eyes on it, and I can assure you it's not in Hagia Sophia or any other church in Constantinople."

Ciarán shook his head; this cannot be right. "Your Beatitude," he said, unable to keep silent, "we have the evidence with us. A letter from Saint Helena to Saint Sylvester that proves the scroll was taken by Constantine and placed beneath the altar of his church on the very site where Hagia Sophia now stands."

"I would like to see this letter," the patriarch said, raising a brow, "if for no reason than to admire the penmanship of Saint Helena. But sadly, she wrote the letter before the Nikka Riots in 532. When the Blues and Greens revolted in the Hippodrome during the reign of Justinian the Great, their violence spread beyond the stadium to engulf most of Constantinople, and the rioters burned the cathedral that stood on the site to the ground. Afterward, Justinian built Hagia Sophia on top of its foundation. But unlike Saint Peter's in Old Rome, there is no passageway to an undercroft containing the remains of the churches that preceded it. And even if there was, the tunnels and undercroft were flooded when Justinian created the great cisterns beneath the city. So even if you could find the altar place of Constantine's old church, the entire area now lies underwater."

Ciarán staggered back a step, his mind reeling at the news. Under his breath, Pietro uttered a phrase. "Blessed Sergius."

Wiping the perspiration from his forehead, Ciarán proposed the only solution he could think of. "We must somehow drain the water and excavate beneath the church."

The patriarch's eyes widened, and so did the emperor's. "Have you gone mad?" the patriarch asked. "There is no way on earth I would desecrate Hagia Sophia by digging a hole in her nave. Not even if the pope himself came here to ask."

"Your Beatitude," Pietro pleaded, "you would defy the Holy See?"

"That is enough, Brother Pietro," the emperor said sternly, "I would not allow it either. Justinian the Great built that church, not the pope." The emperor gestured to Eutropius. "We are done here. Show them out."

A painful lump knotted in Ciarán's throat, and his head began to spin. For in these past few moments, all their plans, if not their entire mission, had shattered like glass.

CHAPTER 49

DESPERATE MEASURES

Alais waited nervously for Pietro and Ciarán to return from their audience with the emperor and the patriarch. So much of their mission depended on that meeting, and it was killing her that she could not be a part of it. Women, it seems, were not worthy of being papal emissaries. And while Alais was well aware this was a man's world, that did not mean she had to like it. At times like this, she grew envious of Breda, for women were the equals of men in Danish society.

Hours had passed since the men left with the eunuchs. The lead eunuch, who held some position of high stature in the Sacred Palace, had arranged for her and Tara to enjoy their own warm baths, which were absolutely lovely. The two of them were dressed now in clean silk tunics and robes with silk slippers on their feet, sharing breakfast at a stone table in a small pavilion near the palace where they slept. But while they were well-fed and the cleanest they had been in weeks, Alais felt ready to crawl out of her skin the longer she waited for Ciarán and Pietro's return.

When she finally spotted them, dressed in their fine new clothes, her heart sank. The broken expressions on the two men's faces were unmistakable, as was the listlessness of their gait.

"How bad was it?" she asked when they reached the pavilion.

"As bad as it could be," Ciarán said. As he told her what had transpired, she found herself holding her head in her hands, trying to make sense of it all. Why would whoever is behind the messages sent through Tara send them all the way here if hope was already lost?

Tara reached across the table and patted Ciarán's arm. "I'm sorry it went so poorly."

Ciarán shrugged his shoulders. "I've been racking my brain for a solution since we parted ways with the Syncellus, who was of no help, by the way."

"Have you come up with anything?" Alais asked.

"Nothing that'll work," he admitted. "When we were rowing into the harbor, Demetrius told me a story of how he once broke into the Hagia Sophia. I suspect he'd even do it again if we asked him. But even if we got inside, then what? I suppose you could use the power to loosen a flagstone or two. If there is an undercroft, we could find it. Yet unless we can hold our breaths long enough to go swimming through some pitch-black tunnels, then what?"

"I suppose I should tell you," Pietro sighed, "I tend to sink. Growing up as an oblate in Rome, the monks didn't exactly teach us how to swim."

Ciarán gave him a tired smile. "I grew up on the River Foyle, so as a lad, I did plenty of swimming. But a lot of good it'll do since I can't breathe underwater."

Alais looked up; Ciarán's words sparked a thought. "What if Sirra could?"

Pietro cocked his head. "Even if she could, how would you know?"

"Her memories are buried deep inside me," Alais explained. "Sometimes, I see flashes of them in my dreams. Other times, like in the Theatre of Pompey, I remind myself that I was her once, and things she knew just come to me."

"Then I think a good moment of self-reflection may be in order," Pietro said.

"You're right," Alais replied. "Give me some time to be with my thoughts. A walk may be good for that."

"Do you want company?" Ciarán asked. "I promise, I won't say a thing."

Alais shook her head. "I need to do this alone."

She left them to stroll through the sprawling gardens, trying to summon any memory of Sirra that might be relevant to their problem. As she walked, she listened to the splashing fountains and the mechanical birds singing in their artificial trees. A breeze whispered over the flower beds, gently rustling the colorful blossoms.

After some time, her wandering took her to a quiet pond. Lily pads with violet flowers that looked like tiny crowns floated on the surface, and deeper down, large fish with brilliant orange and yellow scales swam lazily. She stared at the fish, watching for a while as they wove in and out of the tall grass sprouting from the bottom, sometimes breaking the surface to eat an insect that had landed on the water. Eventually, she drew in a deep breath and closed her eyes. In her mind's eye, she saw larger fish. Giant meandering sharks and dolphins racing beneath the waves in a sea filled with sprawling coral reefs and schools of silvery fish wheeling past enormous sea turtles slowly gliding through the water. She knew she had been there before, or rather Sirra had. She glanced toward the surface twenty feet above, where rays of sunlight lanced into the deep beneath the waves. She had no need to swim to the surface for air, for Sirra knew the secret of breathing underwater and the words of power to make it happen. Those words, born of the language of creation, came to Alais, and she spoke them in her mind.

This might work ...

By the time she returned to the pavilion, Alais walked with an air of confidence. Everyone at the table looked up in anticipation.

"Pietro," she said with a smile. "Go find Demetrius. If he can get us inside Hagia Sophia, I can get us the scroll."

~

THE SCENT of lilac and rose petals filled the air as Demetrius passed the stalls of the royal perfumers upon entering the Chalke Gate. The double pair of towering bronze gates stood in a gatehouse that looked like a gigantic triumphal archway surmounted by a domed turret and crowned with a golden cross. Red-cloaked imperial sentinels stood guard at the gates, which were open to the public until sunset, as was the courtyard of the Sacred Palace. Covered walkways surrounded the courtyard like an enormous cloister, lined with marble pillars and scarlet banners bearing the double-headed golden eagle of Constantinople.

Demetrius leaned against the stone curtain wall attached to the gatehouse as he waited for the bells to toll at Vespers, the hour he agreed to meet Brother Pietro. The corpulent Italian monk had found him earlier in the day at Zosimo's Tavern, while Demetrius was enjoying a light meal of cured meat and salty cheese with Anastasia. The beautiful dancer had stayed with him all night, making up for many lost months during Demetrius's enslavement. After their night of pleasure, Demetrius felt like a new man, albeit a slightly exhausted one.

The monk's request, so soon after their arrival in Constantinople, had come as a surprise, but when he offered a palm-sized sack of golden solidi as a down payment, Demetrius could hardly refuse. This job would make him more money in a single night than he might make in three years of thieving.

When the chorus of bells rang for Vespers, Demetrius spied the portly monk right on time. Demetrius nodded toward a deserted place beneath one of the covered walkways, then strolled over there to greet the monk.

"Did you get it?" Pietro asked.

"The sleeping draught?" Demetrius flashed a smile. "Of course I got it. I know some of the best apothecaries in town." He drew a tiny clay vessel sealed with wax from his belt pouch and placed it in Pietro's palm. "The draught has very little taste. Mix it with wine. It works quickly and will knock out the guards in no time. Later, they will have a headache, as if they had drank a few too many carafes of wine, but otherwise, they'll be fine."

Pietro gave a nervous nod. Eliminating the guardsmen who protected the entrance to the secret passageway to Hagia Sophia was integral to their plans. But by the uncertain look on the monk's face, Demetrius wondered if he was up to the task.

"How, pray tell, do we get the guards to drink the wine?" Pietro asked.

Demetrius gave a slight grimace. "I think you should leave that task to someone else. Alais is as beautiful as they come, and while a bit young, Tara is not hard on the eyes. If the two of them act like they are having an evening stroll through the gardens, with perhaps a carafe of fine wine, I suspect they might convince a pair of lonely guardsmen to join them for a drink. As soon as the guards are unconscious, use the key to open the door. One of them will have it on a ring on his belt. I will meet you on the other side in Hagia Sophia."

"And what if the guards don't take the drink?"

"They have to," Demetrius insisted. "Either that, or you have to kill them, and I don't believe you are built for that kind of thing."

A horrified look spread across Pietro's face. "Blessed Sergius, no!"

Demetrius patted the monk's shoulder. "Don't worry, Alais was determined enough to go with us inside the Varangian's fortress. I've no doubt she'll get this job done."

Cupping the sleeping draught in both hands, Pietro swallowed hard. "Very well."

"Now, listen carefully," Demetrius said. "The entrance to the passageway is a plain-looking postern door in the wall surrounding the gardens, near the exit to the courtyard. The two guards will give it away, but it is thirty paces northeast of the statue of the three-headed serpent."

Pietro nodded as Demetrius spoke. "Three-headed serpent," Pietro repeated, "that can't be too hard to find. So … when do we do this?"

"I'll meet you inside Hagia Sophia. Only the priests have the key that opens the door from the passageway into the baptistry, but I know how to pick the lock. We'll rendezvous after sunset. Tonight is a new moon, so it will be quite dark then, a good night for a burglary."

Pietro winced at the word.

"Do you need this scroll or not?"

"No, you're right," Peter stammered. "It has to be this way. An hour after sunset, we will see you then."

"You'll bring the rest of the payment?"

"Of course," the monk said before turning to leave.

"Excellent—and don't be late."

Pietro nodded again. "Oh, one last thing. Can you bring a rope?"

Demetrius tipped his head to the side. "Why would you need a rope?"

"Just in case," Pietro replied before turning back toward the palace.

As the monk walked away, a smile slowly spread across Demetrius's lips. For life was a beautiful thing. He was a free man with a woman who adored him, and before the day's end, he would be very, very rich.

CHAPTER 50
HAGIA SOPHIA

An hour after sunset, a chorus of chirping crickets murmured through the palace gardens. Their music mixed with the sound of rolling waves crashing against the seawalls. A thick humidity hung in the air, and the distant growl of thunder bore the threat of a coming storm.

Within the garden, an enormous bronze statue of a three-headed serpent rose from a sea of golden pebbles like the biblical Leviathan. And with no moonlight because of the new moon, there was nothing to expose Ciarán and Pietro crouching behind the sculpture. It helped that Ciarán was wearing Pietro's old black habit and cowl, which the eunuchs had washed earlier in the day, while Pietro wore his new habit, also Benedictine black. Together, the pair were nearly invisible to the two imperial guardsmen protecting the nondescript postern door set into the palace walls.

Thirty paces ahead, the glow from Tara's oil lamp illuminated the scene unfolding with the guardsmen. Dressed in a cloak of midnight blue, Alais pretended to laugh, flipping back her raven hair while holding the carafe of spiked wine in one hand and a goblet with good wine in the other. Growing up as a niece of the powerful Duke of Aquitaine, she had had years of practice playing roles at court, and she seemed to relish this one as a tipsy young noblewoman strolling the gardens at night with her servant Tara.

Ciarán could overhear one of the guardsmen laughing along with Alais while Tara translated between the two in Greek. The guardsmen had left their spears leaning against the wall while talking with their hands the way the Greeks tend to do, clearly enjoying Alais' company. She took a sip from her goblet and offered the carafe to one of the burly guardsmen. When he took a slug of the spiked wine, Ciarán let out a relieved breath. "It's working," he whispered.

"Thank the Lord," Pietro muttered.

"Thank Alais," Ciarán replied as the other guardsmen took a long swig from the carafe.

Alais pretended to laugh again when the first guardsman grabbed the carafe and took a second drink. Not to be outdone, the second guardsman followed with an even longer chug.

Meanwhile, as planned, Tara tugged on Alais' sleeve. This was the signal for them to leave. Her ladyship, Tara would explain, has a very early morning tomorrow and needs her rest. The guards encouraged Alais to stay while Tara tried to lead her away. Over Tara's protests, Alais feigned resistance before finally offering the guards her carafe as a consolation prize. When the guardsmen took it and shared another drink, Ciarán knew their plan had worked. And by the time Alais and Tara circled back to the serpent statue, the guards were slumped against the wall with their heads tipped back. One of them was snoring.

"How did we do?" Alais asked, trying to conceal a smile.

"You have them sleeping like wee babes," Ciarán said.

"Well done," Pietro added, giving Tara a pat on her shoulder.

Over the Sea of Marmara to the southwest, lightning flashed, followed a breath later by a rumble of thunder. "We should get going before the storm arrives," Alais said.

"Aye," Ciarán replied. He used Tara's lamp to light his own before the four of them approached the postern door. The carafe lay on its side, spilling its remnants into the manicured grass. Other than the droning snores, neither guardsman moved nor made a sound. Pietro began searching their belt pouches until he found the key on a small brass ring. He slipped it into a keyhole nearly hidden in the dark wood and turned it until they heard the lock release with a click.

Pietro let out an anxious breath. "Are we ready to do this?"

"Ready as we'll ever be," Ciarán replied, grabbing one of the spears leaning against the wall.

Tara's eyes widened nervously. "Are you going to have to use that?"

"Not as a weapon," Ciarán assured her. "Only Demetrius knows we're coming. But this spear will serve as a fine lever for lifting the marble floor slabs when we're looking for the well."

"By Archimedes, that's a good point," Pietro said, taking the other spear before pulling open the door.

Ciarán glanced one last time at the sleeping guardsmen. Fortunately, the parapet atop the curtain wall provided some shelter below so the men would not drown when the rain arrived. Though whether they could sleep through a storm was another matter entirely, and it left Ciarán with a swirl of unease in his stomach as he followed Pietro into the passageway.

Light from Ciarán's oil lamp flickered off the passageway's plain stone walls. Once Alais and Tara had joined them inside, Pietro closed the door. Ahead, the low-ceilinged corridor extended into darkness.

"The passageway must run inside the palace wall," Alais observed.

With the spear in one hand and the oil lamp in the other, Ciarán took the lead down the passageway. After a hundred or so paces, the tunnel ended in a stairwell descending beneath the ground. They climbed down the stairs, which ended in another passageway proceeding straight ahead.

"I suspect we're traveling beneath the Chalke Gate," Pietro noted, glancing at the low ceiling.

The tunnel continued for about a hundred and fifty more paces before turning left into a stairwell leading up. "My guess is these stairs will take us into Hagia Sophia," Ciarán said. "Let's hope Demetrius has unlocked the door, or this will be a short trip."

"I know he's a thief, but I trust him," Pietro remarked. "Besides, I'm still holding half his payment."

"I trust him too," Tara added, looking a bit more at ease.

Ciarán nodded thoughtfully. "Let's hope he's earned that trust."

As he started up the stairs, Ciarán could see that Demetrius had not let them down. For at the top of the stairwell, light from an oil lamp flickered in an open doorway.

When Ciarán reached the doorway, Demetris stood on the threshold carrying the hand-held lamp. A coil of rope was slung over his shoulder. The thief had a pained look in his eyes, though he smiled when he saw Ciarán. "Right on time," Demetrius said. He eyed Ciarán's outfit and shrugged. "Disguised as a monk?"

"I am a monk," Ciarán replied before entering the chamber.

The doorway opened into an elaborate baptistry with slender columns surrounding an octagonal-shaped baptismal font made of marble and inlaid with gold. Ciarán glanced up, watching his lamp-light flickering off a mosaic of Christ and his apostles on the baptistry's domed roof.

Demetrius gestured for the others to join them in the chamber. When they had all assembled there, he quietly closed the door, which was covered with bronze plates on the side facing into the baptistry.

"Thank you," Pietro told Demetrius as he handed him the small purse of coins representing the rest of his payment.

Demetrius weighed the purse in his hand before placing it inside a pouch at his belt. "I trust it's all there."

"Of course," Pietro replied.

A flash of lightning lit up the baptistry, blasting through an array of arched windows made of colored glass. A moment later, thunder rolled louder than before. The storm was getting close.

Demetrius fidgeted for a moment, as though unnerved by the thunder and lightning. Then he drifted to a pair of bronze doors at the far end of the baptistry. "Through here, you'll stand inside Hagia Sophia."

He opened the doors. Inside, the church was eerily quiet and as dark as night, though the darkness fled from the lamplight, illuminating a broad aisle with a gold-plated ceiling thirty feet above the marble floor. Their footsteps echoed within the vast space beyond as they passed through the aisle. When the glow from their oil lamps penetrated the nave, what Ciarán beheld took his breath away. The nave of Hagia Sophia was enormous, at least a hundred feet wide and more than twice that in length. His lamplight reflected off scores of columns, revealing a dazzling array of colors. Some were porphyry, glittering with star-like sprinkles, while others had greenish or yellowish hues. Still others were golden or gray, with swirling veins of crimson, azure, and emerald. The many columns were of slightly different shapes and sizes, as if they had been ripped from the temples of antiquity and repositioned in the cavernous space.

As Ciarán tipped his head toward the ceiling, he sucked in a breath. His lamplight crawled above the columns topped by galleries, vaults, and half-domes, building up to the enormous central dome nearly two-hundred feet above the floor.

"I know now what Justinian meant," Pietro muttered.

"What?" Ciarán asked, still spellbound.

"When he first set foot here," Pietro explained, "he announced, 'Solomon, I have surpassed thee.'"

"I understand why," Ciarán said.

Alais shook her head in awe. "It's so beautiful."

Ciarán wandered towards the chancel, his footsteps echoing through the colossal nave. In the apse, nearly a hundred feet above the floor, stood a huge mosaic of the Virgin Mary holding the Christ child in her lap. Mary appeared to gaze down upon the massive marble altar where Jewel-encrusted candlesticks surrounded an elaborate golden cross. Through an arcade of windows beneath the mosaic, white lightning flared, followed by a boom of thunder that shook the ancient cathedral.

Ignoring the storm, Ciarán focused on the altar, recalling Tara's message about the Fifth Seal.

After the fourth comes the fifth seal,
the slain souls' home it shall reveal.
It lies beneath where they are found,
on the holy emperor's sacred ground.

The slain souls were found under an altar, and Ciarán knew that beneath the floor on which they stood were the remains of holy Emperor Constantine's original church. Though whether his altar was directly beneath the current altar remained a mystery, as did how they would find the well or passageway beneath Hagia Sophia that would lead to the ruins of the original church. He studied the floor. Six-foot-long panels covered every inch of the nave like a sea of gray marble flowing with light blue veins. There must have been hundreds of marble panels, but which one covered the entrance they were looking for?

"How will we ever find it?" Alais asked. "This place is gigantic."

Ciarán sighed. "I was thinking the same thing myself."

Demetrius ran his fingers through his hair, his gaze flitting between the nave and the narthex. "What are you searching for?"

"One of these panels covers the entrance to a well or a passageway to whatever's beneath this nave," Ciarán explained. "It leads to an area that we're told is flooded like the cisterns beneath the city."

"Flooded?" Demetrius cocked his head. "I know of the cisterns, but I did not think there was one beneath Hagia Sophia." He scratched at his beard. "I wonder if it has anything to do with the weeping column?"

"The weeping what?" Ciarán asked.

"There is a column here in Hagia Sophia where water drips from a tiny hole. Some believe these are the tears of the Virgin Mary herself. Pilgrims travel here all the time to touch the water, believing it can heal whatever ails them."

Ciarán glanced at Alais. By the look in her storm-gray eyes, he could tell she was thinking the same thing he was. "Where is it?"

Demetrius pointed to the northwest corner of the nave, near the narthex, shrouded in shadows. Everyone headed in that direction, but Tara reached it first, her lamplight revealing a rectangular column topped by an elaborate capital supporting an archway. "I can see it," she said, lifting a hand to touch the white marble surface. She held up her index finger. "It's wet."

When Ciarán reached the column, Tara showed him a small hole. Ciarán set down his spear and peered at the opening. After a moment, a droplet of water dribbled out of the hollow, landing cold and wet on his fingertip.

"A miracle, no?" Demetrius said.

"It's certainly a sign," Pietro added. "The water must be coming from somewhere."

Ciarán dropped to a knee and began searching the floor for the seam to the marble slab in front of the column.

"Do you think you've found it?" Alais asked.

"Like Pietro said, the water has to be coming from somewhere," Ciarán answered with a shrug.

A determined look settled on Alais' face. "Then let's get started." She drew in a breath, as if summoning the words to her mind before placing a finger on the mortar-filled seam between the marble floor plates. When she began speaking the verse, Ciarán felt a sizzle in the air and noticed the faint, bluish light glimmering in the archways overhead like Saint Elmo's fire before a storm.

"What's she doing?" Demetrius asked with a hint of terror in his voice.

Ciarán rose to his feet and looked Demetrius in the eyes. "You've nothing to fear. We don't have time for long-winded explanations, but consider it white magic, used for good, not evil."

Demetrius went pale.

"The Lord works in mysterious ways," Pietro said, clapping Demetrius on the shoulder.

Ciarán returned his attention to Alais. Wherever her fingertip touched, the centuries-old mortar transformed into a glistening mud. When she had traced her way around the marble slab, he knelt to touch it. The wet mortar slid off his fingertip like sand beneath an ebbing tide. "Amazing," he uttered.

"The power rearranges the particles that make up the mortar, transforming the solid into a liquid," she explained.

"Let's see what's under it," Ciarán said as another flicker of lightning flashed through the arcade of windows in Hagia Sophia's nave. A peal of thunder accompanied the lightning, and Ciarán could see rivulets of rain streaming down the glass windows.

Ciarán handed his oil lamp to Alais before picking up his spear and wedging its tip into the mortar. Using all his strength, he pulled down on the lever, raising the slab two inches, but the marble weighed a ton.

"Let me help," Pietro said, wedging his spear into the gap. Together, they lifted the plate a bit higher. Demetrius jumped in, straining to heft the slab, but pushing it just enough that it came down on an adjacent floor tile. This allowed them to move it a foot aside, revealing a dark hollow underneath.

From the hollow space rose the dank scent of well water. Ciarán's spirits soared.

"Help me widen the gap," he told Pietro and Demetrius before setting down his spear and grabbing the loose slab with both hands. As he threw all his strength into moving the slab, his fingers pressed into condensation covering the rough underside. When the other two joined him, they managed to move the slab some more, widening the opening by a full yard.

Ciarán peered down into what looked like a well shaft. He lowered his oil lamp. Water glimmered at the bottom of the well about forty feet from the opening. "This has to be it."

"By Blessed Saint Sergius," Pietro said, "let's hope so."

Alais gave the oil lamp back to Ciarán. "Let's find out."

Through the windows, another burst of lightning silhouetted Alais as she unclasped her cloak and let it fall onto the marble floor. She slipped off her shoes, standing barefoot, dressed only in her tight-fitting vest and woolen hoes.

"Are you sure you can do this?" Ciarán asked, taking her hand.

"Sirra could," she said confidently. "So can I."

He gave her hand a gentle squeeze before turning to Demetrius. "We could use that rope now."

"I can see why," Demetrius said, removing the coiled rope from around his shoulders. He tied one end around the Weeping Column while Ciarán took the other end and dropped it into the shaft.

Alais sat down on the floor and lowered her feet into the opening. She gazed at Ciarán with her storm-gray eyes as she gripped the rope. "Wish me luck."

Then she pushed off and lowered herself into the well.

CHAPTER 51
INTO THE WELL

Ciarán's oil lamp illuminated the well shaft as Alais slowly climbed down the rope. The walls of the shaft were five feet apart, and the ancient stone bricks were slick and wet.

After she descended twenty feet, the shaft opened into a barrel-vaulted chamber, though how large, she could not tell, for the space was shrouded in shadows. Below her feet, what had looked like a pool of water from the shaft now appeared more like a dark, murky lake.

"I'm in the undercroft," she called up. "In what may have been the nave of the original church."

"Can you see an altar?" Ciarán asked.

"No, everything's underwater."

Carefully, she lowered herself another twelve feet. A dank odor filled the chamber; the water's surface was but eight feet below.

Her arms ached as she climbed to where her toes could touch the water. The water was cold, but so was the river Clain, where she had learned to swim. The best thing to do was to dive right in. So Alais let go of the rope.

As she plunged into the water, the cold enveloped her body. The water, however, was not frigid; she could tolerate it without her limbs going numb. She swam upwards and broke the surface, breathing in one last natural breath before focusing on the verse she would need underwater. Clearing her mind, she closed her eyes and let herself sink while whispering the words of power. The liquid around her nose and lips sizzled into a small explosion of bubbles as the power of her verse transmuted the water into air. She drew in a breath, trying to ignore the fact that she was fully submerged, before uttering the verse again.

When she opened her eyes, she could see nothing in the darkness. She drew in a breath and whispered a different word of power: "*Eoh.*"

Soul light exploded from her palms. As the faint bluish light penetrated the dark water, broken columns came into view, lining the nave of the ancient church. Flagstones covered the floor fifteen feet below her toes.

She began to swim, still reciting the verse that kept her from drowning, while her soul light danced across the ruins. To her left, she spotted a yawning archway, completely submerged, leading to a tunnel of some type. She made a mental note of the exit, wondering where it might lead. But if the riddle of the fifth seal were true, the Jerusalem Scrolls would be here, somewhere beneath the old altar. She kept searching.

As her strokes propelled her through the water, her soul light flickered across the outline of an apse above a chancel at the far end. Yet there was one problem: she saw no altar. Trying to ignore the growing concern knotting in her stomach, she swam toward the floor. Her soul light crawled over the flagstones until she spotted a hollow where one of the enormous stones was missing, near where the altar should have been. The opening reminded her of the entrance to the necropolis in Saint Peter's. Might this one lead to a crypt too?

Sure enough, she spotted a stairwell. Kicking her legs, she dove into the hollow. The deeper she swam, the more pressure built in her ears. She counted fourteen steps as she emerged into another chamber, much smaller than the nave above. The chamber's walls were made of roughly hewn stone; piles of rubble covered much of the floor. There were no other passages leading out of this chamber. She had reached the bottom.

It has to be down here, Alais told herself.

She let her soul light wash over the debris. Most of the wreckage appeared to be pottery of some type—vases, amphoras, and urns—many of which had broken, their jagged remnants strewn across the earthen floor. But from one amphora, intact and sealed with a thick cap of wax, came a shimmering blue glow clinging to the ceramic. Alais let out a relieved sigh, for that is what she had been looking for —a sign of the power. Whatever was inside that vessel had been enchanted.

Her heart thumping in her chest, she swam down and reached for the amphora. As her fingers wrapped around its handle, she prayed to Saint Radegonde that it contained the scrolls.

AT THE EDGE of the well, Ciarán knelt beside Tara on the cold marble floor. Both shined their lamplights down the shaft, waiting for the rope to twitch and Alais to emerge from the murky water below. Nearby, Demetrius tapped his foot, his gaze sifting between the well and the narthex veiled in shadows. Ciarán could tell something was bothering the thief. Might he be worried the guards would discover they had broken into Hagia Sophia? Ciarán doubted that. A man of Demetrius's occupation should have learned to conquer such fears.

Leaning on his spear, Pietro appeared no less concerned as he peered into the well. Alais had been down there longer than they had hoped, and while Ciarán did not doubt her mastery of the power, a lump of apprehension hardened in his stomach.

"What's taking so long?" Tara asked, wrinkling her brow.

"I wish I knew," Ciarán replied. "That undercroft has been sealed up for nearly five hundred years. Who knows what it's like down there?"

Tara let out a long sigh.

342

"If anyone can do it," Pietro said, "it's Alais."

Ciarán combed his fingers through his hair. "I just hope——"

The words caught in his throat when he heard the crack of doors being thrown open. The sound came from the narthex, followed by boots pounding on the marble floor.

Tara seized Ciarán's arm as he felt a sudden stab of fear. "Demetrius, what's happening?"

The thief gave him a despondent look. "I'm sorry it had to end this way."

CHAPTER 52

THE THIEF OF NEW ROME

Three hours before he broke into Hagia Sophia, Demetrius found himself in a cellar staring into the masked face of his guildmaster.

The man's gaze was hard and cruel through the eye-holes of the golden mask forged in the image of Hermes, the god of thieves. It was the only name by which Demetrius had known the Guildmaster; his true identity remained a mystery. But one of his two companions in the cellar was frighteningly familiar: the tall woman with a birthmark shaped like a crescent moon who had chased them through the Hippodrome. With her black hair pulled tight behind her neck, she bore a ruthless expression in the flickering light from the torches burning in iron brackets set into the stone walls. That same light gleamed off the polished dagger she pressed against Anastasia's throat.

Tears streaked down the dancer's cheeks, one red and swollen from a blow to her face. Blood stained her bottom lip beneath the cloth gag tight around her mouth. With her hands tied behind a wooden chair and her ankles bound to the chair's legs, her body was shaking.

"How much does she mean to you?" the guildmaster asked in a

menacing tone. Next to him glared an equally tall man dressed in a black cassock. The man had a stern face framed in a dark beard that ended at a point at his chin, and a medallion hung at his chest, bearing the symbol of the House of Gogam. A fat raven perched on his shoulder, and from a belt at his waist gleamed a sword with a hilt shaped like a dragon's wing. From the shadows of the cellar came the deep, low growl of a mastiff.

Demetrius's heart shattered at the sight of Anastasia, terror welling in her eyes. "She means everything to me," he answered, choking back a sob.

"Then the people you were with should mean nothing at all," the guildmaster said threateningly. "Either tell us their plans and do as we say, or neither she nor you shall wake in the morning. And I promise you, she will be made to suffer. The decision is yours. What will it be?"

Anastasia's tearful eyes widened, pleading with Demetrius.

As much as he knew what must be done, he felt a pain in his soul when he answered the question. "Whatever you ask, Guildmaster."

"KILL THE GIRL!"

At the sound of the woman's shrill voice blaring from the narthex, Tara wanted to jump out of her skin. She clung to Brother Ciarán, who stared slack-jawed at Demetrius. Meanwhile, Brother Pietro's face flared red with fury as he leveled his spear at the thief. "You Judas!"

"They have Anastasia," Demetrius pleaded, raising his hands above his head. "They're going to kill her. I bought you as much time as I could!"

Just then, the double-bronze doors to the narthex flew open. A rush of white-hot fear seized Tara as she glimpsed the horde of black-clad assassins coming toward them.

Brother Ciarán pried her fingers from his arm and grabbed his spear lying on the floor. "Flee to the baptistry!" he said urgently.

Before she could turn to run, the assassins burst into the nave.

They numbered at least a dozen, moving with long-legged strides, their faces masked in the same tight-fitting cloth as their dark tunics. Lamplight glinted off foot-long knives in each of the assassins' hands. Behind them, the woman pointed straight at Tara, screaming with rage. "There she is!"

Tara's legs went weak, and her heart threatened to explode from her chest. The assassins fanned out, racing toward them from both sides. Tara knew she would never make it to the baptistry. Her mind whirling, she did the only thing she could think to do.

She jumped into the well.

THE ATTACK HAPPENED SO FAST that Demetrius struggled to follow it all.

He watched Tara jump into the well, only to have two black-clad assassins dive in after her. Ciarán lunged at a third assassin with his spear, but the assassin grabbed the weapon's shaft and, with one hand, tore it from Ciarán's grip. As he spun to the right, gripping the spear, the assassin delivered a back-handed strike with his left hand, ramming the pommel of his dagger into the side of Ciarán's head. The Irishman's head snapped to the side, and his legs buckled as he collapsed onto the marble floor. Meanwhile, out of the corner of his eye, a well-placed kick swept Pietro off his feet, toppling the heavy-set monk backward. He landed hard on the floor, striking the back of his head as his spear clattered into the shadows of the nave. While this was happening, the man Demetrius had come to know as Naberus, leader of the House of Gogam, strode from the narthex, bellowing, "I want them alive!"

Demetrius's oil lamp was the only one still burning, creating a halo of light amidst the darkness that settled into the rest of Hagia Sophia. In the center of that light sauntered the towering woman named Astarte. She was dressed in the same tight-fitting tunic, hoes, and boots as her assassins, though she remained unmasked. In the lamplight, her crescent-shaped birthmark took on a violet hue, the same color as her eyes. Demetrius had never known a woman with such a look. She was strangely attractive, with a dangerous air about her, like a lioness stalking her prey.

Astarte gazed into the well as another thunderclap boomed outside, and the nave filled with a flash of white light. A moment later, she looked at Naberus. "I know where these waterways lead. I'll take half my men to meet them if they come out the other side. You and the others stay here in case they return up this rope."

Demetrius wondered who this woman was that she could give orders to the ruler of the House of Gogam, but Naberus appeared untroubled by her show of authority.

"If you encounter the woman with the girl, tell her we have the Irishman hostage," Naberus said. "And be careful; the woman is dangerous."

"So am I," Astarte replied.

She gestured to six of the assassins to follow her, then headed for the narthex. Demetris felt a muscular arm wrap around his chest, holding him tight. Strips of black cloth covered the man's forearm and wrapped around his huge hand. With his back pressed against the man's chest, Demetris realized the top of his head did not reach the man's chin. "If the girl and the woman are found," came the stern voice of the Guildmaster, "you might even see your pretty dancer again."

Demetrius let out a shuddering sigh. Anastasia was all that mattered, no matter what they had made him do. As lightning flared, followed by a peal of thunder, he kept his gaze fixed on the rope, hoping he would see it twitch. Hoping this would end soon.

A whirr in the air, followed by a thunking sound, tore his gaze from the rope. The hands of a nearby assassin flew to his neck, where an arrow shaft pierced straight through. Before Demetrius could suck in a breath, three more arrows struck. One plunged into an assassin's eye; the others landed deep in the chests of two more of the black-clad men. A fourth arrow whizzed by Demetrius's ear as his Guildmaster wrenched him back, dragging him toward the narthex. "What the hell is happening?" the Guildmaster demanded.

"I don't know!" Demetrius gasped.

Thunder boomed as another flash of lightning lit the inside of

Hagia Sophia. From the arcade in the gallery above the nave, a host of dark-cloaked bowmen drew arrows from their quivers, nocking them on bowstrings.

Naberus ran for his life, clutching his bleeding left arm where an arrow had grazed him. The man's face was a mask of fury. He slammed into Demetrius and the Guildmaster, pushing them into the narthex as another arrow glanced off the open bronze doors. Stumbling backward, the Guildmaster let go of Demetrius, who tumbled onto the cold floor. Before he could scramble to his knees, two powerful hands grabbed the back of his tunic and hurled him hard into the marble wall.

"You betrayed us!" Naberus roared.

As he looked into the man's eyes, Demetrius's heart pounded with fear. "I didn't, I swear."

"Liar!" Naberus ripped his sword from its sheath.

Demetrius felt a punch to his gut, followed by cold steel slipping inside him. His jaw fell open as the strangest sensation seized him, as if all his blood, and even his spirit, were being sucked into the blade. As the terror overwhelmed him, a soul-rending scream burst from his lungs, only to fade to a dull moan as the life rushed from his body and he slipped into the void.

CHAPTER 53

LÍFTHRASIR

Alais' soul light faded, allowing a murky gloom to return to the cold waters flooding the ruins of the ancient church.

She clutched the wax-sealed amphora in her left arm, using her free arm and legs to propel herself up the ancient stairwell that led back into the remnants of the nave. Under her breath, she continued to utter the words of power that created the pocket of air surrounding her face, the only thing keeping her alive underwater.

As she emerged into the nave, she heard a loud splash as if something heavy had fallen into the flooded undercroft. She looked toward the sound but could not see more than a yard in the dark water. *"Eoh,"* she whispered again, blasting a ray of soul light toward the surface. The light reflected off a storm of bubbles and thrashing slender limbs, only to shine brightly off a white streak running through a mess of dark hair.

Alais gasped. *Tara!*

Before Alais could exhale, two dark figures plunged beneath the surface. Soul light glinted off steel daggers clutched in their hands.

Tara let out a muffled scream as she swam frantically away from her attackers. With powerful strokes of their long arms and long-legged frog kicks, the two shadowy figures pursued Tara like a pair of bull sharks. Despite swimming desperately, Tara had no chance of outpacing them.

Alais reacted with a fierce instinct born of the spirit inside her. Summoning a verse to her mind, she let it roll off her tongue, sending a thrum through the surrounding water. Eldritch blue light flickered off the ancient stone walls and broken columns running down the nave as a sudden current rushed through the water and swirled around the legs of the two attackers. Then, with a surge of anger, Alais drew the current back her way like a riptide. The knife-wielding men flailed their arms as the current sucked them beneath the surface, pulling them toward the rows of jagged pillars. Puffs of bloody mist exploded in the water as the helpless men struck one column after another with muffled screams of pain. After battering them against a half-dozen columns, Alais whipped the current in a new direction. The fast-flowing water tore the bleeding men off the columns and flushed them down the entrance into the crypt. Unless these two knew the secret of breathing underwater, Alais felt certain they were doomed.

She glanced toward the surface and spotted Tara treading water. Holding the amphora, Alais kicked hard, swimming to the girl. Alais broke the surface and let the pocket of air around her nose and mouth dissipate before taking a long breath of dank air. Tara's face was dripping wet and creased with fear.

"You're safe," Alais assured her.

Tara threw her arms around Alais, who had to kick hard just to keep her head above the surface. The muscles in her leg burned, and it did not help that the amphora cradled in his left arm was growing heavier by the minute.

"Where are they?" Tara asked, choking back tears.

"Where they can't hurt us anymore." Alais glanced at the rope dangling from the well shaft. "What happened up there?"

"They stormed into the church. Demetrius betrayed us."

A knot coiled in Alais' stomach. "What of Ciarán and Pietro?"

"I don't know," Tara replied, shaking her head. "We can't go back up the rope."

Alais fought a wave of nausea at the thought of what might be happening up there. Ciarán and Pietro would be little match for these Nephilim. As much as Alais wanted to climb the rope and try to save them, she knew Tara was right. They'd be defenseless on that rope, and who knew how many assassins of the House of Magog were inside Hagia Sophia? The notion stirred a sickening sensation inside her, as did the realization that Demetrius had betrayed them.

"What will we do?" Tara pleaded.

"I found another way out," Alais said. "A tunnel beneath the surface. But we won't make it there by holding our breath. I can use my powers to help us breathe air underwater. It will seem odd at first, but you have to trust me. Can you do that?"

Tara nodded.

"Good. Press your cheek to mine and breathe when you feel me do the same."

The girl gave another brave nod, but her body was shaking.

Once again, Alais cleared her mind and began reciting the verse to transform water into air. Then she let herself sink, pulling Tara down with her. Tara gasped when she took her first breath underwater, but after that, her breathing began to calm.

Alais took a breath of her own before summoning more soul light. *"Eoh."*

Light flashed from the fingertips of her right hand, dancing over the broken pillars and revealing the tunnel Alais had spotted earlier, halfway down the nave. With her soul light illuminating her path, Alais kicked toward the tunnel's arched entranceway. Once inside, they found themselves swimming down a passageway not more than seven feet wide and maybe ten feet high, not unlike the corridor that led from the Hippodrome to the House of the Greens. Only this one was filled with water.

Thirty yards down, the tunnel led to a flight of stairs leading upwards. Alais used her feet to push off the steps, propelling herself up the stairwell. When they reached the top, Alais found she could stand, for the water was no higher than her knees. She breathed a relieved breath. The air was still as dank as it was in the ruined church.

Tara, too, drank in a normal breath. Her dripping wet hair was slick against her forehead. "Where do you think this leads?"

"I don't know," Alais replied. She projected her soul light down the corridor. Forty yards away, the light reflected against a stone wall. Alais' heart sank when it looked like they had reached a dead end, but then she saw her light illuminate the faint outline of a rectangular seam within the stone. "There's a concealed door."

They waded down the tunnel until they reached the door. There were no visible hinges, so Alais assumed it would open into whatever chamber lay beyond. "Help me push."

Tara placed both hands on the door, which looked to be made of the same stone bricks as the rest of the tunnel, while Alais pressed her shoulder against the portal. Together, they pushed, and the door slowly opened. The waterline stayed above Alais' knees; wherever they were going, it, too, was flooded. When the opening was wide enough for each of them to slip inside, Alais took Tara's hand and stepped across the threshold.

The first thing she noticed was the light. Little more than a dim glow, it emanated from a series of oil lamps hanging in what looked like the nave of another church. The light reflected eerily off the water's surface where scores of columns rose from the flooded nave, connected by archways thirty feet above the waterline.

"Where are we?" Tara whispered.

"It looks like someone turned a basilica into a cistern," Alais answered under her breath.

From the shadows at the far end of the nave came a faint splash followed by a second, similar sound. Alais froze. "Someone's here."

Tara's grip tightened on Alais' hand.

"Take this." Alais handed her the amphora, then held a finger to her lips. She listened closely for another sound. A series of subtle splashes followed as if several people had entered the pool filling the basilica. Alais' muscles tensed.

Across the nave, she spotted two of the intruders, shin-deep in the water, darting between the pillars like black-clad phantoms.

"I see them!" cried one of the assassins.

The pair of assassins charged through the water.

"Stand back," Alais warned Tara, her senses honed to a razor's edge as Sirra's ancient energy pulsed through her veins like liquid fire. Three arcane words crystallized in her mind. The first word slipped from her lips, and a powerful current materialized, rippling through the nave like a ghostly serpent. With a quick incantation that vibrated the surrounding air, she guided the undulating current toward her, then swiped her hands through it, spraying a surge of water into the air. With a final, resonant word, she willed the water to freeze. As ethereal blue flames danced across the ancient columns of the basilica, the shards of frozen water sharpened into lethal icicles. They rocketed toward the assailants: one skewered an assassin through the chest, catapulting him back twenty feet into a watery grave; the other tried in vain to dodge, but the ice spear found its mark, puncturing his side and plunging him beneath the water's surface.

Alais spun around as three more assassins charged from the narthex. She chanted words of power, conjuring a gust of wind and a surge of water that coalesced into a swirling tempest. With another incantation, the air thrummed as the waterspout crystallized into ice. She uttered a final word, and the ice exploded outward, sending razor-sharp shards flying like arrows. The icicles struck with deadly precision, piercing necks, chests, arms, and legs. One icicle landed squarely between a man's eyes. All three assassins collapsed, their blood mingling with the water. Around the nave, eldritch blue light flickered beneath the archways.

The basilica fell deathly silent. Alais glanced over her shoulder. Tara was gone. Alais hoped the girl had thought to hide when a massive hand wrapped around her mouth and the cold steel of a blade pressed against her throat.

She felt the heat of the man's breath on the top of her head as he called out in Latin, "I've got the witch!"

HIDING in the shadows of the flooded basilica, Tara watched in horror as one of the towering assassins held a dagger to Alais'

throat. A trickle of blood ran down her neck where the blade had already nicked the skin. The assassin's other hand covered her mouth, and his long fingers pressed into her cheeks.

Tara covered her mouth to prevent herself from screaming. It took everything she had to hold her hands over her lips when she heard the voice of the woman with the crescent-shaped birthmark echo through the basilica.

"Your words can't save you now."

The woman sauntered from the shadows of the narthex into the nave, where five of her assassins floated lifelessly, their blood spreading through the water. She stood nearly as tall as the assassin, with her long dark hair pulled tight behind her head and her slender frame clad in a close-fitting black tunic. The birthmark above her left cheek held a violet-reddish hue in the eerie glow from the hanging oil lamps.

"It's time to surrender the Key," the woman said, drawing a thin dagger. She flipped it, spinning it in the air, only to catch it again. "Your Irish friend is as good as dead, and so is the girl. I know she's hiding somewhere, but there's no way out. I suspect you didn't think it would end this way. But, then again, you should have stayed far away from here. The House of Magog owns this city."

As she stepped toward Alais, clutching her dagger, Alais' eyes widened with fear. Tara felt as if she might jump out of her skin. Without another thought, she splashed from her hiding place into the light of one of the oil lamps. "Stop!"

Twenty feet away, the woman spun toward the sound. When she saw Tara, her lips stretched into a wicked grin. "There you are."

With a blur of motion, the woman flung her dagger. Tara's legs grew weak. She fell backward as a whir of steel flashed, followed by a sharp, burning pain in her shoulder. She splashed into the water, her head striking the stone floor beneath the surface. Pain throbbed as a burst of stars filled her vision. When the motes of lights began to fade, she heard a commanding voice filling her head—the voice of the lion.

"Say the word!"

A surge of energy filled Tara's veins as she bolted upright

through the water, only to see the woman rearing back to strike with a long-bladed dagger in her hand. Around the two of them, the air hummed with unseen energy as the word erupted from Tara's throat.

"BURN!"

The woman's hand gripping the dagger exploded in a burst of flame. The dagger tumbled harmlessly past Tara into the water while the fire, in a series of booming puffs, spread down the woman's arm, to her torso, and up her neck. A scream pealed from her lips only to be cut short when a burst of flames tore through the flesh around her mouth and cheeks, obliterating the birthmark beneath her left eye before another fiery eruption turned her entire head into a flaming brazier. Smoke billowed from where her violet eyes had been as her legs gave way and her body collapsed into the water, where the flames burned on the surface like Greek Fire.

Another scream tore Tara's gaze from the burning woman. In the center of the nave stood the assassin, his hands clutching a spear of ice piercing his chest. Two paces away, a faint blue light flickered from Alais' fingertips as she glared at the dying man.

The sudden energy that had pulsed through Tara's veins when the lion had spoken to her melted away, replaced by an icy tingle in her head. Her shoulder throbbed with a fierce pain, and when Tara glanced at the wound, it was slick with blood streaming down her right arm and flowing over her hand and fingers. The icy numbness in her head spread to her limbs. Her vision blurred, and Tara felt her consciousness slipping away from one world to another.

Where the leaves of a colossal tree burned like fire.

WHEN THE NEPHILIM woman burst into flames, the assassin holding the dagger to Alais' neck let out a horrified gasp. The hand clasped hard around Alais' mouth loosened its grip enough for Alais to reach up and push both hands off her as she ducked to avoid a desperate swing of the dagger from the stunned assassin. Ignoring the woman's hideous wails and the stench of burning flesh, Alais swept her right hand through the water while chanting words of power. The air around her sizzled with arcane energy. A plume of water rose, coiling like a cobra poised to strike. With a final incantation from Alais, the watery cobra's head crystallized into an icy spear tip. It plunged downward, lancing straight through the assassin's chest.

With her attacker reeling from the mortal wound, Alais spun toward Tara. In front of the girl, the woman had collapsed into the water, her whole body ablaze as if she had been doused with Greek Fire. That's when Alais saw the blood pulsing from a wound on Tara's right shoulder. When the girl's eyes rolled back into her head, Alais' heart skipped a beat.

"Tara!"

Alais lunged as Tara collapsed backward into the water. The girl had been underwater for only an instant by the time Alais reached her.

"Talk to me," Alais said.

Tara did not open her eyes, but she sucked in a breath through her nose. A long cut ran from one side of her right shoulder to the other, pulsing blood. Cradling the girl in her arms, Alais placed a hand on the wound and began uttering the words to mend flesh. The warmth spread from her palm into the gash as she pressed the tissue together. With another verse, the bleeding stopped. Once the water cleaned away the blood, only a faint scar remained where the wound had been. Even so, the girl would not awaken.

When she heard footsteps echoing from the direction of the narthex, Alais' muscles tensed. Her heartbeat quickening, she dragged Tara into the shadows behind one of the columns. Alais' calf brushed against the nearly submerged amphora, leaning against the column where Tara must have left it.

The drumming footsteps grew in number. Alais drew a deep breath and steeled her nerves. If another wave of assassins was coming, she would be ready. Though she hoped the sight of six of their brethren floating dead in the water, along with the smoldering corpse of their leader, would stun the intruders long enough to give her the advantage. She had air, water, and fire at her disposal and could feel the power flowing through her veins.

A voice called from the narthex: "Alais?"

Alais could hardly believe her ears. The voice was Ciarán's.

Holding Tara in her arms, Alais stepped out from the shadows as a half dozen cloaked figures waded into the nave. In the glow of the oil lamps, she saw most carried bows with arrows knocked on the strings. All except one wearing an oversized Benedictine habit.

When she saw Ciarán's face, Alais' spirits soared.

"Thank God," Ciarán said with a relieved look, although his forehead creased with concern when he set eyes on Tara. "What happened?"

"She was wounded, but I've healed it. She's breathing well enough, though I fear she's slipped into one of her trances."

Ciarán let out a grateful sigh.

Alais glanced at the men accompanying Ciarán. All wore dark beards, their faces otherwise hidden beneath their hoods. "Who are they?" she asked.

Ciarán gave her a weary smile. "It seems we have some allies here, after all."

CHAPTER 54
THE MAGI REVELATIONS

L ightning painted the night sky as the storm moved west over the Bosporus while curtains of rain lashed the streets outside the nondescript entrance to the Basilica Cistern. Kamran, the leader of the men who had saved them, carried Tara in his arms. The raindrops streaming down the girl's face did nothing to wake her from her slumber.

Ciarán drew his cowl over his head, grimacing from the throbbing pain above his left ear where the assassin had rammed the pommel of a dagger. Beside him, Alais clutched an ancient-looking amphora sealed with a thick wax cap. He hoped the vessel contained the scrolls, but first, they needed to get safely to wherever their rescuers were taking them.

As they followed Kamran and his men down a maze of dark alleyways, Ciarán told Alais what little he knew. "Kamran said they serve the Magus. So it seems Khalil was right all along. The last time the cycle of prophecy came about, the magi fulfilled it. And their descendants have been preparing for this cycle ever since."

Alais shook her head in disbelief. "How did they find us?"

"Through Tara's sister, Sara. She's with them, and it seems she,

358

too, has been having dreams. That's all I know, but thank the Lord they found us, or Pietro and I would both be dead."

"Where's Pietro?"

"With the rest of them. He got the worst of it when the assassins attacked. But he's alive."

Alais looked relieved. "Tara said Demetrius betrayed us. Why?"

Ciarán frowned. "He said they were holding Anastasia hostage. He had no choice, and still, they killed him."

Alais gasped.

"We found his body as we were leaving Hagia Sophia."

A look of grief overcame Alais, and Ciarán understood how she felt. He had taken a liking to Demetrius and could not blame him for the betrayal if his tale was true. Though beneath the feeling of loss simmered anger at the people who did this, and Naberus da Roma was chief among them. Any chance of saving Anastasia was likely beyond their reach, for they would not even know where to begin looking for her. And in their current state, they could hardly risk another encounter with the House of Magog. All they could do was hope the dancer would be released safely now that Demetrius was gone. Though if he ever reclaimed Caladbolg, Ciarán swore to himself Demetrius would be avenged.

Through the driving rain, their party emerged from the alleyways into a narrow street of single-story homes clustered tightly together. Halfway down the street, they stopped at a large house built of stone bricks. Shutters covered a pair of windows facing the street while rainwater cascaded off a roof of terracotta tiles. Kamran turned to Ciarán. "We're here."

The man stood a hand taller than Ciarán, regarding him with sharp, piercing eyes. He was older than Ciarán, too, maybe twice as much, with grey flecking his dark beard and the thick eyebrows above his aquiline nose, while creases ran from the corners of his eyes down the dark olive skin of his face. Cradled in his muscular arms, Tara breathed calmly, still unconscious.

One of his bowmen opened the sturdy wooden door and ushered them into a home aglow with oil lamps, some hanging from the rafters, while others perched on small tables. As soon as Ciarán stepped through the threshold, he inhaled scents of mint and cinnamon. Embroidered carpets covered the floor where a half-dozen men had cast off their wet cloaks. Their bows and quivers leaned against the wall. The men were all dark-bearded, like Kamran, though most were much younger. They looked up as Ciarán and the others entered before some dropped their gaze to a broad alcove at the chamber's far end. Pietro sat on a bed of cushions, resting with his eyes closed as he recovered from hitting his head on the marble floor during the attack. Nearby, on another bed, lay a sleeping girl who was a mirror image of Tara save for her dress of fine blue silk. Two people knelt beside the girl. One was a middle-aged woman with dark hair and an olive complexion, dressed in a deep red stola and gown, while the other was a much older-looking man with a wild mane of gray-white hair, nut-brown skin, and an untamed beard. Over his thin frame, he wore long, dark robes embroidered with patterns of silver thread that gave the appearance of constellations in the evening sky. Ciarán had little doubt this man was the one Kamran had called the Magus.

As they entered the home, the Magus looked up with kind but mischievous eyes that reminded Ciarán of the old rabbi, Isaac ben Ezra. Around those eyes stretched age-worn skin over hollow cheeks and a hooked nose that, along with his flaming white beard and mustache, added to the man's wizened appearance.

"Bring her here, beside her sister," the Magus told Kamran.

The woman rose to her feet and moved aside to allow Kamran to lay Tara next to her twin sister. A look of compassion filled the woman's stately face. While gray strands ran through the woman's dark hair, age had been kind to her. Ciarán imagined she must have been beautiful in her youth, but even in middle age, she was a comely woman with an air of confidence about her, like someone who was used to being in charge.

"When did she slip into this condition?" the woman asked in Greek.

"I don't know," Ciarán replied, gesturing toward Alais. "But she does."

"Does she not speak Greek?"

Ciarán shook his head.

"Then we shall speak in Latin." The woman turned to Alais. "When did this happen?"

"In the cistern," Alais replied, "not long before these men found us. She had been attacked. I thought she had passed out from her wound, but she would not wake up even after I tended to it."

Upon hearing of the attack, the woman's expression hardened. "Show me the wound."

"It's completely healed."

"How?"

Beside the woman, the Magus stood up, stooping over as if his spine were slightly bent. "I sense she has the yazata within her."

The woman's eyes widened, though Alais tipped her head to the side. "Yazata?"

"In your Christian parlance," the Magus explained, "you would call them heavenly spirits or angels. Although, for those who came to Earth long ago, legends call them the Jann. I believe you were once one of them, and your name back then was Sirra."

Alais drew a sharp breath while Ciarán's jaw fell slack. "You know about Sirra?"

"Of course," the Magus replied with a smile that revealed a few missing teeth. "She's the one who must repair the pillar to keep the daevas in their prison. That is why you are all here. Are you not the one born of Virgo's seed?"

Ciarán could hardly believe his ears. "You know the prophecy?"

The Magus shrugged and held out his palms. "Is it not written in the stars?"

Next to him, the woman's face held a look of amusement. "I doubt you will find anyone who knows more about the stars and their meanings than Fereydun Sultani." She gestured toward the old man. "No one is wiser. He is the Magus and the leader of our people in the city."

The old man, Fereydun, waved his hand dismissively. "Compared to one with the yazata inside her, I am but a humble servant."

"And I have been a poor host," the woman said. "I am his daughter, Kira. You have already met my brother Kamran."

Ciarán offered Kira his hand. "I am Ciarán mac Tomás."

"And I'm Alais of Selles-sur-Cher. The monk you are caring for is our companion, Brother Pietro."

Kira greeted Alais warmly, then glanced at the girls sleeping side by side. "I am grateful you returned Tara to us safely. I have prayed a long time for this day."

"Were you the one who saved Sara from the attack that killed their parents?" Alais asked.

"No," Kira said. "Their mother, Shirin, and their father, Yusuf, were trained in the ways of the magi. They saved their children, but they gave their lives doing so. Sara was found on a beach off the Sea of Marmara, clinging to the siding of a rowboat's hull. The man who found her was none other than the emperor, out riding with a company of his soldiers. The emperor is a hard man, but his heart is not made of stone. He took a liking toward Sara and has raised her with his nieces in the Imperial Gynaeceum ever since. When we learned of her fate, I took a job as a chambermaid there, where I've watched over her and helped prepare her for the conflict that would come."

Ciarán looked down at Sara. Her eyes were closed, and her chest rose and fell with each breath in the same rhythm as Tara's. "She sees visions, just like her sister?"

Kira nodded. "That's how we knew when you would come and where to find you. Sara's last message foretold the twins would reunite on the night of the new moon at Wisdom's temple. We found the guards to the passageway asleep and reached Hagia Sophia not long before Magog's assassins found you. I was in the gallery with Sara when she slipped into a trance. I suspect it happened about the same time Tara fell into her own dream."

Fereydun brushed the white streak in Tara's rain-slick hair. "I believe they are together now, speaking with the Amesha Spentas."

"Who?" Ciarán asked.

"The Amesha Spentas, four of them at least," Fereydun said. "In our faith, they are the divine servants of Ahura Mazda, the creator of all good in this world. Their names are Vohu Manah, Kshatra Vairya, Spenta Armaiti, and Asha Vahishta. You know them as the archangels: Gabriel, Raphael, Uriel, and Michael. In this time of conflict, they send us messages through these young women, who are their prophets. So it has been foretold to my people for over a hundred years. That is why these half-daevas who call themselves the people of Magog want them dead."

Fereydun's words lifted Ciarán's spirits, confirming everything he had come to suspect. They were not alone in this war. Divine forces have been aiding them, sending messages through Tara and her sister. So it's no wonder the Dragon's servants want to kill them.

Beside Fereydun, Kira gestured at the amphora in Alais' hands. "Is that what you were seeking beneath Hagia Sophia?"

"My hope," Alais said, "is that it contains what we seek. Tara's last vision told of a scroll hidden under the altar of Constantine's old church. I found this in the undercroft of the ruined church at the bottom of the well. Whatever's inside is touched by the power. I can sense it."

Fereydun clasped his bony hands together. "A scroll, you say?"

"Yes," replied Alais.

"We believe it was written by the Hebrew king, Solomon," Ciarán added. "We discovered another in Rome that helped us find the Key to repair the pillar. While we now know the Key lives within Alais' spirit, the scroll showed us the place where her consciousness would awaken to that reality."

The old man's eyes filled with wonder. "In our legends, the magi in Babylon discovered the scrolls during the reign of Cyrus the Great. The magi-kings of a millennium ago used them in their quest to defeat Ahriman. But afterward, they left them in the care of the one they believed to be the Saoshyant, the savior who would finally bring peace to the world. Though from there, in the land of Judah, the scrolls were lost to the sands of time."

"Not quite," Ciarán said. "In Rome, we found evidence the scrolls were hidden in Jerusalem. Constantine and his mother, Helena, discovered them beneath the place where the Church of the Holy Sepulchre now stands. One—the Testament of Solomon —was given to the pope at the time. That's the one we used. The other three were taken by Constantine to his new church, now the ruins beneath Hagia Sophia."

Kira's eyes narrowed. "What will these scrolls show you?"

"Something we'll need to aid us on the last leg of our journey," Ciarán said.

Fereydun threw up his hands. "Then what are we waiting for? Let's open that amphora."

CHAPTER 55

THE WAR SCROLL

From the corner of the alcove came a groan. "I heard all that," Pietro said, his voice groggy.

"Pietro, you're all right?" Alais asked in a hopeful tone.

Pietro touched the back of his head and grimaced. "I have a lump like Mount Vesuvius on the back of my head, but I'll live." He gave her a weak smile. "If you found the scrolls, I would very much like to see them."

"So would I," Fereydun said impatiently.

Ciarán, too, could hardly wait to open the amphora, and seeing Pietro awake lifted his mood even more. He knew how fascinated the papal librarian had become with King Solomon's scrolls.

"Set it on the table." Fereydun gestured to a circular wooden table to the left of the alcove, where a brass oil lamp burned brightly.

Alais placed the amphora on the table. The ceramic vessel looked hundreds of years old, though its thick wax cap appeared utterly intact.

"Kamran," Fereydun said, "we could use your knife."

Across the chamber, Kamran got up from a long trestle table

where the dozen men who had saved them were snacking on bowls of olives and nuts. Kamran drew a long, thick hunting knife from a sheath on his belt and set its blade against the wax cap. He grunted as he pressed the blade into the hard wax. "It's as hard as stone."

The muscles in his arms bulged as he tried to saw through the wax cap. After several moments, he shook his head, letting out a frustrated sigh. "I can't get through it."

"Allow me," Alais said. She placed a hand on the wax cap and began uttering a verse. The oil lamp flared, and Ciarán could feel a thrum in the surrounding air. Fereydun, Kamran, and Kira watched in awe as the wax cap began to glisten.

"*Yazata,*" Fereydun muttered under his breath.

"Now try it," Alais told Kamran.

Awe lingering in his eyes, Kamran pressed his dagger into the wax. This time, it cut straight through. When his knife had carved a circle around the vessel's neck, he wedged in the blade and pried off the top. As the cap fell onto the table, the amphora emitted a whiff of foul air.

Fereydun reached into the amphora with his thin, bony hand. "There is more than one thing inside." He pulled out an ornate-looking scroll case. It was just like the case Gerbert found in Rome, made of burnished gold and twisted like a rope in a pattern reminiscent of the four columns framing the altar in Saint Peter's Basilica. Emeralds, rubies, and ambers studded the ends of the scroll case before the caps, inlaid with silver and adorned with the symbol of a five-pointed star.

"It's so beautiful," Kira said.

"It could be the twin of the Testament of Solomon," Pietro added.

Fereydun reached into the amphora twice and produced two more scroll cases identical to the first.

"You believe these are touched by the power?" Kira asked Alais.

"At least one of them is," she replied. "Let's find out which." For a heartbeat, Alais closed her eyes, then whispered a word. "*Eoh.*" Light emanated from her palm, washing over the scroll cases on the table. The one in the middle shimmered with a faint blue glow.

Fereydun's eyes widened while Kira sucked in a breath.

Ciarán could already guess which of the three scrolls mentioned in Saint Helena's letter was giving off the light.

His hands shaking slightly, Fereydun picked up the glowing scroll case and twisted off the cap. From the opening, he drew an age-worn papyrus scroll. As he slowly unfurled it, Ciarán could tell the delicate words adorning the papyrus were written in Hebrew.

Pietro leaned over the table, squinting as he read the title aloud.

THE WAR OF THE SONS OF LIGHT AGAINST THE SONS OF DARKNESS

"This will take much time to read," Fereydun said.

"I don't think what we're looking for is in the text," Ciarán replied. "At least that wasn't the case with the Testament of Solomon."

"Turn it over," Pietro told Fereydun.

Carefully, the magus turned over the scroll, revealing a wordless sheet of papyrus.

"My lady," Pietro said, glancing up at Alais, "we need more of your light."

Alais let her soul light flow over the papyrus. Lines of golden glowing light began to appear, spreading from the center of the sheet and snaking outward like the branches of an oak.

Kamran let out a gasp; Fereydun sucked in an excited breath.

Ciarán felt a surge of hope as he watched the image take shape. For just like the Testament of Solomon and the blank pages in the book of Maugis d'Aygremont, this scroll contained hidden imagery revealed only by the glow of soul light. As the image continued to etch itself across the page, some of the spidery branches began to twist and cross over one another, forming a rough circle around the image. Several of the scraggly lines started to widen, while others stayed narrow, giving the image a starker resemblance to the ancient branches one would see above the trunk of a mighty oak, and for a moment, Ciarán wondered if he were gazing upon the tree of fiery leaves that Tara had seen in her dreams. Near the top left of the papyrus, a new image took shape: large, round, and slightly oval. Then letters began to appear, each in Hebrew, forming six words. Five appeared above the thickest branches, while the sixth emerged within the oval.

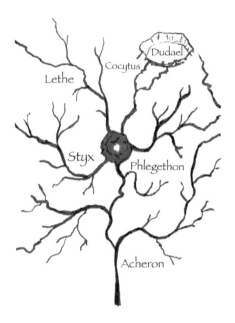

"Blessed Sergius," Pietro said. "Ciarán, your theory was right!"

Ciarán shook his head. "I never had a theory about the image of a tree."

"Those aren't tree branches." Pietro pointed to the thicker lines. "Given the names in Hebrew, those are rivers." He touched each of the five words. "Acheron, Lethe, Cocytus, Phlegethon, and Styx. And this one," he said, pointing to the oval shape, "says Dudael. Just as you had guessed, the slain souls' home is the Otherworld, and Solomon has given us a map!"

"I'll be damned," Ciarán said, studying the image. Pietro was right. What had first appeared as tree branches were actually five primary rivers, along with tributaries and streams branching off from the major waterways, one of which snaked its way to Dudael. Solomon had indeed shown them the way, but one critical detail was missing. "The map tells how to get to Dudael but doesn't show how to get to the Otherworld. I don't know where we go from here."

"There is no need for concern," Fereydun said with a smile. "This is a most miraculous discovery. For while I have long known that the place we must go to is in what you have called the Otherworld, I have always wondered how we would navigate that strange land, and now that question has been answered. It is no mystery why the Amesha Spentas guided you to this scroll through their visions to Tara."

Ciarán gritted his teeth. "But how we get to the Otherworld *is* still a mystery."

"Not if you know how to read the stars," Fereydun replied, waving a bony finger

"The prophecy says nothing about how to get to Dudael," Ciarán insisted.

In the glow of the map's light, the amused look returned to Kira's face. "I warned you, no one knows more about the stars and their meaning than my father."

A mischievous gleam sparked in Fereydun's eyes. "What are the final constellations that comprise the prophecy?"

Ciarán thought for a moment. "Taurus, Gemini, Cancer, and Leo."

"And what is to the right of Leo?"

"The Hydra, a symbol of the Dragon."

Fereydun leaned closer to Ciarán. "True, it is a symbol of Ahriman traveling to the place of the final conflict. But sometimes, symbols can have more than one meaning."

Dual meanings, Ciarán thought. This was not the first time he had encountered one. But what other meaning could the Hydra have?

Just then, Pietro smacked his forehead. "Blessed Sergius!"

"You know the answer?" Fereydun asked with a curious smile.

"I think so," Pietro said. "In Greek mythology, it was called the Lernaean Hydra after the place where Heracles fought the beast. So, the Hydra tells us the location of the gateway. It's in Greece, at Lerna."

Fereydun clapped his hands. "Very good! Not only do we now know where to go, but we can also find our way to Dudael once we get there. Now, there's only one more thing we need to learn."

"What's that?" Alais asked.

Fereydun gazed into the alcove where Tara and Sara slept. "Whatever it is these two need to tell us."

CHAPTER 56

THE FINAL MESSAGE

Within the alcove, beneath the dim light of an oil lamp, Tara and Sara joined hands as they slept, making Alais wonder if Fereydun was right. Perhaps the two sisters were together in whatever dream or vision they found themselves in.

Alais watched them from the trestle table in Fereydun's comfortable home. All the bowmen except for Kamran had retired to an adjacent chamber for the evening. Kamran joined them at the table, along with Ciarán, Pietro, Kira, and Fereydun. Kamran spoke few words, but his sister, Kira, said plenty, acting as the matron of the family. After insisting they eat something while holding vigil for the twins, Kira brought out a platter of flatbread, olives, and a block of tangy white cheese, along with carafes of pale red wine. "Eat up," she said. "We will all need our strength for the upcoming voyage."

Ciarán cocked his head. "Voyage?"

"To the Lerna Gate," Kira replied. "It is only accessible by boat, and we must leave soon to have any hope of getting there in time."

"In time for what?" Alais asked.

"The gateway is only open for three days surrounding the summer solstice," Kira explained.

Alais raised an eyebrow. That sounded much like the gateway they discovered at Stonehenge, if, in fact, it was a portal to the Otherworld. "How do you know this?"

Kira looked at her father, who was sucking on an olive. "You've always relished the role of storyteller, father."

Fereydun spit out the olive pit and set it on the table. "I will tell you our tale, and in time, you will tell me yours, for we have much to learn from one another. But our tale begins with one of the magi's most treasured secrets—our knowledge of the yazatas, for not all of them dwell in the heavens, as you know. In the east, people call them the Jann, and in the west, you refer to them as the Fae. But in truth, they are all yazatas and three of them have instructed me and my forefathers for generations. It was they who told me the time when the Lerna Gate would open to our mortal world, and it was they who gave my ancestors the prophecy concerning the two young women in our care." He gestured to the alcove where Tara and Sara lay sleeping.

It did not surprise Alais to learn there were others like Orionde and Nimue in the world. Though what intrigued her the most was Fereydun's revelation that three of these beings have been aiding him and his people, and even prophesied about twins. She could tell from the wide-eyed look on Ciarán's face that he was equally fascinated by this development.

"A prophecy about Tara and her sister?" he asked.

Fereydun scratched his beard beneath a sunken cheek. "It was why we have known for so long how important the twins will be in the conflict that awaits us. You see, the twins are the descendants of a woman named Nura who lived about two centuries ago. She was not Persian, nor was she Zoroastrian. Rather, she was a Moor who came from the land of al-Andalus. Her father was a famous warrior and poet named Faris al-Basar, and he knew of the prophecy written in the heavens."

Ciarán nearly choked on his wine. "Fierabras—he was one of Charlemagne's paladins, like Maugis d'Aygremont."

"Yes," Fereydun acknowledged, "it appears the servants of the foreign emperor Charles harbored these secrets, and Faris al-Basar passed them on to his daughter. When she lost her father at a fairly young age, Nura took this knowledge with her on a journey to Baghdad and ultimately to the land of Bukhara, where she met a Persian man who also understood the secrets of the prophecy. He was an apprentice, studying the ways of the magi, and eventually became one of our order. After Nura converted to our faith, the two of them wed, and Nura soon became with child. Before the child's birth, the chief Magus at the time, a wise ancestor of mine, went to the vanishing oasis to see Ilat, leader of the Jann. There, she foretold that in two hundred years, around the time the Christians call the millennium, Ahura Mazda would send two prophets, twins born of Nura's bloodline, who will cause great anguish to Ahriman in the mighty conflict written of in the stars. So ever since, my people have protected Nura's descendants, many of whom followed in the ways of the magi."

Fereydun took a sip of wine. "Two generations ago, Ilat told our ancestors that the journey of the prophecy would take our people to Constantinople. So my people moved here and built a life for themselves as they waited for the time of prophecy. However, the one thing we did not know was that the enemy lived here, too. Descendants of Ahriman and his daevas who crossbred with the Greeks of this land, keeping their true nature secret while holding themselves out to the world as wealthy merchants of the House of Gogam.

"My late wife was of Nura's line. Thirteen years ago, when my youngest daughter, Shirin, had twins, I knew the time of prophecy had come. Though seven years ago, I feared everything we had worked for might have been lost in the Sea of Marmara. We thought only Sara had survived the assassins' attack. But Ahura Mazda works in mysterious ways, and he brought Tara into your care. When Sara began having her visions, we learned Tara had survived and that the time of their reunion was near. We have been preparing for this day ever since."

Ciarán cast a sidelong glance to the room where the archers had retired. "Were these men part of your preparations?"

Fereydun's eyes narrowed. "We are preparing for a war, are we not? These men have served as my guardians since the attack that claimed the life of my daughter and son-in-law. But they are not the only ones. My son, Kamran, has been recruiting men to our cause. Many are men of our faith who understand that the conflict between Ahura Mazda and Ahriman continues on Earth. Some are Muslims who find similarities between their faith and ours, and others are Christian Greeks who understand our ways. We call them the Aswaran. In the Persian empire of our ancestors, the Aswaran were noble warriors, servants of the king of kings. Our Aswaran are the warriors of Ahura Mazda, and Kamran is their leader. "

"The Aswaran number nearly a hundred," Kamran interjected. "They are well-trained and have been taught to overcome their fears. These men revere the mysteries of the magi, and they understand the coming conflict will take them to a place beyond the edge of this world. Several of our followers are wealthy enough to own ships. So we have two vessels to take us to the Lerna Gate."

Listening to Kamran and Fereydun, Alais felt a surge of hope. They may have failed to obtain Greek Fire from the emperor, but they gained the assistance of a small army. On top of that, they now had the means to rendezvous with Holger's crew at Myros, where hopefully, Gerbert's ships carrying the Dragonslayers would be waiting.

"That is not all," Fereydun said, holding up his index finger. "Once we pass through the Lerna Gate, Ilat will find us. So, three of the Jann will join our cause."

Alais sucked in a breath. This was more help than they ever could have fathomed. She glanced at Ciarán, whose mouth had fallen open. Pietro looked equally stunned.

"Blessed Sergius," he said under his breath, making the sign of the cross.

A moan from the alcove drew Alais' attention to the twins. Tara sat up and opened her eyes before throwing her arms around her sister. Sara, also awake, held her tight as tears of joy streamed down the twins' faces. Everyone stood from the table. Kira hurried to Tara and wrapped her in an embrace. "It's so good to see you again," Kira said, fighting back her own tears.

Meanwhile, Fereydun's eyes gleamed with excitement. "What did they tell you, my dears?"

Sara looked at him bravely, still holding her sister's hand. "They said, '*Five seals are broken, yet two remain, though aid in these labors you must obtain.*'"

Tara finished the verse. "'*Through Leviathan's breath and Behemoth's teeth, at the center of gloom where the rivers meet.*'"

"What does it mean?" Sara asked.

Alais glanced at Pietro, who was already fumbling with the cap of the scroll case. When he opened it, he spread the blank papyrus on the table and looked up at Alais.

She closed her eyes and drew in a breath. "*Eoh.*" Soul light blazed from her palm, washing over the papyrus and bringing the map to life. When the glowing lines crawling across the papyrus completed the image, the last phrase of the twins' message became clear.

Ciarán pointed to the center of the map. "The place where the rivers meet."

Fereydun clapped his hand. "Now we know what we need to do. Go to that place and discover what further aid awaits us."

Alais could hardly believe this unexpected turn of fate. Yet, from the fleeting memories of her past lives, she had a sense of what awaited them, for they were about to enter the Dragon's lair, the realm of the oldest of all enemies, a being of fire and fury whose terrible might knew no equal.

Down there, they would need all the help they could get.

PART FOUR

When he opened the sixth seal, I looked, and there came a great earthquake; the sun became as sackcloth, the full moon became like blood, and the stars of the sky fell to the earth as the fig tree drops its winter fruit when shaken by a gale.

— Revelation 6:12-13

CHAPTER 57

THE COMING DOOM

The night after the ships departed Constantinople, Ciarán found himself trapped in the billowing gray mists. Vapor coiled around his limbs, holding them outstretched, his bare feet never touching the ground.

He was not alone.

Across from him, through the oppressive gloom, floated the hooded figure, his golden irises gleaming within the hollow of the cowl.

"I see you have found allies in the followers of that long-dead prophet Zoroaster," the Dragon said coldly. "I remember him well. As old as the first Egyptians. He understood this conflict better than most, though he chose the wrong side. So have you."

Ciarán gritted his teeth, anger rising within him. "Your servants couldn't stop us in Constantinople."

The Dragon laughed under his breath. "All you did was cull the unworthy from my ranks. You will meet the strongest among them soon—if you make it that far."

A hiss slithered through the vapor surrounding Ciarán as the Dragon spoke another of his alien words. *"Agrit."*

From the cold mists, a swell of heat surrounded Ciarán's right foot, just shy of burning. He wanted to look down, but the vapor coiling around his neck held his head, forcing him to stare into those golden irises. Around him, ghostly whispers followed as if on cue.

Ozam, odamma, cialpor, mir, agrit …

Ciarán grimaced. "What does it mean?"

"In time, you'll understand."

"Why are you doing this?"

"To show you the truth." The Dragon held out his palms aglow with golden light clinging to his golden skin. "Do you want to know how this journey ends?"

Ciarán tried to shake his head. He did not know if he could bear another vision. "Whatever you show me will be a lie," he insisted.

"See for yourself."

The figure's black robes dissolved into smoke, and in a breath, his entire being disappeared into the mists. Where he had been, another image took shape—large jagged rocks surrounded by freezing mist. Curved wooden beams jutted from the rocks like the rib cage of some long-dead sea beast. Tattered red sailcloth fluttered from the rocks near a gray beach littered with broken oars and a shattered prow bearing a dragon's head, its lifeless black eye staring into the dark gray gloom of the sky.

Ciarán found himself unable to take his gaze off the wreckage. *Lindworm …*

He felt a rush, like a strong wind behind his back, propelling him fast over a dying, gray landscape that reminded him of the barren plains surrounding Rosefleur, except these were shrouded in perpetual dusk. A war chant boomed across the plain.

"OZAM, ODAMMA, CIALPOR, MIR, AGRIT!"

Ahead, a shield wall of Danes braced itself to meet a charging horde of pale-skinned giants. Outnumbering the Danes, the giants crashed through the shield wall like a tidal wave. Bodies flew backward, men screamed, and the air misted with blood. One of the hulking pale giants raised a massive spear in triumph. Impaled on its shaft writhed a dying warrior, his golden hair slick with blood.

Holger!

As the wind at his back pushed Ciarán closer to the battle, he saw so many faces he recognized in the carnage. Freybjorn and Jorundr, Strong Bjorn and Úlfarr. Near them, a woman lay dead, her wild red hair spilling onto the gray earth next to the lifeless form of a boarhound with a spear impaling its barrel chest, pinning it to the ground.

Rosta, Breda!

With a whirr, the wind tore Ciarán to another part of the battlefield. A woman, tall and pale like the giant warriors, with long, black hair pulled tight behind her neck and an obsidian gemstone set into her prominent forehead, trudged across the plane. Her right hand, at the end of a long, lithe arm ringed with bracelets, gripped the hair of two small corpses, dragging them over the ground.

Ciarán gasped when he noticed streaks of white in their otherwise dark hair.

The woman hauled the girls past another corpse—a monk dressed in a Benedictine habit with a sword protruding from his ample stomach.

Ciarán's heartbeat quickened as their names caught in his throat. *Tara, Sara, Pietro …*

The wind whipped Ciarán away from his dead friends, sending him hurtling towards a hill topped with a towering black obelisk. Spidery cracks crawled down the obelisk's surface from its pointed crown to its base atop enormous gray boulders that comprised the hill. As the wind brought him closer, Ciarán saw the hill was not made of boulders but of thousands of mammoth skulls piled atop one another. Few were manlike; most were beastlike, with long tusks, jutting teeth, and curved horns. But neither the nightmarish skulls nor the crumbling obelisk stoked the terror filling Ciarán's veins, for Alais was pressed against one of the titanic skulls, wrestling with a much larger man dressed in dark, close-fitting armor. When the man reared his right arm back, gripping a slender sword, Ciarán recognized the fury on her attacker's familiar face. Naberus da Roma let out a cry followed sharply by Alais' scream as he plunged the blade into her chest. Alais' eyes rolled into the back of her head; the color drained from her skin, which began to dry up and wither like dead winter leaves.

Ciarán's heart sank into his stomach as we watched her spirit drain away.

As Naberus pulled the sword free, Alais' blood, slick on the blade, disappeared as though it was being absorbed into the steel. Naberus puffed out his chest and let out a victorious cry. Then he climbed up the hill of skulls until he reached the obelisk. He placed his hand on its surface. The spidery cracks began to widen and spread until the entire obelisk shook. The cracking of stone filled the air like a peal of thunder the instant before the obelisk imploded, crashing into brittle pieces on the hilltop from where the pillar had stood, followed by a plume of black smoke.

Then the entire hill exploded.

Shards of skulls flew past Ciarán's head. Where the hill had stood was the mouth of a yawning chasm. Out of the abyss crawled a horde of long-limbed, hard-chiseled giants with flesh as dark as night, as if their skin was made of shadows. Their eyes burned red like the fires at the heart of a volcano. Over these beings, as if summoned from the smoke, the Dragon flapped his massive wings, his scales burning like embers, and his molten eyes fixed on Ciarán. Behind dagger-like teeth, fire gathered in the back of the Dragon's throat, emitting a furnace-like heat that pressed against Ciarán's skin.

Ciarán gave a hoarse gasp as a torrent of fire blasted from the Dragon's mouth. Flames engulfed him, searing through his skin, ripping a desperate scream from his throat.

And over his scream and the crackling flames, the Dragon roared in triumph.

~

"You're safe!" Pietro said, wrapping his arms around Ciarán. Cold sweat covered Ciarán's face, and it took a moment for him to stop shaking after the sensation of being burned alive.

He found himself sitting on the gangplanks within the hull of

Fereydun's Byzantine vessel. He must have fallen out of his hammock, one of sixty hanging inside the hull filled with sleeping Aswaran warriors. Kamran and two of his Aswaran knelt beside Ciarán.

"What has happened to him?" Kamran asked.

"The one you call Ahriman torments his dreams," Pietro replied.

Kamran raised a wary eyebrow. "We must tell my father."

"I'll tell him," Ciarán said, scanning his arms, which looked perfectly normal. Though a moment ago, they seemed on fire.

Pietro handed Ciarán a wooden cup of watered ale. "What did he show you?"

Ciarán took a sip of the ale. "He showed me what will happen when we get to Dudael. We can't save the pillar. I saw how each of us is going to die."

The color drained from Pietro's face. "He's the father of lies, remember that."

Ciarán nodded. "But may God help us all, for I don't know how we can defeat him."

Kamran set his jaw. "Do you think this cause is worth risking our lives?"

Ciarán closed his eyes, knowing the answer. They would either die soon in the coming battle or die later after the Dragon and the Watchers brought about the End of Days. But the difference might be the millions of other souls whose lives could be spared in the remote chance they prevailed in Dudael. He looked Kamran in the eyes. "It is," Ciarán admitted.

"Then we will fight him," Kamran said. "And along the way, Ahura Mazda will show us how."

CHAPTER 58

MYROS

The Byzantine galley glided through the Aegean Sea, its rigging creaking as the vessel rocked slightly. The ship was named *Daena* after a holy maiden of the Zoroastrian faith, and it carried Tara toward her destiny.

A second galley, named *Anahita*, sailed alongside *Daena*. Both were twin-masted vessels with sixty oars, longer and broader than Lindworm. With the triangular sails filled with wind, the oarsmen rested on the top deck. A lower deck lay beneath them, filled with supplies and hammocks for the warriors, while a comfortable deckhouse stood in the ship's aft.

Father Michele had told Tara she would go on this voyage, and as dangerous as she knew it would be, she felt as if a deep void inside her had been filled. For as terrifying as it had been to return to Constantinople and confront the assassins who had murdered her parents, Tara had reunited with the twin sister she thought to be long lost, as well as an aunt, an uncle, and a grandfather. She could faintly remember them from her youth. Still, with the love they had already shown her, Tara felt at home, even if that home was a galley sailing toward a mysterious gateway that Lady Alais and Brother Ciarán said would lead to some place called the Otherworld.

Tara's newfound family was so different from the nuns who had raised her. She had grown up in a convent where she was taught all things magic are evil. That oracles and magi are witches, and witchcraft is the work of the Devil. Sara, by contrast, grew up in the Sacred Palace, raised secretly by their aunt Kira in the ways of their people. People of the Zoroastrian faith revere the magi and believe their talents are gifts from the creator, Ahura Mazda. The same creator, Tara thought, that she was taught to call God the Father and Lord. Tara found it mystifying how two religions that worship the same being could have such differing views. But at least among her family, she was no longer a witch to be burned at the stake, but a daughter with gifts to be treasured. Gifts like those that had allowed her to survive the fight inside the basilica cistern, for Tara knew in her heart it had been a power inside her that put an end to the menacing woman. Their mother possessed similar gifts, and so did their father and grandfather. Her aunt Kira shared them too, and under her tutelage, Sara had even learned how to summon a brilliant light into a crystal. Tara could hardly wait to learn how to do that.

Tara stood on the prow with Sara as sea spray blasted up the hull, kissing their faces. "I'm sure Aunt Kira will teach you soon," Sara said as they watched a pair of dolphins play in the ship's bow wave. "Maybe when we get to Myros."

The name of the fishing village on the isle of Lemnos brought a faint smile to Tara's lips. "The captain said we should arrive there before dusk. I'm looking forward to it."

"Why? To finally sleep on steady land instead of this rocking boat?"

Tara shook her head. "Our ship's there. It's called *Lindworm*. There's a dog on board named Rosta. You'll love him, and Lady Breda, too. She helped protect me back in Rome."

"Is she one of the Varangians?" Sara asked, her eyes bright. "In the palace, I grew up with the Varangian Guards. They're a boring lot. But I've never seen a wild Varangian—a Viking, as they call them."

"Lady Breda is one of them, but then, she's not. She's actually from a place called Ireland, like Brother Ciarán."

Sara tilted her head. "You keep calling him that, but he looks nothing like a monk."

Tara thought about that, scraping her fingers through her damp hair. "He used to be a monk, but they still address him like one. Now, he's a warrior, and a good one too. I saw him best a giant of a man back in Rome."

"Why is his hair so white?"

"It didn't use to be," Tara said with a frown. "He has terrible dreams, and after each one, his hair's gotten whiter and whiter."

"How strange."

Tara nodded; she, too, found it very odd. Brother Ciarán had never told her what he saw in those dreams, but it must have been something awful.

"You know," Sara said with a hint of mischief in her voice, "I think he might be Lady Alais' lover."

"Her lover?" Tara blinked. "I think not."

Sara sighed. "And that's where you and I are very different. You grew up in a convent, and I grew up in a palace. I've seen how men look at women and have known more than a few ladies at court who would sneak men into their bed chambers late at night." Sara could not hide the smile on her face.

"Really?" Tara blushed.

"Of course, Aunt Kira disapproves of such things. But they still happened."

Their conversation continued for hours, as it had done every day since being reunited. After all, a seven-year separation left half a lifetime of things to learn about one another. But despite the passage of years, part of Tara felt as if she had known Sara her whole life. Looking at her sister was like gazing at her reflection in a silver mirror, and their similarities did not end with their appearance. They shared similar thoughts and tastes, and even similar mannerisms. Both used their left hand more than their right, hated the idea of eating rabbit, and loved sardines. Fortunately, rabbit was not part of the diet onboard the galley, but sardines packed in salt were a staple, and the two enjoyed some for an early supper in the deckhouse before joining the others before sunset on the prow.

Lady Alais and Brother Ciarán were there, along with their aunt Kira, uncle Kamran, and Brother Pietro. The once blue sky was now a curtain of gray haze which the setting sun's red glow threatened to pierce through. A mile ahead, the mountainous island of Lemnos rose from the Aegean Sea. Tara searched for the fishing village of Myros, but it was concealed by the haze.

As the galley closed in on the island, something delicate and feather-like landed on the tip of Tara's nose. She swiped it away, puzzled, as more descended. At first glance, it seemed like a gentle flurry of gray snowflakes. But accompanying them was a caustic, acrid odor that clawed its way into her nostrils, turning her stomach into a tight coil of dread.

Beside her, Alais inhaled sharply, as if the air itself had turned to poison, while Ciarán's voice, a broken whisper, cut through the tension. "No."

A chill lanced through Tara, crystallizing her disquiet into sheer panic. The "flakes" weren't snow; they were ashes. And where the village of Myros should have stood was instead an immense plume of smoke, smearing the sky in a haunting tapestry of gray.

CHAPTER 59
ASH AND BONES

Despair crashed over Ciarán like a wave as he waded through the knee-deep tide, surveying the devastation as he approached the village of Myros.

The burnt husks of ships lay half-submerged in the harbor, veiled by a haze of smoke and ash. Soot-covered masts jutted from the tidewater while the remains of broken oars littered a beach marred with blackened corpses strewn among mounds of seaweed. His mind shuddered as he wondered which of the burned-out hulls belonged to *Lindworm* and who among its crew lay dead and scattered on that beach.

"Breda and Holger ... Mordechai ... all of them," Alais muttered beside Ciarán, choking back tears.

Ciarán's chin quivered as he tried to fight back the swell of emotion and quell the sickening feeling in his stomach as he breathed in the stench of burnt timber and flesh. As he neared the beach, he counted more than forty corpses burned beyond recognition. If their friends were among them, they would be hard to identify. The thought of having to do so twisted like a knife in Ciarán's heart, and that blade twisted deeper as he realized what this meant for the rest of them. For along with *Lindworm's* crew, Caladbolg was surely gone, and with it went any hope of surviving the coming conflict.

Alais held her hands over her mouth as she trudged through the water toward the beach. Nearby, Tara's face had gone ashen, tears streaming down her cheeks. Her twin, Sara, looked stunned, but she could not have imagined Tara's grief. Their aunt, Kira, gazed stone-faced at the carnage as she waded toward the beach, as did her brother, Kamran. Meanwhile, Fereydun's eyes filled with shock and sorrow, while beside him, Pietro clutched the crucifix that hung around his neck. "Blessed Sergius," he said under his breath.

The piers of Myros had been reduced to smoking piles of timber. Beyond them, through the gray haze, stood the remains of the village, the shops and houses burned down to their stone foundations. Tendrils of smoke wafted from the wreckage. As Ciarán and the others traipsed up the beach, the village square came into view. Dozens of charred bodies lay on the ash-covered ground as if every man, woman, and child in Myros had been put to the torch.

"Why would anyone do this?" Alais sobbed.

"To send a message," Kira replied coldly.

Was that it? Ciarán felt the weight of these lost lives piling onto the burden he already carried, all while Niall's voice from the Dragon's vision echoed in his mind: *"You're going to let them all die ..."*

Ciarán grasped at his chest as dull pain gathered there, then let out a shuddering breath as he gazed upon what stood before the smoking remains of the parish church. A tall wooden post had been erected at the church steps, and affixed to it was a circular shield with a black face. A golden seven-pointed star touched the edges of the shield, and in its center, also painted in gold, was the image of the Dragon shaped like an inverted pentagram. Golden crowns adored each of the pentagram's points next to a letter, all five of which formed a now familiar word:

MAGOG

But that word was not the whole of the message. For slumped against the post was the only corpse left unburned. Ciarán recognized him as the parish priest Pietro had paid when they first arrived in Myros en route to Constantinople. The priest was already old, but the corpse sitting at the foot of the post looked practically ancient. The skin of his face was dried and cracked like a pale sheet of parchment, and his lips and eyes had lost all color, as if the man's lifeblood had been drained from beneath his skin. It was the same look Demetrius had when they found his lifeless body in the vestibule of Hagia Sophia. As if both of their lives had been taken in some terrifying, unnatural way, the product of whatever dark arts Naberus da Roma had learned to wield.

There was more, however. A torn piece of sailcloth was tied to the crucifix hanging from the dead priest's neck. Ciarán pulled it free. Scrawled on the cloth was a phrase he had heard before, and reading it sent an icy shiver up his neck.

"Your God has failed you, and your cause is lost."

"What is it?" Alais asked.

"Something Naberus da Roma said to me when we were attacked off the English coast. When Caladbolg fell into the sea, he said God had abandoned us, and our cause was lost. I fear this time he's right."

Alais clung to Ciarán's arm; he could not stop a tear streaming down his cheek. Meanwhile, Tara began convulsing with sobs as Kira and Sara wrapped her in an embrace.

Fereydun shuffled toward Ciarán and plucked the torn sailcloth from his hand. The Magus crumpled it in his bony fist, then flung it into the smoking remains of the church.

"All you see around you are the husks of a mortal life," Fereydun said angrily. "But their souls have moved on to cross the Chinvat Bridge into the next life. Who do you think gave them that power? Do you see Him here among the dead?" The Magus held out his palms, gesturing to the bodies in the square. "No—which means there is hope. This fight is not over; the enemy has not won!"

Ciarán clenched his jaw. "You don't know what we're facing."

"Rubbish. I have studied the sacred writings about *Him* for two of your lifetimes, and I know our prophecies." He pointed to Tara and Sara. "We have these two, and they will bring great anguish to Ahriman."

Ciarán shook his head. These two young women could not make up for losing Caladbolg—the one weapon the Dragon feared —or the prowess of *Lindworm's* crew. Fereydun had known none of them, nor had he ever seen Caladbolg in all of its fiery glory. Ciarán's gaze wandered over the burned corpses, and the pain grew heavier in his chest.

"You have no idea what we've lost," he said.

Fereydun curled his lips, but before he could speak, one of Kamran's warriors called up from the beach.

"Sails, to the south!" the man cried with a look of alarm. "Four of them—the attackers are coming back!"

CHAPTER 60
REVERSAL OF FORTUNE

Kamran shot Ciarán a look of grim determination. "We must get the ships to sea now!"

Ciarán's heartbeat quickened. "Aye." He peered out to sea and spotted the four vessels, barely silhouettes before the horizon. But if these were Byzantine war galleys, he had little doubt they were moving fast.

To his right, Kira grabbed Tara and Sara by their arms. "Move girls, back to the ships!"

Fereydun glanced at Ciarán. The Magus's eyes, so confident a moment ago, now shimmered with a hint of fear.

Kamran sprinted from the village square to the beach, joining four of his men and gesturing everyone to hurry. "Make haste!"

Ciarán allowed Kira, the twins, and Fereydun to go ahead, then followed them along with Alais. Pietro huffed alongside them, moving as fast as his heavy-set frame would allow.

As they reached the beach, Alais slowed down.

Ciarán turned to her. "What are you doing?"

The stern look in her storm-gray eyes was all the answer he needed. It was the same look he had seen outside the Varangian's fortress. She wiped the tears from her cheeks, holding her chin high. "I can stop them."

Ciarán glanced back at the ships, recalling what she did to the pirate vessel they encountered off the Sicilian coast. The memory of that capsized vessel brought a glimmer of hope. All she needed was a bigger wave, and these four ships might suffer the same fate. "I'll stay by your side."

Pietro had his hands on his knees, catching his breath. "As will I."

Alais took her hand from Ciarán's. He could sense the energy gathering in the air around her. "They'll answer for this carnage."

"Hurry on!" Kamran called back, having reached the ship.

"Come back for us," Ciarán yelled.

"You're staying?" Kamran asked incredulously.

"Remember," Ciarán bellowed, "she has the yazata within her."

Even from the beach, Ciarán saw Kamran's eyes grow wide. Fereydun glanced back; a look of wonder had replaced the fear in his eyes. The Magus raised a fist in the air. "For Ahura Mazda!"

As Kira and the twins scurried up a rope ladder onto the nearest ship, Alais stepped into the surf. Ten yards in, she knelt in the water, placing her hands into the rolling tide. A verse rolled off her tongue with the melody of a song. Around her, the air thrummed, and the tidewater surrounding her hand began to froth and swirl, forming into whirlpools that grew in size with each Fae word uttered from her lips.

Ciarán peered at the enemy ships. They were moving with considerable speed, with churning oars and full sails. However, something struck Ciarán about these sails. They were square-shaped, unlike the triangular sails Ciarán had seen on every Byzantine vessel since they arrived at Constantinople. He squinted his eyes. One of the sails appeared striped, though the other three bore images. His jaw fell when he realized the images were crosses, crimson in color against a white field. As for the vessel with the striped sail, Ciarán recognized its prow: shaped like a sea serpent, rearing back and ready to strike.

His breath caught in his throat. "Alais, stop!"

The seawater surrounding her seethed and swelled. Upon hearing Ciarán's words, she jerked her head toward him, leaving her trance.

"It's *Lindworm!*"

Alais ripped her hands from the water, and the angry sea dissolved into a rolling tide.

"Blessed Sergius," Pietro remarked, his face beaming.

Alais stood up, holding a hand over her mouth. Her eyes widened with joy.

Kamran and the others had not recognized the ships, for their two vessels had raised their anchors and dropped their oars into the water. Ciarán did not worry about them; they would soon deduce what was happening. Instead, he, Alais, and Pietro waded deeper into the water as the four ships neared. Behind *Lindworm's* prow, Ciarán could see Holger's golden hair with Breda by his side. The jarl lifted a sheathed sword above his head, its cross-shaped hilt with a gemstone in its pommel gleaming like a beacon of hope.

Caladbolg!

As the four vessels rowed toward shore, Ciarán recognized another man standing at one of the bows. It was Gaido, the crimson-cloaked captain of the papal guard. The three ships with crosses emblazoned on their sails must have been the ones Gerbert sent carrying the Dragonslayers. Ciarán could hardly believe how quickly their fortunes had turned.

When *Lindworm* had rowed as close as it could in the shallow water, Holger leaped into the tidewater. Breda followed her husband while men gathered in the bow, Jorundr, Strong Bjorn, and Mordechai among them. Breda embraced Alais, and Holger wrapped Ciarán in a bear hug. The jarl handed over Caladbolg. The sword's familiar weight within Ciarán's grasp brought a tremendous wave of relief, as if a void within him had been filled.

"I told you I'd guard it with my life," Holger said.

"I'm grateful you did." Ciarán glanced back at the village. "Did you see what happened?"

"The jötnar happened," Holger replied grimly. "Mordechai spotted them first, two warships, each twice the size of *Lindworm.*

After warning the village, we set out to sea, hoping to draw both warships away. But only one followed us, and she was no match for *Lindworm's* speed. With the wind in our sail, we lost them around one of the other islands and hid in a cove. We sent lookouts to the highest ridge, and when we were certain the warship was gone, we set back out for Myros. It was then, to our surprise, that we encountered Gaido and his ships sailing toward the rendezvous point."

Holger shook his head, eying the devastation. "The second of the two jötnar vessels must have anchored here and razed the village. The only crime these people committed was letting us moor there. There was no reason for this. But then again, we're dealing with monsters."

"We'll make them pay," Breda said with a hard look in her eyes before turning back to Alais. "Is Tara safe?"

Alais nodded. "She is, and she's reunited with her twin sister. It turns out the girl had been living in the palace under the protection of her family for years."

Breda's eyes widened. "Her parents are alive?"

"No," Alais explained, "but her aunt stayed with her in the palace disguised as a chambermaid while her uncle and grandfather aided them from the city. The grandfather is the leader of a religious sect, while the uncle commands a band of warriors who helped us evade our enemies."

"Are those their ships?" Holger asked, peering at the two Byzantine vessels turning back toward shore.

"Aye," Ciarán replied. "They're Persians like Khalil was. I think you'll like them."

Holger's lips twisted into a grin. "If they help us fight these jötnar, I like them already." He combed his fingers through his long, golden hair. "Tell me, did you find the scroll?"

"We did. It contained a map of Dudael, as we had hoped. And we've discovered the location of the gateway that will take us there."

Holger sighed, though his lips curled into a grin. "So we sail toward Ragnarok together, just as Blind Mikkel said."

"There's more you should know," Ciarán said right before a voice called out from the direction of the papal ships.

"Ho, Brother Ciarán!" Wading toward him was Gaido. The normally stern-faced guard captain carried the ghost of a smile. "His Holiness sends his regards."

"Captain, you are a sight for sore eyes," Ciarán said with a grin. "How many men did you muster?"

"Sixty. A third are papal guardsmen, many of whom fought with you and the Danes outside the Temple of Venus and Roma. The rest are men of faith from the towns around Rome and as far north as Umbria and Tuscany. Some had fought among the ranks of their lords at one time or another. Most have no families. The rest are mostly young men with varying degrees of skill with bows or swords, though more than a few began their training after we recruited them. They're driven more by a sense of adventure, hoping to escape a life working on the farms or caring for livestock. But a few are seasoned warriors."

Gaido glanced toward one of the ships where a mail-clad warrior towered over the railing on the bow. The man wore a pointed helm topped with a horsehair plume. Ciarán recognized him at once.

"Gundoald?"

"Thought you'd be surprised to see him," Gaido said. "After the horrors he witnessed in the Theatre of Pompey, he laid down his sword at the gate to the Lateran Palace and volunteered for the mission. I suppose fighting the living dead changes a man."

"Thank the Lord it did. He's a hell of a fighter." Ciarán ran his hand over his chin. "Did His Holiness give these men any sense of where we're going?"

"He told them a story about some ancient king named Odysseus who ventured through strange lands and fought monsters of legends, even going so far as to visit the Underworld, all so he could find his way home and save his family from wicked men. Like King Odysseus, the pope said, this journey would take them to lands off any map, to places spoken of only in legends, not to save a single family, but to save all the kingdoms of men. Not very direct if you ask me. Maybe you can speak to them when the time comes. Most have heard how you defeated Gundoald, and they're eager to fight alongside you. Even Gundoald speaks of you as a hero with a blade that burns like the sun."

"I'll talk to them," Ciarán said. But even as the words left his lips, he felt their unbearable weight crash down upon him. Sixty lives. Nearly a hundred Aswaran in Kamran's crew. Men who were utterly unaware of the nightmare they were about to step into. These men might have heard tales of the Otherworld, but hearing and seeing are oceans apart. The Sisters of Orionde had called it purgatory, but he suspected Dudael was far worse, even more unforgiving than the Otherworld he knew. But the location, dark as it might be, was not the crux of the matter. As brave as these souls might fancy themselves, they had never come face-to-face with the Dragon. Never felt the terror that only his molten gaze could instill. That raw, incomprehensible fear. And yet, despite their naivety, their eyes were on him. They were looking to Ciarán to lead them into the abyss.

In the recesses of Ciarán's mind, Niall's words echoed hauntingly—words never spoken in life, yet chillingly prophetic: *"You're going to let them all die ..."*

Deep down, Ciarán was consumed by the fear that this terrible prophecy would come true—that he would lead these men to their doom, despite their courage. The weight of that potential reality pressed on him, as unyielding as a mountain. Unless he discovered some miraculous strategy to win this war.

Yet there, standing before Gaido with the relentless tide swirling around his knees, Ciarán felt as powerless to change their fate as he would be to leap from a mountaintop and touch the moon.

CHAPTER 61

A CALL TO ARMS

During the four-day voyage through the Greek Isles to Lerna, Alais could not help but feel she had made this voyage before. Not as Alais of Selles-sur-Cher, but in Sirra's past lives.

Fragments of those lives remained buried in her memory, conjured to the surface at times when she dreamed, and sometimes, though rarely, when she lay awake. She remembered a lake surrounded by marshlands and forest, with a mountain in the background. Pietro and Ciarán had told her this lake was famous in the ancient Greek legends, the place where Heracles slew a seven-headed dragon in its waters. The monster was called the Hydra, and it gave its name to the constellation that formed part of the prophecy. Fereydun believed the lake was one of the gateways to the Otherworld that would take them to Dudael. And from the fragments of the lives submerged deep within her memories, Alais felt confident he was right. A thousand years ago, and a thousand years before then, men had known this lake. Brave men who had been her companions in lives long ago. These men had a name for the lake, and it unsettled Alais as their ships neared the end of their voyage. For they had called it the Lake of Darkness.

Equally unsettling was the thought that the two ships of the House of Magog were but a day ahead of them, also heading for the lake at Lerna. Had those ships already entered the gateway, or would they be waiting for them outside it? Yet if they were waiting, what would they do at the sight of six vessels, three of which were papal warships and one a Viking longship? Alais hoped their enemy would choose to avoid such a conflict at Lerna, even though she knew conflict would eventually find them. Of that, she was certain. For, if nothing else, the shards of memories that invaded her dreams had warned her that, at Dudael, the journey always ended with war.

Alais could not quell these thoughts when their small fleet entered the bay that would lead to the lake at Lerna. She stood with Ciarán in *Daena's* bow, gazing at the bay. Beneath a dark gray sky, the bay's waters looked almost black, and the mountains that rimmed the bay took on a dusky hue. A slight breeze rustled Ciarán's hair, now completely white, a stark contrast to his young, handsome face.

He surveyed the bay. "Where do we go from here?"

Alais pointed to a meager settlement on the shore less than a half league away. "North of that village, a narrow river runs from the bay to the marshlands where the lake is."

His lips curled into a smile. "You remember this from Sirra's past lives?"

Alais nodded. "She's been here twice before. I feel certain of it."

"I suppose you don't have any happy memories from this point on."

"I wish I could say yes." Alais ran her fingers through her long, raven hair. "It gets harder from here on."

He turned his head starboard to look at *Lindworm*. The sleek longship glided alongside the Byzantine craft, propelled by its oars, dipping through the dark water in unison. "Holger believes we're sailing toward Ragnarok, the final destiny."

She hooked her arm around his. "Whatever they call it, it's both of our destinies."

Ciarán grimaced. "Saint Paul wrote that God will not let us be tested beyond our strength. I'm not so sure of that."

Alais drew a deep breath. She was unsure, too, but she knew Ciarán needed strength—and hope. Without it, they were doomed.

"Sirra has survived this conflict three times before," she said, "and so have the champions."

For a moment, he looked into her eyes, and a ghost of a smile returned to his lips. He glanced back to the rows of oar benches behind them where forty of Kamran's men rowed shirtless, driving the ship toward the shore.

"What about all these men?" Ciarán asked. "And those who came on the ships from Rome? Will they survive? They don't even know where they're sailing to or what they'll find when they get there. Gaido wants me to talk to them. What would I even say?"

Alais pondered for a moment, her eyes meeting his. In that brief contact, she felt something unspoken, but real. Pushing the thought aside, she focused on what she had to say. "Speak to them as you spoke to the Danes and Gaido's men in Rome before we set off for the battle at the Temple of Venus and Roma. You knew they were heading into danger, but you rallied them. You inspired them."

Her words lingered in the air, a fragile bridge between hope and dread. Ciarán chewed his lip, then finally nodded. "I'll do what I can."

With a tender touch, she caressed his cheek. "You'll be wonderful."

Yet, as she spoke, an unsettling tightness gripped her chest, as if her conscience had sprouted talons that dug deep into her heart. For despite her most fervent wishes, she knew she had just told Ciarán a lie. Because, however fractured they were, her memories of Sirra's past lives had told her one thing.

The champion did not always survive.

WHEN THE SHIPS reached the mouth of the river, they dropped anchors and, at Ciarán's request, gathered their crews on the muddy shore.

For the gathering, Ciarán dressed in the polished mail hauberk that once belonged to Maugis d'Aygremont, which Orionde had given him during the Battle of Rosefleur. Clasped with a brooch beneath his neck was the crimson cloak trimmed in gold he had received as a gift in the Sacred Palace of Constantinople, along with the fine leather boots he wore on his feet. And across his chest hung the leather baldric attached to the scabbard that held Caladbolg, its cross-shaped hilt with the gemstone embedded in its pommel resting just below his chest. He placed a hand on that pommel and gazed upon the assembled men. The crowd numbered less than two hundred. Hardly a horde. Barely even a platoon compared to the four thousand men Duke William of Aquitaine had mustered for the Battle of Brosse or the six thousand warriors Emperor Otto used to besiege Castle Sant'Angelo. But despite the meager size of the company he would lead into the Otherworld, Ciarán felt the heavy weight of all those lives on his soul.

At the front of the crowd, Jarl Holger and the Danes of *Lindworm's* crew stood taller and more imposing than the rest, clad in their chain mail and arm rings of silver and gold. Even the younger ones, like Strong Bjorn, who stood the tallest of them all, wore the hardened expressions of veteran warriors. They had fought Nephilim and demons and monks animated from the dead. More than any in this small platoon, they were prepared for what would come next. But only Jarl Holger had ever stepped foot in the Otherworld, and only he had witnessed the Dragon. It was the rest that worried Ciarán. Gaido and his twenty members of the papal guard dressed the part in their crested helms and crimson tunics over mail coats, and though he had fought alongside some of them at the Temple of Venus and Roma, that battle was against mortal men, not Nephilim. The other men from Rome were just as Gaido had described, a ragtag mix of young and old. All wore mail, thanks, in part, to Gerbert, but less than half had the bearing of warriors of any merit, and many of those were among the oldest. The rest, save one, were young.

Some were younger than Ciarán, and their expressions bothered him the most: youthful, curious, wide-eyed, and eager. Among them, only Gundoald looked as fierce as the Danes, tall and broad-shouldered, cradling his plumed helmet in his muscular left arm. Then there was Kamran and his nearly one-hundred Aswaran warriors. Instead of chain mail, most wore lighter shirts of overlapping metal plates, while others donned vests of padded leather. These were serious-looking men, and well-trained, as they proved at Hagia Sophia. They, too, were mostly young, though some were older, all bearded, like Kamran, sturdy and muscular, and all of Persian, Greek, or Arabic stock. But none had been to the Otherworld, and none had seen the Dragon. And *that* is what Ciarán had the unenviable task of trying to prepare them for.

He glanced at Alais, who stood near the back with Kira, Tara, and Sara alongside Fereydun, who leaned on a long, blackened staff that reminded Ciarán of the one Dónall once owned. Alais caught Ciarán's gaze, then nodded and smiled.

He drew a deep breath, knowing he must speak each sentence three times—first in Greek, then in Latin, and finally in Danish—so all could understand him, assuming he could find the right words. Before the ship set anchor, he had decided how his speech would begin, with words from one of his favorite Psalms. But beyond that, he had prayed to Saint Columcille that the rest of the words would come. They had to.

"Brothers," Ciarán began as he had planned, "a famous king of old once wrote, 'though I walk through the valley of the shadow of death, I will fear no evil, for the Lord is with me.' By whatever name you may call the Lord—God, Ahura Mazda, Allah—you will need all the courage your faith in Him can give you. For we all are about to enter the valley of the shadow of death."

He paused to consider his next words, knowing he must tell them about the Otherworld. As he opened his mouth to speak again, it was as if Saint Columcille had heard his prayer, for the words flowed off his tongue.

"It is a land," he told them, "spoken of in myths and legends, a place few men have gone before. My people, the Irish, call this place the Otherworld. In the legends of the Danes, it might be called Álfheimr or Niflheim. A Persian friend who was like a brother once called it Barzakh. But whatever the name, it is a land hidden in the shadows beyond the edge of our world. I do not know what we will find there or what it will look like, but I know where we are going once there. To a place called Dudael, the Cauldron of God. It is where we shall meet our enemy—the one all of you have volunteered to help fight."

Barely a murmur rippled through the crowd, and Ciarán noted that a more somber look had replaced the eager and wide-eyed expressions of the young men from Rome.

"Our enemy," Ciarán continued, "has had many names throughout time, most of which I will not speak. I call him the Dragon, and I have seen him with my own eyes, and he is every bit the winged, fire-breathing monster of legend you may have heard about in the stories. But those were only stories, and what you will face is far too real. Yet what do those stories tell us, those legends of old? That dragons can be slain! And all of us must be the heroes who strike that blow!"

This brought a roar from the crowd as men clapped their hands and pounded their chests. Their applause filled Ciarán with a surge of hope, and at that moment, the once impossible idea of defeating the Dragon felt suddenly real.

"Our enemy seeks to end the age of men and bring about the End of Days. So we fight for nothing less than the fate of mankind. For a future for your families, your children, and your countrymen!"

More cheers erupted from the assembled warriors. Among the Danes, Jarl Holger gave Ciarán an approving nod. When the cheers died down, Ciarán took a more somber tone. "To win this battle, all of us will need to be brave. And there is no question this will be dangerous. Some of us will not return, and some will give the ultimate sacrifice for our cause. I understand if that is too much to ask, and if it is, walk away now. For once we board those ships, there will be no turning back."

Ciarán held his breath as he looked out at the assembled men. They gazed back at him, many with hard looks of resolve on their faces, though others looked afraid.

Jarl Holder was the first to raise his voice, drawing Curtana and lifting it above his head. "*Lindworm's* crew will sail with you, even if the voyage leads us to the gates of Hell!"

The Danes roared.

Kamran spoke next. "My family and my brethren have prepared for this journey. We know the stakes and will not abandon you!"

The Aswaran answered with a battle cry.

Then Gaido announced, "His Holiness, Pope Sylvester, sent us on this mission. We all swore oaths, and we will not break them!"

As resounding cheers erupted around him, a wave of awe and gratitude washed over Ciarán. It was awe at the sheer loyalty and raw courage exhibited by these men and gratitude at their willingness to face whatever terrifying unknown lay ahead. Remarkably, not a single man had turned back. While Ciarán harbored no illusions about their readiness for the trials they were about to face, the knowledge that they were choosing this path of their own volition lessened the crushing weight he'd felt on his shoulders for so long.

And so, for the first time in an eternity, he realized he wasn't carrying this burden alone. In the sea of resolute faces before him, he found a new truth—whatever fate tomorrow had in store, they would meet it together.

CHAPTER 62

THROUGH THE GATE

From here on, Ciarán decided he would sail on *Lindworm*. Alais and Pietro joined him, nearly reuniting the crew that set out from Rome to Constantinople, except for Tara, who remained with her family on Fereydun's galley.

Standing inside *Lindworm's* hull brought Ciarán a familiar comfort. His round shield bearing the white cross over a crimson field still hung from a strake on the longship's gunwale beside the bench where Ciarán had pulled an oar for the better part of a year now. Mordechai now sat on that bench across from Hári Grayhair, and Ciarán could not help but marvel at how well this young Jewish sailor from France had fit in with this rugged crew of pagan and Christian Danes. Ciarán sat down on the raised platform in the stern along with Alais, Pietro, and Breda, who sat near Jarl Holger manning the steering oar. Meanwhile, Rosta lounged on the deck planks behind Mordechai's oar bench, weary from the summer heat. Ciarán kept on his hauberk, despite that heat, as did Jarl Holger and the rest of the crew, because no one knew if the enemy ships would be waiting for them when they reached the lake.

The river that would take them there was so narrow the ships would have to sail single file. *Lindworm* took the lead, followed by the Byzantine galleys, *Daena* and *Anahita*, and the three papal ships carrying the Dragonslayers, the massive ballistas nicknamed Saint George, Saint Theodore, and Saint Radegonde. In no time, Ciarán began sweating beneath the tunic and padded wool jacket he wore under his hauberk. A slight breeze wafting off the bay provided the only relief from the warm air, which seemed to grow more humid the farther they rowed upriver, where the riverbanks became more marsh-like. Soon, they were surrounded by marsh-lands and the swarms of buzzing, biting insects that dwelt in such fetid places.

Ciarán cursed as he swatted a mosquito feasting on his neck. Beside him, Pietro waved his hands to fend off the hungry insect, and Rosta began to growl, annoyed by the pests. "Do you remember how far these marshes stretch?" Ciarán asked Alais. "We're being eaten alive."

She smacked a mosquito that landed on her arm. "Less than a mile or so. My memories aren't exactly clear, but I feel the lake is close."

It turned out Alais' memories were correct, for after a half-mile traversing the marshlands and fighting off hordes of mosquitos, Ciarán glimpsed the still waters of a lake ahead. Then, from the bow of the longship, Freybjorn called out. "Jarl, Ciarán, you have to see this!"

Holger handed the steering oar to Breda and headed for the bow. As he stood up, Ciarán's stomach tightened. What if Freybjorn had spotted the two galleys of the House of Magog? He dreaded the thought of engaging the enemy in a bloody battle before they even passed through the gate.

As he followed Holger, he placed a hand on Caladbolg's hilt. Yet when he reached the bow, he saw no other vessels on the lake, only a wall of thick gray fog that stretched from one side to the other, obscuring everything beyond it. Ciarán breathed a sigh of relief.

"What is that?" Freybjorn asked, his face growing paler.

"The gate." Ciarán was sure of it, for a similar curtain of mists had marked the gateway to Rosefleur in the forest near Brosse. He remembered what Dónall had told him back then: *The gateways to the*

Otherworld can be disastrous for men who do not know the proper way to enter them.

Holger grimaced, eyeing the imposing wall of fog. "We're supposed to row into that?"

Ciarán shook his head. "I'm afraid if we just row into it, we'll be lost. We'll likely crash *Lindworm* into rocks or the lakeshore. To pass through the gate, we're going to need a little help."

As he spoke those words, he felt Alais' gentle touch on his shoulder. Ciarán glanced at her and smiled before turning back to Holger. "Seems our help's just arrived."

"You know how to guide us through that fog?" Holger asked Alais.

"I do," she replied. "Row straight toward it, and I'll do the rest."

Holger gave her a wary nod before turning to his crew. "You heard her, row!"

The jarl returned to the steering oar, but Ciarán stayed in the bow with Alais, peering around *Lindworm's* dragon-headed prow at the wall of fog that became more imposing the closer the longship came to it. By the time they reached the fog, the wall towered more than a hundred feet into the air, a ghostly, billowing mass that gave off an audible hiss that sent a chill through Ciarán's bones. He had little doubt they would be devoured if they plowed into that vapor.

From *Daena's* prow, Kamran bellowed an anxious question. "Do you know what you're doing?"

"Aye," Ciarán called back. "Follow us through!"

He looked at Alais. "Time to work your magic."

"Let's just hope it works." She reached her hand toward the hissing wall of fog and uttered a word. *"Eoh."*

A ray of pearlescent light blasted from her palm into the enormous wall of fog. At first, it seemed the wall fought back against her light, the gray fog darkening in color and swirling angrily. The hiss emanating from the vapor rose into a ghastly howl. Alais clenched her jaw, and the light projecting from her palm grew brighter. As her light pierced the fog, the wall let out a wail like a banshee's cry. Then a seam began to form where her light had struck, spreading from the lake's surface and crawling up the wall. Soon, the power of her soul-light bored through the mountain of fog, parting the vapors and creating a tunnel large enough for their ships to pass through.

Ciarán's eyes widened in awe while behind them, whispers of *"Lifthrasir"* broke out among the crew.

"We sail to Ragnarok!" Holger hollered from the stern.

Ciarán glanced back at the Danes manning their oars. Their expressions were a mix of trepidation and grim resolve. When *Lindworm's* dragon-shaped prow passed through the tunnel's threshold, Ciarán drew a sharp breath. He gripped Caladbolg's pommel, feeling a tinge of warmth from the embedded gemstone, and tried to steel his nerves. For through that gateway, there was no turning back.

The voyage would take them to Ragnarok—to Armageddon—where their final destiny awaited.

WHEN *LINDWORM* EMERGED from the tunnel through the fog, Alais let the soul light fade from her palm. Where it had been daylight when they entered the tunnel, they now found themselves in a dusk-like gloom with no hint of stars in the sky and no sign of the moon. A sudden coldness seized the air, as did a deathly silence save for the splash of oars dipping into the water.

They were in a river as narrow as the one that had led to the lake. Yet, unlike the marshes around that waterway, there was no sign of anything alive on or near this river. Not even a blade of grass grew from the crevasses on the shallow basalt cliffs that flanked the banks of the river, whose waters looked as dark as the ocean.

Beside her, Ciarán let out a relieved sigh. "They're still behind us."

Alais craned her neck to see where Ciarán was looking just as the two Byzantine galleys departed the tunnel.

"Thank goodness," she replied, feeling a sense of relief. For she did not know how long the passageway would remain open when no longer exposed to her soul light.

The shifting wall of fog surrounded the tunnel, stretching in both directions as far as her eyes could see. In the gloom, she could barely glimpse the last of the papal vessels leaving the tunnel, but once they did, the tunnel collapsed in a rush of vapor, and, in a breath, only a titanic curtain of fog remained behind them. All six ships had made it through, and for that, Alais was grateful.

She returned her attention to the river beyond *Lindworm's* serpentine prow. The rugged cliffs on each side of the river climbed higher ahead, and Alais sensed the waterway ran through a ravine. The oppressive gloom of this strange land made it hard to see too far in front of them, but eventually, she realized the river forked ahead, split by a promontory of some sort that vaguely resembled the silhouette of a man.

Alais narrowed her gaze to get a better look, then sucked in a sharp breath. For the longship was heading toward a giant. Not one of flesh and blood, but one chiseled from the same basalt rock that comprised the cliffs. The colossal carving must have stood three hundred feet tall, the image of a muscular titan wearing little more than a loincloth and a towering headdress. The titan's face was stern, almost angry, with piercing eyes and a narrow, rectangular beard that drooped from the bottom of his chin to the top of his chest. His massive arms were outstretched with equally massive hands, each gesturing toward one of the forks in the river.

"Dear God," Ciarán muttered. "Do you remember *that* from your dreams?"

Alais shook her head, still in awe of the gigantic statue. "It's asking us to choose which way to go."

Mutters of astonishment and concern percolated from the Danes on the oar benches behind them. "Black Surt," murmured Freybjorn.

"No," Jorundr said in a harsh whisper. "Ymir."

"What is it?" Holger called out from the stern.

"Jarl, you'll need to see this to believe it," Ciarán hollered back.

Holger strode up the aisle between the oar benches, where the men in the front rows gaped in disbelief at the colossus. "By the gods," Holger uttered, his jaw slack.

Following Holger, Pietro stopped in his tracks. "Blessed Sergius …"

"Who could create such a thing?" Holger asked.

"Not men," Ciarán replied.

Alais had little doubt that was true. From everything she could recall about Sirra's past lives and everything she had learned since that fateful day Ciarán and his companions saved her from burning at the stake in Selles-sur-Cher, there was a time when the gods of old ruled the world of men. But like Sirra, they were not true gods, but rather the celestial beings who had followed Samyaza to Earth. These beings had spawned the Nephilim, many of which were banished to the Otherworld. Perhaps they sculpted this statue ages ago to honor one of their divine ancestors now imprisoned beneath Dudael. Yet the colossus, no matter how awe-inspiring—or terrifying—was not the pressing issue. Rather, it was the fork in the river and the path they must choose.

"We need the map," Alais told them.

"Right," Pietro said, trying to pull his gaze away from the statue. He returned to the stern, where they stored the iron-bound chest containing the coins and relics they had brought from Rome. Before the galleys departed the city, Kira had obtained the chest from the eunuchs in the Sacred Palace, and once Alais, Pietro, and Ciarán rejoined *Lindworm's* crew, they had moved the chest here. Pietro opened it and removed one of the three ornate scroll cases Alais had retrieved from the flooded undercroft of Hagia Sophia.

When Pietro returned to the bow, he unscrewed the cap and pulled out the two-thousand-year-old papyrus scroll titled *The War of the Sons of Light Against the Sons of Darkness*.

"This is a map?" Holger asked.

"The map's hidden on the back," Ciarán explained. "But you have to read it in the proper light." He looked to Alais. With a word, she summoned her soul light, and as it touched the papyrus, the glowing image of a land crisscrossed by rivers took shape.

Pietro pointed to a word near the mouth of one of the rivers. "This is the gate through which we entered, and there's a label for

410

this river, but it's written in Hebrew, so give me a moment." He squinted his eyes as he focused on the map."

"The river's called the Acheron," Alais said. The name had come to her from the recesses of her memory—*Sirra's memory.* "It's one of five rivers in this land. I'm certain of it; I've been here before."

Pietro glanced up and raised an eyebrow. "The Acheron?" He thought for a moment. "I believe Plato called it the River of Woe."

"Sounds delightful," Ciarán quipped.

Holger did not crack a smile. "What about the fork?"

"Of course." Pietro traced a thick finger up what must have been the river they were traveling until he reached the fork. From there, the direction they must take became clear. "Go left," Pietro said.

So, Holger steered the longship to the left. As the two Byzantine galleys and the trio of papal ships meandered in their wake, the river snaked through a sinuous canyon, its towering walls almost suffocating in their closeness. Along the left bank, unnatural hollows were gouged into the cliffside like gaping maws, perched ominously twenty yards above the Acheron's winding course. Shadowy figures flitted in and out of these dark cavities, their movements too quick to be natural, as if unwilling to be fully seen. They seemed to scrutinize the passing fleet with an intent that couldn't bode well. As Alais caught sight of them, a chill swept through her, so intense it was as though her very blood had turned to ice within her veins.

"What ... are they?" Pietro's voice trembled.

Ciarán's face tightened into a grimace, his eyes narrowing. "Tara's message named this place as the dwelling of slain souls."

"Or perhaps a home for the damned,' Alais whispered, clutching her arms tightly around her chest as if to ward off the chilling atmosphere that seemed to grow heavier with each heartbeat. From the hushed murmurs and stifled breaths of the men trailing behind them, she sensed an escalating tension in the air—a collective wariness bordering on dread, as if they all innately understood the sinister nature of the entities lurking in those shadowed caverns.

411

"*Draugar,*" some whispered.

"The Grim," others said uneasily.

As *Lindworm* navigated the labyrinthine bends of the river, snaking its way through the towering basalt canyon walls, Alais took note of an unsettling pattern: the caves pockmarking the cliffs were only on the left side, as though the Acheron itself served as a final boundary trapping whatever malevolent entities lurked within those warrens. The river's meandering course seemed to stretch endlessly through the abyss of this sunless world, where time itself felt unreliable. Hours—or what should have been hours—unspooled like a twisted thread. All the while, Alais, Pietro, and Ciarán maintained a vigilant watch on those shadow-strewn caves, bracing for the moment when the concealed inhabitants might finally reveal their true natures. A moment that, fortunately, never came.

In time, the river forked again, though instead of a colossal statute guarding the fork, the rock had been hewed into the shape of a mammoth, skull-like head that looked as if it were rising from the dark waters. The tips of its ears ended in sharp points, flanking a massive nose, halfway submerged beneath a pair of hate-filled eyes. Alais had the unnerving feeling the stone head was staring straight at her.

She peeled her gaze from the disturbing carving when Pietro needed, once again, to consult the map. With a word, her soul light brought the glowing image of these riverlands to life.

"Go right this time," Pietro remarked.

Ciarán' hollered the direction back to Holger at the steering oar. With a slow, creaking turn, the vessel veered into another shadowy gorge, this one devoid of the unsettling warrens but awash in a different breed of dread. Here, monolithic faces—less human and more avian—were carved into the towering limestone cliffs. These grotesque visages seemed to leer down like gargantuan raptors, their beady, stone eyes fixated hungrily on the vulnerable vessels below. As the ship moved deeper into the gorge, each chiseled face appeared more menacing than the last.

"Why birds?" Ciarán wondered.

"Not birds," Pietro said, "but gods. In the Reading Room, we have numerous scrolls from ancient Egypt. Many of their gods—Ra, Horus, Thoth—had the bodies of men, but the heads of birds."

"So this place is some type of shrine to them?" Alais wondered.

Ciarán studied the carvings. "Maybe whatever lives in the caves around here, these were their gods."

The river curved around the desolate cliffs; with each passing moment, Alais' unease seemed to grow. Just when she thought the scenery couldn't get any more unsettling, an imposing shape materialized in the gloom ahead. At first, it appeared to be an immense cave studded with stalagmites. Yet, as the vessel inched closer, the horrifying truth snapped into focus. It wasn't a cave at all—it was the massive skull of some ungodly creature carved from bone as pale as moonlight. Its cavernous jaws gaped open, stretching at least a hundred feet high, revealing what she'd mistaken for stalactites and stalagmites: these were towering, saber-like teeth, each rivaling the height of *Lindworm's* mast. Two elongated, tusk-like incisors projected menacingly, far exceeding the others in length. A jagged crown of horn-like ridges adorned the skull's crest, sweeping back like a regal mane and disappearing into the murky distance. The unholy amalgamation of features—part mythical dragon, part colossal lion—gave the titanic skull an aura of both majesty and malice. Its empty eye sockets seemed to pierce the semidarkness, eliciting audible gasps from the already-tense crew behind them as they realized the river was flowing straight through the beast's gigantic maw.

"Blessed Sergius," Pietro muttered before making the sign of the cross.

"What in all of Midgard is that?" Holger asked grimly, striding toward the bow.

Ciarán shook his head in awe. "Not what I imagined, but I believe we've found Behemoth's teeth. Tara told of it in one of her visions."

"I think you're right," Alais replied breathlessly, recalling the words Tara and Sara had spoken when they awoke from their dream.

Five seals are broken, yet two remain,
Though aid in these labors you must obtain.
Through Leviathan's breath and Behemoth's teeth,
At the center of gloom where the rivers meet.

Holger's face went pale. "We're supposed to sail into that?"

Ciarán nodded solemnly. "I fear so."

As Alais gazed upon the enormous skull, a chill shot up her spine at the thought of what it would be like to sail into its cavernous jaws. She kept her eyes on the monstrosity when Holger ordered his anxious crew to row.

Then suddenly, within the skull's massive left eye socket, she saw a glimmer of movement, as if Behemoth had winked at them.

CHAPTER 63
THE DARKNESS WITHIN

N aberus stood at the prow of his galley, firmly gripping the railing as the ship slowly continued its path up the dark river that meandered through a pair of towering basalt cliffs. An endless gloom covered the landscape, as if this world were in a perpetual state of twilight, without any stars or moon. Many of his crewmates found the atmosphere oppressive and disconcerting, but not Naberus. The gloom of this place fit his mood.

Ever since the disaster that had been his last few days in Constantinople, he had felt a darkening in his soul. Not only had he lost men, and nearly his own life, in the ambush inside Hagia Sophia, but he had failed to kill the twins or capture the woman who held the Key in her veins. Lovetar had warned him of their new enemy, this sect of magi who operated in the city as covertly as his own kind. And still, with all his resources and spies, he had failed to see the ambush coming. Yet it was the discovery within the Sunken Palace that had affected him the most. The sight of his mother's body, half submerged in the water, her skin burned and blackened as if she had been doused in Greek Fire. His mother had been one of the strongest, most cunning, and most capable people he had ever known, yet they destroyed her.

It had been all he could think about, his mind churning with questions about how it could have happened. He knew the woman, Alais, and one of the twins had gone down into the well and made their way into the Sunken Palace. Then, somehow, they killed his mother and six of their assassins. How the woman and a child had accomplished such a seemingly impossible feat eluded him, but one thing was certain—they would pay for those actions with their lives.

By the time he embarked on the voyage to the Lerna Gate, the anger and hatred had swelled inside him to the point it threatened to explode in a torrent of rage. And after a boat full of fishermen informed him and his crew that a Danish longship had moored at a village named Myros, he finally unleashed that rage. The longship escaped, evading his second galley, but Naberus's fury washed over the treacherous people of Myros like the Dragon's breath. Everyone burned as his mother had burned. Everyone except for that fool of a priest whose corpse would deliver a message to the Celt, his woman, and those horrible twins. A warning that their lives were Naberus's to take, and their God could not save them.

Yet even all those lives taken at his command could not quell the burning hatred inside him. He would not rest until the two that killed his mother were dead. Though that time would not come until they reached Dudael, and before then, he needed to rendezvous with his master's vessel. As he peered past the galley's curved prow, he realized the rendezvous would come soon when he spotted another landmark from Lovetar's map. On the map, she had called them the "Queen and the King"—two mammoth faces carved into the cliffs, one on each side of the river. The Queen bore the image of a woman with strong cheekbones and narrow lips wearing a headdress similar to a coiled serpent. At the same time, the King was a stern-looking man with a sharp nose and pointed beard that had a vague resemblance to Naberus. He surmised the King was Asmodeus, an ancient god-king whom Naberus's grandfather had sworn was one of their family's most esteemed ancestors.

Behind him, Naberus heard footsteps on the deck planks and turned to find Saleos. Like Naberus, the Guildmaster wore a dark, heavy cloak to ward off the chill of this place.

"Incredible," Saleos murmured, staring at the giant sculptures of the Queen and the King. Each of them had to be at least sixty feet tall. "Who do you think could have created these?"

"Our cousins of Gog," Naberus replied. "While our ancestors were clever enough to blend in with the world of men, the race of Gog was banished here eons ago. I suspect these sculptures reminded them of their lost paradise when our forefathers ruled as gods and kings. It's the paradise Samyaza will bring about again after we prevail at Dudael. And men like you and I, we will be princes in that world."

As they remained at the bow, the galley moved past the stately carvings of the Queen and King, entering a widening expanse of the river that blossomed into a small, dark lake. Anchored at its heart was *Mesektet*, the dreaded Ship of the Night, flanked by a half-dozen mastless war galleys. Even from this distance, Naberus could discern the lumbering figures of Gog's giants pacing their decks.

A tumultuous mix of anticipation and apprehension swirled within him. There was no doubt in his mind that his master was aware of their failure to assassinate the twins and secure the Key in Byzantium. How would he and Lovetar react? The thought chilled him, yet he steeled himself for whatever punishment awaited him, so long as he could reach Dudael and exact his vengeance.

Drawing a deep, steadying breath as his galley pulled within sight of *Mesektet's* menacing, spear-like bowsprit, he spotted Lovetar standing sternly at the prow. Her expression was impenetrable, but he felt the weight of the jet-black stone embedded in her forehead drilling into him as though her third eye had locked onto the very core of his being.

As soon as the two vessels were within earshot of one another, Naberus made his confession. "I have failed you, my lady."

"No," Lovetar replied, shaking her head. "Astarte was the one who failed, and she has already paid for her transgressions."

Naberus swallowed hard. He did not like the thought that his mother was to blame and what it might mean if Samyaza held that same view. "Will the master see me?"

"In time," Lovetar said. "He's not here."

A flutter roiled through Naberus's stomach. "Not here?"

"No." Lovetar's lips spread into a fiendish smile. "The Dragon has gone hunting."

CHAPTER 64

BEHEMOTH AND LEVIATHAN

T he gaps between Behemoth's enormous teeth were wide enough for *Lindworm* to pass through without the crew having to draw in their oars. From the bow, Alais gazed up at the teeth lining the beast's upper jaw, aiming down at them like forty-foot-long daggers. If the ancient jaws suddenly closed, they would snap *Lindworm* in two. And anyone not crushed or impaled by the gigantic teeth would be left to drown in the river's dark waters.

This thought never left Alais' mind as the longship glided beneath the creature's snout, and the gloom over the canyons turned into darkness. Behind her, several of the oarsmen hissed in a breath. The darkness was unnerving.

"Light some torches!" Holger called from the stern.

The crew did as their jarl commanded, and soon, six or seven torches flared into existence.

"That's a bit more comforting," Ciarán remarked, standing beside Alais. Though he kept his left hand firmly gripped around Caladbolg's pommel, and she could hear the trepidation in his voice.

The flickering torchlight cut through the darkness, revealing what appeared to be a barrel-vaulted ceiling a hundred feet above made of pale gray bone. The splash of the oars echoed through the tunnel created by the beast's snout, and the cold air became thicker and more humid, carrying a stench of decay. Alais glanced back to see *Daena* maneuver through the jutting teeth. In the torchlight, she saw Kamran standing behind the ship's prow, along with Fereydun, leaning on his blackened staff. The older man's gaze was a mix of fear and awe.

Alais turned back toward *Lindworm's* dragon-headed prow, where Pietro clung to the gunwale with both hands, muttering a prayer. As the torchlight danced down the tunnel, Alais saw that twenty yards away, it opened into the cavernous hollow of Behemoth's skull. The rowers propelled the longship through the opening. Alais looked around. The darkness was so thick she could not see the top of the skull, though a semi-dark gloom lingered in the massive opening of the beast's eye sockets. Then, again, in one of them, she saw something move.

A second later, her blood ran cold as a hideous squeal echoed through the skull. In the gloom of the eye socket, scores of creatures erupted into the air as if a murder of crows had suddenly taken flight.

"What in God's name?" Ciarán stammered as the creatures came into the torchlight, pale and birdlike, with long, narrow beaks. An entire flock dove toward *Lindworm*, flapping emaciated wings like rabid bats and emitting an ear-splitting squeal that blended with a chorus of frightened cries from the longship's crew. Alais gasped as one of the birdlike creatures sped toward her, its alien eyes filled with a hungry look. She raised her arms instinctively to protect herself when an arrow flew over her head and impaled the creature before it could reach the prow. A second arrow felled another one, and out of the corner of Alais' eyes, she saw Mordechai, bow in hand, draw another shaft from his quiver.

Ciarán tore Caladbolg from its scabbard just in time to arc its blade through one of the descending creatures, cutting it clean in two and misting the air with blood. Beside him, Pietro cried out as one of the birds clawed its talons into the monk's shoulder and sunk its needle-like beak into the ample flesh of Pietro's neck. Alais

420

watched in horror as the creature, whose small, round head looked to be covered more in fur than feathers, slurped up Pietro's blood like a giant mosquito. Pietro yowled in pain before Ciarán grabbed the creature with his free hand and ripped it off Pietro's neck. Meanwhile, the Danes swatted at the oncoming swarm, some battering them with round shields, others whacking them with flaming torches or swiping at them with swords. Other Danes tried to tear the creatures off of them as the needle-like beaks pierced through chain mail into flesh.

One creature landed on Ciarán's back and sunk its beak into his bare neck. Ciarán screamed. Alais lunged at the monster, which was the size of a raven, and grabbed its wings with both hands. With a grunt, she tore it off Ciarán, but the creature jerked its wings with tremendous strength. The next thing Alais knew, it was free of her grip, flapping its emaciated wings and pecking its bloodstained beak toward her face. She braced for the strike, but Strong Bjorn was there, catching the creature with his huge hands before wringing its neck. Yet as soon as they killed one, three more were swooping in to take their place. Mordechai's arrows dropped two of the birds gliding haphazardly toward the prow, and behind her, Alais sensed a pulse in the air as Ciarán whispered a word. *"Eoh."*

Alais felt the heat as Caladbolg's blade burst into white flames. The fire engulfed the first creature that came in contact with the sword. But unlike human foes who knew fear, the sword's power did nothing to deter the incoming swarms of flying beasts. However, as Ciarán swung the fiery sword in broad arcs, it brought a quick death to a half-dozen of the creatures. The air filled with the stench of the scorched birds and the acrid smell of blood.

A flurry of arrows sped through the air as Kamran's archers joined the battle from *Daena's* deck, dropping scores of the slain creatures into the dark waters. Just as it looked like they were thinning the flock, another loud, vicious squeal sounded from the other eye socket, and the gloom in its hollow became blotted out by a new horde of creatures taking flight. Alais' heart sank as she realized that without help, everyone on board would soon be overwhelmed. *I am Sirra,* Alais reminded herself, stretching her fingers from her palms.

"Keep them off me," she told Ciarán before beginning a verse born of the language of creation. The power gave her command over the elements—fire, earth, and water—but her favorite element was wind, and as the air thrummed around her, she summoned it now. Alais thrust her right hand toward the oncoming swarm and felt the wind whip off the water before blasting skyward. The wind howled as it struck the cloud of bird-like creatures, throwing them in every direction. Though Alais knew that would not be enough. She spun her hand in the air, reciting the words to transform the wind into a cyclone. As it grew, the whirlwind swallowed up the flying creatures until it was a swirling mass of feathers and wings, expanding until it threatened to consume the entire flock. Then, with power and anger coursing through her veins, Alais pointed her right hand toward the river and sent the cyclone crashing into the dark waters. The whirling mass of creatures hit the river with a sound like a thunderclap, blasting a torrent of water that washed over *Lindworm*, spraying everyone on board. A wave followed, rocking the longship so violently that Alais had to cling to Ciarán to stay on her feet. The dark waters frothed and boiled as whatever dwelt beneath the surface began feasting on the horde of bird-like monsters that had plunged into their lair.

With the threat of a second flock eliminated, all that remained were a dozen or so of the flying beasts still harassing *Lindworm's* crew. Although the lingering creatures did not last long as the Danes stabbed them with daggers or cleaved them into the deck planks with their longswords. When it was over, whispers of *"Lifthrasir"* broke out among the crew while Ciarán let the flames on Calad-bolg's blade die out and wrapped his free arm around Alais. She held onto him tightly as her breathing calmed and her heartbeat settled into a normal rhythm.

Nearby, Pietro slumped against the gunwale, pressing his hand over the wound on his neck, smeared with blood.

"Let me see that," Alais said, rushing to his side.

Pietro removed his hand, and red liquid pulsed from the puncture wound. Alais thought he might bleed to death if she didn't fix it now. With the word *"Eoh,"* she summoned soul light into her palm and touched it to Pietro's wound. Reciting the words of another verse, she felt the wound close beneath her palm, and Pietro let out a groan of relief. She tended to Ciarán's wound next, which was far less serious. The creature's beak had missed an artery, puncturing muscle more than anything else.

"Thank you," Ciarán said with a grateful smile.

"What the hell were those things?" Holger asked, making his way toward the prow. Blood marred the chest of his mail, but judging by the swagger in his step, Alais guessed the blood was not his own. Behind him, Breda looked no worse for the wear.

Pietro bent over and studied the creature whose neck Strong Bjorn had wrung. Its round head was covered in coarse, pale fur while feathers adorned parts of its emaciated wings. Lying there, the creature looked like a grotesque combination of a bat and a bird with a beak like a mosquito's proboscis.

"If I'm not mistaken," Pietro said, "this is what Ovid described as a strix or a stirge in one of his writings on mythological creatures. He believed they haled from the marshes of Hades."

"Is that where we are now?" Holger asked.

"Otherworld, underworld—I suppose it's all the same down here," Ciarán suggested.

Alais glanced at the gigantic eye sockets looming above like enormous windows into the gloom. "Wherever this is," she said, "I'd like to get out of here in case there's another nest of these things up there."

"I wholeheartedly agree, My Lady," Pietro replied. "Besides, we still need to find Leviathan's breath."

"Then let's get going," Ciarán said. "And hope whatever that may be, it's a bit more hospitable than these creatures living above Behemoth's teeth."

HOLGER GRIPPED THE STEERING OAR, guiding *Lindworm* upriver through another ravine of basalt cliffs. It seemed like an hour since their small fleet sailed out of the tunnel created by the titanic ribcage of a beast Pietro had called a Behemoth, and according to the map, they would encounter one more fork in the Acheron before they reached the lake where all five rivers of this Otherworldly land converged.

He remained alert for more dangers and was grateful that his men had donned their armor before entering this realm. The chainmail had proven effective against the flying beasts Pietro called stirges. While the creatures' sharp, pointed beaks could pierce the mail coats, as well as the leather vests beneath them, all that material blunted the stirges' attack, and their beaks rarely punctured much further than muscle. Most of the crew escaped the attack without serious injuries except for Stóri Red Beard and Ormr, who suffered wounds to their unarmored necks. Those wounds could have been fatal, but Alais healed them with her magic before their situations became too dire. Otherwise, the crew had fared well during the chaotic attack.

For his part, Holger had killed nine of the stirges with Curtana, while Breda slew five of her own, and Rosta tore apart three of them. Jorundr boasted the most kills, having smashed four creatures to death with his shield and cleaved six more into pieces with his blade. However, Mordechai took issue with that, claiming to have felled eighteen stirges with his arrows. But Jorundr insisted that when it came to battling stirges, only hand-to-hand combat should count. He also dismissed Ciarán's total because his flaming sword gave him an unfair advantage and Alais' because her magic allowed her to wreak widespread destruction, which was unsportsmanlike. Holger found the entire debate amusing. It was not the first time Jorundr had rigged the rules of a game to ensure he came out the winner. But then again, no one could question the man's creativity when it came to arguments or his competitiveness in contests, rigged or otherwise.

Another hour passed before they reached the last fork in the river identified on Pietro's map. Holger steered the longship to the left, following the meandering waterway without a sound except for the lapping of oars in the river. The cliffs that had bordered them disappeared, and the ravine flattened into rolling hills made from dark volcanic stone. Meanwhile, the air, which had settled back into a dry, bone-numbing cold since leaving the stirges' lair, began to warm again, with the source of the heat coming from upriver.

Ahead, a faint glow cut through the gloom. "What do you see up there?" Holger called to Ciarán, who was standing watch on the bow.

"About thirty yards ahead," Ciarán replied, "there's steam rising from the river, and whatever's causing that glow, it's coming from beneath the water."

Alais, who was sitting beside Breda on the shallow platform in the stern, ran her fingers through her raven hair. "We must be nearing the place where the rivers meet," she said. "That glow in the water could be coming from the Lethe."

"The what?" Breda asked.

"It's one of the rivers down here," Alais explained. "It flowed through Avalon, and the water glows brightly."

Holger grunted. He'd seen water as black as squid ink in the strange harbor beneath Rome and the endlessly dark waters of the Acheron. But he'd never imagined seeing a river that glowed.

From the bow, Ciarán yelled back. "Stop rowing for a moment!"

The crew rested their oars as *Lindworm's* dragon-headed prow neared a wall of thick steam rising from the river. Holger found it vaguely similar to the barrier of fog that marked the gateway to this realm.

"Let me see if I can do something about that," Alais said before getting up from the platform and heading toward the prow. When she reached Ciarán and Pietro at the ship's bow, she held out her right hand. A flash of light burst from her palm, but instead of blasting through the vapor and creating a tunnel as she had through the wall of fog, her soul light disappeared into the rising steam.

Alais turned around and shook her head.

"I think we may have found Leviathan's breath," Pietro announced.

Holger grimaced. Ahead of them, the steam rose in every direction, suggesting they had reached the lake marked on Pietro's map.

But rowing through that steam was the last thing Holger wanted to do, though it seemed they had no choice.

As the longship drew nearer to the steaming lake, sulfurous fumes saturated the air and caused several crew members to curse and groan. Steam rose on every side of the longship's hull, engulfing Holger and the others in a suffocating heat that turned Holger's brow to perspiration in moments. Breda wiped her forehead as her hair stuck to her face while Rosta shifted restlessly on the deck planks. For an instant, Holger wondered if they might choke on the foul-smelling vapor until he managed to draw in a breath. Even worse than the heat and the smell was his vision, for the steam was so thick he could see barely a few feet beyond *Lindworm's* prow.

"Freybjorn," Holger shouted, "give Ciarán your oar and stand lookout."

"Aye," Freybjorn answered from his oar bench at the front of the ship.

Good, Holger thought. No one in the crew had better eyes than Freybjorn.

Alais and Pietro, their hair and faces slick with sweat, returned to the shallow platform in the stern. They took a seat beside Breda as the crew rowed slowly through the hot, humid vapor.

"What's causing this?" Breda asked.

"I don't know," Alais replied, "but whatever it may be, this steam is not affected by my soul light."

"I have a theory," Pietro said. "The five rivers on the map were known to the ancient Greek philosophers, like Plato, who wrote about them. One of those rivers, called Phlegethon, is supposedly a river of fire. Another river, Cocytus, is said to be filled with ice. So when the fire and ice converge and mix with the waters of the Acheron and the other two rivers, I suspect they create this steam we're caught in."

"So you don't think this is the breath of some sea monster?" Holger asked, sharing his deepest concern. After all, the monk had called it "Leviathan's breath."

Pietro shook his head. "Perhaps Leviathan's breath is just a *metaphora*, as the pope would say."

426

"I hope you're right," Holger said with a nod. Though now he needed to worry about some river of fire, which would not bode well for *Lindworm's* wooden hull.

Oars splashed in the water as the longship slowly advanced into the lake. The unrelenting steam was as thick as a morning fog. After some time, Freybjorn began to shout. "Draw in the oars! Steer left!"

Holger yanked the steering oar left to avoid a looming obstacle. His muscles tensed as his crew worked quickly to bring their oars inside. Holger nearly lost his balance when their vessel's prow collided with something rising through the steam like a gigantic rock. The frightened cries of his crew mates filled the air; some were thrown forward while Freybjorn clung to *Lindworm's* serpentine prow. As Holger tried to make sense of what had happened, he realized they were surrounded by rocky formations jutting from the river. Just then, more cries rose from behind them, and everyone at the back rushed away before the Byzantine galley slammed into *Lindworm's* stern, its spear-like foremast narrowly missing Holger's shoulder.

It took a moment for *Lindworm* to stop its violent rocking as men clutched the gunwales or the rigging to keep their balance. Kamran and a host of his men looked down from *Daena's* prow, gesturing apologetically. Then Strong Bjorn cried out, "gods!"

Holger's eyes widened when he, too, saw what had alarmed his friend, for up close, the rocks were covered in massive, dark gray scales, and what appeared to be jutting ridges now looked like the fins or spines of some gigantic sea beast.

"Midgard's Serpent," some whispered.

Freybjorn reached out and touched the creature. "It's as dead and hard as stone," he said.

Holger extended a hand to the obstacle. It had the feel of wet stone. "Whatever this Leviathan had been, it's only a fossil now."

"Remarkable," Pietro said, touching one of the enormous fins.

After checking for damage, Holger confirmed that *Lindworm's* badly scraped hull had not been breached, and no oars had been broken. But he ordered his men to row even more cautiously now. They did so, slowly maneuvering around the Leviathan's fossilized corpse. The beast's serpentine form rose and fell into the water in great twists and turns as if its body had formed a massive labyrinth for the ships to navigate. The constant steam made the voyage even more nerve-wracking, and Holger's muscles tensed with every stroke of the oars. He worried they would collide with another of the creature's towering fins. Or worse, a portion of its body lying just below the surface like a jagged reef that could quickly sink a ship.

An hour passed before Holger could breathe easier—when the steam began to thin, and the last sign of Leviathan's corpse disappeared beneath the water.

"Something's up ahead," Freybjorn yelled back. "It looks like an island."

Pietro glanced up, his eyes bright. "There's an island on the map in the center where the rivers meet."

Holger squinted to see through the thinning fog. The island's silhouette looked like a rounded hill rising from the lake.

"I see mooring posts and a stone pier," Freybjorn reported.

Holger raised an eyebrow. "Does the island look inhabited?"

"Hard to say," Freybjorn called back.

Then Ciarán's voice rang out from one of the front oar benches. "My lord, there's a wall encircling the base of the hillside. And an entrance with double doors."

As the longship closed in on the pier, Holger's eyes took in the scene before him. A towering wall of rough-hewn stones, thirty feet high, enfolded the hill like a ringfort. The hill itself was clad in a carpet of deep mauve grass that seemed almost unnatural in its hue. At the wall's heart stood a foreboding structure, much like a gatehouse, its entrance guarded by what looked like twin doors of an ominous make.

A visceral unease churned in Holger's stomach as the doors let out a loud, almost sentient groan and began to swing open.

CHAPTER 65
THE INNER SANCTUM

From the yawning doors in the island's stone wall, a flickering glow spilled forth, reminding Ciarán of a cooking hearth's flames. It was both welcoming and unsettling, leaving him to wonder what awaited them within.

The island's stone pier was cramped, barely offering enough berth for two ships. Ciarán proposed that *Lindworm* and *Daena* anchor there, while the remaining four ships could drop their anchors into the eerily placid waters of the lagoon. The twilight air hung heavy, infused with a sulfurous, humid stench emanating from the steaming lake. Uncertainty laced the atmosphere. Pietro and Fereydun insisted that benevolence awaited beyond those gaping doors, citing the twins' vision of aid "where the rivers meet." Holger, however, wasn't so sure. He argued for taking his entire war band through the ominous entrance. Fereydun countered that a company of warriors might be perceived as a threat. A tension-laden pause filled the air before Ciarán finally brokered a compromise. From *Lindworm*, he would lead Alais and Pietro, joining Holger, Breda, Jorundr, and Strong Bjorn to cautiously explore the unknown. While Fereydun would take Kamran, along with the twins and Kira.

A pathway of flagstones led from the pier to the open doors. Ciarán took the lead alongside Holger, who had drawn Curtana from its scabbard, earning a disapproving glare from Fereydun. Twenty yards away stood the gatehouse, a blunt, square-shaped structure housing the thick doors, each nearly thirty feet tall. Three shallow steps ascended to the doors, and as Ciarán began to climb them, he felt warm air radiating from beyond the doorway. He peered through the entrance, where the strange glow danced off the stone walls.

"It looks like a tunnel," Ciarán observed. The passageway was wide enough for six or seven men to stand side-by-side, reminding him vaguely of the tunnel that spiraled up Castle Sant'Angelo, except this one ran straight, about thirty paces toward the source of the light. Jorundr and Strong Bjorn joined Ciarán and Holger in the front. Each of the Danes had drawn his blade. Ciarán resisted the urge to unsheathe Caladbolg to avoid upsetting Fereydun more than he already was. But Ciarán's nerves were tense, and he kept a firm hand on the sword's pommel.

"Be calm, my friends," Fereydun said behind them. "We are heading into the light, not away from it. The ones sending the twins these messages do not mean to ambush us, but to aid us."

"I'll believe that when I see it," Holger grumbled.

"Fereydun's right," Alais said. "I feel like I've been here before."

Ciarán stopped and turned to Alais. "Are you sure?"

She nodded. "The memory seems real."

Her words eased Ciarán's nerves, but did nothing to change Holger's disposition. "Keep your guard up," the jarl told Jorundr and Strong Bjorn.

As they neared the end of the tunnel, the glow grew brighter, and they could hear a faint crackle of flames from the chamber beyond. Ciarán held up a hand to shield his eye from the intense glare as he crossed the threshold. Finally, the glow dimmed slightly, and Ciarán gasped in awe. He found himself in a meadow encircled by rough-hewn stone walls thirty feet tall, like those of an Irish ring-fort. But where the ceiling should have been beneath the dome of this hill was a night sky with hundreds of glimmering stars. The flagstones paving the tunnel gave way to golden grass, and in the meadow's center stood the most enormous, ancient-looking oak Ciarán had ever set eyes on, but instead of leaves on its outstretched limbs were tongues of flickering fire as if the tree were a titanic candelabra with thousands of candles.

Holger stood beside Ciarán, gaping at the oak, while Jorundr muttered a word. *"Yggdrasil."*

"Ahura Mazda," Kira said under her breath.

Ciarán pulled his gaze away from the tree and glanced at Tara and Sara, who stared wonderstruck at the scene before them.

"The tree from your visions?" Alais asked them.

The twins nodded in unison.

"But where are the four creatures?" Pietro asked, marveling at the oak.

"We most certainly are not alone," Fereydun said.

Just as the words left his lips, a figure emerged from behind the colossal oak, its trunk so broad it must have spanned thirty feet, and its roots, like gnarled fingers, seemed to clutch the golden grass. The figure was tall and lean, swathed in midnight-black robes that seemed to swallow the light around him. A wide-brimmed black hat sat atop his head, casting a veil of mystery over his features. As the figure stepped over the gnarled roots, Ciarán caught sight of a long nose above a bushy gray beard. Drawing closer, the man's face became increasingly clear—and familiar. His skin was deeply etched by the years and framed by the wrinkles of a life that had known laughter. The bright blue eyes that met Ciarán's were unmistakable, filling him with a sense of surreal recognition. For the figure making his way toward them was none other than Father Michele.

The old priest spoke with a wizened voice and a friendly smile. "My dear Alais, it's been too long."

Alais nodded, her eyes widening in disbelief.

Then Father Michele turned to Tara. "And my sweet child, I said you'd go on this adventure if you only had the courage to do so, and I'm very pleased you did."

Clutching her hand to her chest, Tara gazed upon the old priest with a look of awe. Sara's face mirrored her twin's expression.

Next, the old priest addressed Fereydun. "Magus Fereydun, I've not had the pleasure of making your acquaintance, but your friends have arrived."

As the Magus raised his thick brows, three more figures emerged from behind the oak. Each was tall, long-limbed, and graceful in their movements, with long hair that shone like precious metals. At once, Ciarán knew they were among the Fae—or the Jann, as Fereydun had called them.

Upon witnessing their arrival, Fereydun dropped to one knee, a gesture swiftly followed by Kira, Kamran, and Sara. "My lady, Ilat," the Magus intoned with deep reverence. "And Ladies Asira and Ashta."

Ilat stood a head taller than her companions, her oval face emanating an ethereal beauty rivaled only by Orionde's. Her eyes, ancient yet vibrant, locked onto theirs, carrying the wisdom and weight of millennia. Her skin glowed with a burnished bronze hue, and her raven-black hair shimmered like polished zirconium. Clad in a tunic of tightly woven silver scale mail, she bore a scimitar at her hip, its ornate bronze hilt catching the light. Her appearance evoked memories for Ciarán of the Sisters of Orionde, dressed for combat in the tower of Rosefleur.

Her companions, Asira and Ashta, were similarly armed and dressed, yet unique in their own right. Asira possessed an angular face, her narrow eyes captivating, her dark hair kissed with silver strands. Ashta, on the other hand, boasted a mane of coppery locks twisted into tight braids. Her face had a fierce quality, less tradition-ally beautiful but no less mesmerizing, in line with every Fae Ciarán had ever encountered.

"Rise, Fereydun," Ilat said in a sonorous voice. "Did you doubt we would come?"

"Never once, my lady," Fereydun replied humbly as he rose to his feet.

Stepping forward, Father Michele gave the Danes a stern look. "You can put those away now," he said, gesturing to their swords.

Jorundr and Strong Bjorn glanced at Holger, who nodded

before sheathing Curtana. His eyes narrowed slightly as he studied the priest. "Have we met before?"

"Indeed, we have," the old priest said, "in a cave outside the temple at Uppsala. Though, to be fair, my appearance was a bit different back then."

Holger's mouth fell slack. "You're Blind Mikkel …"

"When I need to be," Father Michele replied with a wry grin.

A question gnawed at Ciarán's mind, and as much as he suspected the answer, it would be so incredible—so momentous—he had to confirm it. "Who are you?"

Father Michele raised an eyebrow. "You don't believe me to be an old priest of the Roman Church? Of course, you don't, though I think you can guess who I am. I was a general once, a long time ago, in the days when war broke out in heaven. And as it's written, I return when I'm most needed. When humanity stands at the precipice of the end times with but one chance to prevent them."

Ciarán nearly staggered at the man's answer, even though he had suspected the truth. But the mind-blowing thought that Michael —*Saint Michael*—stood before him, even in this most humble guise, was hard to comprehend as real. Yet there he was in flesh and blood, and with three of the Fae, too. It was far more than Ciarán could have hoped when they entered the Otherworld. "You're here to help us?" he asked, realizing the question was foolish the instant it left his lips.

"My boy," Father Michele replied in an amused tone, "I've been helping you all along, at least as much as I could without breaking the rules."

Ciarán tilted his head. "Rules?"

"Every contest has its rules, but you've known that ever since Orionde told you about one of them in the tower of Rosefleur. Do you remember?"

Ciarán thought for a moment. "She said only the champion could take Enoch's device."

Father Michele nodded. "That was one of the rules. Another was that the Key would only be revealed at the place of the awakening, when Sirra's awareness blossomed again in our dear Alais at the

Temple of Venus and Roma. And a third rule is that I—or rather, *we*—cannot intervene directly in this contest, though I've skirted that rule as much as I can, offering you words of wisdom, subtle clues, and guidance as indirectly as I could without making a mess of things. But all that changes here, in the Inner Sanctum."

Ciarán slowly shook his head. "Why?"

"It's another of the rules. Have you wondered why your ships weren't burnt to cinders by dragonfire as soon as you passed through the Lerna Gate? Or why an armada from Gog was not waiting there to sink your small fleet with its canons? Samyaza knew you were coming, but he could do nothing about it because of the Rule of Safe Passage. Once you entered the Otherworld, he was bound to let you come here unmolested, for we have some business to attend to presently. However, now that you've made it here, your safe passage has ended. So from here on, you'll be without protection."

"Who makes these bloody rules?" Ciarán asked in frustration.

Father Michele clasped his hands together below his chest. "The who and the why are not relevant now, but let's just say this cycle of conflict began with a war, and in every war, surrender has its terms."

Ciarán did not like that answer; he did not want to believe they were but pieces on a board in some cosmic game of Tables. "Are there any other of these rules we should know about?"

"Only one," Father Michele replied, holding up his index finger. "That the outcome of this conflict will decide the fate of the world as you know it, at least for the next thousand years. It's the reason the prophecy was etched in the heavens before the world was young. As we speak, the power of the great pillar in Dudael that seals the Watchers' prison is fading, and when it's gone, the Watchers will be freed. Only our dear Alais here has the power to restore the pillar to its full strength. But if the enemy were to steal that power, the pillar would collapse with a single touch, and all would be lost. Beyond that, there's just the matter of Samyaza—the Dragon, if you will. You must defeat him and send him back to his prison. Or again, all will be lost. Once the Watchers are freed, their collective power, combined with Samyaza's, would allow them to tear a rift through the barrier between the Otherworld and the mortal world, and no one on Earth will be safe from the destruction they would unleash there."

Even though Ciarán had believed the truth of everything the old priest said, Father Michele's words felt like a millstone weighing on Ciarán's chest. Every time he thought about the task ahead, it seemed impossible. "How do we possibly defeat him?"

Father Michele gave Ciarán a harsh look. "I gave you the means when I left that sword you're wearing at the ends of the Earth, so the first champion could find it, albeit in another guise."

Ciarán's eyes flew wide. *Saint Michael's sword—no wonder the Dragon fears it.*

"On top of that," the old priest continued, "Sirra sacrificed her immortal form so she could be with us now. And then God Himself gave you these two." He gestured toward Tara and Sara. "Two of the most important players of them all."

Tara's gaze filled with awe, though Sara appeared more ready for this revelation.

Then, to Ciarán's surprise, Breda stepped forward, a defiant expression on her face. "What role do they have in all this?"

A ghost of a smile touched the old priest's lips. "They will cause great anguish to Ahriman."

"As it has been prophesied," Fereydun added reverently.

"Yes, Magus Fereydun," Father Michele said, "as it has been prophesied. Now, all I need to do is unlock their potential."

Ciarán's gaze shifted between the twins and the old priest. He could not fathom how these two young girls could pose a real threat to the Dragon or somehow change the odds stacked against them. Even so, he held his breath in anticipation as Father Michele beckoned the twins to step forward.

"Tara and Sara," he said, "it's time to realize your destiny."

CHAPTER 66
THE SIXTH SEAL

Tara felt as though she were drowning in a sea of disbelief. It was challenging enough to grasp that she was physically standing where she had once only stood in her visions—before the colossal tree whose thousands of leaves burned like flames. As if that weren't disorienting enough, she found herself looking upward into an open sky dotted with stars, despite the hill she had seen outside suggesting an enclosed chamber. And then there was Father Michele. The same Father Michele who had discovered her on the lakeshore seven years prior and left her in the nurturing care of Minerva's nuns. His countenance was as kind and as stalwart as she remembered. Yet, the man before her had just insinuated that he might not even be a man, or at least not a mortal one. He claimed to be a general from an age when heaven itself was torn by war. Tara's mind was spinning, struggling to reconcile these bewildering revelations.

Moreover, Father Michele had summoned her and Sara forward to unlock some latent power within them. Tara knew her mother possessed certain powers, and so did her aunt and grandfather. Even Sara was learning to harness such powers, too. But Tara was the odd one out—incapable of the mystical feats her family could perform. She had summoned fire from thin air on three separate occasions, but each instance was accompanied by a lion's roaring voice inside her head. She couldn't be sure the power truly originated from within her rather than from the lion—despite what Brother Pietro had suggested during their voyage to Constantinople. Yet Father Michele spoke with unwavering certainty. Both she and her sister harbored hidden abilities, and the time had come to reveal them.

A tingling sensation crawled across Tara's skin as she clasped Sara's hand. Together, they stepped toward Father Michele. As they advanced, the three ethereal women—towering figures in armor more exquisite than Lady Breda's—shifted to stand beside their aunt and grandfather. This left Tara and Sara alone, standing in front of Father Michele. Behind him, the tree blazed like a living inferno, its fiery foliage illuminating the moment with an otherworldly glow.

"My dears," the old priest said, "you are the youngest oracles to ever appear in this conflict. Had you been older, you undoubtedly would have discovered more of your gifts, and through training, you likely would have honed them by now into powerful weapons. But it's no fault of yours that you were chosen at such a young age. However, this means that you'll need something to help focus your power and unleash its potential. Just like your family has used those blackened staves and small silver cups to help focus theirs."

Father Michelle reached into the pockets of his black priestly robes and removed two bronze armbands, each long enough to cover half of Tara's forearm. The light from the fiery leaves reflected off the metal, illuminating silver symbols that ran the length of the armband to each silver-trimmed edge.

"There's one for each of you," Father Michele continued. "When you wear them, they help connect your mind to the power lying deep inside you. All I need you to do is to be brave. Only a few words are needed to summon the power, then let your will be its guide. As for the nature of that power, it has been written that the oracles—or witnesses, if you will—can summon forth thunderstorms of hail and fire that can change the tide of this war."

Tara glanced at Sara. Her sister's eyes held the same look of awe and uncertainty that Tara felt inside herself. What Father Michele said did not seem possible, but she had never known him to speak of anything that had not come true.

He held up the armbands, one in each hand. "To access this power, you must put these on and speak seven words, just as I tell you now." But before he could utter the first word, his voice was drowned out by a deafening boom that shook the world around them.

Tara's breath caught in her throat as the celestial tapestry above splintered into chaos, as if the very heavens were sundered by some divine wrath. Hundreds of glimmering stars cascaded in bits and pieces, raining down like the shards of a shattered mosaic on a cathedral dome. Instinctively, Tara raised her arms, bracing for the celestial onslaught, a scream suspended in the air. Where the sky had been torn asunder, a column of incandescent fire erupted, giving form to an awe-inspiring figure—an angelic giant, standing nearly eight feet tall. His skin radiated with a celestial golden luminance, his eyes aflame with an otherworldly intensity. From his back unfurled wings, each feather wrought from molten embers, stretching an astonishing twenty feet from tip to tip. Before Tara's stunned consciousness could fully comprehend what was happening, and before Father Michele could muster any response, the winged being coiled like a striking serpent. A massive trident gleamed wickedly in his powerful hands. The next thing Tara knew, the man rammed the weapon through the old priest's back.

Three pointed prongs burst through the old priest's chest, splattering Tara with blood. Father Michele's face twisted in pain and shock, his mouth open in a silent cry as the armbands flew from his hands.

A piercing scream erupted from Tara's lungs as Father Michele let out a final, labored gasp. Tara's legs almost buckled as the earth trembled beneath the weight of his last breath. The flaming leaves burning in the massive oak vanished in a hiss of smoke, and Sara's hand closed around Tara's like a vise. Sara, too, was screaming, as were others, and cries rang out around them. Then, the golden being, who wore a tunic of black steel armor, lifted the impaled priest off the ground, gripping the shaft of his trident. A fierce look of triumph filled the being's face, but his eyes were not fixed on the man he'd just killed.

Instead, those eyes, with their searing golden irises, stared straight at Tara.

~

ALAIS' heart hammered in her chest as her mind raced to comprehend everything that had happened.

Samyaza stood before them, hefting the body of Father Michele impaled on a massive trident of obsidian-black steel. The golden hue of his skin shone even brighter in the Otherworldly gloom that filled the chamber now that the giant oak had lost its fiery leaves. As screams echoed off the stone walls, Samyaza jerked back his trident, and Father Michele slid off the prongs, his limp body crumpling at Samyaza's feet.

A flurry of motion followed. Samyaza reared back his trident as if to hurl the weapon, his gaze fixed on the twins. Breda lunged at Tara, who staggered backward. The three Fae standing near the twins reacted with lightning speed. Ilat reached for Sara while the fierce-looking Fae named Ashta darted between the twins and Samyaza, ripping a gleaming scimitar from a sheath at her waist.

With a roar, Samyaza launched his trident. Ashta swung her scimitar and, with a clang that reverberated through the chamber, altered the weapon's path so that it struck the ground inches from where Tara had stood. Breda had the girl in her arms and pulled her back as the third Fae, Asira, dove onto the grass to claim one of the fallen armbands. "Sirra," she urged, "grab the other one!"

The sound of her true name spurred Alais into action. She spotted the second armband lying on the grass a yard away and scrambled to grab it. The armband's metal felt cold in her hand as a new roar filled the chamber. She glanced up to see a dozen pale-skinned giants repelling rapidly down ropes dangling from the circular opening where the starlit roof had been. Alais' blood froze as she recognized the Nephilim from Gog, like the ones who butchered the Sisters of Orionde at Rosefleur.

"Blessed Sergius!" Pietro cried out behind her.

"Ahura Mazda!" Kira exclaimed in alarm.

Before Alais could climb to her feet, muscular arms wrapped around her torso and lifted her off the ground. She realized the arms belonged to Strong Bjorn an instant before Ilat's voice cut through the chaos.

Holding a terror-stricken Sara like a child, the leader of the Fae had a desperate look on her face. "For the love of God, run!"

As soon as Ciarán's mind grasped what was happening, his hand wrapped around Caladbolg's hilt.

He pulled the sword from its scabbard as everyone around him scattered. Out of the corner of his eye, he glimpsed Breda and one of the Fae rescuing the twins, a breath before Ashta let out a battle cry. The Fae warrior charged at Samyaza, who drew in one of his fiery wings like a shield. The scimitar clashed against the wing's ember-like scales, sending a shower of sparks into the air. But then Samyaza opened the wing wide, using it now as a weapon that struck the Fae hard and threw her ten yards onto the grass.

As Ciarán brought Caladbolg's pommel to his lips, he watched Samyaza reach for his trident, stuck into the ground ten yards away. The trident flew backward as if pulled by some invisible force until Samyaza held its shaft in his hands again. By the time Ciarán spoke the word *"Eoh,"* and a surge of power raced up the blade, the Nephilim of Gog had reached the ground. Each wore breastplates with more armored plates strapped to their arms and thighs, and together, they drew huge, curved blades from sheaths on their backs.

White fire exploded from Caladbolg's blade. The fire gave the Nephilim pause and revealed something that widened Ciarán's gaze. Where Father Michele's body had been was a large, lion-like creature with wings like a raptor covered in feathers of reddish bronze.

The beast lay motionless, and blood spilled from three puncture wounds on its back, wetting its fur and pooling in the grass.

Ciarán drew in a sharp breath. They were outnumbered, but his enemy stood before him, not as the Dragon, but as the manlike being who had visited him in his dreams. A being who had feared this weapon since the day war broke out in heaven. With one good strike, Ciarán thought, he could end this war here and now.

Before he could charge, Ashta clambered to her feet. With preternatural speed, she sprung toward Samyaza, raising her scimitar above her head, ready to bring it down with a thunderous blow. But Samyaza moved even faster. He whipped his trident into her path, catching her in her abdomen. The sharp prongs pierced through steel and flesh as Ashta's fierce expression melted away, and her blade fell from her fingers.

Her sacrifice, however, may have been the distraction Ciarán needed. As he readied himself to charge, Samyaza turned toward him with a cruel smile.

Something in that smile caused Ciarán to hesitate. Whatever fear Samyaza may have had for the sword, it was nowhere to be seen in his savage expression. Instead, his golden irises flared as he uttered five familiar words.

"OZAM, ODAMMA, CIALPOR, MIR, AGRIT!"

Pain exploded inside Ciarán with a blinding fury. Pain so great it felt like his blood had turned to molten fire, burning through muscle, skin, and bone. A pain so intense it brought him to his knees. A pain so extreme, so all-consuming, that Ciarán hoped death might take him to end the overwhelming agony.

As a torturous wail burst from his lungs, Caladbolg fell from his grasp. A thousand stars filled his vision before fading into deep darkness.

Desperate to escape the pain, Ciarán collapsed into the void.

CHAPTER 67

INFERNO

S tanding in the gloom-filled ringfort, Holger had no doubt he gazed upon the Dragon. Although now, with the creature's humanlike form, luminescent skin, and slender wings, it took the guise of the being who fled from them a half-year ago in the Otherworldly place beneath the Etruscan shrine on the Palatine Hill.

Back then, the Holy Lance Holger had thrown like a javelin still pierced the being's side, wounding him gravely. But now, in his black armor, wielding his black trident, backed by a platoon of pale-skinned giants clad similarly in breastplates and plate-like mail, the Dragon seemed invincible.

In the chaos, shock and indecision had kept Holger rooted in place. Breda had pulled Tara from the fray, and Strong Bjorn held Alais in his arms. Then, the bronze-skinned woman, who looked like one of the Valkyrie in her scale mail, yelled for all of them to run. Jorundr grabbed Holger by the shoulder, trying to pull him back. But Holger shook him off, his eyes on Ciarán. His friend had drawn Caladbolg and ignited its blade. However, as soon as he moved to charge, the Dragon uttered a string of foreign words that sent a shudder through the surrounding air. Ciarán fell to his knees; Caladbolg slipped from his grasp. Then Ciarán let out a scream so filled with agony it sent a chill through Holger's veins.

"Lord," Jorundr cried, "we must go!"

Anger flushed up Holger's neck. "And leave him?"

When Ciarán collapsed onto his back, Holger knew he had no choice but to drag him from the battle. "I'll get Ciarán," Holger barked at Jorundr. "You get Caladbolg."

Before Holger could step toward Ciarán, the sprawling oak, whose twisted branches were bare a second ago, burst into flames, its limbs again covered in leaves of fire. Amid the near-blinding burst of light, three fiery columns blasted through the shattered roof onto the grass between Ciarán's body and the Dragon and his host of giants. Where the columns landed stood three huge, cat-like creatures with broad wings of reddish bronze. One, with the head of a giant eagle, sprung at three of the pale, armored giants. A second, with the head of an ox, plowed its long horns into another group of giants, while the third, which Holger swore had the head of a man, raked its claws into the Dragon's side. The claws struck the Dragon's breastplate beneath the ribs and tore through black steel like it was made of wool. The Dragon cried out; a hand flew to the gash. Holger could hardly believe his eyes. It was the same place where he had thrown the Holy Lance, and luminescent blood flowed from the wound!

Using his free hand, the Dragon stabbed at the beast with his trident, but now the creature used its wings like shields to parry the blow. Meanwhile, Holger watched in awe as the other two creatures tore through the giants, one ripping through armor and flesh with its raptor's beak, the other goring enemies with its horns, and both rending terrible wounds with their lion-like claws. In the background, the titanic oak blazed like a miniature sun, cutting through the gloom as the air shimmered with a fine mist of blood.

With a frustrated roar, the Dragon clutched his trident and leaped into the air. With two flaps of his slender wings, he disappeared through the open roof into the gloom, but the creature with the human-like head bolted after him, spreading its raptor-like wings as they propelled it skyward.

"Come on!" Holger cried as he rushed toward Ciarán. The jarl dropped to a knee and touched Ciarán's chest. He was breathing, but just barely. As Holger gathered Ciarán in his arms, he noticed the body of the man who had been Blind Mikkel was gone, and instead, a fourth cat-like creature, with the head of a lion, lay dead in his place. Even more, the lion's corpse was slowly disintegrating into tiny particles that wafted into the air like dead leaves in an autumn breeze before they disappeared into the light of the blazing tree.

Using all his strength, Holger hefted Ciarán off the ground while Jorundr grabbed Caladbolg. At the entrance to the tunnel that led outside stood Kamran, waving for them to move with haste. The rest of their party had already fled. Holger ran as fast as he could while carrying Ciarán's weight; Jorundr stayed by his side, gripping his longsword in one hand and Caladbolg in the other. As they entered the tunnel, the shrieks and roars from the two creatures mixed with the panicked cries of the pale giants, echoing off the ringfort's stone walls.

"To the ships!" Kamran said hastily.

Holger nodded as his heart pounded in his chest and sweat beaded his brow. His muscles burned carrying Ciarán's dead weight, but he willed himself to move.

When they emerged from the tunnel, the stone pier was alive with motion. Pietro, Fereydun, and Kira were climbing *Daena's* gangplank, which Alais, the twins, and one of the Valkyrie-like Fae had already boarded. On *Lindworm*, Rosta was barking fiercely while in the bow, Freybjorn was urging them to hurry; other crewmen—Úlfarr, Askil, Ormr, and Hári Grayhair—were scrambling to lower the sail. To Holger's surprise, the dark-haired leader of the Fae named Ilat was climbing on board the longship and commanding the crew in Danish with an accent that suggested she'd been speaking the language her entire life. As soon as she was on board, she glanced at him. "Jarl Holger, we must row away from here now, or we won't make it to Dudael."

She reached for Ciarán, and Holger exhaled a relieved breath as she took his weight off his arms, lifting Ciarán's body as if he weighed no more than a child. Jorundr handed Caladbolg to Mordechai and climbed aboard.

"Where do we go?" Holger asked Ilat, for there was no doubt she was the one in charge now.

"I know the way," she said, "where Cocytus feeds into the marsh."

Before he could ask what she was talking about, an explosion filled the air, rocking *Lindworm* and slamming its side against the stone pier. Holger's hands flew to protect his ears. His gaze darted to the source of the sound, his eyes widening at what he saw.

For anchored in the lagoon, one of the papal ships was going up in flames.

THE FIRST THING Alais felt from the explosion was the heat. It washed over her back as *Daena* pitched starboard, colliding with the stone pier. She struggled to keep her feet on the swaying deck; Kira grabbed Alais' arm to maintain her balance. Amid a chorus of gasps and cries, Alais craned her neck toward the source of the blast. One of the papal ships anchored in the lagoon had burst into flames. Fire raced up the ship's rigging, consuming its sail as the mast collapsed onto the deck. Oar benches had been blasted into tinder while crew members, at least the ones not lying dead among the flames, screamed in agony. The remains of one of the Dragon-slayers lay shattered in the hull while black smoke and the stench of burning wood filled the air.

"What's happening?" Sara cried, clinging to her terrified sister's hand. The same question raced through Alais' mind an instant before the answer presented itself. A half-score of the pale-skinned giants, each at least seven feet tall and dressed for battle in iron breastplates and long mail tunics, had emerged from around the ringfort.

"Nephilim!" the Fae, Asira, hollered.

445

Many of the Nephilim held spears as long as a ship's oar, though several gripped strange-looking weapons on thick iron chains. At each weapon's head, a circular iron cage surrounded an opaque globe that glowed faintly, as if filled with some luminescent liquid. One giant spun this weapon like a lasso over his head. Then he let his go. The weapon sped toward one of the other papal ships. When the cage-encased globe struck the deck, it burst into a flash of heat and light with a loud boom that rocked the ships in the lagoon. Fire exploded through the papal vessel and ripped through hull boards, deck planks, and oar benches along with the terrified men sitting on them. A torrent of flames rushed up the mast while an icy chill pulsed through Alais' veins as she realized their enemy had their own form of Greek Fire.

"We must save the ships!" Fereydun yelled.

Asira shot Alais a desperate glance. "Sirra, use the wind!"

Two more giants launched their chain weapons, hurling them toward the Byzantine galleys. As soon as the weapons left the giants' hands, Alais and Asira were reciting words of power as they summoned the wind, sending a sizzle through the smoky air. Asira attacked the weapon spiraling toward their galley. The air around the weapon's deadly globe flared with a ghostly blue fire as her wind changed its path so that it flew over the galley and splashed into the lagoon. Alais willed her air into a gale-force blast that struck the other weapon, altering its course, too. But the end of the chain struck *Anahita's* sternpost, whipping the chain's links into the globe, causing it to shatter. Liquid fire sprayed onto the stern and erupted into flames as the globe's contents mixed with the air. The aft-most rowers cried out in terror as they were splattered with the fiery liquid while fire spread throughout the ship's stern.

Alais let out a horrified gasp. Then, over her shoulder, she heard more words of power that sent a thrum through the air. The speaker was Fereydun, reciting words to manipulate the fire. The flames on the galley's stern leaped into the air and streamed toward the blackened staff clutched in Fereydun's hands. Everyone around him backed away as he drew the flames into a swirling tempest of fire around the staff's tip. Then, with another three words, the

446

Magus whipped his staff toward the Nephilim, hurling a ball of fire that exploded into their ranks. The fireball ignited one of the other chain weapons, and the resulting explosion blasted the giants into the ringfort's stone walls and across the mauve-colored turf. When the smoke thinned, Alais could hardly believe her eyes when most of the giants staggered to their feet. Rage filled their pale faces as they readied to hurl their long spears. But then a bull-like roar and a raptor's cry sounded from the ringfort, where two of the winged, cat-like beasts bounded over the top of the wall and fell upon the Nephilim.

"Flee now!" Ilat commanded from *Lindworm*.

"Oars in the water!" Kamran bellowed as his crewmen cut the mooring ropes to free the galley from the stone pier.

Lindworm had already pushed off into the lagoon, its crew rowing urgently. As the roars from the battle on shore echoed through the lagoon, Alais turned her head toward the carnage. The smoldering remains of two of the papal ships were sinking into the water, but the third vessel appeared unscathed. *Anahita* had drawn in its anchor, and crew members were hurrying to drop their oars, but the stern, blackened from the fire, looked severely damaged.

Forty men, Alais thought, as a wave of dread washed over her. That's how many crew were on the two papal ships now lost to the inferno. And who knew how many of *Anahita's* Aswaran were injured or dead? But those around her on *Daena* were safe, especially Tara and Sara. Pietro was with them, and so were Breda and Kira. But where was Ciarán? In her haste to save the twins and their armbands, Alais realized she had lost track of him when they fled the ringfort. A swell of panic overwhelmed her as she rushed to the bow. She did not see Ciarán with his pale, white hair working among the crew. Her heart pounded in her chest. "Do you have Ciarán?" she cried.

The grim look Holger gave her from his perch beside the steering oar made her stomach sink. Then she noticed the body of a man with a head of white hair slumped in *Lindworm's* stern. Ilat stood over him. Alais' lower lip began to tremble.

"The champion has succumbed to Samyaza's curse," Ilat called out from the longship, her ethereal face filled with compassion. "And if we don't reach Dudael soon, there will be nothing I can do to save him."

PART FIVE

When the Lamb opened the seventh seal, there was silence in heaven for about half an hour. And I saw the seven angels who stand before God, and seven trumpets were given to them.

— Revelation 8:1-2

CHAPTER 68
THE DEVIL'S FURY

N aberus stood on *Mesektet's* blackened deck planks, his mind whirling with emotions. He felt exuberance at the thought of Samyaza's bold move to strike against their enemy when they least expected it. A gambit to slay the twins and possibly seize the Key to the Abyss. A move so bold it could win the war before they'd even reached Dudael. But with these thoughts came a simmer of anger and dread. For his master may have robbed Naberus of his chance at revenge, to take the lives of the woman, Alais, and the twin who killed his mother. He yearned for Murgleis to feast on their souls and feel the ecstasy of their life forces pulsing through his veins. At times, it was all he could think about, but the possibility this vengeance could be denied him left a bitter taste in his mouth.

From *Mesektet's* foredeck, Naberus gazed upon his two Byzantine galleys and the fleet of warships from Gog anchored in the black waters beneath the twilight of the Otherworld. Lanterns glowed on the vessels like will-o'-the-wisps floating above a haunted fen. He waited there with Lovetar and a new arrival to his master's galley— the prince of Gog. Prince Menoetius was a stoic giant. He stood seven and a half feet tall, with a long face, a close-cropped beard,

451

and a mane of black hair pulled back into a braid tied with golden cords. He looked two decades younger than Naberus, though the prince was nearly two hundred years his senior and appeared every bit the warrior. He wore a black steel breastplate, with similar mail plates covering his muscular arms and legs. Rings of ivory and gold dangled from his pale ears, and a necklace of blood-red gemstones hung from his neck. There was an arrogance about the prince, who spoke few words, and the occasional glances he gave Naberus carried looks of disdain.

Down the galley's narrow deck, forty-one of Samyaza's oarsmen stood at attention as still as pale statues. Each was seven feet tall, shaven of any hair, and wore only loin cloths on their heavily muscled torsos. In unison, they looked up when a pair of wings glowing with fire appeared in the semi-dark sky.

Naberus watched in awe as Samyaza glided like an angel on those wings, his golden skin shining like a beacon through the Otherworldly gloom. His wings made two rapid flaps to slow his descent before he landed on *Mesektet's* foredeck. With a shake of his shoulders, his wings sloughed off his back, dissolving into a shower of sparks and embers that fell hissing into the river. Samyaza gripped a trident of black steel in his right hand. His face was unreadable, and his eyes, with their piercing golden irises, surveyed everyone on board.

Following Lovetar's lead, Naberus, Menoetius, and all but one of the oarsmen knelt before their master. Naberus waited breathlessly for Samyaza to speak. The chief oarsman, who remained standing, approached Samyaza and gave a formal bow. "My lord," he said, "we pray your mission was successful."

Samyaza answered his servant by seizing his neck with his free hand and lifting the oarsman, who must have weighed three hundred pounds, off the deck. The oarsman gasped for breath as Samyaza tightened his grip, his eyes blazing with a fury unlike anything Naberus had ever seen. The oarsman clawed futilely at the fingers of Samyaza's massive left hand before flames sprouted beneath Samyaza's palm, and fire began crawling up the oarsman's face. Samyaza squeezed harder; the oarsman's eyes bulged, and a horrified whimper escaped his lips. Neck bones cracked as fire engulfed the oarsman's head, blackening his pale flesh. When the oarsman went limp, Samyaza tossed his body into the water, which frothed and boiled as whatever swam beneath the black surface devoured the oarsman like chum.

Watching the execution, Naberus struggled to steel his nerves. His master's fury was terrifying to behold, yet his raw strength and godlike power left Naberus in awe. He remained unclear on how the mission had gone. But given his master's anger, Naberus suspected something less than ideal had occurred, which left hope that he might yet realize his revenge.

Samyaza's eyes were still blazing when his gaze returned to those assembled on the ship. Naberus felt a sudden chill when that gaze washed over him and settled on the Prince of Gog. "MENOETIUS," Samyaza bellowed, "UNLEASH THE TARASQUE!"

Prince Menoetius, whose already pale face had drained of any color, hesitated before he answered. "But my lord, the tarasque will serve us best on the battlefield once we reach Dudael."

"NOW, MENOETIUS! OUR ENEMY IS WOUNDED —*NOW* IS THE TIME TO STRIKE!"

"Yes, my lord," Menoetius stammered.

Naberus glanced sideways at Lovetar, whose eyes flickered with eager anticipation. The tarasque was a creature of legend. According to the myths, it was the monstrous offspring of the biblical Leviathan, a monster used in stories to frighten children. Could one really exist in this Otherworld? Naberus soon discovered the answer to that question.

Menoetius summoned one of his war barges to anchor beside *Mesektet*, and when it arrived, Naberus got his first look at the creature called the tarasque. Sitting in the barge, the enormous creature must have been twenty feet tall and massively muscled, looking somewhat like a cross between a great ape and a crocodile. Thick, plate-like scales covered its arms and legs, each ending in three curved claws as long as a man is tall. Horned ridges exploded down its back, and the scales there thickened into a stone-like armor. A giant iron hood like one a falconer would put on a bird of prey covered its eyes and most of its head save for two bull-like horns that jutted six feet from circular openings near the top of its skull. Its uncovered snout revealed huge fangs on its upper and lower jaws, each tooth the length of a longsword. From that snout, Naberus could hear the creature's breath like wind being sucked into a cave, and even from *Mesektet's* foredeck, his nose wrinkled at the beast's pungent stench.

"Remove its hood," Samyaza commanded in a more measured tone, though anger lingered in his voice.

Four of the barge's crew members, each dressed similarly to *Mesektet's* oarsmen, used long poles to undo latches along the sides of the massive hood. When they were finished, the hood fell onto the barge's deck with a loud clang. The beast opened its jaws and its dark eyes filled with a savage gleam.

"Listen to me," Samyaza said as his luminescent skin gave off a more intense golden glow. The tarasque closed its jaws and fixed its gaze on Samyaza. "There are ships sailing upriver to the west of here. They are your prey."

The tarasque gave a nod of understanding.

"HUNT THEM DOWN, AND KILL THEM ALL!"

The beast answered with a roar that reverberated off the surrounding cliffs like rolling thunder. Then, flexing its enormous muscles, the tarasque leaped off the barge, nearly capsizing the vessel. The creature bounded a hundred yards through the air before landing on one of the cliff sides, its terrible claws digging into the basalt rock. As the tarasque climbed to the cliff top and leaped again, disappearing into the gloom, Naberus felt his dreams of revenge slipping away.

For he could not imagine anyone surviving once the tarasque found its prey.

CHAPTER 69
THE RIVER COCYTUS

The moment *Lindworm* entered the new river, Holger felt an icy chill crawl up his spine, as if the very air had been kissed by a Danish winter. Puffs of mist billowed from the mouths of his crew, each exhale a testament to the biting cold. The water had lost its darker hue, now resembling a nearly frozen fjord. Fist-sized chunks of ice bobbed and jostled in the river, thudding against the ship's hull in a dissonant melody of cracks and groans. The crew muttered curses, their oars meeting resistance with each icy obstruction, turning every stroke into a battle.

"Why did we enter this frozen river?" Holger questioned Ilat, his eyes narrowing as he scanned the icy waters.

"The Cocytus is the sole river that will lead us to Dudael," Ilat responded, her words crystallizing in the frigid air as she spoke. "We have no alternative but to forge ahead."

Holger ran his fingers over his coarse beard. His eyes flitted to the basalt cliffsides flanking the river, noticing how they glittered with ice crystals as if speckled with jewels from a frozen realm. Then his gaze lowered to Ciarán, lying still and barely breathing on the platform at his feet. Rosta had nestled close, his body providing the young man with a bit of warmth. Holger turned back to Ilat, his eyes searching hers. "If we make it to Dudael, can you save him?"

Ilat looked down at Ciarán and then met Holger's gaze. "He is one of the seven prophesied to meet at the Cauldron of God," she began, her voice imbued with a solemn tone. "In a sense, he is fated to be there. The very magic of Dudael should give him strength. Once there, I'll do everything within my power to lift the curse Samyaza has placed on him."

"Samyaza?" Holger asked. "That's the name of the Dragon?"

"It is one of his many names. In the mythology of your people, he is Loki. In other myths, he is known as Set or Hades, Ahriman or Lucifer. He is the ancient one, the original betrayer, and the champion is the only one who can defeat him in the coming battle. But until we can free Ciarán from this curse, you must be the one to lead these men. It is why you were chosen."

Holger narrowed his gaze. "Chosen?"

Ilat gave him a nod. "Blind Mikkel sent you dreams that guided you down this path. But, in truth, you were chosen long before then when you inherited that sword." Her gaze fell to Curtana's hilt.

"That blade belonged to my forefather, Sigfred, king of the Danes."

"Before then, it belonged to Sigfred's brother, your namesake—Holger, prince of the Danes. However, during his time in exile from Denmark, he was known as Ogier the Dane, one of the twelve paladins of the Frankish emperor men called Charlemagne. Ogier's sword was forged by Orionde, of whom I'm sure Ciarán has spoken. It was one of three swords created by her, as you know from the runes etched on its blade."

Holger recalled the time Blind Mikkel had translated those runes. "They read, *My name is Curtana, of the same steel and temper as Joyeuse and Durandal.*"

"Joyeuse was the sword of Charlemagne," Ilat said, "and Durandal belonged to Roland, his finest warrior. He, too, was one of the paladins who, along with Ogier, Maugis d'Aygremont, and their companions, fought the first skirmish in this war more than two hundred years ago. Thereafter, the paladins protected the secrets of the prophecy for the heroes of your age, and through them, more than a few of you were chosen. Ciarán's father and mentor, along with Gerbert of Aurillac, discovered the book of Maugis d'Aygremont, which contained the secrets of the prophecy, and set Ciarán on the journey that has taken him here. Another of the paladins, a Moorish poet and swordsman called Fierabras, passed these same secrets to his daughter Nura, who became one of the magi and the ancestor of the twins. His writings also inspired your late companion, Kahlil al-Pârsâ. It was how he was chosen. And when the sword of Ogier the Dane passed to you, you, too, were chosen.

Holger slowly shook his head. "How do you know all this?"

Ilat gave him a warm smile. "We have scrying pools that allow us to watch over this world. Before this cycle began, it was decided that Orionde would oversee events in the west, and I would watch over things in the east until both sides came together en route to Dudael. That is how Michael wanted it."

Michael, Holger thought, another name for Mikkel. "The old priest said he was Blind Mikkel, but he was not blind." Holger recalled the old man crumpled at Samyaza's feet and the lion-like creature with wings that seemed to take his place. "Now he's dead, too, whatever he was."

Anger gathered on the Fae woman's forehead. "Never before has Samyaza been so brazen. To attack the Inner Sanctum ..." She shook her head in disgust. "But, then, the two of Gemini have never been so young and inexperienced. He must have thought he could stop Michael from unlocking their powers. Had we not saved the twins and those armbands, all would have been lost."

So much has already been lost, Holger thought. Two entire crews and two of the Dragonslayers. Of the three ships that had sailed from Rome, only Gaido's ship remained, and who knew how many had been killed or wounded in *Anahita* after she was struck by Greek fire? And now Ilat wanted him to lead those who survived? Holger never feared leadership. Indeed, he embraced being the jarl, the one in command. But never, going into a battle, had he felt so hopelessly outmatched.

Holger's thoughts were abruptly cut short by Freybjorn's voice, tinged with urgency, calling out from the prow. "My lord, another fork in the river looms ahead!"

Straining his eyes past *Lindworm's* dragon-shaped stempost, Holger took in the looming promontory of ice-encrusted rock that jutted out ahead. Its jagged outline was so sharp that it resembled the blade of some titanic battle-ax, ready to cleave the world in two. Ilat, her gaze fixed on the bifurcating path, spoke without hesitation. "Both forks will lead us to Dudael. The path on the left is quicker but fraught with peril. Choose the right."

Holger hesitated and glanced at Ciarán's limp form. "The left path is faster, you say? Could it not be worth the risk to get Ciarán aid sooner?"

"No," Ilat responded, her voice edged with a finality that would tolerate no further argument. "The left path leads to the Ice Rapids of Cocytus. To venture that way would be to gamble not just your ship, but the lives of everyone on board."

Holger met her gaze and nodded, the gravity of the choice weighing heavily on him. "Steer to the right fork," he bellowed to his crew.

Holger pulled his bearskin cloak from the hollow beneath the sternpost and draped it over his broad shoulders. One by one, he noticed, his crew had followed suit, their cloaks billowing as they rowed through the river cluttered with floating ice. As they closed in on the jagged promontory, Holger cast his eyes to the right. The river snaked through a narrow ravine, its basalt cliffs crowned with a frosty sheen. Just then, an earsplitting roar reverberated from the depths of the canyon, a sound so terrifying it could freeze the marrow in a man's bones.

A chill of primal fear ran down Holger's spine. "By all the gods …"

The crew's collective gaze was drawn to the ravine's edge. Launching itself from one side to the other was a monstrosity—a creature rivaling the Dragon in size and ferocity. Ridges as sharp as spearheads adorned its massive shoulders, and colossal horns crowned its head. Its cavernous maw bristled with fangs that could skewer a man, while its gigantic paws, tipped with enormous curved claws, punched holes into the basalt as it hurtled toward them. It roared again, a sound like the legendary Fenrir wolf unbound.

The crew's collective cry of terror sliced through the air, echoing the creature's own monstrous call. Realizing they had mere moments, Holger gripped the steering oar and wrenched it with all his might, sending *Lindworm* veering sharply into the left fork.

"The other ships!" Ilat cried out, her voice tinged with a dire urgency. Without a moment's hesitation, she launched herself into the air, soaring higher and farther than any mortal could until she landed thirty yards away on *Daena's* foredeck.

BEFORE THE ROAR echoed from the ravine, Tara found herself still shaken after their escape from the Inner Sanctum. The image of the trident's sharp prongs bursting through Father Michele's chest was seared into her memory, and she and her sister were still covered in the old priest's blood.

"Put this on," Breda told her, handing her a cloak. "This river we're on is filled with ice." As she spoke, her breath froze in puffs.

Tara clutched her cloak close, shivering not just from the cold but from the lingering dread of their flight from the Inner Sanctum. Breda had remained a steadfast presence at her side, as had her grandfather Fereydun and her Aunt Kira, who enveloped Sara in a protective embrace. Brother Pietro stood with them, sharing the foredeck with the imposing figure of Asira, her hair a captivating cascade of black steel and molten silver. At the prow, Lady Alais stared at the longship ahead, while behind them, Uncle Kamran's voice thundered, urging his rowers onward.

Fereydun weighed the heavy bronze armbands in his hands. "These symbols are etched in silver, seven in total—three on one armband and four on the other. They look like the language of creation, but I can only decipher some," he said, his brow furrowing in concentration.

Asira leaned in, scrutinizing the inscriptions. "I can read them.

If Michael is to be believed, these seven words are the key to the twins unlocking their power. They translate to, '*Upon the wicked, rain fire and hail.*'"

Fereydun's eyebrows shot up in astonishment. He turned his gaze to Tara and Sara. "Can you commit these words to memory?"

Before Tara could answer, a roar unlike anything she had ever heard reverberated off the cliffs where the river forked right. Ahead, *Lindworm* turned sharply left as cries rang out from the vessel. A chorus of frightened shouts erupted from their galley, and Breda grabbed Tara's arm to steady her as their galley swerved to the left.

"Blessed Sergius!" Pietro cried out, his eyes wide with terror, while Sara let out a horrified gasp. Tara's scream got caught in her throat as her muscles froze at the sight of the enormous beast bounding across the ravine. Tara had only seen drawings of dragons, but this beast could have been a dragon, except that its massively muscular body seemed more manlike, as if the mythical wyrm had bred with an ogre or a giant. Its face appeared vaguely wolflike, but only if wolves had great horns like a bull's, grayish scales instead of fur, and were ten times their normal size. Shards of ice and basalt flew into the air, where its huge, curved claws gorged into the cliffside, tearing across the landscape. As it leaped into the air toward the ships, Tara's heart slammed into her stomach.

With the oarsmen rowing for their lives, *Daena* continued its leftward path, curving enough that the bounding monstrosity flew past the ship's stern only to land on *Anahita's* foredeck. With a sweep of its enormous hand, it shattered *Anahita's* mast, sending the yard, sail, and rigging into the river and taking with it the oarsmen working the galley's larboard side. The claws of its right hand raked men from their starboard oar benches. Those who weren't killed instantly by its claws went flying into the freezing river. A sweep of its wicked tail tore through the stempost and ravaged the ship's prow. Meanwhile, the monster's massive jaws bit down on more terrified crew members, filling the air with blood and screams.

"Now, children!" Fereydun cried as he handed the armbands to Tara and Sara. Tara's hands were shaking so badly that Breda had to help her slide the armband over her left wrist. Sara slid her armband onto her right forearm and grabbed Tara's free hand. When their skin touched, a swell of energy pulsed through Tara's veins.

"Focus on the tarasque," Asira urged.

Tara peered at the monster, who was roaring like a giant bear, tearing off the siding of the other galley and hurling men into the river.

"Now, speak the words!" Fereydun said.

Tara drew in a breath, her lungs filling with the power flowing through her veins. *"Upon the wicked,"* she said.

"Rain fire and hail!" Sara cried, finishing the verse.

Holding her sister's hand, Tara felt a thrum of power as a peal of thunder echoed through the sky. Lightning followed, a jagged bolt from the gloom that struck the beast in the back. The monster roared in pain as a second and third bolt struck with deafening booms, filling the air with the smell of ozone. A fourth bolt sizzled down, blasting some of the bony ridges on the creature's shoulders into pieces. Then, a loud hiss filled the air as a shower of hailstones blistered the flailing beast, smoke drifting from the stones as they fell. The monster writhed in agony. What portions of the ship's siding that had not been torn into shards by the beast's enormous claws were now riddled with the rain of smoky hail. For an instant, Tara felt seized with sudden fear for the men on board, but her eyes told her there were no living men in the galley when the hailstones struck. The monster had killed them all, but now it was the one suffering under the constant barrage of fiery hail.

Over her shoulder, Tara heard the voice of the Fae woman Ilat, though Tara did not know how she had suddenly gotten on board the galley.

"Asira," Ilat commanded, "it's wounded. Let's finish it before it leaps onto another ship."

Tara watched in awe as Asira vaulted herself into the air, gripping a long curved blade in each hand. Ilat followed with her own high jump, her gleaming scimitar drawn from its scabbard. The Fae let out battle cries as they fell upon the beast. Asira landed a sweeping strike that blinded one of the creature's eyes while Ilat drove her scimitar into the back of its massive skull. The beast groped behind its neck for Ilat but grasped only air as the Fae somersaulted onto the remains of *Anahita's* deck, which was rapidly filling with the river's freezing water. Asira, meanwhile, bounced off the roof of the smashed deckhouse where she had landed and leaped back into the air, swords crossed. She uncrossed her blades in a violent strike that sheared through the beast's throat. The monster's huge hands wrapped around the wound, which flowed with blackish blood.

The next thing Tara knew, Asira had vaulted onto the papal ship trailing the ruined galley while Ilat leaped backward onto *Daena's* stern. "Tara, Sara," she called out, "again!"

Tara's heartbeat was racing. *"Upon the wicked!"* she shouted.

"Rain fire and hail!" Sara finished.

With a thrum of power and a chorus of thunder, a torrent of lightning lit up the gloom. A half-dozen searing bolts blasted into the monster, followed by another storm of hailstones. What remained of the galley collapsed under the beast's weight as it toppled backward into the river. Clouds of steam billowed off the water as the monster's burning hide struck the icy river, obscuring Tara's view.

Fereydun pulled Tara and Sara into his embrace. "You did it!" Their grandfather's face was beaming.

"We did," Sara said, exhaling.

Tara could hardly believe what had happened, but her sister was right. When the steam cleared, where the monster and *Anahita* had been, only the wreckage of broken deck planks and hull boards remained floating on the ice-choked river.

A swell of joy flowed through Tara's veins—right before a burst of alarmed cries rang out from *Lindworm* at the head of the fleet.

CHAPTER 70

THE EDGE OF THE OTHERWORLD

The shock of seeing the enormous monstrosity leap onto *Anahita* stole the breath from Holger's lungs. Terrified screams from the galley's crew echoed through the ravine, though *Daena*, having turned into *Lindworm's* wake, blocked Holger's view of the carnage. But the speed at which the longship was now moving snapped Holger's attention back to the danger of his own situation.

The sight of the rampaging beast had forced Holger to steer the ship into the left fork against Ilat's warning. The crew was rowing as fast as they could to escape the abomination. Though in doing so, the longship had entered a fast-moving current that had doubled the vessel's speed. Ahead, the ice-filled water was frothing over boulder-sized basalt rocks jutting out of the water, and the river itself appeared to be dropping in elevation. Even with his considerable strength, Holger found it nearly impossible to steady the steering oar as the ship sped toward the rocks.

"Draw in the oars!" Holger cried. The crew scrambled to abide by the order, but some weren't fast enough. Holger felt a sickening feeling in his stomach when he heard the crack of oar blades snapping against rocks.

Chunks of rapidly streaming ice banged against the hull, which made a loud crack as the current carried the ship over one of the larger rocks. The impact bounced *Lindworm* momentarily into the air, and his stomach dropped as the longship plunged several feet down the first rapid.

Men clung to their oar benches as the longship clattered through the rushing water, blasting a spray of freezing liquid into the hull. The current's roar nearly drowned out the screams behind them until even that roar was eclipsed by a peal of thunder that reverberated through the gloom-filled sky. Flashes of lightning preceded the hiss of rain or hail, followed by a pain-filled roar from the beast, wherever it was. Holger, however, did not have time to figure out what was happening behind them, for the longship struck a rock and careened into the increasingly furious rapids.

A wave of icy water washed over Holger and everyone near the stern as the vessel plunged down another drop. Then, to Holger's horror, he felt the steering oar snap in two. Near his feet, Rosta's head jerked up, fear welling in the boarhound's eyes. Ahead, a crewman cried out as the rudderless vessel pitched violently at the whim of the fast-moving river.

Spray blasted over the dragon-headed prow as the ship dove into another rapid. In the sky, more lightning flared, and thunder boomed, mixing with the roar of the river. Swells of freezing liquid spilled over the gunwales along with fist-sized chunks of ice; frost clung to Holger's beard, and the cold burned his skin. Meanwhile, hull boards creaked and groaned each time the ship, caught in the racing current, collided with basalt rock or became bartered against the ice-crusted cliffside. Water pooled at the crews' feet, and Holger feared the hull might have been breached.

His heart pounded, and his stomach dropped each time the ship fell into another rapid. *Lindworm* had lost all control. Holger grabbed the cross hanging at his chest and prayed, for they were at the mercy of these rapids, and only God could save them now.

But God did not answer that prayer. Instead, Freybjorn called out a word that chilled Holger's blood.

"Waterfall!"

Holger let out a panicked cry when the bottom fell out beneath him. A deafening torrent of water roared around them, filling the air with a freezing mist as they plunged downward. Men were thrown from their oar benches, and shields were shaken from their strakes along the ship's sides. Then, suddenly, the dragonhead snapped in two as a wall of water blasted toward them. It hit Holger like a blow to the face, punching the air from his lungs and enveloping him entirely. All he felt was freezing cold, and all he saw was darkness.

ALAIS FELT as if she were trapped in a whirlwind of chaos, each moment superseding the last in its urgency. One second, her eyes widened in horror at the sight of the monstrous beast shredding the neighboring galley, its guttural roar and the crew's terrified screams reverberating through the ravine. The next, her disbelief melted into awe. Tara and Sara unleashed a spectacle of lightning and hail, wounding the creature enough for Ilat and Asira to carve into it with their blades. After another cascade of elemental fury from the twins, the behemoth collapsed. Just as Alais exhaled, her ears caught a cacophony of shouts from *Lindworm's* crew. She glanced ahead and realized they were speeding toward a menacing stretch of rapids.

Alais gripped the rail to steady herself when Kamran ordered his crew to pull in their oars before the galley hit the first rapids. Freezing spray misted over the gunwales, and through that mist, Alais could see *Lindworm* moving farther away. But the longship had lost all control and was captive to the rushing waters.

Her muscles tensed as the galley plunged over the next rapid. Rowers cried out in alarm, as did the twins. Alais glanced back to see Breda clinging to Tara with one hand while her other gripped the larboard rigging. Sara held tight to her sister and grandfather while Pietro and Kira hugged the rigging on the starboard side. Alais' attention returned to the prow when the galley glanced off one of the enormous basalt rocks jutting out of the frothing, ice-filled river. The thud of the collision sent a flutter through her stomach.

Clutching the rail, her knuckles whitened with each sway of the galley, and drop in the river sickened her stomach. Blasts of frigid water swelled over the rail each time the rapids blasted over the rocks. Alais felt crystals of ice on her fingers when she brushed a wet lock of hair off her forehead. Ahead, *Lindworm* was careening off the rapids. For an instant, she lost sight of the vessel in another fog of frozen spray, but then glimpsed it again as it plunged down another drop. Another blast of water stung her eyes, and ice burned her skin. She wiped the water from her eyes, only to see *Lindworm* for a second. Then she watched in horror as the vessel appeared to fall off the edge of the world.

It took Alais a breath to realize what had happened. Fifty yards ahead, *Lindworm*, carrying its crew and Ciarán, had gone over a waterfall, and now the galley was heading straight for it! At that moment, time seemed to stop. Alais conjured an image from her memory of the trials Nimue put her through during her apprenticeship in Avalon. Of the day she froze the surface of the river Lethe to save an infant from a serpent. Alais imagined the Cocytus would be even easier to freeze. She glanced back at Fereydun and Kira. "Use the power to freeze the river!"

Alais extended her hand over the rail and began reciting the words of power—a verse to solidify the water. As the air thrummed around her, she saw the surface of the rushing river take on a whiter hue. Swiftly flowing chunks of ice began to slow and thicken around one other. Frost spread across the water's surface as words spoken by Fereydun and Kira joined Alais' own. Then Ilat was at Alais' side, repeating the same verse. Blue eldritch light flickered off the basalt cliffs as the icy river hardened before Alais' eyes. The galley, speeding through the rapids but a moment ago, slowed to a stop, then shuddered violently as the papal ship behind it slammed into the galley's stern.

Ahead, twenty yards of frozen river ended at the waterfall's crest. Alais's stomach clenched at the thought of what must have happened to *Lindworm* and everyone on board. "Lower the gangplank!" she cried out desperately. But as the crew scrambled to follow her order, Ilat did not wait. Instead, she leaped over the rail and landed ten yards away on the river's frozen surface before rushing to the waterfall's edge.

As soon as the gangplank was in place, Alais and Breda climbed down onto the ice. They moved as fast as they could to the edge while maintaining their balance on the slick surface. When they reached Ilat, Alais felt a weight on her chest as she peered over the frozen waterfall. Beside her, Breda let out a gasp.

For sixty feet below the falls, through a cloud of frozen mist, *Lindworm* lay in wreckage.

CHAPTER 71

AFTERMATH

Piercing cold engulfed Ciarán, each frigid sensation a needle prick against his skin. Opening his eyes was like inviting shards of ice to sting his pupils, and the freezing water rushed up his nostrils and invaded his mouth. His mind screamed that he was drowning, but his limbs lacked the strength to fight. *So this is how it ends*, he thought, surrendering to the icy embrace.

Just as Ciarán felt himself being swallowed by the numbing abyss, muscular arms encircled his torso, hoisting him upward. His head breached the surface, and he coughed out the icy liquid that filled his mouth. His blurred vision kept him from making out details as he blinked away the water in his eyes. But when he was laid on the frigid, hard-packed earth, his vision started to clear. His eyes met those of Jarl Holger. The Danish lord was soaked to the bone, yet exuding fierce determination. "We don't die this day," Holger declared.

Ciarán tried to nod before a sudden dizziness washed through his head. He closed his eyes. For how long, he did not know. But when he opened them again, Holger was still there. "Take this," he said.

The jarl grasped Ciarán's hand and pressed the leather-wrapped

468

hilt of a sword into his palm. A peculiar warmth radiated from the grip, crawling up his arm like living fire. *Caladbolg.* When the warmth surged into his chest, Ciarán mustered the strength to lift his head, and a haunting scene met his gaze. A terrible image that reminded him of his last vision with Samyaza.

Lindworm's hull was shattered into three or four pieces, and its curved hull-boards jutted from the basalt rocks like the rib cage of a whale. A frigid mist hung in the air, and *Lindworm's* sail, still lashed to the yard, floated in a vast pool choked with large chunks of ice. Ten feet away, the top half of the ship's dragon-headed prow lay on the rocky shore, its dull black eyes staring lifelessly at Ciarán. Near him, three other figures were laid out on the ground. He strained his neck for a better look and recognized their faces, pale and still as death: Úlfarr, Askil, and Halfdan.

What's happened? The last thing he remembered was Samyaza speaking those five strange words: *Ozam, odamma, cialpor, mir, agrit.* Then came the pain. Pain so intense that Ciarán would have chosen death to escape the agony. And the next thing he knew, he was drowning in that freezing pool. He closed his eyes again and slipped into unconsciousness.

Ciarán was roused once more by the sound of boots crunching against gravel. Fluttering open his eyelids, he found himself staring up at an ethereal face. It was the Fae woman, the one Fereydun had named Lady Ilat, her skin glowing like polished bronze and her hair a cascade of black steel. She leaned over him, her amber eyes locking onto his.

"Where are we?" he rasped.

Her lips curved into the barest semblance of a smile. "We are in Dudael."

Alais felt a growing sense of dread as she peered down at *Lindworm's* wreckage amidst the frozen mist. The wreckage was half submerged in a broad pool where the frozen falls met another branch of the Cocytus that snaked around a towering wall of basalt cliffs hundreds of feet high and stretching for miles in either direction. The cliffs loomed over the falls like a ring of high mountains whose peaks disappeared into the perpetual gloom of the Otherworld.

A moment earlier, Ilat had launched herself over the edge of the falls and disappeared into the mists below. Breda, her face ashen, clasped her hands together in a desperate gesture of prayer. "No," she whispered.

A lump formed in Alais' throat. All she could think about was Ciarán, and her thoughts were a tangled mix of fear and hope. She breathed a silent prayer to Saint Radegonde. *Let them be alive.* But she knew that standing there would not bring answers. "We need to find a way down there."

The shieldmaiden nodded, holding back tears.

They located a pathway down the cliffside, flanking the left bank of the falls. The path was a narrow, crude flight of stairs, but whether they had been carved into the basalt rock or formed naturally, Alais could not tell. The descent looked steep and treacherous, but it was the only path they had.

Breda went first, clinging to the rugged cliffside as she descended the rocky steps, one by one. Alais followed. The rock was frigid to the touch, and so was the air filled with icy mist. A layer of frost coated the rocks, but the two stepped down carefully enough to avoid slipping and falling to their doom.

Halfway down the slope, figures materialized through the mist. Three lifeless bodies lay sprawled on the ashen shore. Alais' heart sank as she recognized them: the young, handsome Dane named Askil, along with Úlfarr and Halfdan. But no sign of Ciarán. Other survivors of *Lindworm's* crew were salvaging shields and weapons. About thirty yards away, Mordechai stood, his bow clenched in his right hand.

Breda opened her mouth to speak but faltered, unable to say his name.

"The jarl is alive, my lady," Mordechai said, his face a map of relief and gratitude. "And so is Ciarán. Today, death claimed only three of us."

A surge of joy overwhelmed Alais, only to be immediately tempered by a wave of guilt. Their journey had already been so costly, so fraught with loss. *Anahita's* crew had been taken by the monstrous creature, two papal ships had been obliterated during their harrowing escape from the Inner Sanctum, and now three more had perished. And there was Father Michele. If he was indeed who they believed, then Samyaza had murdered an archangel. Why hadn't the demon gone directly for her or the twins? Did he fear Father Michele would stop him? Whatever the reason, Father Michele was gone, and now half of their fleet lay in ruins. The gravity of facing Samyaza without them seemed almost too over-whelming to bear. But at least Ciarán had survived.

"Where are they?" Breda's voice trembled as she questioned Mordechai.

"We've found shelter," Mordechai said. "The woman, Ilat, had Jarl Holger take Ciarán there. He's conscious, but very weak."

Mordechai helped Alais and Breda reach the ground. The path down the side of the falls led to a stretch of ash-gray earth that rounded the curve of the icy pool and continued along the edge of the mountainous wall on the far side. Freybjorn, Ormr, and Hári Grayhair were lining painted round shields on the ground next to spears and swords rescued from the wreckage. Stóri Red Beard knelt beside the bodies of Úlfarr, Halfdan, and Askil, while a stocky Dane named Skarde and a young warrior named Knut used oars to fish out more shields floating amid the ice chunks in the pool. When they passed a portion of *Lindworm's* shattered hull half-submerged in the water, Alais noticed a tear welling in the corner of Breda's eye as she surveyed the remains of the longship and its crew.

The women followed Mordechai to a cave mouth two yards up the side of the mountain, accessible by several steps of fallen basalt rock. The opening was large enough for a carriage to pass through, and Alais shuddered at the thought that some otherworldly beast once made the cave its home. As Mordechai led them into the cave, they were struck by the odor of burning timber and the warmth of the air. Jorundr, Strong Bjorn, and several other drenched crew members huddled around a blazing fire in the center of the cave.

Rosta lay beside them as they fed fragments of the longship's siding and shards of its oars into the blaze, sending smoke curling dozens of feet into the air, where it disappeared into the darkness.

When Breda spotted Holger standing near one of the curved walls of the cave, she rushed to him and threw her arms around her husband. Ilat knelt beside Holger, tending to Ciarán, who sat propped up against the wall. His eyes were open. Alais hurried to him and knelt beside Ilat.

Ciarán's face was haggard and as pale as a ghost's. With his white hair, he looked as if he had aged another ten years. Alais placed a hand on his thigh. "What happened?"

"Samyaza," he said in a weak voice. "When he spoke those words, it triggered something, like the ward I encountered back in Rome in the Book of Giants. But the pain was a thousand times worse."

"A curse like that should have killed you," Ilat said. "I can only imagine it was because you were holding Enoch's device that you are alive. The power of the stone saved your life."

Ciarán glanced down to Caladbolg in his right hand, with the gemstone embedded in its pommel etched with the one true name of God.

Alais looked to Ilat. "What can we do to help him?"

"To figure that out," Ilat replied, "we must understand the nature of this curse and how it was applied. To do that, we will need the light."

Ilat reached out her palm as a familiar word of power rolled off her tongue: "*Eoh.*" A blueish light flickered from Ilat's palm and washed over Ciarán. Alais gasped, for its glow revealed an even brighter rune etched into Ciarán's forehead. The rune appeared vaguely shaped like the letter E but with flares and curves that made it look like the profile of a grinning skull. Alais had seen symbols like that in the books Nimue kept at Avalon. She remembered they were dangerous.

"*Mir,*" Ilat hissed under her breath.

Alais noticed a second symbol glowing on the palm of Ciarán's left hand. This one looked somewhat like a diagonal letter V. She gestured towards it. Ciarán stared wide-eyed at the symbol emblazoned on his hand.

Ilat narrowed her gaze. "Ciarán, show us your right palm."

He let go of Caladbolg and held up his right hand. His jaw fell open when he saw an O-shaped rune seared into his palm.

"*Ozam,*" Ilat whispered. "We must remove his boots."

Alais and Ilat each grabbed one of his leather boots and pulled them off. The tops of each foot were glowing in Ilat's blue light, with a different rune burned onto each foot.

"How did this happen?" Ilat's eyes searched their faces as if probing for an answer.

"The visions!" Alais gasped, her fingers clenching in realization. "Samyaza has been tormenting him in his dreams."

Ciarán nodded. His eyes were wide, his face flushed with a look of shock. "Each time he spoke one of those words, I felt something. A strange sensation on my hand or foot. Once, on my forehead. I never imagined ..."

Ilat's eyes narrowed, and she grimaced as if in pain. "The runes form a pentagram. From your right palm to your left, down to your right foot, up to your forehead, and then down to your left foot. The pentagram binds the curse. If only I had known about these visions sooner ..."

"What happens now?" Ciarán asked.

Ilat drew a sharp breath. "Those runes are now a part of you. My power isn't enough to erase them. When you next encounter Samyaza, merely speaking those words will activate the curse. And this time, I have no doubt it will kill you."

A sickening feeling twisted in Alais' stomach. "There has to be something we can do. There must be!"

Ciarán slumped against the wall, drained of hope. His gaze shifted to Ilat as if seeking an answer.

Ilat sighed, her voice heavy with regret. "There is one thing that might save you. But it will be a terrible decision for you to make."

CHAPTER 72
THE WAR PLAN

s Ciarán lay on the brink of sleep, Alais filled him in on the harrowing ordeals their forces had endured: the destruction of the papal ships outside the Inner Sanctum, the demise of *Anahita* and her crew to a monstrosity that Ilat had named a "tarasque." And then there were the twins, who had unlocked their dormant powers, raining destruction upon the beast. The knowledge that Alais and the twins had survived gave him a sliver of relief, yet the weight of so many lost lives pressed down on him, dragging him further into the darkness that loomed at the edges of his consciousness. Tangled up in all of this was the terrible choice Ilat had said he would need to make—one so agonizing he could scarcely bring himself to ponder it. With these heavy thoughts as his cold comfort, he yielded to the insistent tug of exhaustion and sank into slumber.

Ciarán awoke to the sound of commotion in their makeshift campsite. The coarse texture of a wool blanket chafed against his skin. Nearby, Pietro hunched over, a candle flickering beside him as he pored over one of the Jerusalem scrolls. Ciarán rubbed the sleep from his eyes and took a deep breath; the air was smoky, laced with the scent of burning wood. Three campfires glowed in the spacious cave, their light casting golden shadows on its bronze walls. Aswaran warriors and Danes huddled around the flames, their voices hushed but tense. A sudden commotion at the cave's entrance snapped the men to attention, many leaping to their feet.

"What's happening?" Ciarán asked Pietro.

"Kamran and his men have returned."

"Returned? Where did they go?"

"They set out on a scouting mission shortly after you passed out."

Ciarán rubbed his temples, which were still sore, along with every inch of his body. "How long was I out?"

Pietro shrugged. "It's hard to measure time down here without a sun or a moon. But I've eaten twice and slept myself for a few hours. So, a day, perhaps?"

"A day?" Ciarán shook his head. "Bloody hell."

"You look like hell," Pietro said with a hint of a smile. "How do you feel?"

"However hell must feel like."

Pietro stood up and smoothed his wrinkled habit when Kira approached them. "My brother has returned," she said, "and my father wants to gather the leaders to hear what Kamran has discovered."

Ciarán nodded before Pietro helped him to his feet. He staggered with his first step, realizing how weak his legs felt. *I'm in no condition to charge off to battle,* he thought as he gingerly took the next step. Pietro helped steady him as they followed Kira to one of the three campfires. Kamran stood by the fire with Fereydun, Alais, and the twins on one side, while Holger, Jorundr, and Breda stood on the other. The two Fae, Ilat and Asira, along with Gaido, soon joined them.

"My son," Fereydun beckoned as soon as they were assembled around the fire, "tell us what you learned."

Kamran's face held a grim expression. "We found a path up a series of hills that climbed to a ridge about seven miles from here. From there, we could peer down into the valley, where we spotted the enemy's camp. It stands before a slender, dark tower at the far end of the valley before the strange cliffs of bronze that surround this place."

"That's not a tower," Alais said. "It's an obelisk. I've seen it before."

"It's the pillar that imprisons the Watchers," Ilat explained. "And soon, it will fall. Time is not our ally."

"What of the enemy?" Gaido asked. "How many are we facing?"

Kamran grimaced. "We are greatly outnumbered. Of the pale-skinned giants like the ones who attacked us at the Inner Sanctum, we counted three hundred and fifteen. But those were only the ones we could see. Undoubtedly, there are more. Then there is the House of Magog. In their camp, we counted a hundred and sixty-one, though I do not doubt there are more of them, too."

Gaido rubbed a hand over his face while Ciarán could not help but throw back his head and let out a hopeless laugh. "How in heaven's name are we supposed to deal with an army that large? Just how many men do we have left?"

Gaido sighed. "My crew numbers but ten, plus Saint Rade-gonde. Though Gundoald of Pavia is as good as two men, by my estimation."

"The Aswaran are fifty strong," Kamran said.

"*Lindworm's* crew numbers fifteen now," Holger added, "counting myself and Breda."

Ciarán held his head in his hands. "That's less than eighty men," he said, remembering nearly twice that many had entered the Lerna Gate. "While our enemy likely numbers more than five hundred. And not men either, but Nephilim. Not to mention the Dragon himself."

"This is no time to lose faith," Fereydun said sternly. "The smallest among us are the mightiest. We all saw what the twins did to that monster, a beast greater in size and mightier than twenty Nephilim. Imagine their rain of fire and hail upon the enemy's ranks."

"I suspect we would need to get them close to the battle," Alais remarked. "But somewhere where the enemy could not find them."

Kamran narrowed his gaze. "The ridge we found was surrounded by a parapet of rocks. They'd be close to the battle, but safe up there."

"We'll go where we're needed," Sara announced bravely. However, Ciarán could see hesitance in her sister's eyes.

"That would require us to split up," Kira said. "Yet our numbers are already small."

Pietro cleared his throat. "What if we are *supposed* to split up?"

Ciarán raised his eyebrows. "What do you mean?"

Pietro held up the scroll he had been reading. "It's written here." He unfurled the scroll and turned his body so the firelight would illuminate the papyrus. Then, he read: "*On the day of battle, the congregation of the gods and the congregation of men shall engage one another, and the outcome will be great carnage. The Sons of Light and the forces of Darkness shall fight one another to show the strength of God ...*" He traced his finger down the scroll. "*In three groups, the Sons of Light will stand firm to strike a blow at wickedness ...*" Pietro glanced up. "So, maybe we don't split into two, but break into three."

When Ciarán noticed the hint of a smile on Ilat's lips, he knew Pietro was on to something. "Three groups."

Fereydun held up a finger. "One could take the girls to the ridge and protect them once they get there."

"But if they're to do any good," Breda said, "we'll need a second group to lure the enemy onto the battlefield."

"It will have to be the largest force," Holger added. "We'll have to taunt the enemy into engaging us in battle, like we did at Maldon."

Jorundr grunted in approval. "Like Maldon."

"Then the twins will rain lightning and hail upon the wicked," Fereydun said with a half-toothed grin.

The more Ciarán listened, the more encouraged he felt. "But what of the third group?"

"That's the group that will go with me to the pillar," Alais said. "I'm the only one that can heal it."

Ciarán shot her a look of alarm and mouthed a word: "*No.*"

"Ciarán," she said, "it has to be this way, and you know that's true."

"It has always been this way," Ilat interjected. "Only Sirra holds the Key to the Abyss. Yet the question remains: which group will you join, Ciarán mac Tomás?"

He pressed his palms against the side of his head. More than anything, he wanted to stay with Alais, to use Caladbolg and whatever strength he had left to make sure she reached the obelisk safely. But in the Inner Sanctum, Father Michele had told him what he must do—face the Dragon and defeat him, or all will be lost. *The Dragon knows this too,* Ciarán told himself. *He'll seek me out on the battlefield. I can't be anywhere near Alais or the twins.*

When Ciarán looked up, he knew what must be done. "I'll fight with the main force alongside Jarl Holger."

Holger nodded while Ilat's lips stretched into a grin. From the understanding look on Alais' face, Ciarán knew she agreed with his decision.

"But who goes in the other two groups?" Pietro asked.

"I shall go with my granddaughters," Fereydun announced.

"And I will go too," Kira said.

Pietro ran a hand over his chin. "I won't be much use in the main force, so I'll go with you."

"I can go as well," Kamran said, earning a frown from Fereydun.

"No, my son," Fereydun said, shaking his head. "You are the leader of the Aswaran, and they will need you on the battlefield. Give me six of your best warriors. That should do. Your sister and I are magi, and we're not easily trifled with."

Kamran gave his father a reluctant nod. "Very well."

"Can Rosta go with us?" Tara asked.

Breda raised her eyebrows, then grinned, "I'm sure he'd like that."

The answer brought a smile to Tara's lips.

Ilat looked at Alais. "Asira and I will go with you to the pillar."

Hearing that, Ciarán breathed an inward sigh of relief. The two

Fae were the most powerful in their group by a broad measure. No one could protect Alais better.

Finally, Gaido spoke. "We have but ten men, but they've been trained to operate the Dragonslayer. We will go with the main force."

Holger and Jorundr nodded their approval.

Gaido's face cracked into a rare smile. "And as luck would have it, my ship carried the pope's chests with those white cloaks he had made. We have three-score of them, enough for most of the men who shall stand on the front line."

Ciarán had forgotten about the white tablecloth and the cloaks Gerbert promised to make. But hearing the news raised his spirits. "Protection from fire," he said under his breath.

"Then it's decided," Ilat announced. "We have our battle plan."

When their group dispersed to tell the other men the plan, Ciarán lingered by Ilat until they were alone. The conclusion Ciarán had come to after learning about Samyaza's curse had sickened his stomach, and even now, he felt ill at having to say the words he knew he must speak.

Summoning his courage, Ciarán inhaled deeply before exhaling a shaky breath. "I've made my decision," he finally said, locking eyes with Ilat. "But I'll need your help to do it."

CHAPTER 73

THE CAULDRON OF GOD

I n the cave that had become their sanctuary, the Aswaran, the
Danes, and Gaido's small band of men readied themselves for
battle.

Light from the campfires reflected off their chainmail coats and
scalemail vests while the men donned the white hooded cloaks
Gerbert had designed based on Charlemagne's fireproof tablecloth.
Each cloak was long and broad enough to wrap completely around
a man, providing a small glimmer of hope that its wearer might
survive a blast of dragonfire. After they dressed and sheathed swords
at their belts or slung bows and quivers over their shoulders, many
gathered in prayer. Soon, somber appeals to God and to Christ, to
Allah and to Ahura Mazda, and to Odin and to Thor, murmured
throughout the cavern. They were prayers for courage and protection, for good fortune and divine aid, for the families they had left
behind and the fate of their souls, for these were the prayers of men
who knew this might be their last battle. Men who may leave their
lives on the gray wasteland of Dudael.

As Ciarán listened to these prayers, he remembered one of his
own, the one he recited back in Rome on the morning of the siege
of Castel Sant'Angelo. It was a verse written by Saint Columcille: *Be*

480

a bright flame before me, my God. For we have nothing to fear when you are near, O Lord of day and night. As he did back then, while trying to summon whatever courage he could muster before the harrowing siege, he remembered his companions who had given their lives in pursuit of the prophecy: Dónall and Remi, Rabbi Isaac and Josua's son Eli, and his good friend, Khalil. He also recalled those he lost before them, including his mother and father and his brothers at Derry: Bran and Murchad, Fintan and Senach, Áed and Ailil, and his dearest friend, Niall. And now, since entering the Otherworld, half the Aswaran, two-thirds of Gaido's men, and three of *Lindworm's* crew had sacrificed their lives for this cause. Ciarán clenched his jaw and made the sign of the cross. *I cannot let their sacrifices be in vain.*

He stood near one of the cave's strange bronze-colored walls while Pietro helped him dress. Pietro placed the leather baldric strapped to Caladbolg's scabbard over the mail hauberk that once belonged to Maugis d'Aygremont. Over that, Pietro pinned the white cloak made of Asbestus stone, spun as soft as wool, then strapped Ciarán's shield tightly onto his left arm. It was the same round shield painted with a white cross over a crimson field that Ciarán used during the trial by combat back in Rome. Ciarán winced when Pietro tightened the straps.

"You don't want it to fall off, do you?" Pietro asked.

"I suppose not," Ciarán admitted, gritting his teeth.

Next, Pietro picked Caladbolg off the ground and slid the sword into its scabbard. "Can you reach it?"

Ciarán touched the pommel with his right hand, brushing his thumb against the gemstone. "As well as always."

"Now, you only need your helmet, and you'll look just like one of Emperor Charlemagne's paladins." Pietro lifted the helmet off the ground. It was the same one, slightly pointed at the top with a triangular nasal, that Ciarán wore during his fight with Gundoald of Pavia. Before Pietro could place it on Ciarán's head, Alais approached them. Her long raven hair was tied behind her neck, and she wore the tight-fitting leather vest over a long-sleeved tunic with woolen hose and high leather boots. To Ciarán, she looked as beautiful as ever.

She took the helmet from Pietro and regarded Ciarán with her storm-gray eyes. He saw emotions for him in those eyes, a feeling he shared with all of his heart. She placed the helmet on his head, straightening it so the nasal shielded his nose. "Thank you," she said, "for always being so brave." A flicker of tears formed in her eyes. "I hate that you have to do this."

"You said it yourself," he replied. "It has to be this way, and you were right."

"I know." Then she drew him into an embrace. Her touch filled him with a sensation so warm, so comforting, he wished they could stay in this embrace forever. When they finally let go, Ciarán swallowed hard and noticed tears staining her cheeks.

"When this is over," she said, "let's find the most peaceful place on Earth and stay there."

Ciarán nodded. He wanted nothing more than to wait out the rest of his days with her. But before he could respond, a series of booming sounds echoed through the cavern as if someone had blared some titanic trumpet across Dudael. He counted seven of the ominous horn blows.

"What is that?" Alais asked.

"The pillar is failing," Ilat said, striding toward them, dressed for battle in her gleaming scalemail like the armor worn by the Sisters of Orionde. "The enemy is celebrating this fact, and those horn blows are a countdown to their victory. We have perhaps seven hours before the pillar falls, and all is lost."

Ciarán shook his head. "How's this happening so fast?"

"Time moves differently in the Otherworld," Ilat responded. "The closer one gets to the center—to Dudael—the faster it moves. In what may pass for an hour down here, two or three days would pass in the mortal world. You've been here long enough that the millennium is nearly upon us."

Alais shot Ciarán a look of concern.

"Sirra," Ilat said sternly, "it's time we go."

A TUNNEL from the cavern led to another cavemouth that opened onto the plains of Dudael. The second and third groups departed first so that the twins could gain position on the ridge before the first group—the diversionary force—neared the enemy encampment to lure out the legions of Gog and Magog. Their small but resolute army numbered eighty-one warriors, a force far too small to take on the legions that awaited them. Most wore Gerbert's billowing white cloaks, along with determined expressions. Yet, as brave and resolute as these men were, Ciarán knew their mission would end in disaster if the twins did not reach the ridge.

When Ciarán stepped from the threshold of the cave, he found himself in a desolate valley of gray, hard-packed earth, surrounded by towering bronze cliffs beneath a sunless sky. The air was cold and still, as if nature itself held its breath in the face of the coming storm. Meanwhile, the sight of the sheer bronze cliffs forming a rough circle around the valley made it clear how this place got its name—the Cauldron of God.

The warriors marched across the valley in two ranks behind its four leaders, along with Breda, who stayed by her husband's side. Most were the Aswaran, strong, disciplined men whom Kamran had trained for years to prepare for this moment. Holger's Danes were a smaller lot, but the most battle-hardened of the group. These were the men who triumphed over the English at Maldon and plundered half of Dorsetshire. They were the sea wolves, spear Danes and sword Danes who defeated Jarl Orn's crew at Stonehenge, fought Naberus da Roma's men at the Temple of Venus and Roma, and slew a band of Nephilim warriors from the House of Magog on the Palatine Hill. These were men resigned to fight—and possibly die—at the battle they called Ragnarok, the conflict that awaited them now. Alongside the Danes strode Gundoald of Pavia with his horsehair-plumed helm and shield bearing the symbol of the marble horse, along with three of the papal guardsmen, all veterans of the fight against Naberus's forces at the Temple of Venus and Roma. The rest of Gaido's men gripped ropes pulling Saint Radegonde, the only one of the three Dragonslayers to make it to Dudael. The wheels of the giant ballista groaned as they rumbled over the hard gray earth.

An hour into the march, six horn blasts echoed off the cliff walls, an ominous booming sound: *"BWOM, BWOM, BWOM— BWOM, BWOM, BWOM!"* Ciarán could not see where the sound came from, though he could tell it originated miles ahead of them down the desolate plain. But the sound of the horns sent a chill down his neck.

"What does it mean?" Breda asked.

Ciarán sighed. "It means we have only six hours before the pillar that imprisons the fallen angels collapses, and all hell breaks loose."

Holger peered at the miles of wasteland that lay before them. "In our legends, the great horn Gjallarhorn heralds the beginning of Ragnarok."

"In my faith," Kamran said, "a trumpet sounds at the end times before the day of judgment."

Gaido grimaced. "I may not know much of myths and legends, but I know when an enemy is trying to intimidate its opponent. And that's exactly what these horns are meant to do."

With these sobering thoughts, the small army continued its procession through the valley. Two more hours passed, for the great horns blew five times, and then sometime after, four horn blasts followed. Long before then, Ciarán's muscles began to ache from the weight of his armor and the distance they had traveled over the hard ground. Despite the cold air, sweat dampened his hair beneath his helmet and beaded on his brow, adding to his discomfort and the lingering weariness from Samyaza's curse.

As they trudged on, Ciarán noticed the jagged hills to the right about a half mile away, climbing to the ridge Kamran had discovered during his scouting mission. Ciarán could only hope that the second group, led by Fereydun, had made it there safely by now. Alais, Ilat, and Asira were traveling with the second group but planned to separate from them at the ridge and use stealth to approach the pillar. Ciarán tried not to think about Alais. He had to trust that the two Fae would protect her, for he knew that if he let his thoughts dwell on her, he wouldn't be able to lead the men who needed him now. So, keeping his mind on the mission at hand, he soldiered on at the head of the army.

"BWOM, BWOM, BWOM!"

The horns rang out for a third time before the enemy encampment came into view, sprawling like a dark stain in the distance. Banners waved ominously above a sea of tents, all dwarfed by a towering black spire. A hellish glow of firelight reflected off the surface of the spire, which came to a point at its crown, resembling a gigantic version of the Egyptian obelisks scattered throughout Rome. Ciarán knew that the obelisk was the only barrier keeping Samyaza's followers trapped in their abysmal prison.

The army advanced a few hundred yards closer to the camp before Jarl Holger hollered for Freybjorn to join them at the front. "What do you see?" he asked.

Freybjorn narrowed his gaze, studying the enemy encampment. "Lots of tents and hordes of those pale-skinned jötnar. I see the horns. Three of them curved like a good Danish horn, but ten times the size. And then there's ..." He paused for a moment, his eyes widening. "Big pot-bellied beasts. Looks like they're made of iron, with open jaws like a dragon's. There are five of them, and they sit on carts with wheels. What in the gods' names are they?"

Ciarán knew what Freybjorn was describing. He had seen them unleash their fury at Rosefleur, and the thought of facing them sent a swell of dread through his stomach. "They're war engines," he said. "They hurl great balls of fire and smoke. I once saw them take down an entire tower, and they'll slaughter anyone in their path." He glanced back at the army. "We need to spread the men out. When they see a flash or hear a boom like thunder, they have to scatter. The farther apart they are, the harder they'll be to hit."

After receiving Ciarán's warning, Holger, Kamran, and Gaido informed their troops. Soon, the army arranged itself in a single row, with each man positioned seven feet away from the other. The line of warriors extended for one hundred eighty yards from one side to the other.

"Is it time to get the enemy's attention?" Holger asked Ciarán.

Ciarán drew in a deep breath. As soon as he gave the order, he would draw the fight to them, risking the lives of all these men. But he had to do it; their plan depended on it. "Aye," he told Holger.

Holger turned toward the army. "Beat on your shields!" he ordered. "Let the enemy know we are here, and we're ready for a fight!"

Jorundr was the first to comply, hammering the pommel of his sword onto the willow boards of his round shield. Strong Bjorn followed, banging on his shield until the rest of the Danes joined in. Kamran's Aswaran, each of whom wore smaller round bucklers compared to the Danes' larger shields, pounded the shafts of their bows against the bucklers while Gaido's men drummed on their own shields, creating a clamor loud enough to wake the dead.

"That got their attention!" Freybjorn hollered over the din of beating shields.

"So will this," Ciarán said. He drew Caladbolg from its scabbard, the scrape of steel ringing through the noise. He brought its pommel to his lips and breathed in slowly, clearing his mind. Then he whispered a word, *"Eoh."* Energy surged down his arm as the blade erupted with the light of a thousand torches. A flare of white fire surrounded the sword as he raised the weapon above his head, summoning gasps of awe from the Aswaran, who had never witnessed Enoch's device in all its glory.

In the enemy encampment, a thousand yards away, the Nephilim began scrambling into action. "They're gathering around those iron beasts!" Freybjorn warned.

"Get ready!" Ciarán called back to the men. "When you see something, scatter!"

An instant later, the iron beasts roared to life, accompanied by bright flashes of flame and thunder-like booms. A hot and sulfurous blast filled the air, and Ciarán darted to his right as something whizzed past him, smoke trailing behind it. Men scattered as four more streaking missiles tore through the air. Only one man cried out in pain as an explosion followed. Ciarán glanced toward the sound. Where one of the Aswaran had stood, almost nothing remained but blasted earth, and a body obliterated beyond recognition.

The surviving warriors roared in triumph. "Keep banging those shields!" Holger commanded.

Ciarán's heart pounded in his chest as he waited for the haze of smoke to clear. He knew the enemy would keep trying, and they did. Five more flares of light and thunderous booms sent five more smoking projectiles speeding into the line of dispersed warriors. This time, none hit their mark, earning even louder roars from the army.

The air stank of sulfur and smoke as hordes of pale-skinned Nephilim emerged from the camp, forming into ranks. The enemy's sheer number and hulking stature sent a flutter through Ciarán's heart.

"The front ranks are arming themselves with gods-dammed crossbows!" Freybjorn hollered. "And they're bloody giant ones, too!"

With a look of alarm on his face, Kamran turned to his Aswaran. "Bows at the ready!"

On command, the Aswaran reached into their quivers and knocked arrows onto bowstrings.

"Let's hope our bows have better range than those crossbows," Kamran said.

Ciarán prayed they did, for in the distance, the enemy was amassing. The sight was like nothing he had ever seen, and he felt an unsettling mixture of awe and terror. For before him, an army of Nephilim, nearly six hundred strong, stretched across the battlefield carrying a host of foreboding banners. Most of the enemy warriors were pale-skinned giants, their immense figures a stark contrast against the gloom-filled sky. Clad in black iron breastplates that glistened under the faint light, they looked less like men and more like monstrous statues carved from pale stone and iron. Some wore intimidating helms that enveloped their entire heads and carried menacingly long spears while the front ranks gripped massive crossbows. Another group of Nephilim gathered beneath a black banner bearing the symbol of the House of Magog. Though a half-head shorter than their stronger comrades, the warriors of Magog looked no less formidable. They were clad in mail hauberks, their armor glinting darkly under the gloom-filled sky. Round shields were strapped to their arms or backs, while helmets concealed their features. Most wielded crossbows, though some held spears or poleaxes.

As the enemy marched forward, their war chants drifted across the plain, filling the valley with an ominous cadence. Ciarán tightly gripped Caladbolg's hilt, trying to swallow his fear. But his heart raced with each long stride taken by the opposing forces through the desolate plain.

"Take aim!" Kamran commanded.

His Aswaran archers drew back their bowstrings and lifted their weapons.

Ciarán sucked in a breath as Kamran waited for the advancing Nephilim to get into range. When they were five hundred yards away, Kamran bellowed: "Fire!"

A flurry of arrows filled the air, hissing as they flew. They soared high, arcing as they dropped and fell upon the enemy ranks. The arrows landed with a shuddering thud, but the warriors of Gog did not even try to scatter. Some swatted away the arrow shafts as if they were nothing more than pesky mosquitos, while other shafts clanged off black iron armor. The arrows that landed in flesh were plucked from the wounds like they were pine needles.

"Gods," Holger muttered as an icy dread crept down Ciarán's spine.

The enemy continued forward, their rippling banners coming more clearly into view. Prominent among them was a banner bearing the image of a seven-headed dragon, a monstrous creature rendered in hues of crimson and obsidian. Others featured coiled serpents or malevolent skulls, some with horns jutting from their foreheads. Another banner showed a symbol of a black ram with twisted horns, a stark image against the gloom. From their ranks, a harrowing command resonated across the battlefield. With a swift, terrifying ease, the Nephilim hefted up massive crossbows, each a monstrous weapon of war. A dreadful silence fell over the battlefield as the giants took aim. Ciarán's breath hitched in his chest as the Nephilim, with a chillingly synchronized motion, unleashed a storm of bolts that sliced through the air, blurring into a rain of deadly iron.

"Shields!" Holger yelled, his voice swallowed by the deafening rush of crossbow bolts.

Ciarán crouched and ducked behind his shield. A bolt struck it so hard it split the willow boards a hair above Ciarán's arm. The other bolts landed with a staccato of thuds and screams. Bolts protruded from shields and bucklers like porcupine spines, but to Ciarán's horror, at least ten of the Aswaran took bolts through their unarmored limbs or, worse, their mail-clad chests. Among the Danes, Hári Grayhair toppled backward, a bolt jutting right above his heart, while Ormr slumped to the ground from a bolt that pierced his gut.

"Where are they!" Breda hissed. She had two bolts lodged in her shield.

Ciarán gritted his teeth and turned his gaze towards the ridge, his mind racing with thoughts of what could have happened up there with the second and third groups. He had not heard even a rumble in the gloom-filled sky, but he saw ominous trails of smoke rising from the top of the ridge.

Then suddenly, his heart sank as he heard the unmistakable sound of the Nephilim reloading their weapons.

CHAPTER 74

THE SONS OF LIGHT AGAINST THE SONS OF DARKNESS

Naberus da Roma watched the entire encampment come alive as soon as the enemy's army began beating on their shields.

Prince Menoetius ordered his troops to man the war engines. They were huge iron beasts, each larger than an African elephant, and forged in the image of a roaring dragon. From their gaping mouths, the engines used Greek Fire to launch iron balls filled with more of the deadly liquid. They could blast these projectiles a thousand yards into the enemy ranks, and Naberus marveled at the engines' craftsmanship. They were far more advanced than anything existing in the mortal world. But then again, the race of Gog had learned how to build such weapons from the angel Azazel thousands of years before, in the age when god-kings ruled the earth.

Azazel and the rest of the Watchers were imprisoned nearby, beneath the black pillar that towered three hundred feet into the sunless sky. The pillar stood on a hill of monstrous skulls around which Lovetar had constructed a moat ten yards wide and then filled it with Greek Fire. The moat now blazed like an inferno.

Heat radiating from the hellish moat cut through the chill but filled the air with the acrid odor of sulfur and pitch. Firelight reflected off the thousands of gigantic skulls piled around the pillar. Among the heap, Naberus noticed tarasque skulls with their long, curved horns and dagger-like teeth. There were skulls of other strange beasts, too, with tusks and jutting horns, some on their heads and others on the tips of their snouts. All belonged to beasts of legends, many of which had faded into myths.

Atop this macabre hill rose the pillar. Its shaft was fifteen yards wide on each side, made of smooth obsidian-like stone. The flaming moat reflected off its surface, where enormous runes were etched up the shaft to its obelisk-like peak. Spidery fissures now marred those runes along the pillar's black surface, climbing to its summit. Every hour, the fissures spread and widened, and it would not be long before the pillar collapsed. But before then, there was the enemy to deal with in the inevitable battle to come.

Naberus had dressed for that battle in a long mail hauberk with Murgleis sheathed in a scabbard strapped to his belt. Over his shoulders, he wore a black cloak that protected him from Dudael's cold air but was becoming a burden in the stifling heat emanating from the moat. On his head, he wore a helmet of dark, polished steel that covered his cheeks and nose. His raven, Hermes, perched on his left shoulder, and his two mastiffs, Set and Grim, sat at attention to his right.

Nearby, Lovetar paced like a lioness eager to embark on a hunt. She had traded her gossamer robes for a tight-fitting tunic of polished scalemail, and a long dagger with a jeweled hilt hung from a sheath belted to her slender waist. Her long hair was tied tightly behind her head, and the gemstone above her eyes gleamed with the firelight's orange hue. That same light illuminated the black symbols painted down her arms and legs, and the severe expression she wore on her face.

Fifty yards from the two of them stood Menoetius. He would lead the forces of Gog against the enemy's feeble army, whose ranks had been thinned by the tarasque and the ambush at the Inner Sanctum. Saleos would lead the smaller legion of Magog against that same army. Naberus, however, would have nothing to do with the fighting on the field. Rather, Samyaza had tasked him and Lovetar with protecting the pillar until its collapse. As much as Naberus longed to witness the release of the Watchers from their prison, he also lusted for revenge. He knew the woman, Alais, would come for the pillar, and when she did, he planned to kill her himself.

He glanced up at the pillar's summit. Samyaza crouched there like a gargoyle with his wings forged of magic and fire folded behind his back. For hours he had perched there, as if he were waiting for the moment when the Dragon would enter the arena in all his fiery glory.

Moments later, the war engines erupted with a deafening boom that reverberated through the encampment. Naberus's hands flew to his ears. Thick smoke billowed from the roaring maws of the war machines, wafting through the surrounding area and leaving behind a pungent odor of sulfur. But when the smoke cleared, Naberus realized the attack had not had its desired effect. Across the battle-field, a chorus of jeers echoed from the enemy line. A furious Menoetius barked orders to his war leaders, who began forming their groups into ranks armed with massive crossbows and long spears.

Naberus was watching Saleos organize their own legion into formations when a fluttering sound caught his attention, causing him to look up. He sucked in a sharp breath as he saw Samyaza had spread his fiery wings and taken flight. He glided downward, circling the pillar twice before landing gracefully on the balls of his feet. Naberus and Lovetar bent their knees as their master regarded them sternly with his golden eyes. He clutched his black steel trident in his right hand. Its prongs aimed casually at the two kneeling before him.

"There's a smaller group climbing the hills toward that ridge." He gestured towards a ridge of jagged rocks that stood alongside the towering bronze cliffs in the distance, roughly half a mile from the encampment.

"My lord," Lovetar replied, avoiding Samyaza's gaze, "I sent nine sentries to guard that ridge two hours ago. They are among my finest warriors."

Towering over them, Samyaza's expression hardened. "Your sentries will not be enough. The traitors Ilat and Asira are among the group, and so is the incarnation of Sirra. The magi's twins are with them, too. I want all of them dead." His lips twisted into a snarl. "And I want both of you to take care of it."

As Naberus listened, he was struck with a sudden realization—the revenge he longed for may come sooner than expected.

"My lord," he replied, feeling a surge of exhilaration. "I'll gather a cadre of my most elite warriors. And I swear to you, it shall be done."

Tara gazed up the steep and foreboding path that led to the ridge. The echoes of the war horns still chilled her ears, and a shiver of fear clawed at her insides. Fear at knowing the small army led by Brother Ciarán would be slaughtered if she and her sister did not reach the ridge and invoke the terrible power Father Michele had unlocked inside them. As she ran her fingers over the bronze armband on her left forearm, she couldn't help but feel the weight of the responsibility it had given her and Sara. But if they didn't reach the ridge in time, all the power it allowed them to wield would be for naught.

She glanced at Rosta, padding alongside her. The massive boarhound served as a comforting presence, as did the six Aswaran warriors with their scale mail vests, curved bows, and sheathed scimitars. The handsome young sailor named Mordechai joined the archers' ranks, having asked Brother Ciarán permission to escort her and her sister to the ridge. Brother Pietro trailed behind them, huffing as he trudged up the hill.

At the forefront of their party strode her aunt Kira and her grandfather Fereydun, using his tall, blackened staff as a walking stick. They walked alongside Lady Alais, who wore one of Asira's curved swords at her waist, strapped to a sword belt that had belonged to one of the fallen Danes. Joining Alais were the beautiful and mysterious Ilat and Asira. Those two were taller than any of the men and could do things that Tara had not thought were humanly possible. But, then again, she knew these two were not human. Her grandfather had called them yazata. Sara had said they were of the Jann, legendary beings whose veins were filled with fire and light instead of blood. Whatever the truth, Tara was glad they were on her side of this conflict.

After some time, a drumming sound echoed from the valley. "They're beating on their shields," Mordechai told Tara and her sister, "to draw the enemy onto the battlefield." Tara could not help but notice the eager look of excitement in his eyes—a feeling she did not share. Instead, she felt a nagging dread at what would happen if they didn't reach the ridge in time.

A moment later, Tara nearly jumped out of her skin when a series of thunder-like booms shook the nearby cliff walls and sent a painful ringing through her ears.

"What was that!" Sara cried.

Ilat glanced over her shoulder. "War engines," she told them. "The battle is starting."

An icy knot formed in Tara's stomach at the thought the battle had begun. Yet the crest of the ridge was still fifty yards away up the rugged pathway climbing the hill.

"I'll make sure the ridge is clear," Asira said.

With several long strides, she bound up the path, leaping twenty yards at a time before disappearing over the crest. But then, suddenly, she came flying backward, crashing down the hill in a whirl of motion before coming to a stop ten feet from where their party stood.

Sara's hand flew to her mouth while Tara gasped in horror as a platoon of giant warriors loomed on the crest of the ridge. They were hulking, pale-skinned men towering over seven feet tall, wearing heavy iron breastplates, with more armor plating strapped to their forearms and legs. The giants held huge spears in their hands.

And three of those spears were now pointed straight at Tara and her party, their wielders' arms pulled back, ready to throw.

~

THE SECOND ALAIS saw the Nephilim on the ridge, Sirra's instincts took over. With a word, she thrust out her palm. *"Eoh!"* A searing ray of soul light blasted into the spearmen as they released their weapons.

Screams erupted around her. Alais spun in time to see a spear whiz by Tara's head, though the other two struck a pair of the Aswaran warriors in their chests. Alais whirled back toward their attackers, unleashing another blast of soul light into the eyes of another spearman. With a blur of motion, Ilat joined her attack. She struck with a blast of her own soul light from her left hand before sliding into a blinded Nephilim and slicing her scimitar across its waist. The next thing Alais knew, Asira had leaped to her feet and bound into another of their attackers. Her curved blade flew in a graceful stroke that sheared through one of the giant's necks.

Kira had a crystal in her hand, sending her own ray of soul light into another giant's eyes. Alais followed with a similar attack, but her breath stuck in her throat as one of the Nephilim leaped into the air, driving his spear toward the twins. Alais had no way to stop him, and Ilat and Asira were too far away, engaging other giants atop the ridge. Mordechai managed to loose an arrow at the leaping giant, but the shaft bounced off its breastplate as the Nephilim drove the spear home. But the spear never landed, for with a terrified cry, the twins screamed: "Burn!"

Pietro pulled the twins away as the spear's shaft exploded into flames, disintegrating into ash. The giant's skin blackened as flames erupted across its body, consuming flesh and bone. The four surviving Aswaran leaped backward as the burning giant crashed onto the rocky path. A second later, Fereydun was there, chanting words to control the fire and summoning a plume of flames from the giant's corpse onto the tip of his blackened staff. With an angry shout, Fereydun flung the fire into a flaming ball that exploded into one of the Nephilim on the ridge. Flames spread over its skin as if it were made of dry parchment.

As the giant roared in agony, Alais realized her opportunity, for there was more than enough fire here to work her magic. Reciting a verse to control the flames, she willed the fire into a wide arc that leaped from the burning Nephilim and struck four more of its comrades. Flames spread over the giants as Ilat and Asira continued their deadly handiwork. The head of one giant flew clean off its shoulders, severed by Asira's curved sword, while Ilat gutted another with her scimitar. Only one Nephilim remained, and with a roar, he charged at the twins. But after three huge strides, he staggered with an arrow jutting from one of his eye sockets. Twenty yards away, Mordechai aimed a second arrow before firing it into the base of the giant's neck. With a huge hand, the giant grasped at the shaft as he toppled forward. Rosta was there before the Nephilim hit the ground, growling fiercely as his teeth tore into the giant's flesh. Meanwhile, the four surviving Aswaran joined in, having traded their bows for curved scimitars that gleamed amidst the gloom.

As quickly as it had started, the battle had ended. Alais fought to catch her breath, her heart beating rapidly. Downhill on the path, Pietro clung to the twins, whose faces had drained of color. They both stared wide-eyed at the giant, lying face down, felled by Mordechai, Rosta, and the Aswaran. Nearby, tendrils of smoke curled from the smoldering corpse of the Nephilim they had told to burn. Atop the ridge, the air reeked of burnt hide as more smoke wafted from the other four giants killed by Fereydun and Alais' fire.

"Hurry, children!" Fereydun urged, a plume of flame still clinging to the tip of his staff.

Pietro let go of the twins, and they hurried toward their grandfather, following him to the ridge. Alais strode with them to the parapet of jagged rocks Kamran had described from his scouting mission. There was indeed a curved wall of basalt about four feet high, rimming the ridge as if they were standing in a shallow crater. From that vantage, Alais peered down at two armies about a half-mile away in the valley. Ciarán's meager force was spread out in a broken line while two much larger armies stood their ground four of five hundred yards away. The larger war band consisted of hundreds of pale-skinned Nephilim armored like the ones they had just slain. The other army was fewer in number and smaller in stature, dressed more traditionally in chain armor with round shields. But from the symbol on the banner this army flew, Alais knew this lesser force—which was still larger than Ciarán's—were troops from the House of Magog. Which meant they were still Nephilim, so they were still deadly.

"Girls," Fereydun said to the twins, "you know what you must do."

"Yes, grandfather," Sara said, taking Tara's hand.

The twins fixed their gaze on the enemy armies in the valley. Alais felt a sizzle in the air as they began reciting the words emblazoned on their armbands.

"Upon the wicked," Tara said.

"Rain fire and hail!" Sara shouted.

Then, as if answering their call, a deep rumble of thunder echoed across Dudael.

～

"SHIELD WALL!" Holger cried after Kamran's archers fired another volley of arrows into the Nephilim horde.

The Danes scrambled to assemble the wall, aligning their shields edge-to-edge, the metal rims meeting with a series of decisive clanks. Ciarán hurried to join them, as did Gaido, Gundoald, and the papal guardsmen. The front ranks crouched low, their shields forming the base of the wall. Behind them, the next line stood taller, their shields raised to cover the heads of the first rank and protect against the rain of crossbow bolts.

After a tense moment, the air was suddenly filled with the whistling rush. When the bolts hit the shield wall, the deep "thud" of impact echoed across the battlefield as iron-tipped bolts slammed into the hardwood of the shields. Even bracing himself for the impact, pain shot down Ciarán's shield arm as it was hammered backward amid the clang of bolts meeting the iron rims and the crack of wood under the furious assault. Beneath the noise came a muted grunt from the men whose shields bore the brunt of the attack. Though not far away came cries of pain from the Aswaran, whose smaller bucklers were not suitable for a shield wall. But then another sound joined the screams and curses—one that gave Ciarán a surge of hope. For a loud growl of thunder shuddered through the surrounding air and shook the ground beneath their boots.

Ciarán lowered his shield and watched in awe as the first bolt struck. A half-dozen giants near the center of the army were blasted off their feet, briefly etched in a halo of blinding light. Meanwhile, the banner bearing the seven-headed dragon erupted into sparks. Then, with a deafening boom, the sky tore open, and the very wrath of the heavens was unleashed upon the enemy. Furious bolts of lightning tore through the murk, illuminating the battlefield in flashes of stark white and cobalt blue. They struck down with ruthless precision, turning the warriors of Gog into flaming pillars that screamed and fell, leaving nothing behind but charred remains. The incessant booming of thunder swallowed their cries of shock and pain. With each impact, bright veins of electricity raced across their bodies, illuminating their horrified faces and transforming them into flickering silhouettes. And amid the relentless percussion of the storm, smoke rose from the scorched victims into the bleak, sunless sky.

Then came the hail. Fist-sized chunks of ice rained down like a volley of celestial arrows. Each hailstone hit with a sickening thud; the echo of ice meeting flesh resonated over the howling thunder. Shields cracked and banners shattered under the relentless onslaught while icy stones struck metallic armor with resounding clangs. Soon, the battlefield became a chaotic portrait of scrambling figures ducking for cover, raising shields over their heads. The ground quickly became littered with fallen warriors, their bodies strewn about with plumes of steam rising from the corpses.

"Blessed gods," Jorundr muttered behind Ciarán. Though most of their companions in the shield wall watched in stunned silence as the once formidable armies of Gog and Magog were being reduced to a haggard, battered assembly buried under the violence raging from the sky.

But then, as suddenly as it had started, the storm stopped.

Ciarán sucked in a breath as an eerie silence fell over the battlefield. He glanced toward the ridge, now shrouded in an ominous red mist. A fog the color of blood. The sight sent a chill through Ciarán's veins, and he swallowed hard as he watched the enemy pick itself off the ground.

Across the battlefield, about a quarter of the enemy warriors climbed to their feet, though only one banner now flew among their ranks—the banner of the black ram. Near it, a group of Nephilim had used huge iron shields to form a barrier that looked vaguely like a tortoise shell. When the shields began to lower, opening the carapace, Ciarán could see they were protecting a single Nephilim warrior, clearly their leader. The imposing giant was encased in a breastplate of black steel, which extended as mail plates over his muscular arms and legs. A mane of black hair, bound with golden cords, contrasted with the pale skin of his face, while a necklace of blood-red gemstones against his sternum added to his formidable appearance. The giant gripped a wickedly long spear, and Ciarán knew he was gazing upon the Nephilim prince Samyaza had warned him about in one of their visions—the sibling of the being that had become Adémar of Blois. The one eager to avenge his brother's death.

As if to dispel any doubt, the Nephilim prince fixed his gaze on Ciarán, pointing the spear toward him while he roared three bitter words: "You die now!"

CHAPTER 75

ARMAGEDDON

From atop the ridge, Alais watched in amazement as the twins summoned the storm of lightning and hail. The silver runes on their bronze armbands glowed with eldritch light, and Tara and Sara's intense gazes never left the armies in the valley below.

As thunderous booms filled the sky, Alais' left hand rested on the pommel of the curved sword Asira had lent her. The Fae woman had called it a katana, and it was the twin of Asira's other sword—a fine weapon of polished steel with a round guard and a long hilt wrapped in black ribbon. Alais had no training with swords beyond the short, leaf-shaped blade that Nimue had taught her to wield when summoning the wind. But Asira assured Alais that Sirra was a swordswoman without equal, and when the time came, her spirit would guide the blade.

The four Aswaran warriors stood guard at the far end of the ridge, facing the massive black obelisk that rose ominously in the distance. The rest of their party leaned over the parapet of jagged basalt rock, observing the enormous destruction the maelstrom of hail and lightning was wreaking on the forces of Gog and Magog. Alais' spirits soared, for it appeared as if they might destroy the entire enemy army before it even reached Ciarán and his small force.

But then the red mist came.

It began as a cold, wet, haunting fog that washed over the Aswaran warriors standing guard and filled the ridge with its blood-red hue. The mist even carried the scent of blood, a metallic tang that hung heavy in the air.

"What sorcery is this?" Asira asked, alarm in her voice.

"The kind fueled by blood," Ilat replied from somewhere in the dense mist.

Alais' muscles tensed. The mist was so thick she could no longer see her hands in front of her face. It was affecting Tara and Sara, too, for the thunder had stopped, and through the mist came the frightened voice of one of the twins. "What's happening?"

Instead of an answer came gasps and groans, followed by the thudding sound of bodies dropping to the ground.

"Ilat," Fereydun urged fearfully, "do something."

Ilat whispered, "*Eoh,*" followed by several more words of power. The air thrummed as blueish light burst through the mist, burning away the vapor that touched its preternatural luminescence.

As a pocket of fog began to clear, Alais gasped at the sight of the four Aswaran warriors lying dead on their backs with daggers protruding from their chests. Another weapon burst through the thinning mist—a spinning silver flash that landed with a sickening sound in Sara's right shoulder. The jeweled hilt of a dagger jutted inches above her heart. A cry caught in Alais' throat as Sara toppled backward, and Tara let out a bloodcurdling scream. Kira, Fereydun, and Pietro rushed to protect the twins.

Next, seven shadows burst through the fading mist where the Aswaran had been guarding the ridge. They charged like mailed demons with dark steel helms, long hauberks, and sharp, gleaming blades.

Without a second thought, Alais ripped her katana from its scabbard and raised it just in time to parry one of the enemies' blades. Steel met steel with a resounding clang. The warrior stood a head taller than Alais, and with his superior strength, he pushed on his blade, knocking her back a step. Through the opening in his helmet stared the eyes of a killer, and Alais had little doubt he was one of the Nephilim from the House of Magog. He struck again, but once more, Alais instinctively parried the attack. With a roar, he swung his sword in a powerful arc, but this time, Alais ducked beneath the wild blow and sliced her katana across her attacker's abdomen. The Fae-steel blade sheared through his chainmail hauberk into flesh and muscle, and with a groan, the swordsman slunk to a knee, trying to hold in his guts.

To Alais' right, Asira wielded her own katana with deadly precision. Her blade danced in her grip as it parried a sword blow before she spun with the grace of a dancer and carved a gaping wound through the man's ribs. Ilat, meanwhile, sparred with two more Nephilim. Her scimitar became a blur of steel that moved in swift, lethal strikes. The twang of a bowstring mixed with the clash of metal as Mordechai fired an arrow through the neck of one of their attackers before lodging a second shaft in the chest of another swordsman. All the while, Rosta barked ferociously, forming a defiant barrier between the twins and their attackers.

Despite the wound in his side, Asira's assailant fought on, roaring as he hammered his sword onto her katana. She spun again and, this time, thrust her blade back into the wound until her steel was embedded a foot deep into his torso. The man gasped, then so did Asira.

Alais' jaw fell open as a seventh warrior drew a narrow blade from Asira's lower back. The air sizzled as her blood seemed to be absorbed into the steel blade, and a reddish vapor hissed from the wound up the sword. Asira collapsed onto the hard ground while its wielder roared in triumph as he ripped the steel helmet from his head. Alais found herself looking into the eyes of Naberus da Roma, his face flushing red and his gaze holding a gleam of near madness.

"I'll take the Key," he roared, "with your life!"

Moving as fast as Asira had moved a moment before, Naberus charged. His narrow blade hissed through the air as Alais struggled to parry it. Naberus fought on, moving with preternatural speed and striking with supernatural strength, driving her back toward the parapet of basalt rock at the edge of the ridge. Alais' heart pounded as she swung desperately to block his relentless attacks until she finally missed. His narrow blade sliced through her leather vest into the flesh of her shoulder. The wound stung, followed by a strange, icy sensation as if a piece of her soul was being drawn into the blade. Alais screamed as she realized what was happening.

He's stealing the Key!

Naberus let out a victorious roar, his eyes burning with a mix of ecstasy and triumph. Gripping the hilt with both hands, he lifted his sword above his head and hammered it down on Alais. She raised her katana to parry the strike, but the force of the blow slammed her hard against the basalt parapet. As the clang of metal rang in her ears, she heard the crack of rock and felt the parapet give way.

The next thing Alais knew, she was falling backward with nothing but air beneath her.

~

THE STORM of lightning and hail had shattered the Nephilim's massive crossbows, along with any discipline and order their army once had. Their roars filled the air and their eyes gleamed with a feral light. They were no longer an army, but an angry mob of muscle and steel charging forward like a wave of primal fury.

The enemy outnumbered Ciarán's force by more than two to one, but Jarl Holger was already accounting for those odds. He stood amidst the Danes and Gaido's men, who had broken their shield wall once the storm had begun. With Curtana held high above his head, he surveyed his troops with the commanding presence of a Danish lord. "Three to one!" he hollered. "Engage them, three men to each jötunn!"

"My lord," Freybjorn replied, "their numbers are already twice ours—we'll be overwhelmed."

Holger shook his head decisively. "That's what Kamran's bloody archers are for! The jötnar are weakened; let's hope those arrows thin their ranks."

Ciarán was grateful Holger took command of the group, but his attention remained locked on the Nephilim prince, three hundred yards away, charging toward him like an enraged bull.

Meanwhile, the ground trembled beneath the thunderous advance of the ragged Nephilim horde and their enraged war cries. But then, a different sound resonated over the battlefield—the sound of Kamran's archers releasing their arrows. It began as a soft whoosh that quickly amplified into a deadly hiss as the arrows sliced through the air. The first line of giants was met with a barrage of razor-sharp points, impacting their armored skin with a resounding thud. Their war cries fell briefly silent as the arrows found flesh, and their targets, already battered by the hailstorm, either slowed their advance or collapsed onto the battlefield. A second volley followed, and then a third and a fourth. With a hundred yards to go, the Aswaran archers had culled the oncoming Nephilim horde by half, just as Holger had hoped. But the enraged roars of the surviving Nephilim reached a new pitch, as if the volleys of arrows had only fueled their bloodlust.

At Holger's command, the Danes and Gaido's men formed themselves into teams of three. Holger stood with Breda and Jorundr, shields and swords at the ready. Strong Bjorn joined with Freybjorn and Stóri Red Beard, and so it went with three more trios of Danes and a fourth trio comprised of papal guardsmen.

Gaido stood with Ciarán, and, to Ciarán's surprise, so did Gundoald of Pavia. The enormous Lombard glanced down at Ciarán. "It will be good to fight by your side this time," Gundoald said.

"Aye," Ciarán replied, his heart pounding faster, for the Nephilim prince and his comrades looked taller and more ferocious the closer they came. He gripped Caladbolg tightly with his right hand as white fire crawled like scrollwork up the blade.

"He's mine!" the Nephilim prince roared. Besides the spear in his right hand, the prince had drawn a sword with a blade over five feet long. He bound forward with massive strides.

"Ciarán," Gaido cried, "duck!"

Ciarán gave Gaido a confused sideways glance, but then, out of the corner of his eye, he spotted Saint Radegonde. Gaido's crew had the massive ballista aimed straight at the Nephilim prince.

"Vengeance is mine!" the prince roared as Ciarán dropped to the ground. A loud, familiar *ka-chunk* followed as the ballista bolt whizzed overhead. Ciarán glanced up as the mammoth shaft roared through the air before catching the Nephilim prince mid-stride. The sheer force of the impact lifted him off his feet, his massive form hurtling backward, crashing into the charging giants behind him. The huge bolt protruded from the prince's armored chest as he slammed, unmoving, onto the hard-packed ground.

Ciarán exhaled an astonished breath. One of the seven had fallen. But that was the only thought he had time to muster before the stampede of giants was upon them.

Of all the times Holger dreamt of Ragnarok, he never imagined this. The ground rumbled beneath his feet as the monstrous jötnar bore down on them. While he had no time to count their numbers, there seemed to be two jötnar to each mortal man. Each jötunn was a head taller than even Strong Bjorn and twice as broad. What skin was not protected by black iron plates was covered in a macabre patchwork of burns, bruises, and frostbite. They roared as they charged, their faces twisted with unbridled rage.

In the seconds before the jötnar were upon them, Holger recalled Gerbert's words after Magnus's funeral. *You are a weapon of God, and your destiny awaits at Dudael.* Clenching his jaw, Holger readied his shield, waiting to embrace that destiny.

The first jötunn to meet him leaped into the air, bringing down his spiked club with a force to shatter stone. Holger caught the blow with his shield, but the pain of the impact reverberated up his arm. With all of his strength, Holger thrust Curtana, finding a gap between the giant's breastplate and his mail skirt. The Fae-forged blade punched through the jötunn's thick skin and slid into his gut. The giant's roar became a mewing cry as Holger wrenched the blade free just as Breda sliced her sword across the tendons behind its left knee. For good measure, Jorundr hammered his blade into the side of the jötunn's head.

As the giant doubled over and slumped to a knee, two more jötnar took its place while all around them, the battle raged. The air was filled with the sounds of grunts and cries, the clashing of steel on steel, the thud of weapons on flesh, and gasps of pain. One of the jötnar slammed his club so hard into Jorundr's shield it knocked the hulking Dane three feet backward. Not far from where he stood, another giant drove his spear into Stóri Red Beard's chest. But there was no time to mourn his loss, for the second jötunn chopped a blade as long as a bastard sword down on Holger. He parried the blow again with his shield, though this time, the shield boards cracked, and pain shot up his left arm. Again, he hacked at the giant while his heart drummed in his chest. Breda lashed out with her sword, catching the giant in the knee, but with a roar of pain, he swatted his free arm, knocking her violently to the ground.

Fueled by a surge of anger, Holger hacked with Curtana as if he were chopping wood. Some blows clanged against the giant's breastplate, but one caught the giant in the jaw, sending a font of blood into the air. The giant hacked back, cleaving off a third of Holger's shield. But Holger struck again, hewing Curtana into the burnt flesh of the giant's biceps. The blade cut deep, and the giant's right arm fell limp. By then, Breda had scrambled to her feet, her cheek bruised and her lip bleeding. But with a furious cry, she rammed her sword up the giant's skirt straight into its loins. As the giant gasped, Holger drove Curtana into the flesh beneath the giant's chin until the tip of the blade punched through the top of its mouth.

To Holger's left, Jorundr cried out. He was landing mighty sword blows, but his opponent carried one of the long iron shields and used it to his advantage. The giant backhanded his shield arm, hurling Jorundr backward. Before the Dane could find his footing, the giant brought down a spiked club onto Jorundr's helmet with a resounding clang. Jorundr staggered back, fell to a knee, and slumped onto the ground. As the giant moved in for the kill, Holger swung Curtana in a wide arc, hitting the giant in the side. The jötunn's iron breastplate absorbed much of the blow, but the blade opened a gash in the flesh around the giant's ribs. The air was tinged with a fine spray of blood. Gritting its teeth, the giant spun toward Holger, raising its club to deliver a hammer-like blow. But the blow never landed, for Strong Bjorn was behind him and cleaved his sword into the back of the giant's skull.

Sweat stinging his eyes, Holger gave Strong Bjorn a grateful nod, but his heart sunk when, behind his friend, he saw the corpses of two jötnar lying amid the lifeless bodies of Stóri and Freybjorn, who had been impaled by one of the giant's spears. By now, the Aswaran warriors had traded their bows for scimitars and joined the fray, hacking and chopping their blades at the horde of giants who fought back with a vengeance. Screams and cries mixed with clanging steel and the sickening sound of blades sinking into flesh.

To Holger's right, Breda screamed. "Watch out!"

Holger whirled around in time to catch an arcing sword strike with the flat of Curtana's blade. But the force of the blow was powerful enough to knock Holger back. As the giant lunged toward him, Holger saw a flare of white fire as Caladbolg sheared into the enemy's side, tearing through metal and filling the wound with flames. The giant yowled in agony, and Holger watched, huffing for breath, as it collapsed onto its side.

Ciarán also struggled to catch his breath, his face spattered by blood that Holger hoped was not Ciarán's own. Beyond him, Gaido and Gundoald were battling another jötunn. The towering Lombard was trading blow for blow with the giant as they hammered on each other's shields. With a frustrated sigh, Ciarán stormed over to the distracted giant and hewed Caladbolg's fiery blade into the giant's back, cutting its spine clean through before the jötunn collapsed into a heap.

Holger took this moment to survey the field. Along with Strong Bjorn, six of his crew remained standing, fighting alongside the Aswaran swordsmen. Their ranks, however, had suffered badly, for the ground was littered with weapons and the bodies of Aswaran warriors lying in pools of blood with the fallen jötnar. But the giants still outnumbered them, and the longer the battle lasted, the worse their situation would become.

To Holger's left, Ciarán cleaved his sword through the spear of a giant who had tried to parry the blow. The blade continued until it shore through the giant's knee, crippling its leg and filling the wound with fire that blazed up its thigh. With a cry, Ciarán buried his sword into the giant's chest, piercing the iron breastplate. Nothing, it seemed, could stand against the might of Ciarán's blade—not iron, steel, or their enemies' thick hide.

"Fall back," Holger cried. "Rally around Ciarán!"

Holger and Breda hurried to Ciarán's side. Gundoald, Strong Bjorn, and Gaido joined them. The guard captain gritted his teeth, pressing a hand against his ribs. His chainmail coat was torn open, and the wound was bleeding heavily.

"How are you holding up," Holger asked Ciarán.

The Irishman clenched his teeth. "As well as I must."

"That blade of yours is doing just fine. Lead the way, and we'll follow you."

Ciarán nodded and sucked in a deep breath. Then he charged.

Ahead, a half-dozen giants stood over the bodies of three Aswaran, and a fair-haired Dane named Ulf. Their eyes widened when they saw Ciarán running at them with his flaming blade held high while Holger, Breda, Strong Bjorn, Gaido, and Gundoald bellowed battle cries, charging alongside him. Ciarán swung Caladbolg in a wide arc that severed an enemy's sword and cut a yawning wound into its chest. Holger used the remnant of his shield to parry a club strike before scraping Curtana across the giant's face, opening a gash in its cheek, and exposing a mouthful of bloodstained teeth. Breda went low, hacking at another giant's legs, while Strong Bjorn cleaved his blade into the giant's right arm. However, as one giant fell, another took its place. One landed a violent blow that cut out Gaido's legs, slamming his backside into the ground, while another plunged a spear through Strong Bjorn's shoulder. The tall Dane cried out in pain before Holger hammered Curtana into his attacker's skull, cracking bone and spewing blood.

Soon, only Holger, Breda, and Gundoald remained standing alongside Ciarán, but Caladbolg was slowly changing the tide. Each blow Ciarán struck with the sword landed with lethal precision, filling wounds with white fire that burned the enemy alive from within. By the time the last of the six giants fell to their blades, Holger's muscles ached and burned, and he had to grit his teeth to fight the overwhelming feeling of exhaustion.

But the fight was far from over. Groups of giants engaged pockets of brave Aswaran warriors and what few remained of *Lindworm's* stalwart crew. Around them, a tableau of devastation sprawled across the rugged landscape. Fallen Aswaran and Danish warriors lay among the debris of shattered shields and broken swords scattered haphazardly over the ground while the bodies of the pale giants, their flesh burnt, frostbitten, and marred with blood, sprawled lifelessly along with warriors of the House of Magog, clad in their dark mail, lying twisted and broken among the fray. The smell of blood, sweat, and fear lingered heavily in the air, and the din of the remaining battle echoed through the valley until it was drowned out by a far more ominous sound.

"BWOM, BWOM!"

Holger turned his head toward the sound, and his gaze caught sight of something that chilled his blood—for in the sky above the enemy encampment flapped enormous wings of fire, bearing aloft the Dragon. The giant winged serpent sped across the length of the battlefield before banking sharply, letting out a roar and a torrent of fiery breath. The fire consumed a band of helpless Aswaran, along with the trio of giants they had been fighting, their dying screams extinguished by the roar of the Dragon's breath.

From Holger's vantage, the Dragon was an enormous creature of primal fury. Scales glowing like ten thousand smoldering embers covered its massive form, and its open jaws revealed an array of dagger-like teeth. Each movement of the terrifying creature was marked by the cracking sound of those shifting scales, and each beat of its colossal wings gave rise to smoky tendrils and wisps of flame that danced in the dusky air. Its eyes blazed like molten slits in the gloom and, within those fiery orbs, burned a hatred, unlike anything Holger had ever seen.

He grabbed the edge of his white cloak, stained with the enemies' blood, and pulled it over Breda. "Hide under the cloaks," he hissed. Gundoald crouched beside Holger, wrapping his white cloak over the jarl while Breda shared hers with Ciarán. An instant later, a deafening explosion filled their world, coupled with a searing heat. But their flesh did not burn. As quickly as it came, the heat dissipated while, overhead, they heard the powerful whoosh of the Dragon's wings.

When Holger pulled his cloak off his head, he grimaced at the sight of Gaido and Strong Bjorn charred almost beyond recognition amid the flames still flickering across the burnt ground. He glanced at Breda's cloak. The once-white fabric was covered in gray ash. His cloak was, too, as was everyone else's who had survived. Gundoald shot him a concerned look when the hem of his cloak crumbled beneath his fingers.

"These won't survive a second round," Ciarán said through gritted teeth.

"Well, that's one bloody hell of a problem," Holger sighed, gazing at the sky.

For in the gloom of Dudael, the Dragon flapped his mighty wings, then glided ominously as he wheeled back in their direction, with the glow of fire burning from his open jaws.

CHAPTER 76

THE PILLAR AT THE PRECIPICE OF OBLIVION

When Alais fell off the edge of the ridge, Naberus could hardly believe his good fortune. His sword blow, powerful enough to crack the basalt rock behind her, had sent her to her death, and now, the Key to the Abyss belonged to him.

With the slain Jann's spirit coursing through his veins, he felt stronger and faster than ever before. But he had to keep his wits about him, for the other Jann, with skin the color of bronze and hair as black as zirconium, remained a threat. As if sensing her attack, he whirled in time to parry a vicious strike from her scimitar, its steel clanging against Murgleis's gleaming blade. Naberus crouched, ready for a second attack, but the Jann ran straight past him and leaped off the ridge. Naberus's jaw fell open as she disappeared beyond the edge of the cliff.

His mind whirling from everything that had just happened, he suddenly remembered the others on the ridge. The most immediate threat was the strapping young archer who, in a flurry of motion, fired an arrow straight at his heart. Drawing upon his preternatural speed, Naberus dodged the shaft and, in the same motion, pulled a dagger from his belt. Before the archer could nock another arrow,

Naberus hurled the weapon. It struck the young man in the abdomen with an impact so hard it slammed him into the basalt parapet. The boy groped hopelessly at the dagger as he slumped to the ground, drawing a horrified scream from one of the twins.

Surveying the situation, only the Magus, his daughter, a monk, the twins, and the boarhound remained. The portly monk and the Magus's daughter knelt beside the injured girl while the child's sister, who was crying and screaming, clutched her hand. The boarhound crouched beside the girl, barring its teeth as a deep growl rumbled from his throat. Naberus could kill them all right now, and he marveled at the thought of it. Though he hesitated when the Magus turned toward him, leveling his blackened staff, its tip blazing with a torch-like plume of flame.

"One step, and I'll burn you to the ground," the old man growled, his age-worn face a mask of grim determination.

"Leave them to me," called a voice from across the ridge. Naberus glanced toward the sound as Lovetar's slender figure emerged through the fading remnants of her blood mist. "Naberus, you have the Key—use it to free our ancestors!"

Naberus was a storm of conflicting desires. There was one of the twins, someone he blamed for his mother's murder. Her blood called to him, screaming for justice. And then there was Alais; her death had been a sweet taste of vengeance, yet he craved more. His sword practically vibrated in his grip, eager to claim more lives. He remembered that same thrill of anticipation he'd once felt before inhaling the euphoria-inducing fumes of opium in distant Eastern lands.

But there was another side to him. Naberus had always been the cold tactician, the unflappable consigliere who manipulated the strings of Rome's power for nearly a century. Emotion was anathema to reason, and reason reminded him why he was here: to free the Watchers, his ancient forefathers, and, through that, find his salvation. It was then, in the crucible of his indecision, that clarity emerged.

"Kill them for me," he told Lovetar before sprinting past her down the rugged path that would take him to the black pillar.

And from there, to his salvation.

~

ALAIS FELT the ground rushing toward her as she plunged down the basalt cliffside.

Time seemed to slow, strangely, with death so near. However, in her mind, she realized she was not alone at that moment. There was another voice, the same one she heard in her head at the Theatre of Pompey. *"Remember,"* the voice said, *"you are Sirra—and angels can fly!"*

Those words ripped Alais back into reality. Instead of the inevitable resignation that she was going to die, she had a fierce realization that she could live as the words to a long-forgotten verse emerged from the shadows of her memory. She began reciting them, a hauntingly beautiful stanza that sent an audible thrum through the air and caused wisps of blue flames to crawl up the basalt cliff. Suddenly, her descent slowed as her body felt as light as air. She twisted her torso, looking down at the ground. But instead of the hard-packed earth rushing to meet her, she was drifting slowly downward as if she and the air had become one and the same.

Alais exhaled slowly, letting herself drift down until the toe of her boot touched the ground. It was only then that she remembered the wound across her chest. Naberus's blade had sheared through the leather and cut a gash into her flesh, but the wound barely bled. Instead, it burned with an icy cold that made her feel weak inside. The sword had taken something from her—a portion of her spirit and part of the Key.

Moments later, Alais heard a faint noise coming from above. She tilted her neck back and spotted Ilat gracefully descending from above. Once Ilat had touched the ground, she gave Alais a comforting smile. "I was hoping you'd remember how to do that."

"Better late than never."

Alais glanced across the valley. A half-mile away, the Nephilim army was charging the ragged line of Jarl Holger and Ciarán's men.

As their battle cries blared across the valley, Alais felt a surge of dread. "We have to help them."

Ilat's expression hardened. "No, Sirra, we cannot help them. Through the power of that accursed blade, Naberus da Roma now possesses part of the Key—enough, I believe, to destroy the pillar. He'll be heading there now, and we cannot let him topple it."

~

A MAELSTROM of emotions swirled through Tara. She felt a bone-deep dread as she watched Sara lying pale and still with a dagger lodged in her shoulder. Meanwhile, each shallow breath Sara drew sent a fresh wave of fear coursing through Tara, who was still reeling from watching the basalt parapet crumble away, causing Lady Alais to plunge off the cliff. Mordechai's sudden death was the latest wound, sending a raw, stinging pain through her heart. And now, a nightmare of a woman had appeared, threatening to kill them all.

Beside Tara, Rosta barred his teeth and barked furiously at the tall, thin woman with intricate symbols painted down her arms and legs. An ominous black gemstone was set into the woman's forehead, and her pale skin was drawn taut over her face, adding to her severe appearance.

Fereydun spun to face the woman, a plume of fire blazing from the tip of his black staff. Between them, the bodies of six of their attackers, along with four of her grandfather's warriors and Lady Asira, lay motionless on the ground, their weapons strewn among them.

"Stay back, demon!" her grandfather shouted above Rosta's barking.

Across from him, the woman smirked as she reached into a belt pouch and produced a ruby red crystal. In her fingers, a red light filled the crystal, which she moved around, tracing a glowing red circle into the air. She began to draw a symbol within the ring— right when Rosta charged. The boarhound leaped, spittle flying and jaws snapping. The attack startled the woman, but she reacted with inhuman speed, striking out with her lithe arm and hammering her palm into Rosta's side. The blow drew a loud yelp from the boarhound and sent him flying over the basalt parapet.

Tara gaped in horror as the dog disappeared over the edge. The next thing she knew, she felt a pang of betrayal as Brother Pietro, who had been right beside her, scurried away toward the other side of the ridge. Then a roar of flames snapped Tara's attention back to her grandfather. A jet of fire blasted from his staff onto the woman, who cried out in pain. Her flesh began to sizzle and burn, yet she kept pushing forward in defiance of the flames.

"I'll rip your head from your neck!" she screamed.

Fereydun's brow creased with rage. He rattled off more words of power, and the flames intensified. Tara could feel the heat from a dozen feet away, but still, the woman pressed on, hatred blazing in her eyes. With bony fingers tipped by long, sharp nails, she reached for her grandfather's throat. He thrust out his staff to knock her back, but she caught it with her left hand and squeezed. Wood splintered and cracked as she crushed the staff in her grip, and with a loud whoosh, the fire vanished.

The woman tossed away the shattered staff while striking out with her right hand and wrapping her fingers around Fereydun's throat. His hands flew to hers, but he could not pry away her grip as she lifted the Magus off his feet. Fereydun let out a choking gasp, his feet kicking in the air.

"Die, Magus," the woman sneered.

Tara heard a loud grunt, followed by a sickening sound. She grimaced in fear as she imagined her grandfather's neck crushed within the woman's grasp. But then she saw the blade. The curved blade protruded through the scalemail, covering the woman's abdomen, its tip slick with blood. The woman's eyes filled with a look of confusion as she let go of Fereydun. Her mouth fell open as the blade twisted in her stomach, and a bloody drool trickled down her chin. Then the sword was wrenched free from the wound. The woman staggered backward, revealing Brother Pietro gripping Asira's bloodied katana with both hands. Sweat beaded on his forehead, and he was huffing to catch his breath. Yet the sight of the woman dropping to her knees made his eyes widen in shock.

Fereydun gritted his teeth in pain. Holding his left hand to his injured neck, he drew a leaf-shaped sword from a sheath at his hip. The woman hissed at him as he swung the blade with an angry cry and sliced it through her throat.

"Blessed Sergius," Brother Pietro muttered with a grateful sigh.

Tara felt her heart pounding in her chest when she heard her aunt Kira's voice. "Tara," she said. "I need your help. You have to remove the dagger."

Sara's eyes were closed, and the color had drained from her face. "Will it hurt her?"

"She's still breathing," her aunt said. "The blade missed her heart, but before I can do anything, I need it gone."

Her hand shaking, Tara wrapped her fingers around the dagger's jeweled hilt. As soon as she touched it, Sara winced.

"Pull it straight out," her aunt urged calmly.

Tara sucked in a breath, recalling Father Michele's words in the ringfort. *All I need you to do is be brave.* He had said similar words long ago when he informed her she would go on a fantastic voyage. And since then, after surviving Cardinal Bishop Beno and his mob, the abbess of Minerva and her priests, the pirates in the sea around Sicily, and the woman with the crescent birthmark, Tara had learned what it meant to be brave. And she could be brave now. Summoning her courage, she pulled the dagger free.

Blood pulsed from the wound, and for an instant, Tara feared she might have killed her sister.

"Talk to her now," her aunt urged as she tore open Sara's tunic to get a better look at the wound. "Keep her with us."

Sara's eyelids flickered as their aunt pressed a glowing crystal onto Sara's wound, reciting a series of words with the melody of a song.

Kneeling beside her sister, Tara spoke softly, her hand trembling as she brushed a white strand of hair away from Sara's forehead. "Stay with us," Tara whispered. "That night on the boat, when we were attacked, Mother saved me. The last thing she said to me was that she always loved us. I know it's true. I thought I had lost all of you, but that wasn't so. You were always here; I just didn't know it. You have to be here now!" A tear rolled down Tara's cheek. "I love you, sister. Be strong!"

When the bleeding finally stopped, Tara gasped in amazement. Aunt Kira responded by pressing her hand against the wound and kneading the open skin together while reciting more of the songlike words. Slowly, beneath her crystal's warm glow, the once-open wound began to heal until only a thin white scar remained.

Sara squeezed Tara's hand; then her eyes blinked open. She sucked in a deep breath as her aunt helped her sit up.

Their grandfather knelt beside them. His neck was red and raw, but his face was beaming. "Welcome back, Sara," he said right before two thunderous horn blasts echoed through the valley.

"BWOM, BWOM!"

Sara's eyes widened with fear. "What's happening?"

"The battle rages on," their grandfather said matter-of-factly.

"What about Brother Ciarán and the army!" Tara exclaimed.

Fereydun pursed his lips. "We need to help them."

"That we do," Aunt Kira said. "So, stand up, girls. It's time to bring great anguish to Ahriman."

NABERUS STOOD in the shadow of the colossal black pillar.

It loomed three hundred feet high, a dark silhouette against the fiery glow of the surrounding moat. The pillar's polished obsidian surface captured the moat's orange-red blaze, a river of Greek Fire whose shimmering radiance danced over the hill of monstrous skulls supporting the obelisk.

Samyaza's towering oarsmen stood at attention around the moat, their pale skin reflecting the firelight.

"Lower the bridge!" Naberus commanded.

The oarsmen sprung into action, gathering around a huge metal contraption with a winch and enormous, gear-like wheels. A bridge forged of iron and curved like a tall arch jutted into the air, but it began to move when the oarsmen cranked the winch. The groan of metal gears mixed with the roar of the flames as the oarsmen lowered the bridge until it settled with a loud crash at the base of the hill.

Naberus could feel the searing heat of the fiery moat as he crossed the bridge, inhaling the acrid stench of pitch and sulfur. *Salvation is near,* he told himself.

He regarded the massive mound of skulls. They rose from the ground like the remnants of some ancient cataclysm, an undulating landscape of hollowed eye sockets and cavernous jawlines bathed in the moat's fiery glow. The entire hill seemed to pulse with a palpable energy, and from beneath its surface came desperate whispers.

"Naberus," hissed a chorus of ghostly voices, *"save us!"*

"Help us!" came a ghastly plea, rising to a crescendo.

"FREE US!"

The haunting whispers prickled his skin, but as he began climbing the hill of skulls, he made a solemn promise. "I will, I swear it."

He stared up at the pillar and the sequence of towering runes marching relentlessly toward its apex. The runes, indecipherable and mysterious, bore a network of creeping fissures devouring the symbols with each passing hour. Even in the time since he left for the ridge, more cracks had spread across the obsidian surface.

Summoning the stolen power coursing through his veins, Naberus placed his hands on the cold obsidian pillar. With an echoing cry of "Shatter!" he unleashed a shockwave of energy that split the surface of the stone.

Cracks raced up its sides like lightning while the entire structure groaned and shook. As if in answer to his call, chunks of rock began raining down from the pillar's pinnacle, crashing into the hill of skulls with sickening thuds. His eyes gleamed with delirious triumph as he cried out, "Salvation!"

And watched as the pillar crumbled.

CHAPTER 77

THE LAST STAND

T he Dragon roared through the twilight sky, banking and
wheeling, preparing to rain down another torrent of fiery
destruction. Wisps of smoke trailed from the serpent's vast
wings as they beat rhythmically, and each flap sent sparks of flame
flitting into the gloom.

A hundred yards away, Ciarán stood steadfast with Holger,
Breda, and Gundoald. Ciarán's shield was still strapped to his left
arm, the broken shafts of crossbow quarrels jutting from its face,
while Caladbolg, gripped firmly in his right hand, blazed with a
halo of white fire. His once polished hauberk was stained red with
enemy blood. Somewhere during the battle, he had lost his helmet,
leaving his pale hair exposed and slick with sweat. His limbs ached
from fighting, and his heart pounded in his chest, knowing that his
white cloak, now covered in gray ash, might be worthless against
another blast of the Dragon's fire.

The Dragon sped toward them when, suddenly, the battlefield
echoed with a resonating *ka-chunk!* Ciarán spun toward the sound
where, fifty yards away, Saint Radegonde sent its massive ballista
bolt tearing through the sky. So many times before, Ciarán had seen
the giant ballistas miss the practice dragon in the sky above the

519

Baths of Diocletian, and he half-expected the weapon to miss again. But the projectile found its mark, ripping through one of the Dragon's wings near its chest and sending a shower of sparks and embers into the dusky sky.

With a deafening roar, the Dragon banked left, veering toward the ballista and its crew. The operator scrambled out of his wooden seat, joining his two comrades as they ran for their lives. Ciarán recognized them as three of Gaido's youthful recruits from the lands around Rome. They were young and fast, but not nearly fast enough to outrun the diving Dragon before it unleashed a storm of dragon-fire. Saint Radegonde disappeared in an explosion of fire and ash, and the fiery torrent continued, blazing a scar of flames across the gray landscape, chasing the terrified crewmen. When the fire overcame them, it swallowed them in an inferno, charring armor and flesh until nothing remained but three blackened husks.

With an effortless beat of its wings, and despite the spear-long ballista bolt jutting from the hollow between its wing and its broad chest, the Dragon ascended back into the sky, fixing its molten gaze on Ciarán. Beneath the heat of that gaze, any sense of hope Ciarán had melted away like snow beneath a relentless sun. Breda squeezed Holger's hand, unable to hide her fear behind her usually defiant face, while Holger's eyes gleamed with a warrior's courage, ready to accept his fate with unwavering resolve. Beside them, Gundoald grimaced and made the sign of the cross.

An eerie calm swept over Ciarán, knowing he would soon be with Dónall and Khalil and his brothers at Derry who had given their lives for this cause. Then a rumble of thunder sounded from the ridge. The storm that followed erupted with a raw, primal intensity that stole Ciarán's breath. Streaks of white-hot lightning tore across the gloom. Each blinding bolt bore into the Dragon's massive form, the raw energy crackling over its scales, illuminating the sky in its fury. The Dragon's roars reverberated through the air as a storm of fist-sized hail struck with unrelenting force. Each icy stone that slammed into the Dragon's ember-like scales hissed and evaporated almost instantly, creating plumes of steam that mingled with the smoke wafting from the beast's wings. The pounding hail, the booming thunder, and the Dragon's pained roars blared like a symphony of destruction over Dudael.

Ciarán glanced toward the ridge, experiencing a newfound glimmer of hope. Lightning and hail rained down on the Dragon while the blood-red mist that had enveloped the cliff was nowhere to be seen.

"The twins are alive," Breda said. The fear disappeared from her face, replaced by a look of awe.

Above, the hail hammered at the Dragon, forcing it to wheel and twist in the sky, its wings laboring heavily against the relentless assault. It staggered in the air, struggling to rise uneasily against the icy barrage. Then, with a crash of thunder, another array of lightning struck the beast, turning the Dragon into a tortured silhouette against the storm-ravaged sky. It fought to stay aloft, before stumbling mid-air and falling. As it lost altitude, Ciarán realized the onslaught of lightning and hail was driving the Dragon straight toward them.

"Get back!" Ciarán cried.

They turned to run just as the Dragon came crashing to the ground. A cloud of rocks and dust billowed into the air as the beast landed with an impact that shook the earth beneath their boots. The massive creature was only twenty yards away, and as suddenly as he landed, the storm of lightning and hail began to die. A stray bolt seared into the beast one last time, blasting through its ember-like hide. The Dragon grimaced in pain but then began sloughing off his bestial form. With a shake of its shoulders, its wings crumbled into a heap of coals and smoke. The rest of its body fell away in huge chunks, as if it were shedding all of its skin, and the ballista bolt lodged in its side fell to the ground with a thud.

"He's too close to us," Ciarán realized. "The twins can't continue their assault without the risk of striking us, too."

"Then let's keep running," Gundoald said.

Holger clenched his jaw. "We'll never outrun him."

Gundoald gestured toward the Dragon. "Look how badly it's weakened—it's falling to pieces, for Christ's sake! He's going to catch us?"

"His Dragon form is like armor," Ciarán explained. "He doesn't need to wear it."

As if proving Ciarán's point, the beast shook one last time. The rest of its hide dissolved into a billowing cloud of smoke and ash. From the haze emerged a towering figure, naked and muscular, with hair the color of spun copper. His hair fell to his shoulders, framing a flawless face with sharp eyes that burned like golden suns. His golden skin shone immaculately in the gloom as if the storm of lightning and hail had not scathed it, except for a dull, thin scar above his left hip. It was the being who killed Father Michele and the one who tormented Ciarán's dreams; the being scripture called "the Morning Star," the one Fereydun named "Ahriman," and the one the Book of Enoch called "Samyaza."

Samyaza reached toward the ground and, with a command, summoned a burst of sand-like ore into his grasp. It coalesced and crystallized into the shape of a menacing trident. As he strode forward, clutching the weapon, the eight-foot-tall immortal was both magnificent and terrifying. He moved with the air of an emperor, striding through a world he had long ago conquered.

Gripping Caladbolg in his right hand, Ciarán planted his feet firmly apart, knowing this would be their last stand.

"CIARÁN MAC TOMÁS," Samyaza roared in a voice that sent a quake across the battlefield, "IT ENDS NOW!"

UNDER THE GLOOM-FILLED SKY, Alais gazed on in horror as she watched the fissures crawl up the towering pillar and pieces of its surface cascade like rain onto the hill of skulls. Then a final horn blast sounded from the enemy camp.

"BWOMMM!"

"We're too late!" she said, shaking her head.

"No," Ilat insisted. "We have little time, but you can save it. Though you must reclaim the portion of the Key he has stolen."

Alais noticed the fiery moat encircling the hill, a blazing inferno amid the twilight. A score of hulking Nephilim had also positioned themselves around the canal. With a deep sigh of frustration, she wondered aloud, "How do we get past them?"

Ilat placed her hands on Alais' shoulders and looked her in the eyes. "Sirra, remember *who* you are. Unlike myself, and Orionde, and Nimue, and the rest of our sisters, you did not join Samyaza's rebellion. You *infiltrated* it. You have always fought on the side of Michael and his archangels, and your power is second only to theirs!"

Alais blinked in disbelief.

"Deep inside, you *know* this is true," Ilat pressed. "You can soar over those flames, and the wind and fire are yours to command!"

Alais clenched her fists, frowning as she pressed them against her temples. *Remember!* she begged herself, desperately trying to recall her past life. Every muscle in her body tensed as if waiting for the answer to come. And then, suddenly, it was there—a moment of clarity like a blazing sun, burning away the morning fog that had filled all her thoughts. "I am Sirra," she told herself, feeling the truth course through her veins like liquid fire.

When she opened her eyes, she turned to Ilat. "How will we deal with those warriors?"

Ilat gave a quiet laugh. "Do you see how much fire I'll have at my disposal?"

Alais lifted her shoulders in response. "True."

"Now, we have no time to waste," Ilat said urgently. "I'll clear the way for you."

Then, with two long strides, Ilat leaped into the air, bellowing a battle cry as she soared over the plains of Dudael. Alais sprinted after her, but she could not keep up with the Fae woman, who was covering thirty or forty yards with each leap. When Ilat landed twenty yards from the moat, the Nephilim warriors, chiseled like statues of ancient gods, leveled their massive spears in her direction and began closing in. Across the flaming moat, a flicker of blue light, like Saint Elmo's fire before a storm, shimmered over the tops of the enormous skulls an instant before a tidal wave of Greek Fire exploded from the trench and crashed down on the Nephilim. Roars of pain erupted from the monstrous warriors as the flames spread across their pale skin as if it were made of parchment. By the time Alais reached Ilat, the warriors were slumped over and burning like hay stacks as the stench of smoke and burnt flesh mixed with the sulphuric reek of the moat.

Wide cracks spread up the three-hundred-foot pillar, creeping like vines toward its summit. The runes scrawled across its obsidian face were fractured into pieces, crumbling away as the obsidian siding fell and crashed atop the hill of skulls. At the base of the pillar, Naberus da Roma pressed his hands into the dark stone, raving like a madman.

"Come, forefathers!" he shouted. "This world is yours. Taste freedom once again!"

As if in response, a haunting moan emanated from the nightmarish hill as fractures began to crawl across the skulls.

Ilat's brow furrowed in sudden alarm. "Now, Sirra!"

Drawing in a deep breath, Alais darted toward the fiery moat. When she was ten yards away, she jumped as high as she could while uttering the words to make her body lighter than air. A heartbeat later, she was flying over the moat, her body rising into the sky, propelled by the power that sizzled through the surrounding air. She willed herself to hover there, twenty feet away from the pillar's base, where Naberus stared up at her, his face twisted with a look of shock and horror.

"How are you alive?" he gasped.

"Because today's not my day to die," Alais said, feeling the power pulse through her veins. "And I'm here to take back what you've stolen!"

Naberus's face hardened into a fierce scowl. "You'll not deny me my salvation." He stretched out his hands, his fingers curling into talon-like arcs. "Forefathers, she's come to keep you in this prison. With all of your divine power, don't let her do it!"

A chorus of ghostly shrieks rose from beneath the skulls. Scores of shadowy arms reached up from the cracks forming between the skulls. They grasped at the sky, gaunt and emancipated, their fingers sharpened like claws, reaching for Alais.

"Show her what you can do!" Naberus cried.

"Stop her," the voices hissed in unison, rising to a crescendo. *"Hurt her. KILL HER!"*

Wisps of energy sparked from within their grasping fingers, flaring up into tendrils of violet eldritch light. The tendrils lashed out at Alais, coiling around her legs and ankles and wrapping around her arms. The touch of the eldritch tentacles burned her skin, and she felt a surge of panic as they began pulling her toward the shadowy arms reaching up from the hill of skulls.

Alais let out a panicked cry when a sound rose above the ghostly voices—the sound of a battle cry. Ilat came flying through the air, cleaving her scimitar into the eldritch tentacles. Her blade sheared straight through them, causing them to dissipate into wisps of purplish smoke. She struck at another array of tentacles, severing each one as she landed on the hill. The tendrils coiled around Alais' limbs dissolved into vapor. But below her, Ilat let out a cry, for a horde of shadowy claws was tearing into her bronze flesh and pulling her onto the skulls.

As she watched Ilat being enveloped by the shadowy claws, Alais knew she had to end this. With a swell of determination, she began reciting the words to summon the wind, and with it, the fire. She felt a blast of air whip past her legs and sent it streaming across the surface of the moat, gathering flames as it sped in an arc around the pillar. The raging tempest of fire and wind howled as it whipped over the hill of skulls before Alais willed it into Naberus da Roma.

Naberus's face twisted into a mask of dismay and terror as Alais' creation struck like a fiery serpent with the force of a gale. The storm of fire and wind engulfed him, blackening his skin and sweeping him off his feet. His limbs flailing, he let out a final, desperate scream as the storm drove him into the moat of Greek Fire. Smoke and steam exploded from the moat. Whatever remained of Naberus da Roma was consumed by the flames like a condemned soul cast into the Lake of Fire.

From the billowing smoke came a wisp of blue light that flickered in the air as it flowed into Alais. *The rest of the Key,* she realized, feeling its power seep into her veins.

Without hesitating, she glided to the base of the pillar, casting a sidelong glance at Ilat, who was now buried beneath a pile of claw-ing, shadowy limbs. Alais knew she had but seconds to save her. Pressing her hands against the obsidian surface, Alais willed all of her power into the pillar. "Heal, dammit!"

Around her, the air thrummed amid the crack of stone as the pillar seemed to come alive under Alais' touch. The huge fissures marring the pillar's surface began to shrink and close, scraping and grinding into place. Three hundred feet of obsidian rock shifted and rippled as the cracks retreated, and the symbols etched on its surface were repaired and started to glow. Shards of stone littering the hill rose into the air and reattached themselves to the pillar as if the Key to the Abyss had reversed the flow of time.

Behind her came a ghastly wail as the Watchers' shadowy limbs receded into the hill. They thrashed and clawed at the air as they disappeared beneath the giant skulls, whose cracks began to mend. Ilat, her face and limbs cut and scratched, rose to a knee. On the pillar, the remaining fissures sealed themselves with a deep sigh of stone, and the last of the spidery cracks vanished into the obsidian. In moments, the structure, which had appeared damaged beyond recognition, was completely restored, its glossy black surface broken only by the symbols that now blazed like massive hieroglyphs down a titanic Egyptian obelisk.

Alais walked over to Ilat and helped her to her feet.

"What do we do now?" Alais asked.

Ilat turned her head toward the distant battlefield. "Pray that Ciarán still stands—and that he ends this."

SAMYAZA GESTURED with his trident to the scene of carnage sprawled across the battlefield behind him. A small army of Danes and Aswaran lay dead among the corpses of giants, while an amused grin spread across Samyaza's face. "You let them all die, just like Niall said you would."

Ciarán straightened his back, standing tall in defiance. "Those weren't Niall's words; those were your lies." He pointed his flaming blade at the carnage. "These men gave their lives to make sure your army would lose today. And it has."

Samyaza snarled. "You will know in a moment what it means to lose." He stretched out his arms and filled his lungs with air. "*OZAM, ODAMMA, CIALPOR, MIR, AGRIT!*"

As those words burned into his ears, Ciarán gritted his teeth, prepared for what would come. He felt the heat blaze into his forehead and burn atop his feet and his right hand. But the overwhelming pain never came.

Samyaza cocked his head, a look of confusion filling his golden eyes.

Ciarán jerked his left arm and let the shield strapped to it slide off and fall to the ground. Where his left hand had been, only a stump remained, wrapped in a bandage stained with blood. Back in the cave, Ilat had convinced him it was his only choice—lose his hand to shatter the pentagram and break the curse. So before they left for the battle, he had asked her to cut it off, and she did, with one swift blow of her scimitar.

Surprise flickered in Samyaza's eyes, quickly replaced by a burning rage. "THEN YOU'LL DIE THE OLD-FASHIONED WAY!"

Ciarán's heartbeat quickened the moment Samyaza took a long-legged stride toward him. From the corner of his eye, Ciarán saw Holger standing next to him, with Breda by his side.

"Do you see the scar from the old wound I gave him below his ribs," Holger said under his breath. "It still bleeds. I saw it back at the ringfort."

Ciarán nodded, eyeing the dull scar above Samyaza's left hip before tightening his grip around Caladbolg's hilt.

"Let the bastard come," Gundoald growled from behind the cheek pieces of his horse-plumed helmet. Then, with a roar, Gundoald charged. The towering Lombard raised his sword as he bore down on Samyaza, who reacted with devastating speed. Before Gundoald could raise his shield, the trident's razor-sharp prongs pierced through the Lombard's mail and drove deep into his chest. Gundoald made a desperate swipe with his sword, but its blade merely scraped off Samyaza's golden chest as if the mortal steel of his sword was incapable of piercing the immortal's flesh.

"That's the distraction we needed!" Holger cried. "Move!"

Holger and Breda bellowed battle cries as they stormed forward, while a familiar shout burst from Ciarán's lungs.

"Columcille!"

Holger swung high for Samyaza's free arm; Breda chopped low at his legs. Her sword sliced harmlessly across Samyaza's golden skin. But Curtana, with its Fae-forged blade, struck with greater effect. The sword bit into Samyaza's forearm, misting the air with luminescent blood. Meanwhile, Ciarán charged straight at Samyaza, trying to land a blow on the being's left side, but he twisted, causing Caladbolg to graze the top of his thigh.

Samyaza roared as he tried to wrench his trident free of Gundoald while sending a backhanded strike into Ciarán and Holger. The blow struck Ciarán in his chest hard enough to knock the wind from his lungs and send him crashing ten yards away onto his back. Holger crashed down beside him. He grimaced in pain, clutching his ribs. Then Breda screamed. A powerful kick from Samyaza's left leg sent her flying a full twenty yards before she smashed onto the hard-packed ground.

With his free hand, Samyaza grabbed Gundoald by the throat and ripped him free of the trident's prongs. Then he flung the massive Lombard to the side like a slain hare.

Lying on the ground, Ciarán struggled to catch his breath when Samyaza hurled his trident. It sped toward Ciarán's chest, but then Holger grabbed hold of him and wrenched him to the side a breath before the trident slammed into the ground and impaled itself in the hard gray earth. As Samyaza extended a hand to summon the trident back to his grasp, Holger wrapped his arms around the weapon, grunting as he exerted all his strength to keep it from Samyaza.

Ciarán climbed to his feet as Breda staggered toward Samyaza, whose face had become a canvas of fury. Breda stopped halfway and pointed to the enemy encampment. "Look!" she yelled. Beyond the tents, a black spire stretched to the sky, and the crisp, clean runes etched upon its face glowed white like beacons in the night. A smile stretched between her cheeks. "The pillar's healed!"

Samyaza's features contorted into a storm of rage, his eyes blazing with a primordial fire as he realized what had happened. A similar realization washed over Ciarán, and it filled him with hope. For if the pillar was healed, that meant Alais was alive, and the third group had fulfilled its mission. But he knew he would not see her again unless he survived this conflict. This last battle—the culmination of a prophecy so many of his friends had died for. And their names were burned forever into his soul: *Dónall mac Taidg, Isaac ben Ezra,* and *Khalil al-Pârsâ; Évrard, Brother Remi,* and *Josua's son Eli;* and his brothers at Derry—*Bran* and *Murchad, Fintan* and *Senach, Áed* and *Ailil,* and, of course, *Niall.* He had not cost them their lives, for they had given their lives to aid this cause. And he would not let their sacrifices be in vain.

As Samyaza's eyes remained fixated on the pillar, a flash of realization shot through Ciarán. He knew right then what he needed to do. Gathering every ounce of courage he'd ever mustered, he broke into a sprint. His sword was aimed like a lance, its tip poised to pierce right below the creature's ribs. But just as he neared, Samyaza pivoted with the speed of a striking viper, his hand shooting out to seize Ciarán by the throat. Fingers tightened, unyielding as iron, choking off air and life. Samyaza's golden irises ignited, glowing with infernal fury as he hissed, "DIE!"

His vision blurring, Ciarán felt himself lifted off his feet. He grimaced through the choking pain, calling upon his last reserves of willpower, and drove Caladbolg forward. The blade sank into the pale scar above Samyaza's hip. A torrent of power flooded Ciarán's veins as white fire roared up the blade into the gash, searing the wound from the inside. Samyaza's vise-like grip slackened, and the cry that escaped his lips shook both heaven and earth.

When Samyaza's fingers fell from Ciarán's neck, Caladbolg's blade slid free of the wound, and Ciarán tumbled onto the ground. Samyaza staggered back. The golden sheen of his skin began to peel and melt away, revealing scarred and burnt flesh. His mane of copper hair hissed into smoke, and his once flawless face twisted into a ghastly, beast-like visage. The light bringer of scripture had become the creature Ciarán always envisioned him to be, a ghoulish demon with skin burnt by Hell's fires.

Then came the horns, a sound that rang through the valley like the blast of ten thousand trumpets blaring down from the heavens. At that sound, Samyaza dropped to a knee, his hand clutching the wound at its side. Luminescent blood seeped through his fingers, and Samyaza let out a sigh that hissed like a bitter wind before he collapsed onto the ground.

Ciarán watched in stunned silence, still grasping at the reality of what had happened. Across the battlefield, the remaining pockets of Nephilim were in full retreat, heading toward the encampment. He spotted Kamran and a half-dozen battle-weary Aswaran limping toward them. By their side was Jorundr, his hand rubbing a prominent lump on his head. But there was someone else, too, farther away. He appeared clad in black robes, moving with the aid of a walking staff, and for an instant, Ciarán thought this must be Fereydun, before remembering that he had gone to the ridge with the second group. As the man came closer, Ciarán squinted his eyes. When he noticed the man was wearing a broad-brimmed hat, his mouth fell open in disbelief.

For Father Michele, alive and well, was crossing the battle-scarred plains of Dudael.

CHAPTER 78

THE SEVENTH SEAL

F ather Michele navigated the rugged landscape, moving slowly with the clack of his walking staff heralding each step of his boots. Beneath the shadow cast by the priest's wide-brimmed hat, Ciarán caught a glimpse of his familiar face— the long nose, the lushly silvered beard, and the sun-kissed skin creased by the decades, or the centuries, perhaps.

Standing around Ciarán, Holger, Breda, Kamran, and Jorundr watched in various states of disbelief and wonder, for all of them had been in the ringfort when Samyaza rammed his trident through the old priest's back.

When he reached the group, Father Michele regarded Ciarán with his blue eyes twinkling with a hint of amusement.

You can close your mouth, lad," Father Michele said. "Did you truly think I was that easy to kill?"

"We all saw it happen," Ciarán stammered. "It looked real enough then."

"Ah," the old priest said with a warm smile. "Perception is a relative concept. To you, seeing a man stabbed with a trident naturally meant he died. But what you perceive as death is merely a change in one's state of being. The body appears to die only for the spirit to live on in a different place. And the place my spirit goes allows me to be reformed—or re-born—in whatever shape I please. It's happened more times than I can remember."

He gestured toward the battlefield behind him. "All of those who fell today are already on their way to different places. Some better, some worse, but then, everyone reaps what they sow in life."

As Ciarán gazed upon the battlefield, his eyes grew wide as fragments of the fallen warriors began wafting into the air. Soon, it looked like a snowstorm falling upside down as the corpses dissolved into millions of tiny pieces, drifting skyward until they disappeared into the gloom.

Soon, the only people in eyeshot were Father Michele, Ciarán's surviving comrades, and Samyaza, who lay on the ground, his chest slowly rising and falling with each strained breath.

Father Michele glanced at the Devil sprawled on the hard gray plain. "I commend you for this—all of you. For now, the Seventh Seal shall remain unbroken, and the world will live on, at least for another thousand years." He reached for something at his hip, which was the first time Ciarán noticed the old priest had a leather book satchel slung over his shoulder. It was a familiar satchel, too—the one belonging to Brother Dónall.

From the satchel, the priest produced an old, weathered book with a symbol pressed into its dark leather cover. It was a cross with a loop at its head—a *crux anasta*—also known as an Ankh. Ciarán sucked in a breath as he recognized the Book of Maugis d'Aygremont, the tome that set him on this journey three years ago.

"You'll want to keep this somewhere safe," Father Michelle said, handing him the book. "That weapon too." He pointed to Caladbolg. "As well as all the scrolls you've accumulated from Solomon's library. My hope is that the next time the cycle of prophecy comes around, whoever carries your mantel won't have such a bloody hard time finding it all."

Ciarán nodded as Father Michele slid the book into the satchel and handed it to him.

"I happen to know of a secret archive," Ciarán said with a

shrug, "where quite a few rare relics have been stored over the years."

Father Michele gave him a wink. "I know, lad—and that would be good."

Glancing at Samyaza, Ciarán asked the priest, "So, what happens next?"

Father Michele chewed his lip as he regarded the demon-like creature sprawled on the ground. "He has another thousand years of isolation and torment to look forward to."

Then the old priest scratched the chin of his beard. "All we need now is the Key to unlock his prison."

WHEN THE HORNS blared from the heavens, everything atop the ridge began to change. The bodies of the Aswaran and Lady Asira, along with the hulking pale-skinned giants and the chainmail-clad assassins, began to disintegrate before Tara's eyes.

Tiny bits of skin and bone floated like ashes into the sky as if some celestial power were calling them home. Soon, the air around the entire ridge was a cloud of mortal remnants rising into the gloom. The only one who didn't disintegrate was Mordechai, who slumped unconscious against the basalt rock with a dagger protruding from his stomach.

"He's still alive!" Tara shouted, hurrying to him. She placed a hand on his chest and felt the faintest sense of it rising.

Aunt Kira knelt beside the young man, drawing out her crystal and infusing it with her soul light. "I'll need you to do the same thing you did for your sister," she told Tara.

Tara nodded briskly and brushed a lock of hair from Mordechai's forehead. She had believed they had lost the handsome young archer, but the thought that they might save him filled her with a swell of hope. She took his right hand in hers. It was cold to the touch. "Hurry," she said as her stomach twisted into a knot. "He's slipping away."

Sara sat beside him and took his other hand, giving Tara a worried look.

Brother Pietro and her grandfather looked intently over Aunt Kira's shoulder as she bathed Mordechai's wound in her soul light, pressing gently on Mordechai's stomach. "Remove the dagger, Tara."

Tara's hand was not shaking this time when she pulled the dagger free. Aunt Kira's soul light flooded the wound, and blood that should have pulsed from the gash stayed within Mordechai. Using her slender fingers aglow in her soul light, Aunt Kira kneaded the wound closed.

Mordechai groaned, and his eyelids fluttered.

"You're safe," Tara told him.

He looked around, bewildered. "Did we win?"

"Yes," Tara said, overjoyed to look into his brown eyes. "We won!"

ALAIS AND ILAT headed toward the base of the ridge. To their surprise, a pair of enormous mastiffs had cornered another animal lying wounded where the ridge descended into a shallow hillock of basalt rock. Hackles rose on the mastiffs' necks. A fat black raven perched on a nearby boulder, cawed incessantly while a chorus of growls filled the air.

As Alais and Ilat neared the scene, one of the massive dogs glanced back, its sharp teeth bared in a vicious snarl, with foam frothing from the sides of its mouth. That's when Alais saw the other animal—it was Rosta! The huge boarhound was crouched down, protecting one of its hind legs, growling defiantly despite being outnumbered.

"I'll handle this," Ilat said calmly. She made a whistling sound as light sprung from her palms, forming a glowing halo around her outstretched hands. When the mastiffs turned toward the sound, their vicious demeanor became suddenly submissive in the soft glow of her soul light, and the raven stopped its screeching. Tails were tucked between legs, and the mastiffs looked on sheepishly as Ilat uttered three words of power and pointed toward the enemy camp. One of the mastiffs glanced back at Rosta and then whimpered before following the other dog, who had already started padding toward the tents. With the flutter of wings, the raven flew after them.

Alais hurried to Rosta. She knelt beside the boarhound, who licked her hand. His large brown eyes showed a look of worry, and she could tell that his left hind leg was broken.

"Let's get that fixed," Alais said before uttering *"Eoh"* and summoning her soul light. She placed her hands gently on Rosta's leg, bathing his fur in her light's warm aura. She ran her fingers down his leg until she found the break and began reciting the words to mend bones. After several minutes of setting the leg and uttering a few more words to reinforce the bone, the limb was as good as new. Rosta stood and shook himself vigorously as if shaking away invisible fetters of pain. He licked Alais' hand again, then cocked his head when he heard his name called from the pathway behind them.

"Rosta!" Tara's face was beaming as she ran up to the boarhound and gave him a big hug.

Coming down the path, Kira smiled at Alais, and the look on Fereydun's face was almost giddy. Mordechai was with them, walking alongside Sara with the relieved look of a man grateful to be alive. Behind them sauntered Brother Pietro, and he waved when he saw the two women. "Well done, ladies. Well done!"

That's when it hit Alais—she was done. The whole reason Sirra's spirit lived from life to life over thousands of years was to heal the pillar when the cycle of prophecy came full circle. Her mission was to keep the Watchers in their prison, and that would be her mission again, a millennium from now, but not in this life. For the rest of her days, this life belonged to Alais of Selles-sur-Cher. To the woman who spent her childhood on the banks of the river Clain and in the palace of Poitiers, and who ruled a small village after Geoffrey passed away from sickness. Ever since then, when Adémar of Blois arrived at Selles-sur-Cher, Alais had been carried away by this prophecy like a ship lost in a storm. But now, the seas were calm. Her mission was over, and her life was her own.

There was one piece missing, however, something she had lost years ago when Geoffrey succumbed to Saint Anthony's Fire. For six years, she had known love—the true, deep, lasting kind of love she had shared with Geoffrey. And while she knew that could never be replaced, she had felt a glimmer of it again in the person who had meant more than anything to her since that harrowing day when she had fled Selles-sur-Cher. She had found that glimmer in Ciarán, and more than anything, she wanted to be with him now.

"I'll see you soon," Alais told Ilat and the others. Then she started running as fast as she could while mustering the words of power in her mind. When she leaped into the air, those words began to flow, summoning the wind. The wind lifted her up as her body became lighter, and soon, she was soaring over the gray plains. When she saw the gathering of warriors around the blackened body of a demon, she slowed her descent and landed gracefully ten yards away.

Ciarán was staring at her as if he'd just witnessed an angel descending from heaven. His once polished hauberk was stained with the grime of battle, and his hair looked slick with sweat. His gaze held onto her, as if he'd been waiting for this very moment amidst the chaos of the battlefield.

With a surge of courage, Alais found herself sprinting the remaining distance. Ciarán rushed to meet her. When they collided, Ciarán's arms enfolded Alais, lifting her slightly off the ground, and she wrapped her own around his neck, holding onto him as if he was her anchor. Leaning down, he kissed her gently, and she kissed him back. It was a passionate kiss, sweet and soft, that brought tears to her eyes and filled her with the promise of their life to come.

She looked him in the eyes. "Do you remember what I asked you back in the cave?"

"Aye," he said. "How could I ever forget?"

"Then will you do it?"

"Ten thousand horses couldn't keep me from doing it," he

admitted. "So, you have my word. When we're gone from here, we'll find the most peaceful place on earth, and we'll stay there."

With a smile filled with pure joy, Alais kissed him again. Then, nearby, someone loudly cleared his throat. She glanced toward the sound and could hardly believe her eyes. It was Father Michele, and he was alive!

"My dear," he said with a grin, "it was so very good of you to show up. We have one piece of unfinished business to attend to." He gestured toward Samyaza.

"Of course," she realized. There was one more thing Sirra had to do beyond keeping the Watchers in their prison. She had to send Samyaza to a prison of his own.

She walked with Ciarán and Father Michele to where Samyaza lay on the cold, hard ground. His eight-foot frame was covered in blackened and burnt flesh, gauntly stretched over muscles clinging tightly to his bones. His face was more bat-like than man-like, as if the endless exposure to hellfire had melted his features into the abomination that lay before them.

Alais knelt ten feet away and pressed her palm against the hard-packed earth. As she did with the pillar, she let the power coursing within her flow into the ground. With a loud crack, like a splitting stone, a fissure spread from her palm, branching out like a spider's web until a hundred jagged cracks surrounded Samyaza. The ground buckled and shook before collapsing beneath him.

Samyaza opened his eyes and gave one last defeated groan before disappearing into the abyss.

~

Daena was right where they had left her, with her anchors buried into the basalt cliffside near the edge of the falls. The river Cocytus had thawed enough that chunks of ice once again cascaded over the edge with an undying roar. The air was so cold their breath froze in white puffs.

With a crew as small as theirs, there would be no way to row a galley this size upriver, but Ilat assured them she and Alais could summon enough wind to get them out of here.

After Kamran and his men worked with Ilat and Alais to free the anchors from the rocks, the ship was underway. Ilat volunteered for the first shift, standing on the deck behind the mast and filling the sail with wind. Ciarán sat on an oar bench on the quarterdeck next to Alais, who rested her head on his shoulder. Pietro, Holger, and Breda joined them on adjacent benches on the larboard side while Fereydun, Kira, and the twins perched on the starboard benches across the aisle where Rosta rested at Tara's feet. Mordechai and Jorundr were off with Kamran and the rest of his Aswaran crew manning the rudders, keeping lookout, and otherwise helping to navigate the galley up the river.

"So," Fereydun asked the group, "where will everyone go from here?"

Holger ran his fingers through his hair. "Jorundr tells me that back in Miklagard, your emperor keeps a Varangian Guard of Northmen. I thought Jorundr and I might offer our services to him until we've earned enough money to buy a new ship and recruit a new crew."

"With my position in the palace, I can help make that happen," Kira said.

Sara glanced up with a hopeful look in her eyes. "So we're going home?"

"Of course we are," Kira replied.

Tara crossed her arms, appearing far less excited than her sister. "Aren't you worried about the House of Magog?"

Fereydun raised a brow. "You mean what's left of them? I think your hailstorm depleted enough of their forces that, with a little help from your sister's friend, Emperor Basil, we can rid our city of their scourge before next summer."

The answer earned a smile from Tara, who returned to scratching the scruff of Rosta's neck.

"What about the rest of you?" Kira asked.

"My duties lie with His Holiness, the pope," Pietro told her. "So it is back to Rome for me."

"We'll be joining you," Ciarán said, "at least for a short while." He patted the satchel at his side containing the Book of Maugis d'Aygremont. "We have a few things to drop off in the secret archives."

Pietro furrowed his brow. "I'm sure the pope will let you stay as long as you want. And he needs a new captain of the papal guard."

Alais gave him a look, and he answered it with a slight shake of his head. "So long as there are families like the Crescentii, Rome will remain a tumultuous place."

"We're actually looking for someplace a bit more peaceful," Alais added.

Ciarán squeezed her hand and gave her a loving smile. "And I know just where to find it."

EPILOGUE

On the brightest day of November 1009, with nary a cloud in the sky, a white-hulled ship arrived at Derry. It appeared on the glistening waters of the river Foyle after the holy hour of Vespers, preceded by a trio of greylag geese who heralded the vessel's approach before it moored on the sturdy oak pier outside the monastery.

Alais stood on a meadow of emerald grass, along with three dozen villagers from the nearby settlement that had grown up beside the monastery since she and Ciarán arrived there eight years ago. They were joined by nearly a hundred monks, all clad in fleece-gray robes, who gathered on the riverbank to greet the ship. Beside Alais, her eight-year-old son, Niall, craned his neck to get a glimpse of the black-robed cleric standing in the bow while her five-year-old daughter, Breda, gazed upon the ship with wide, curious eyes.

"Where do you think the ship's from?" Niall asked.

Alais glanced at Ciarán, who gave her a warm smile. While he was only thirty-two, his white hair painted him as a much older man. Although with his close-cropped beard and his merchant's hat with its upturned brim, he looked as handsome as ever. He bent down, put his arm around their son, and pointed to the strip of scarlet cloth fluttering from the ship's masthead. Two crossed keys, one silver and one gold, adorned the fabric.

"Do you see that pennant?" Ciarán said. "That ship's from Rome. It's a papal vessel."

"What's a papal vessel?" Breda wondered while clinging to Alais' slate-gray dress.

"It means that ship belongs to our new pope," Alais told her.

The *new pope*. Ever since they learned of his coronation, Alais had remained both amazed and heartened by the tidings. For in July of this past year, Pietro Buccaporci had been crowned Pope Sergius the Fourth, and there was no finer man she could imagine for the job. Still, she felt a pang of apprehension in her stomach as she wondered what message the ship had brought from the Eternal City. News from that place was not always good.

A thickset man wearing the scarlet cloak and crested helmet of a papal guardsman lowered the end of a short, wide ramp to the pier. A murmur of speculation percolated from the throng of monks, and Alais clutched her hands together in nervous anticipation.

The priest disembarked next, and Alais let out a relieved breath when she recognized the man. The spear-thin cleric, dressed in a black cassock, was older than she remembered. The wisps of hair beneath his black skull cap were now entirely silver, and thicker bags hung beneath his bulbous eyes, but his usually pinched expression remained unchanged. Archdeacon Niccolo surveyed the crowd, and his face brightened when he spied Alais and Ciarán.

The abba of Derry stepped from the crowd. "Peace be with you, Father. Welcome to our humble home. But please tell us, what is the reason for your voyage?"

"I'm here," Niccolo replied, "to see some old friends."

As Niccolo shared more words with the abba, Niall asked, "Do you know him, Father?"

"Aye," Ciarán replied. "He's a good man."

Niccolo made his way through the crowd of curious monks, followed by two younger priests, one of whom cradled a bundle in his arms wrapped in black velvet cloth. "Captain Ciarán," Niccolo said with a wink and a thin smile, "and Lady Alais, looking as splendid as ever." His eyes widened at the sight of the two children by their side. "And who would these two be?"

"Our son, Niall," Alais said, "and our daughter Breda."

Niccolo's smile widened. "You'll be a feisty lass, I suspect," he said to Breda before turning back to Alais, his gaze settling on her swollen belly. "And you'll have another sibling soon."

"After Midwinter, most likely," Alais said.

"Then I suspect I already know the answer to my first question." Niccolo clasped his hands together and addressed the children. "May I borrow your mother and father for a moment?"

Niall nodded, but Breda gave Alais a wary glance.

"It will be all right," Alais said, touching her daughter gently on the shoulder. "Stay with your brother."

Ciarán led Niccolo away from the crowd to the shadows of a broad oak, heavily flecked with moss. The two young priests trailed after the archdeacon, but before Alais moved to follow them, she glanced back at the village of thatch-roofed cottages standing on the green hillside east of the monastery's earthen wall. Her and Ciarán's house stood prominently among the cottages, built of stone and wood instead of wattle and daub, with a sturdy slate roof. It was not the manor house she enjoyed in Selles-sur-Cher, but it was more comfortable to Alais than any manor or palace she had ever known. She suspected Pietro would want them to leave this place and return to Rome, and she knew Ciarán would refuse. For Derry had become their home.

As Alais set off to join them across a shallow meadow thick with clover, she felt as if the roots of her life had grown deep beneath this land. And as she watched Ciarán trade pleasantries with Niccolo, she knew more than anything this was where they belonged. She had known love once with Geoffrey, but what she had here was different. It was a deeper love than she ever could have imagined— love born from bringing life into the world and building a family. Her love for Ciarán felt different, too. He had rescued her from the pyre at Selles-sur-Cher and risked his life for her in trial by combat. She had saved his life, too, and more than a few times. But she realized that after everything the world had thrown at them, they had rescued each other.

When she reached Ciarán and the priests, Niccolo cleared his throat. "His Holiness, Pope Sergius, would very much like the two of you to return to Rome. Being pope is an awfully challenging endeavor, and His Holiness could use all the help he can get."

Alais glanced at Ciarán, who shook his head. "Our life's here, in Derry," he said. "It's a good life and a peaceful one."

Niccolo shrugged. "His Holiness expected you to say that, and he specifically instructed me not to persuade you otherwise. After all the two of you have been through, you've earned your peace." He turned to the young priest holding the bundle wrapped in black cloth. "The pope wanted me to give you this."

The priest handed the bundle to Ciarán. He unwrapped it to reveal a leather book satchel—Dónall's old book satchel. His eyes grew wide as he pulled out a familiar book with a dark leather cover impressed with a *crux anasta*.

"Maugis' book!" The words escaped Alais' lips as soon as she recognized the old tome.

Ciarán gave Niccolo a confused look. "Why? We had left it in the archives with Caladbolg, for the next time the cycle comes around."

"Our late friend Gerbert had the critical parts copied not long after you and Alais were married and left Rome," Niccolo explained. "They're hidden securely in the archives, along with the device. But His Holiness—our dear friend Pietro—grew concerned about having everything associated with the prophecy hidden in one place, particularly if the papacy were to succumb again to corrupt and ignoble men, as it had in the last century. His Holiness felt certain that you were the worthiest protector for the Book of Maugis d'Aygremont."

Ciarán nodded.

"But there's one more thing," Niccolo said. "Something our pope feels strongly about."

"What's that?" Ciarán asked.

Niccolo arched an eyebrow. "When the cycle comes around

again, a thousand years from now, humanity will need a new champion. And by the look of things, you and Lady Alais appear well on your way to forging a new bloodline."

Alais took a moment to absorb the weight of Niccolo's words as the sun began its descent, casting a golden hue over Derry. Turning to Ciarán, their eyes met, sharing a silent understanding of the responsibility they now bore. As he drew her close to him, she glanced across the meadow at Niall and Breda, their innocent faces alight with curiosity.

"It looks like our legacy will live on in more ways than one," she said softly.

"Then together," Ciarán replied, with the bright smile she had grown to love, "we will teach them well."

HISTORICAL NOTE

M y deep appreciation for both fantasy and historical fiction has been the compass guiding the creation of the trilogy that started with *Enoch's Device* and reached its conclusion with the book you've just completed. While the fantasy elements stand out, the strands of historical truth woven throughout may not be as immediately apparent. As I have done in the past, I will shed light on these historical aspects here.

On April 2, 999, Gerbert of Aurillac, perhaps the most brilliant scholar in all of Christendom, was appointed pope by his former student, the nineteen-year-old Holy Roman Emperor, Otto III. As pope, Gerbert took the name Sylvester II in honor of Saint Sylvester, the pope during the imperial reign of Constantine the Great who constructed the Lateran Palace, the Basilica of Saint John Lateran, and the original Saint Peter's Basilica on the Vatican Hill. Because of Gerbert's passion for science, which many in the Middle Ages believed to be a form of sorcery, he had numerous detractors among the clergy. Some mistook his scientific experiments as dabbling in the occult arts. Others even went so far as to suggest he was the antichrist who had come to usher in the End of Days.

Rumors of Gerbert's occult dealings worsened after his death in 1003. In the twelfth century, a courtier of King Henry II of England named Walter Map suggested Gerbert had made an immoral pact with a beautiful sorceress named Meridiana, who turned out to be a demoness and a servant of the devil. So, Meridiana naturally became Cardinal Bishop Beno's nickname for Alais in the novel. As for Beno, he's a fictional character inspired by a real-life Cardinal Beno who lived in the eleventh century. Cardinal Beno deemed the former pope "Gerbert the Wizard," who made a pact with the devil. After all, what else could explain Gerbert's seemingly magical powers?

As pope, Gerbert's papal librarian was a man named Pietro Buccaporci, the son of a shoemaker who became a Benedictine monk and quickly rose through the ecclesiastical ranks. By 1004, Pietro was named bishop of Albano and, in 1009, was eventually elected bishop of Rome. As pope, Pietro took the name Sergius IV because he did not want to have the same name as Saint Peter. Although little is known of his reign, Sergius IV supposedly acted to alleviate famine in the city. However, his papacy was overshadowed by the influence of John II Crescentius, leader of the powerful Crescentii family. In 1012, both Crescentius and the pope disappeared during a violent revolt in Rome, and some suspect both may have been murdered, perhaps by a rival family who supported the pope's successor. Sergius IV is buried in the Basilica of Saint John Lateran and, while never canonized, may have been considered a saint by some members of the Benedictine order.

In Pietro and Gerbert's day, Rome was a shadow of its former glory. A city built for a million people had a population of barely fifty-thousand by the tenth century, mostly clustered around the Tiber River after the aqueducts had been destroyed centuries before. Many of the most famous Imperial Roman buildings were ruins by then, with the marble that hung on their once glorious facades used to build churches throughout the city. The Theatre of Pompey, where Alais' trial takes place in the book, was the first theatre built in Rome by Pompey the Great. In addition to the huge open-air theatre, the site contained a garden and the Curia of

Pompey, the building where Julius Caesar was famously assassinated in 44 BC. According to a ninth-century pilgrim's guidebook, the theatre was still standing, and may have stood in the tenth century, too. Although, one imagines that had the Theatre of Pompey collapsed during an attack on the pope, that would have made the history books. Suffice it to say, that part was fictional.

While tenth-century Rome was a half-ruined city long past its prime, Constantinople stood at the height of its Imperial glory. It was the most magnificent city in Christendom, a metropolis with a population of nearly four hundred thousand and more wealth than anywhere in the Western world. One of the city's greatest wonders, the Hippodrome, was estimated to seat up to a hundred thousand spectators—twice the population of tenth-century Rome. Chariot racing was an integral part of Byzantine life, and the Greens and the Blues comprised its most famous teams. The emperor of Constantinople was a frequent spectator from his box called the Kathisma, which contained a passageway connected to the Sacred Palace. All the wondrous details of that palace featured in the novel, including the fantastic gardens, the animal statues, the mechanical singing birds, and the golden roaring lions, are based on historical accounts.

The palace's primary resident, Basil II, nicknamed Basil the Bulgar-slayer, was one of the most significant emperors in Byzantine history. He was a heralded military leader who secured the empire's borders and defeated its enemies during his forty-nine-year reign. That said, stories of his greatness are mixed with legends of his cruelty, including the supposed blinding of 15,000 Bulgar prisoners after the battle of Kleidion, which Samyaza reveals in one of his visions to Ciarán in the book. Some historians, however, contest the accuracy of this legend. And since Samyaza tells the tale in the book, you never know if it's the truth or a lie.

While Basil II was an important ruler, the most famed emperor of Constantinople was Justinian the Great, who tried to restore the Roman Empire in the sixth century. Justinian was a prolific and ambitious builder, and his most renowned accomplishment, the Hagia Sophia, still stands as the city's finest architectural marvel.

Hagia Sophia was built on the site of several prior churches, including one constructed next to the imperial palace by Constantius II. However, some rumors suggest that the original church had been built by Constantius's father, Constantine the Great, and I embraced those rumors for this novel. While no one has definitively determined what lies beneath Hagia Sophia, studies in 2005 and 2009 confirmed the existence of a system of wells and waterways under the structure. Though it is pure speculation whether these waterways connect to the Sunken Palace, known today as the Basilica Cistern, a dazzling structure also built by Justinian.

Constantine the Great and his mother, Saint Helena, made pilgrimages to Jerusalem and, according to some accounts, returned with several holy relics, including treasures from the ruins of Solomon's temple. Though it's pure conjecture whether what I've called the "Jerusalem Scrolls" were among them. Three of those scrolls have a legendary connection to King Solomon, although it is doubtful he authored them. I invented that connection for the fourth scroll, titled *The War of the Sons of Light Against the Sons of Darkness*. Also known as *The War Scroll*, the writing was discovered in either 1947 or 1956 among the Dead Sea Scrolls along with copies of the Book of Enoch and the Book of Giants.

As I explained in the Historical Note to *Enoch's Device*, the Book of Enoch is an ancient Hebrew text once considered a lost book of scripture. While the book is cited in the New Testament Letter of Jude and the First Letter of Peter, it has been excluded as biblical canon by most churches, even though it expands on a story in chapter 6 of the book of Genesis. That chapter begins: *"When people began to multiply on the face of the ground and daughters were born to them, the sons of God saw that they were fair, and they took wives for themselves of all that they chose."* In the Book of Enoch, these Sons of God are known as the Watchers, rogue angels who traveled to Earth to mate with mortal women, spawning the race of Nephilim, who are also mentioned in Genesis 6:4. Samyaza was the leader of these fallen angels, and the Book of Enoch tells his story, culminating with his defeat and that of the Watchers at the hands of the archangels, led by Michael. In the end, the archangels cast the Watchers into a prison beneath Dudael, a place whose name translates into the Cauldron of God. This fascinating story became the mythology underlying *Enoch's Device* and the rest of the *Dragon-Myth Cycle*.

The Cauldron of God is the culmination of many years of historical research, a whole lot of writing, and a tremendous amount of fun for this humble fan of historical and fantasy fiction. Thank you very much for reading it, and I truly hope you enjoyed it!

DISCOVER the origins of the Book of Maugis d'Aygremont in ***The Fae Dealings*** ...

BOOKS BY JOSEPH FINLEY

The Dragon-Myth Cycle

Enoch's Device

The Key to the Abyss

The Cauldron of God

Dragon-Myth Prequels

Hela's Bane

The Fae Dealings

Other Tales

Mava's Echo: A Short Story of Celtic Myth and Magic

ABOUT THE AUTHOR

Joseph Finley is a writer of historical fantasy fiction. Following a tour as an officer in the U.S. Navy Judge Advocate General's Corps, he returned to Atlanta where he lives with his wife, daughter, and two mischievous rescue dogs. A lifelong love of medieval history, vintage fantasy, and historical mysteries helped inspire his writing, along with a penchant for European travel. Joseph is a member of the Science Fiction and Fantasy Writers of America, and posts frequently about historical and fantasy fiction on his blog. He can be found most nights enjoying a hearty glass of wine, and in the wee hours of most mornings surrounded by history books and plugging away on his next story.

To receive a **free novella**, as well as emails with updates on Joseph's next novel and special offers, join his Reader List by signing up **here** or at his website, below:

www.authorjosephfinley.com

Lastly, if you enjoyed this book, please consider leaving a review (even if it's only a line or two) at Amazon or Goodreads. Word-of-mouth is essential to an author's success, so your input is greatly appreciated!

f facebook.com/AuthorJosephFinley

X x.com/joseph_finley

instagram.com/josephfinley

Printed in Great Britain
by Amazon

45083713R00320